The Design

G. Lloyd Helm

ISBN: 978-1-62420-465-4

Credits
Cover Artist: Designs by Ms G
Editor: Deborah C. Day

Dedication

This book, like all my other work, is dedicated to Michele, who believed.

Part I

One

22 (B)efore the (C)oming of the (G)ods

In the seventeenth year of the reign of Whidbis IV over the city of Peshar, Indi Ransis, short, skinny, and green-eyed with an infectious grin, strolled through Tapestry Plaza idly looking at the tapestries displayed there. He was supposed to be hurrying to the far side of the Plaza where the best Houses displayed their work. He was to relieve his sister Atris, who was minding the three tapestries House Ransis was displaying. But somehow Indi's feet would not move faster than a stroll.

The plaza was alive with noise and color and aromas; but not the same as the market squares. Those were alive too, but they were filled with commerce. Tapestry Plaza was filled with—life? With spirit? With…Indi could not say with what else, but he could feel the power and joy of it wash over him like the warm breeze that ruffled his hair as he walked. All of Peshar could feel it, for at one time or another, all of Peshar passed through Tapestry Plaza.

"About time," Atris snapped at her brother. "I'm starving."

"I doubt that," Indi said, smiling at his younger sister.

"I am. And where have you been anyway?"

"Looking around the plaza. Taking in the air," he answered, knowing it would annoy her.

"While I sat here in the hot sun, practically fainting from hunger!" she said outrage in her voice.

"I am here now Atris, so why waste time scolding me? You might drop dead from starvation."

"Why…" she sputtered. "I'll tell Papa. I'll tell him you left me sitting out here while you wandered around the plaza."

Atris huffed and fumed and boiled for a few more moments, but Indi ignored her, and when she saw he was not listening, she flounced away and disappeared into the crowd.

Indi was sure she would tell Papa, and he was sure he would catch the sharp edge of the old man's tongue when he got home, but he didn't let it bother him much. He stretched his arms wide and yawned, then settled himself upon the short stool beside the tapestries. He did not glance at them. He already knew them well. One of them he knew far more intimately than he would have liked. He had strung most of the warp thread for it on the medium loom in the Ransis tapestry factory. It was a tedious, eye-straining, patience-trying job at the best of times, and much worse when the workman hated the work to begin with.

Young Ransis tried not to think about the factory. Thoughts of it made his stomach knot, as did thoughts of the dye works, the spinnery, or the sheep and goats on the farms that supplied House Ransis with wool. His stomach knotted with dread when he thought of the life which was planned out for him. He was the eldest son of House Ransis, and as such, was fated to take over as Patriarch when his father decided to retire and begin weaving his *Memoria*. That would not happen for many years, if the Gods were kind. The old man was strong and vigorous. But when the *Memoria* was woven Indi would be expected to bring it here to Tapestry Plaza to display it. That would be his first act as Patriarch of House Ransis.

"A life well planned," which could make Indi's mood bleak if he thought about it for more than a few moments.

He looked around the plaza. The day was beautiful. Blue sky with puffy white clouds slowly drifting by on a warm breeze. Bright golden sun which gave everything it touched a tasty aura of brightness. Small groups of people moved slowly from display to café, to teahouse, talking and nodding. Everything seemed right to Indi except for a group of people too large to be friends talking. Above the heads of this gathering a single head rose, facing the others.

Young Ransis glanced around, saw that no one was near the House Ransis display, and left his stool to find out what was going on. He pushed up to the outside of the crowd and turned an ear toward the man who was standing on something to raise him above the people so he could be heard.

"All things are in the hands of the Great Designer." the man said.

He was youngish, but not a boy, for he had a considerable growth of beard. Much more than the scraggly fuzz Indi's chin could boast.

"The Designer is like a weaver of tapestries, like these here, only his weaving is the world and all that is in it. We are only threads within the Design, and can no more understand the fullness of it than can one thread in a House Ransis weaving perceive the greatness of the whole work."

"We poor children of this world go through our lives thinking we control what goes on around us. We think that with enough gold, or land, or herds we will have say over our lives, but it is not so. We prepare our lives and suddenly, without warning, the Great Designer speaks and all we have, all we are, comes to nothing. Our fortunes are lost. Our lives are changed. Our very hearts are pulled out and put back different than ever before. And it happens in the blink of an eye. It happens between one breath and the next. The Designer and Maker of All crooks his finger and a breath of wind comes to stir a puff of dust, which blows into a wagoner's eye and causes him to pull tight upon the reins, which causes his animals to rear up in their harness and, though they be the most gentle of beasts, they paw the air and strike the head of one passing and he dies. Perhaps he is rich. Perhaps he is poor. But rich or poor, high born or low born, he is dead, and all his illusion of controlling his life is gone as fog before sunlight. Or perhaps a blind beggar sleeping in a ruin beside the refuse pit turns in his sleep rolling upon a lump of rock. The beggar pulls the stone from beneath him and casts it away with a curse; but a scavenger child, trying to stay alive upon the garbage of Peshar finds the stone and sees that it is a lump of stone with nodes of gold in it. He rejoices thinking that now he can control his life. He will no more have to dig in the refuse pit. But his control is illusion also. In fact, he has found this gold because the Great Designer wanted him to find it. The Great Designer has a purpose in the scavenger child's finding of the gold, just as there was purpose in the accidental death of the man beneath the hooves of the horses. Just as there was purpose in the curl of wind. All is in the hands of the Great Designer."

"But you can see tomorrow, I suppose," a voice sneered from the crowd, "and you will be more than happy to tell us what our tomorrows will be—for a zari or two."

Many of the crowd laughed and hooted.

The speaker grinned a twisted grin. It was not the shamefaced smile of one caught in a fortune telling scheme. "Even you, my friend, are moved by the Designer to his purpose."

"No doubt." answered the heckler.

"No doubt," said the speaker. "No, I am no teller of fortunes. I cannot see tomorrow any more than you can. I only know that I am in His hands, and He will deal with me in some way which will enhance the Design. My life will be a part of the Design and I will be a willing thread."

"I do not understand, oh thread," another voice called. "What would you have us do?"

The speaker turned toward the questioner. "I would have you believe. I would have you leave off your belief in the old gods, and your dedication to their temples as did Macar Holis when the Great Designer spoke to him from the flame. I would have you know in the depths of your heart that everything you do, everything you think, every breath you take, is at the behest of the Great Designer. Believe that you serve a purpose, and submit yourself to that purpose."

"And what will it cost us, oh thread?" the mocking voice asked.

"Nothing, and everything. When you acknowledge the Designer your life suddenly changes, for you no longer have the illusion of control. You find yourself completely at peace, knowing that you are truly a part of the Great Design. A willing thread, playing out your part with joy. Knowing that you have no control of life, but happy that you are controlled by the hand of the mighty Creator of All."

The crowd murmured and shifted, almost ready to turn away and go about their business.

"And suppose, oh thread," the mocking voice spoke, and the crowd calmed again, hoping for more amusement. "Suppose, oh thread that your part of this great weaving is to stain it with your blood, when some servant of the true Gods separates your head from your neck? "

The crowd, half anxious for such an execution to add a little excitement to their dull lives, laughed and leaned forward to hear how the speaker would answer.

"I will not look forward to it," he said. "But, if that is in the Design, that is what will happen. It will serve some purpose though I will not live to see that purpose worked out."

The crowd broke up after a little more baiting by the heckler. The speaker refused to rise to grow angry or answer spitefully.

Indi noticed that several acolytes from the Temple of Pesh had been among those listening to the Servant of the Design. It did not surprise him. The Temple of Pesh had been assaulted by this cult of the Design before. They did not talk about it, but almost everyone knew that some time back the Macar Holis the preacher had mentioned, who had been a righteous believer in Pesh, had claimed to have received a vision from some other god, telling him that Pesh was not a god. These Designers returned now and then from wherever they hid to preach their god. It almost always ended badly for the preacher.

Young Ransis went back to his stool and parked himself upon it once more. *This Designer sounds like Papa,* Indi thought. *He has all the future planned out and I have no say in it.*

The thought left a bitter taste, but as Indi rolled it around in his mind, he saw that it was probably true. No one truly controlled his own life, even Papa. He was only doing what his own father had set him up to do and would only do what he thought best.

"They are very beautiful," a voice said.

Indi looked up, and then shaded his eyes from the glare of the sun to see who stood before the display racks. It was the Designer cultist.

"They are House Ransis works, are they not?"

"Yes," Indi answered.

"The workmanship is something to be proud of."

"House Ransis is very proud of its work. That is why we have them displayed here in the plaza."

"Yes, of course." He continued to stand before the tapestry for which Indi had strung the warp threads. "This one seems somehow different though," he said.

"Different?"

"Yes. More—pained than the others." He turned to face Indi who had risen and now stood close. "It is your work, is it not, Indi Ransis?"

"Not…" Indi stopped short. "How do you know my name?"

The man smiled his twisted smile. Now that he was close enough, Indi saw that the twist was caused by a scar on the left side of the man's mouth. It was almost hidden by his beard, but not quite.

The man noticed the direction of Indi's eyes. "The Designer decreed that one who listened would be a strong believer in another god, and would demonstrate his belief with a large stone," he said with wry humor.

"How do you know my name?" Indi asked again.

"A dream. Your name and face came to me in a dream."

Indi snorted. "Those in the crowd who jibed were right. You're only a sooth-sayer and a dreamer of dreams. Go away. Leave me alone. I want nothing to do with your Designer."

"It does not matter. Your wants are of no consequence. The Designer has a special purpose for you, and it will be worked out as surely as the pattern of thread and colors are worked into your tapestry."

The laugh rose bitter as bile from Indi's heart. "Much your Designer knows. I have a part in a Design right enough, and not one of my own making either. I was born eldest son of House Ransis, and nothing I can do, except perhaps die, can change my life from what is set out for me."

The other shrugged, unperturbed. "As you wish. Nevertheless, when the time comes, travel north to Keep Holis. It is not difficult to find. On foot the journey took me a little more than three months. You will know you are near when the mountains called the Three Needles are the last thing touched with the light of evening, and the first thing touched with the light of dawn. Ask for guidance then. You are expected."

Indi could think of no answer for the surety of the man. He could only stare open mouthed as the man turned and disappeared into the crowd.

~ * ~

Design and Designers and what the Servant of the Design had said were never far from Indi's thoughts. He talked with no one about the visit to the display racks, or about anything else. He kept his own counsel and shrugged off the sharp words of his father who told Indi to pay attention to what he was doing, lest he knot the threads or string them backward.

Seven days after Indi had talked with the Servant of the Design he sat at a table outside a tea house in Tapestry Plaza, a cup of tea going cold in his hands and watched ten men in the robes of the Temple of Pesh haul the Designer from the stool which lifted him above the crowd who listened to him. Indi joined the crowd which trailed the priests and their captive to the square at the foot of the broad steps leading up to the colonnade of the Temple of Pesh. A hooded priest dressed all in white came down the temple steps to join them. He carried a heavy bronze sword with shaft long enough to be gripped with two hands.

"By order of Whidbis, Ruler of Peshar, Protector of the Ancient Faith, Chief Worshiper of Mighty Pesh, Father of Gods, you are accused of the crime of blasphemy. Will you answer this charge?"

The Servant of the Design did not smile, but the smile was in his voice when he said, "How can one blaspheme something which does not exist?"

The crowd gasped. This was blasphemy thrown into the very face of Mighty Pesh and his servants.

Indi found a catch in his throat that made him want to cry out NO…NO…NO…Do not say that. They will kill you! Do you not see the sword? But he said nothing, only watched like the rest of the silent crowd.

"By your own mouth you stand condemned," the priest said, cutting off any further words from the Servant of the Design. "Bind him," he commanded.

The priests began winding strips of cloth round the Servant of the Design. They bound him into a cocoon of cloth so that he could not move. The man did not resist or speak.

Indi watched, horrified. He had seen executions before, but not like this. He could not take his eyes away from the face of the Servant of the Design. It seemed that the other's eyes were locked onto Indi's.

At last the man was bound, leaving only his head and neck exposed. He stood still, held steady by three priests. These knelt in their positions, and the executioner stepped forward. He lifted the sword to the heavens and cried, "Behold, Mighty Pesh, we protect thy temple." He lowered the sword and let it rest broadside upon the left shoulder of the Servant of the Design who still stood upright. The executioner drew the sword back, coiling himself to strike.

In the half heartbeat between the executioner's drawing back his sword and the cut, Indi saw the Servant of the Design draw a deep, calm breath, and he knew the man's last thought was, *All is in the Design.*

The sword swung clean and flat, and the head of the blasphemer leapt to the right and rolled down the back of one of the priests who knelt holding the body. Blood pulsed in a fountain from the severed neck and washed down over all the kneeling priests.

The executioner stepped to the severed head and lifted it by the hair. "Thus, ever Blasphemers," he shouted.

The following morning Indi Ransis told his father that he was going to Keep Holis to study the Design.

~ * ~

All who studied the Design at Keep Holis changed their names. Indi chose to be called Javi, which meant seeker, and added Holis in honor of Macar Holis who had first heard the voice of the Designer.

Javi began his training as did all novices. He cleaned endlessly. Common rooms, yards, gardens, dwelling rooms of the Masters. He also helped in the kitchen and worked in the fields which fed those of the community of the Design. He slept and ate in the common rooms with other novices. He learned to look within himself for privacy, for there was no physical privacy in Keep Holis for novices. In the hours of the day not taken up with work he contemplated the drawings and writings of those who had lived and died in submission to the Design.

The Mandalai were Designs of incredible intricacy. They often took the form of wheels with the artist who had drawn them at the center. The artist's personal perceptions of the Design radiated out from this personal center. Other Mandalai had trees or the sun at their centers. All these were magnetic to Javi the tapestry maker. He could almost feel the stir such designs would make if they were displayed in Tapestry Plaza.

Some of the Mandalai he understood. They were celebrations of family, growing things, the changing of season, but others, called *dark,* he did not understand. He went to his masters to ask what they meant.

"We do not know," Master Aram told him. "That is why they are called the *Dark Mandalai.*"

"But they have meaning, Master Aram," Javi said. "I can feel that."

"Yes. You are not the first to feel that they have meaning, but thus far no one has been given the understanding of them."

"But how did those who drew them know what to draw?" Javi asked.

"How does a mother bird know what she must do to hatch her eggs? How does the egg know that it must become a bird not a turtle?" Master Aram shrugged. "It simply knows. That is the way of the Mandalai, and not just those called *Dark*. The Master of the Design whispered to the makers in their dreams or while they sat quietly listening for his words."

Javi sat a long time, and Master Aram did not disturb his thoughts.

Aram remembered the man who had first told him of the Design. That man had spoken of dreams and voices too, and student Aram had thought that man a fool at first. Now he sat, saying the same things to his student.

At last Javi came back from his contemplation and said, "Master, I think I have heard the voice of the Designer."

Master Aram blinked at this. He could hardly believe such effrontery. "Go on," he said.

"The words are not clear," Javi said. "I cannot see the full meaning of them, but I am sure the Designer has told me something of the power of the Dark Mandalai."

Master Aram did not quite succeed in keeping his doubts out of his voice.

"That is the way of the Designer," he said pulling his cloak tighter around him against the cold. "He knows our needs and our capacities, and gives us only that which he knows we are ready to know." He stretched out his hand and patted Javi on the shoulder. "Wait upon the Designer, Javi. He is preparing something for you. But do not be too quick to declare the whisperings of your own mind to be the voice of the Maker of All."

Javi bowed his head. "Yes, Master Aram. I will be careful."

The old man nodded. "Open your mind to the Designer," he said. "Allow yourself to be his instrument. Understanding will come to you, but do not be in too much of a hurry for it to come. Sometimes understanding brings more pain than satisfaction."

"Yes Master," he said, and went back to his duties.

Winter's depths closed over the Keep. The already restricted life became even narrower. No fire seemed able to shield against the knife-like cold which hemmed the Servants of the Design into Keep Holis.

It was during one such bout of cold that Javi, with a wry thought, took the Dark Mandala called The Fire, and began to study it. He carried the velum sheet with care to the hearthstone of the common room and sat down to study it. After many hours of contemplation of the Mandala he found himself nodding, heavy with sleep. The fire in the hearth had burned low, and the room was cold.

Javi stood, stretched, rubbed his eyes, and shivered. He thought of his cold pallet at the other side of the room and decided to make a cup of tea to fortify himself against the chill. He shivered yet more as he broke the thick skin of ice which had formed on the water jar near the door. Javi dipped water into the teakettle and hung it on the pot hook above the fire, then punched up the flames with a poker and added a few sticks. When the blaze merrily licked at the bottom of the teakettle, he sat down on the hearth again. His mind wandered back to the Mandala he had been studying. The meaning of it seemed just on the edge of his comprehension, but he could not pull it into the full light of understanding. After a little while he forcibly shoved the thoughts from his mind and leaned over to check the teakettle.

The fire's warming tongue licked up around the teakettle's bottom and thin wisps of steam rose from the spout. The picture it formed stopped Javi as though he had been struck in the face. This was the meaning of the Mandala. It was the fire, whereby the steam of the spirit could be released from the teakettle of the body. The meaning was so clear Javi was astonished and ashamed that he had not understood before.

With his heart pounding in excitement, the young Servant of the Design lay down upon the hearth and closed his eyes. The hiss of the steaming kettle made a soft background which blanked out the sounds of wind and the crackling of ice from outside.

Javi brought the Dark Mandala called The Fire before his mind's eye. It was fire licking up around him, as fire licked the bottom of the kettle. It heated that part of him which was the real Javi Holis. The essence of him.

After a time, the Mandala began to have an effect. Javi felt his spirit warm and bubble-like heated water, and steam began to rise; the conscious steam of his essence, his spirit.

There was lightness to him. He felt himself drift up like steam from the kettle and he wondered if indeed he was rising like steam. He opened his eyes.

Below him, lying on the hearth was the body of a skinny young man with a ragged beard who was wrapped in a battered cloak. At first glance he looked dead, but a moment's observation showed slow, shallow movement of breath.

Javi wondered who the young man was. He did not remember seeing him among the students. There was something familiar about him though. He looked like—he looked like Javi's father. But that couldn't be. Papa was old.

Realization came to him like a slap. The body on the hearth was his own body! The Mandala had done its work He had separated spirit from body through concentration upon the Mandala.

Shock and surprise robbed Javi of control and his essence was drawn back into his body with a snap. In a moment he sat up and rubbed his eyes wondering if what had just happened was only a dream. He had often dreamed of flying like a bird when he was a child, but never so vividly that he could see his body below him.

Suddenly, Javi was shaking, and not with cold. He was sure this had not been a dream. He had separated his essence from the vessel created to contain it and the very thought of it was overwhelming. Frightening.

Javi drew in a deep breath and tried to calm the shaking of his hands and the quivering of his stomach. He set about finishing the tea he had started to make, not because he really wanted it, but because his mind needed the refuge of common things in order to keep sanity.

Sunlight had barely touched the peaks of the Three Needles when Javi presented himself to Master Aram. He explained what had happened.

"Perhaps it was a dream, Javi," the master said doubtfully

"It was no dream Master Aram," Javi answered positively.

"But have you tried this separation again to be sure?" the old man asked.

"No Master. I wanted you to help me in the test. And...I am afraid."

Master studied his student for a moment, looking for the truth of what had happened. If the boy had been dreaming, then the dream might very well have come from the Maker of All. What else had Master been telling the student? Now Master Aram was being put to the test. Did he truly believe what he had been telling young Javi?

"If this is a real power, then there is reason to be cautious Javi, just as there is cause for caution when using fire or knives or medicines. But all those things are gifts of the Designer and when they are controlled, they are beneficial. I believe that this power, if it is real, is the same. Controlled, it may be of great benefit. Uncontrolled, it may be very dangerous."

"Then, shall I try to use it again, Master?"

The old man thought a moment. "Yes. I do not think the Master of Design would allow understanding if he did not wish the power used."

"I will go back to the hearth, and when the thing is done, I will come to you in my essence."

Master Aram nodded, and wondered if he had done right as he watched his student go.

Javi returned to the hearth, placed the teakettle upon its pot hook and punched up the fire. When steam was rising thick from the spout, he lay down and brought the Mandala of The Fire before his mind's eye. He was so nervous that he had trouble concentrating. Several times he opened his eyes and drew deep breaths, trying to calm himself. At first, he feared to relax too much, lest sleep, rather than the deep relaxation of meditation overtake him.

After what seemed hours, he was ready to give up the attempt. He rose from the hearth and went to Master Aram's chamber to confess his inability.

At the closed door of the master's chamber he stopped, and lifted his hand to knock. His hand disappeared through the door.

Javi snatched his hand back and stared at the solid wood of the door. Then he slowly reached out…and put his hand through it.

It was an odd, watery feeling upon his wrist where it remained within the precinct of the door. He pulled his hand back. After a moment Javi drew in a deep breath, then laughed at the incongruity of a man without a body drawing in breath and stepped through the door.

Master Aram sat at his desk studying another of the Dark Mandalai. He looked up toward the door a second after Javi entered as though the entrance of the student's essence had disturbed him.

"Master Aram, I am here," Javi said.

The old man did not react to the voice, but his dark gray eyes seemed to deepen into their bony sockets and his lined face took on a haunted expression, as though something frightening were just on the edge of his vision.

"Javi, I cannot see you, but I feel the truth of your presence. Can you make yourself known somehow?"

Javi hesitated a moment, then moved to the desk and put his hand into the hand of his master.

The old man snatched his hand away as if he had been burned, but after a moment he returned his hand to the position it had been in before and said, "Javi, if it was you who touched me, touch me again."

Javi did as he was told, and again Master Aram snatched his hand away. "Your touch is like ice, and your presence makes my stomach queasy. Please go before I am unable to control myself. Return to me when you are again joined to your body."

Javi found that he was glad to return to his body. He had begun to feel cold and watery all over, almost as the steam rising from the kettle must feel as it was longer and longer away from the source of heat. He hurried back to the hearth and felt the chilly liquidity growing. When he reached the hearth, he had a moment of panic when he realized he did not know how to reunite with his body. He suppressed the fear and lay down on top of his waiting body, hoping this was the way to reunite body and spirit.

Minutes passed and the chill began to dissipate. Javi could feel the warmth of the fire, and knew he was no longer in two parts. With a corner of his mind he could see the Mandala of The Fire and realized that during his separation he had focused on it from time to time. Now he consciously closed that compartment of his mind and opened his eyes to the physical world.

Javi squeezed his eyes shut once more and flexed all his muscles to assure himself that they still worked, then stood and went to Master Aram's quarters. He knocked and entered when the old man called to him.

"Is all well, Javi?" the master asked.

"Yes Master. I am fully restored."

"It was you who touched me," the old man said, no question in his voice.

"Yes. I spoke also, but you could not hear me."

"The instant you entered I felt your presence. There was a chill, but not from the winter's cold. Deeper, more bone freezing. And there was a sense of...like being at sea in a small boat. I felt sick."

"Yes, I understand."

The old man was in awe of his student. No one until now had understood any of the Dark Mandalai. Now this young man, hardly more than a boy, had been granted understanding by the Master of the Design. "What was it like, Javi? How did it feel?"

Javi tried to explain, but found it impossible. "There is no way to tell you, Master," he said at last. "And I do not know how I did it. I was unable to achieve the separation at first, but when I stopped trying, I suddenly found myself in two parts."

Master looked at student and found himself humbled. All the doubts he had harbored. All the silent laughter he had heaped upon what he thought was a pretentious child. All came back to haunt him now, and he was ashamed.

"Javi," Master Aram began, "The Maker of All truly has a special part of the Design for you to work out. I can only ask your forgiveness for my doubts. You must continue studying the Dark Mandalai. We have known for a long time that they were filled with great power, but we did not know, until now, what that power might be."

Javi, feeling suddenly alone and incompetent, swallowed hard. "Master Aram, I am only a student. I must have your guidance in this."

The old man was silent for a time, then said, "Perhaps I can help you in your studies, Master Javi."

Javi's eyes widened in surprise and he began to protest the title, but Master Aram waved him to silence. After a few moments Javi smiled, shyly. "Then we shall be students together, Master Aram."

Two

15 B.C.G. thru 1 A.C.G

Javi became Master Javi to all and he, above all of them, studied the Mandalai. He also taught all who could learn the technique of holding a mental picture of the Mandalai before the mind's eye, but still being able to function with the rest of the mind.

The young master was puzzled and saddened that not everyone who wished to use the Mandalai could do so. Some simply could not keep the Mandalai firmly in mind, or, if they could, that was the only thing they could do. All other tasks were beyond them. Javi talked with many other masters about this, but none gave him as good an answer as did Master Aram.

"The Maker of All has given each of us talents. Some can write well, some draw well, some have talent with cooking or keeping gardens. We cannot understand why everyone is not given every talent, but it is so; therefore, we must say, 'All is in the Design', and continue to seek and use whatever talents we have."

Javi sighed. "Sometimes I think the Great Designer is cruel to his creations in things like this. Would it not be better for us not to know of these powers, if we cannot all use them?"

"I do not think the Maker of All is cruel, Javi. When things hurt us, or when things are hard to understand, I think the Designer also feels our pain. I think he regrets any pain we must suffer to serve the Design, but, alas, there is pain and we servants must suffer it, if the Design is to go on."

"But why must the Design go on if it causes pain?" the young master asked.

"I cannot tell you, Javi. I do not know. Perhaps, someday I will be wise enough to answer, but now I am not. I can only say, 'All is in the Design.'"

~ * ~

Of the thirty-three Dark Mandalai, only five allowed understanding and use. Those were: The Fire, which separated the essence of being from the vessel of the body. The Enfolding Arms, which gave the effect of reaching out to people and embracing them with a calming force, as a parent's embrace could calm a fretting child. The Hand, which allowed the mind to reach out and move some things; things that could be moved would have to be small enough for one person to move in the physical world. The fourth power was The Ear. This allowed one to hear the thoughts of another, if the other did not know that there was such a power, or if the other allowed his thoughts to be heard. There was a moral dilemma attached to this power. The Masters Council, which now included Javi, discussed this power, and the fifth power, The Whisper, for days.

The Whisper was the power to reach into the mind of another and speak to it. This power had much potential for evil. An unsuspecting person could be influenced to thoughts not his own by use of it. Madness might come of this, or undue power over one who did not know what was happening.

It was decided that The Ear and The Whisper would only be used among those consenting. The council was not unanimous in the decision, but all agreed they would be bound by these rules even as the powers were being further discussed.

"But why can only five of the Dark Mandalai be understood?" many of the masters asked. "We can feel the power of them, but we cannot use them."

"Because all is in the Design," Aram, Javi and other masters said. "The Maker of All has no need for us to understand these others yet. Were not the five powers dark for many years, even from those who drew them?"

The council agreed.

"When the Maker of All sees fit, our minds will be quickened to understand others. In the meantime, the Mandalai of Power should be gathered together and protected."

This suggestion started uproar. "What of those Mandalai which are painted upon walls, or wood? How can they be 'gathered together?'"

Master Kalin Holis, librarian and Master of ink and paint, had been granted visions of new Mandalai by the Maker of All. He spoke now. "My students and I can make copies of the Mandalai. These copies can be bound into a book and preserved. That will also make them more convenient to study."

After much further discussion it was agreed that the copies should be made. "Knowledge of the five powers must be preserved and guarded, and all the Mandalai must be available to students of the future when understanding will surely come," they said.

Javi, still uncomfortable with his status as a master, shyly addressed the council. "We cannot let those who do not serve the Great Designer know of the powers. These must be kept close among the Servants. If someone unscrupulous should find them and learn their use they might harm their brother men for the sake of profit or hatred. That would be a great evil and, though even that be within the Design, I cannot believe the Maker of All would wish evil on his creations if it can be avoided."

"But if it is not the will of the Designer how can knowledge of the uses of the Mandalai come to anyone?" many asked.

"That is true," Javi answered. "Nevertheless, I feel that we must protect these Mandalai of power."

The council argued over this for hours but finally decided Master Javi was right. "The will of the Designer is the will of the Designer, and we cannot change it by anything we may do, but we will guard this knowledge. If it is within the Design that these powers be widely known, there is nothing we can do about it, but we will keep this knowledge within us until such time that the will of the Designer is clear otherwise."

So, it was done. The thirty-three Mandalai of Power were copied and bound and that volume was placed with other volumes of history and philosophy and science. It was studied by all within the keep, but no one outside was ever given knowledge of its existence.

~ * ~

The black ships of the new gods came out of the sky when Javi Holis was forty-two years old. The students of the Design at Keep Holis knew nothing of the landings until refugees began filtering into the mountains. These fugitives were a battered, fear-driven stream of misery who had no clear idea of what was happening, but they told tales of unbelievable terror. Tales of things which flew through the air and black-armored beings with magic sticks which made things – and people – burst into flame.

"They came from across the sky," one who had stumbled and crawled to the gate of Keep Holis told Javi. The man was horribly burned, but not by any fire Javi recognized.

"They are not men," the burned man said. "They look like men, but they are Gods with great power. They fly without wings, and no weapon can harm them."

"But where do they come from?"

"Across the sky," he said again, though what he said made no sense. Everyone knew that the sky was only the cloth the Maker of All stretched over the world to shield it from his glory.

"But how? From whence?" Javi asked, but the burned man's mind skipped away to other miseries.

"Gone… All gone." The man moaned, delirious with pain. "My babies, my babies. All dead. All dead."

All who reached Keep Holis told much the same stories, even those not apparently hurt, but it all seemed like delirious ranting. "Can this be true Master Aram?" Javi asked. "Can these beings have come from across the sky? Are they gods?"

Master Aram was old and feeble but still possessed of a mind sharp as January wind. He shook his head at the question.

"I do not see how this could be true, but those who study the sky say new stars have appeared. Stars which rise in the west and fall in the east. And they rise and fall many times during the night."

"But are they gods?" Javi asked again.

The Servants of the Design had taught that the Design was huge, encompassing everything. So huge that even the most careful study could not understand more than a tiny portion. But even the most astute, most imaginative of them had not considered how big, BIG really was.

"I must go and see for myself whether the poor wretches who have found their way here are right or wrong, Master Aram," Javi said. "I am a student of the Design, and surely this is a great new portion of it."

Master Aram looked at the man who was no longer young and no longer his student. "Since I began to serve the Designer and study his Design, I have believed the Maker of All whispered his secrets in my ear. I believed that the Design was not really so complex. Now, in my old age, I find that the voice I heard was my own puffing. Words to make myself believe I was heir to all the secrets of the Design. What a fool. What a fool I was. I did not listen to my Masters, nor to myself, when I taught my students that we are all only poor instruments of the Designer's will. Poor ignorant instruments. Yet we think that because we study the Design, we are somehow better than the other instruments of the world. Fools!"

The old man fell silent again. Javi did not know what to say to comfort him.

"You must go Javi. You must study this new part of the Design and you must remember that, whether these new creatures are men or something else, they too are part of the Design. They exist to work out some portion of which they know not."

Javi patted the old man's hand. "Thank you for your council. I will go." He stood and Master Aram took hold of his wrist.

"I fear I will not see you again, Javi."

The younger man smiled. "Perhaps that is so. It is in the hands of the Maker of All."

"See that you remember that. Do not be a fool like your master."

Feeling as though he had been caught filching sugar, Javi grinned. "I am caught in haughtiness, Master. But I will try to remember."

~ * ~

Ribbons of smoke still rose from sectors of Peshar when Javi arrived a month later, but the beings from the…sky ships…? had stopped their wholesale destruction in favor of more surgical violence.

During the weeks of travel from Keep Holis, Javi had asked everyone he met what they had seen or heard. All told basically the same story as those refugees who had reached Keep Holis. Flying things shaped round like dishes and black-armored beings. He could hardly credit them until he saw for himself. When he did, he could only stand open-mouthed and watch as the ship passed over head.

Others on the road ran at the first sight of the thing in the sky, but Javi was so astonished he only stood and watched. Nothing happened. The thing passed over like a bird on its own errand and when it was out of sight, people came from ditches and out from under trees to look after it for a moment before hurrying about their business.

The black-armored beings were something else again. Javi saw none of them during the whole trip. Until he reached Peshar he only heard of the "Sky Gods." In the outskirts of the city he saw his first one. This one was almost as impressive as the flying ship had been. It was flying too, but it was clearly human in shape: two arms, two legs, one head. In the hands was a thing which must have been the magic burning stick he had heard of. This creature drifted across the sky at about twice the height of a man above the earth. It moved slowly, turning its head from side to side, looking for something.

Javi did not try to hide, but stopped to watch its progress.

Suddenly, from a burned-out ruin, a man with a bow rose and let fly an arrow at the drifting black thing. The arrow clanged against the armor and shattered. The being whirled in midair and pointed his stick (*more like a tube than a stick,* Javi thought), and the bowman burst into flame. One sharp scream came from the man and then there was nothing.

The black-armored being swung around seeking other targets. It stopped at the sight of Javi, but when he made no hostile move, it continued its survey, looking for other targets. After a few moments of looking around the flying being continued its slow drift and constant scan.

Javi watched until it was out of sight.

Javi saw no more than a hundred of the black armored figures, yet they seemed to have total control of the city. There was a constant patrol by the flying beings. They fired upon anything which looked suspicious, and it hadn't taken a long time for them to control the city and the population.

Javi worked his way toward House Ransis asking questions of any who would stand long enough to answer. Most gave short furtive answers, looking around as if one of the sky creatures would suddenly appear and gobble them up, but from them Javi pieced together a little more of what happened.

The Sky Gods—for that was what people were calling these creatures, had come to Peshar because the people had offended them by failing to worship them. They had destroyed all the government which extended from the palace of King Matir, and swept aside the king's army as if it were nothing.

"Like harvesting wheat," one man told him. "The Sky Gods swept their hands in the direction of the armies and the soldiers died. They never so much as loosed an arrow or spear before they fell."

"They also destroyed all the temples," another volunteered, "even that of Mighty Pesh."

"Not so mighty now," the first said bitterly. "The altar flame is out and the temple is dust and shards. Priests and temple servants lined up to resist, but it was as with the king's troops."

"They would have destroyed the whole city, maybe the whole world if not for the tapestry in the plaza."

"What tapestry?" Javi asked.

"Old Ransis' *Memoria*. The beauty of it stopped the gods' destruction," they said in awed tones. "The gods said any such beauty made it clear that Peshar was redeemable."

"Redeemable," someone snorted. "There was no more sport in killing us. The tapestry was just an excuse to stop."

Javi was stunned, more by reference to his father's *Memoria* than anything else. "When did old Ransis die?" he asked.

"Didn't, so far as I know. The old braggart wouldn't have gone to his grave without seeing all Peshar 'Ooh and Ahh' over his final work."

"The gods spared him," someone else said. "Lucky bastard is one of the few old Lords left. The Sky Gods called most of the others."

"Called them?" Javi asked, not understanding.

"Those not killed outright were gathered up into a sky ship and taken away. Maybe executed."

"Naw, not executed. They would have just done that where they stood. After the thousands of others, why would they worry about a few more? They took 'em back to wherever they came from in the first place. Back across the sky."

"But not Lord Ransis?"

"Even for gods it would not look well to say a man's work was reason for salvation, and then not save that very man."

There were grunts of agreement.

A slow-flying god patroller drifted into the small square where the men had been talking, and the little group melted away, leaving Javi standing alone.

Javi made his way across the river to House Ransis, but found only a burned-out ruin. The gardens looked as though a battle had been fought there.

Javi kicked at a pile of ashes. A stick which looked suspiciously like a leg bone turned up. He did not stoop to see if its appearance was reality. The very possibility made his stomach churn.

But they said Papa was alive, he thought, *or was a few days ago if rumor could be trusted. Where is everyone then?*

Then he thought of the tapestry factory.

The streets were growing dark, and those few brave souls who had dared travel anywhere were quickly getting indoors. Javi hurried on, puzzled by what he was observing. That section of Peshar which had been given over to large manufactories was almost intact. Very little destruction of any sort had come here. Much of the rest of Peshar was in ruin. The Sky Gods had wiped out the government and philosophical base of the city, but left the infrastructure mostly intact. Why was that? Why would gods be concerned with glassmakers and weavers and potters and metal smiths?

House Ransis tapestry factory had not been touched. The entry door, which was cut into the larger doors through which goods were carried, stood open. The rhythmic hiss, hiss, clack, thunk, thunk, clack of a loom being operated drifted out. Even after more than twenty years Javi recognized the sound of the smallest loom being worked. He listened for other signs of life but heard none. He stepped inside the door and shouted, "Hello. Who is here?"

The sound of the loom stopped. After a moment a figure came from the dark, dusty heart of the building. "Who are you? What do you want?" the man demanded. He stumped to Javi as though prepared to toss the intruder back into the street if need be.

"My father. I wish to see my father if he is here?"

"And who might your father be?" the man demanded, still belligerent.

"Nephar Ransis, Patriarch of House Ransis," Javi said with some arrogance, forgetting that no one in the factory would remember him after so many years. "I am Javi Holis...I mean I am Indi Ransis."

The man was instantly alert. "Holis is a name to be feared. Mention of it or of the Design could earn a man a beating in this factory in times past."

Javi smiled crookedly. "My father was less than pleased when I left to study the Design."

The weaver relaxed a little at the newcomer's openness. "Yes, indeed. Lord Ransis could come to a boil in a breath's length over his foolish son."

Javi blushed and looked at the ground. "I went to the old house, but it is only a ruin. Where is the family?"

"Lord Ransis, your mother, and your brothers are here, in the old quarters."

"And my sisters?"

The man's eyes darted away and came to rest in the space above Javi's head. "They..." he began and stopped.

"My sisters?" Javi asked again, afraid of what he was about to hear.

"Gone," the weaver said. "They are gone."

"Dead?"

The man shrugged. "Many young women were herded together and taken into a sky ship. After that…" he shrugged again and looked down at his feet.

Javi drew a deep breath and let it waver out, trying to take in this news. After a little he said, "The old quarters were crammed with stored goods. There was hardly room to turn around. How can they…"

"The gods decreed it," he said making a face as though he smelled something long dead. "The goods are now stacked beneath tents in the dye yard." He paused a moment. "At that, House Ransis has been luckier than many. Other great houses have no one left to mourn them. Come, I will take you."

"I know the way," Javi said.

"I had best go first, all the same. A stranger is likely to be met with fists. Times are hard."

Javi nodded and allowed the weaver to lead the way and tried not to think of hunting rats with a sharpened stick in the old quarters when he was a child.

A bead curtain was drawn over the door. The weaver held it aside and said, "It is me," then stepped through. Javi followed close behind him.

An old woman crouched before the hearth, tending to a cook pot hung over the small fire. She turned with a little scream. It took Javi a moment to realize that this shrunken crone was his mother.

Lauri Ransis did not recognize her son, but was grateful this intruder was not a black-armored god. "Who are you?" she asked, voice cracking with fear.

"Mother… It is me, Indi."

The old woman stood and came closer. She peered into Javi's face, seeking the young man she had last seen twenty years before. "Indi? It is you," she breathed. "It is you." Her skinny arms went round his neck, and she began to cry. "I had given you up for dead. After so many years…and now with the coming of the new gods…"

Javi stroked the old woman's hair. It was stiff with dirt and sweat. She smelled of many days without washing. It wrung his heart to find her so. She had always been fastidious. She had always smelled of flowers when he was a child.

"Where is Papa?" Javi asked after a moment.

The weaver had watched this greeting with growing emotion.

"You truly are Indi," he said, his voice choking a little. "Welcome back to your place, Lord Ransis."

Javi turned to the man. "Thank you, but I do not know if I can stay. My Father?"

"He will not be glad to see you, Indi," the old woman said. "He blames you for all that has happened."

"But you have come home," the weaver said with finality. He turned toward the door. "We have one more thing for which to be thankful." he said and went out.

"That man is not far from belief in the Design," Javi said.

"Do not speak of it," his mother said. "Already your father blames you and your Design for all that has happened."

"Blames me? But why, after all the years? Does he think I called these creatures from out of the sky?" Javi was hurt and angry, and relief at finding any of his family alive allowed him to let the hurt and anger out.

His mother slumped onto a bench beside the hearth. "He is not well Indi. When these. . ." she hesitated. "When they took your sisters, Papa began saying it was all this Design talk that was to blame. Many of your people—Designers—had been preaching in Peshar just before… Many young people said the old gods were false and that this Designer was the true God."

Javi slumped beside his mother. "I am sorry, mother. I, we, had nothing to do with this."

She smiled, thin-lipped. "I know. I know."

They sat in silence for a time then Javi said, "But why are you here? What happened?"

The old woman's hands fluttered as she lifted them from her lap. "The black ships came and the gods came. They destroyed…if not for Papa's *Memoria,* they would have killed us all. I think that is why they let us live. Maybe why they let Peshar live. They came to the house and herded us all into the garden. They asked if we were House Ransis. We were afraid, but Papa stood up to them. They asked if all were blood of Ransis, and when we said 'no,' they made us point out which were not. They separated all the servants out and killed them." She began to weep quietly. "We thought they would kill us all, but they didn't. They took your sisters away. Maybe they killed them later, I don't know. I pray to mighty Pesh that they are alive, but maybe it would be better if they were not."

A man burst through the bead curtain. "Mother?" he called, then stopped dead at sight of Javi sitting beside the old woman, holding her hand. "Are you all right mother?" he asked.

"Bai," she said, "This is your brother Indi."

"Nomer told me someone calling himself Indi Ransis had come here. I do not believe it. Indi Ransis is dead. Long dead."

"No," Javi shook his head. "I am truly your elder brother, Bai."

Bai examined the man beside his mother for a long time. "Papa said you were dead."

Javi shrugged. "Perhaps it would have been better, but I am not. And now the Design has brought me back."

The younger man looked around quickly as though fearing his elder brother might be heard. "Do not mention this Design, whoever you are. Papa will fly into a rage if he hears, and the new gods do not deal kindly with believers in any gods but them."

"Are they truly gods then?" Javi asked.

Bai started to say yes, but stopped, thought a moment and said, "They have the power of gods."

"But does that make them gods?"

~ * ~

Javi left the factory without an answer to his last question, and without having seen his father. He felt loss, as if the old man had died, but he did not want to cause any more pain or trouble for his mother and brothers, so he left. He joined the growing number of beggars in the streets. At night he slept in the alleys with them and found that it was possible for a beggar to go places other citizens could not.

The Servant of the Design played his part well. He begged from everyone who looked prosperous enough to have an extra tenth zari. He even boldly shook his bowl under the noses of the new servants of the new gods when they began appearing upon the streets of Peshar.

The gods set up a clerical hierarchy with one of their own, called the God-Resident, at the top. His power was exercised through hand-picked Pesharis called Priests. These commanded a small army who called themselves Temple Servants. These were Peshari men who had gone over to the service of the new gods. Whether true believers in the new gods or mere opportunists, they were willing to carry out the orders of the new gods against their own people. Many more were employed overseeing Peshari prisoners who were being used as labor to build a new temple.

This new temple was puzzlement to Javi. It was being built the way all buildings in Peshar had been built before. Hewn stone blocks were stacked one atop the other to build walls, but the stone cutting was done by god machines which sliced huge slabs of stone from the face of a mountain and laid them down as gently as a man might lay down a single brick. The slab was then cut into building stones and the stones were transported as by magic from quarry to temple sight. There Pesharis overseers drove slave labor by the old method of lash and kick to erect the walls.

Javi could not understand this. Clearly these creatures from the sky had power that could raise this temple much faster and probably stronger than hand labor could, yet they did not use it. Instead they forced the people of Peshar to work. It made no sense. Nor could anyone he asked about it give him any kind of answer. But in his questioning and watching Javi discovered that one section of the gigantic temple was forbidden to any, save the gods. This section was made of uncut slabs of stone brought whole from the quarry.

Javi hid himself outside the forbidden area and watched as three god machines lifted and placed slabs. Two would set the slab in place, then the third emitted a red light which caused smoke to rise from the seam between the stone slabs. When the machine moved on, Javi could not see where one slab of stone ended and the next began. Soon the area was walled off so thoroughly that he could not see anything more. I must get inside there, he thought. Inside is the answer to whether these are gods or not.

The power of The Fire would have been perfect for such entry into the forbidden place, but Javi dared not use it. He did not know if he would be invisible to the gods (he called them that for he did not know what else to call them, and everyone was calling them gods). He knew that some of the other powers did have effect on gods as well as men, but the effects seemed limited on the gods. With The Ear he had touched a gods' mind, but he could not make sense of the confused patterns and mental noise there. He had used the Enfolding Arms once, and was fairly sure he had stopped a god from killing a Peshari, but he was not positive. But more, he worried about leaving his body unprotected if he used the power of The Fire. At Keep Holis he had never worried about such a thing, but here he was surrounded by enemies. There was no one he could trust. The beggars he knew, of whom he was one, were in a permanent state of hunger and despair. They would sell one another to the gods or the Temple servants for a crust of bread. If they found his unprotected body, they might try to sell it, or they might simply strip it of what little they could steal and make sure it was really dead. Still, he must see inside the forbidden area. The truth, or at least part of it was hidden there.

Javi could see no way to do what he thought must be done. That was when the final warning from Master Aram came back to his mind, and he remembered that he could only wait upon the Design; only trust that the Maker of All controlled everything to his own ends; only possess himself in patience until the Designer showed him what to do.

Usually, Javi took up his beggar's pitch near food sellers. Those spending money for food often felt the hunger of the beggars they passed, but a few weeks after he had decided he must get into the forbidden area, he felt too tired to go all the way to his usual pitch and seated himself beside a wall near a potter's booth. He didn't expect to gain much here, only rest a bit before going on.

The weather was chilly, and the thin crowd huddled into its cloaks and moved along with determination and heads down out of the wind. Javi half-heartedly shook his begging bowl under a few noses, but had gotten only a tenth zari. He was preparing to move on when the Design made itself known.

A man, hooded and cloaked against the chill wind, was shoved by someone so that he stumbled right in front of Javi.

Many hands reached out to help the man rise, and sellers hoping to tempt the stumbler into their booths brushed his clothes and inquired if he was hurt. One brushing pair of hands though, was not helpful. These snaked themselves toward the purse tied by thongs to the stumbler's belt.

Javi caught the glint of the cut-purse's blade as it stretched toward the purse strings. More by instinct than intent, he grabbed the thief's wrist.

The cut-purse jerked himself around, half in fear at being caught and half in rage at being defeated by a ragged beggar. He would have run, but the rage outweighed his fear. He lunged at Javi, intent on driving his blade between the prominent ribs, but the hooded man whose purse Javi had saved grabbed the thief in mid-charge, cuffed him hard on the side of the head and spun him away into the crowd.

The cut-purse sprang up and turned toward Javi again, but he hesitated. Rage and fear showed in his face as he considered whether to try again for the beggar's life, but he thought better of it and fled. A moment later there was no evidence that anything had happened, save that the hooded man was kneeling before Javi.

"Are you all right, Old One?" the man asked.

Javi did not realize the man was speaking to him at first since he did not think of himself as aged enough to be called 'Old One', but the hooded man meant him to answer so he said, "I am unmarked, my Lord. And yourself?"

The man threw back his hood and Javi's mouth dropped open. The man was Bai, his brother.

"Bai," he said. "Do you not recognize me? I am Indi."

Bai's eyebrows lowered in confusion, and he scanned the bearded, emaciated face of the beggar for a long time before he recognized the man he had seen only once in the last twenty years.

"But why are you here, Indi? I thought you returned to your mountain and your precious Design," he said, too loud. Realizing it, he glanced around and was relieved when no one seemed to have noticed

Javi looked around too, and after a little he rose and pulled Bai along into a less populated alley.

"I study the Design in the streets of Peshar now," he said. "I study to discover whether or not these so-called gods are truly gods."

"It looks as though your studies have not helped you to live well. Your bones show."

Javi smiled. "My body is under-nourished, but my mind is much better filled than it was."

For the first time Bai Ransis smiled. "Your fat mind would have been attached to a corpse if that cut purse had driven his blade home."

Javi shrugged. "But your purse is fatter for my stupidity."

"True enough, and for that I think I should help your skinny body to become a little fatter. Come."

"Where?"

"Home, of course. Where else?"

"But father… and I do not want to put you into any danger."

Bai grimaced. "Danger is a thing which cannot be avoided since the coming of the gods. We were not safe in our home then, and we certainly are not now. As to Papa, I doubt he would know you in any case. He is nearly blind and his mind is not so clear. If I tell him you are a fugitive from the gods that will anger him enough to protect you no matter what."

Javi tried to resist even so, but the decision was made for him a moment later when he suddenly felt faint and leaned rather heavily against the alley wall. He had not eaten for two days and the meals before that had been sparse at best. Bai put his arm around his brother's waist and steadied him until the faintness passed.

"Just don't mention Designs, or that you are Indi, or anything about any Holis. You are Javi Mendic now."

"But…" Javi protested.

"No buts. Shut up and walk."

Three

1 A.C.G.

Javi regained his strength and became re-acquainted with his younger brother. Bai had seemed a child when Javi left for Keep Holis. He was, in fact, only five years younger than Javi, and he was the eldest remaining male child of House Ransis, so the Patriarchy of House Ransis had passed to him.

Bai had been young for responsibility of such weight, but House Ransis had done well under his guidance. House Ransis was now better known than it had been under Javi and Bai's father, Nephar. That was because Bai paid more attention to the business of contracts and money, and let the truly skilled weavers, dyers and stitchers handle the manufacture of tapestries. Under Bai's management House Ransis hired artists to weave from their own designs, but more than just paying these artists for their work, Bai began to share the profits of the sale with the artists. This was revolutionary. It also made many artists willing to work for subsistence on the chance that their work might reap a good profit and so make their reputations.

"But that was all before the coming of the Gods," Bai said.

The brothers were sipping tea while sitting in the sun of the court yard, trying to stave off the winter's chill.

"So many artists are dead now," Bai went on. "So many plain simple weavers are dead, or scattered to the winds... It is hard to find anyone to work. Since the sky ships came, only three weavers remain and they have no heart for work. Besides, few have money for anything except food and clothing."

"Perhaps House Ransis should put aside tapestry for the moment and consider something more basic—like food and clothing," Javi said.

Bai looked speculatively at his brother. "I have been thinking that," he said. "The market for tapestries has all but dried up, but there is always a market for plain cloth. Gods or no gods, people still need clothes."

Javi nodded his head in agreement.

"Cloth makers are doing themselves harm," Bai went on. "They continue to price their wares as though Peshar were still rich."

Again, Javi agreed, and he noted a new gleam in his brother's eye.

"Perhaps I should seek out some tailors and seamstresses and hire them," Bai said. "We could have the market covered from raw wool to finished robes."

Javi (all in the house were careful to call him Javi, lest his father hear and go into a fit of rage) disagreed. "I know it is not my place to say anything about the business, but I think you would be better off to let the tailors and seamstress work as they have always worked. You might advance them the cloth against any profit they make, but if they work independently, there would be little on-going burden for House Ransis."

Bai pulled at his ear thoughtfully. "That is true, but how would these tailors know we have changed from tapestry to cloth making?"

"I will take care of that," Javi said.

And so, House Ransis changed from tapestry to cloth making, and Javi Holis changed from beggar to seller. He went from shop to shop, drinking cup after cup of tea, while telling the shop keepers that House Ransis would supply the cloth at no cost to any maker of robes who wanted it. In return, when cloth was made into robes the tailors would pay for the cloth and ten percent of their profit

The idea was new and dangerous. There was ample chance for the shopkeepers to take the cloth and then lie about their profits, but Javi was such a likable fellow, and yet so astute in his dealings, that there was little cheating.

As Javi moved through Peshar on business, he kept an eye on the rising temple building, and on the gods as they solidified their power.

A new class of people began to emerge. Temple guards had been a fact of life almost since the coming of the gods. Then a priesthood developed. These had been outcasts from regular society for a time, but now they began to emerge as powerful, even respected men. They were protected by the reputation of the gods for being swift in the punishment of those who abused their servants. Early on, some of the priests were set upon by thieves or partisans of the old gods or those who had lost loved ones to the new gods' power. But those who attacked the priests were summarily dealt with in god-powerful ways. They were incinerated in Tapestry Plaza with the merest wave of the God-Resident's hand. And punishment was not for the offender alone. Families and friends were incinerated beside the offender with equal swiftness. It did not take long for the people of Peshar to decide that the gods and their servants could not be resisted.

Javi still could not decide if these were gods or simply powerful men. His mind saw their power and he was awed, but something in his heart would not believe that such cruel creatures could be gods. Gods, even the old gods of Peshar, might demand some sacrifice, but there was always some benefit derived from the sacrifice, not simply being allowed to continue living. These gods only took. They gave nothing back, and Javi could not believe that this was godlike.

And along with this, Javi's curiosity about what was in the forbidden part of the temple grew. He felt some part of the answers to his questions was within those walls, but there was no way to assuage that curiosity save by use of the Mandala of The Fire, and he hesitated to use that power. There was still no place safe to leave his helpless body. There must be someone to watch over it like the Servants of the Design did for one another at Keep Holis. That is why he finally approached Bai about it.

"I need to ask a favor of you, Bai."

The other was instantly alert because of Javi's tone. "Very well. Ask it."

"There may be risk to you…and perhaps to House Ransis as well."

Bai stopped his tea cup halfway to his mouth. "Risk?" He said.

"Yes."

Bai sipped his tea and set the cup down. "Say on then." He set his face to show no emotion, no matter what was asked of him.

"My study of the Design…" Javi began, "Is more than an exercise in learning. In my studies the Designer has led me to something which could help resolve whether or not the gods are truly gods."

Javi hesitated a moment, still not sure if he was doing right. He sipped his tea and Bai said, "Go on. I have wondered about this myself."

The servant of the Design took a deep breath and plunged ahead. "In my studies I found a Mandala which allows me to separate my spirit from my body. When my spirit is loosed, no wall or door can stop me. I move through them as though they are air. No one can see me. They may feel my presence, but unless they have knowledge of what is happening, they will not know what the feeling is."

Bai's eyebrows had been crawling upward despite his attempt to remain unemotional, and they were arched very high indeed by the time his brother finished. "You mean you can go into the temple without being detected?"

"I think so. I have never been able to try since I have been in the presence of the gods. I do not think they can see me either, but I do not know. That is the risk. If I am invisible to them as I am to other humans then I can go where I will and learn what I can."

Perplexity and disbelief crossed Bai's face despite all his resolve. "I find this—difficult to believe," he said.

Javi smiled. "I do not blame you. Had I not been a part of discovering the powers I would not believe it either, but is it any more impossible than gods coming across the sky? Everyone knew the sky was only a sheet to protect the world from the glory of the gods which lived beyond."

Now it was Bai's turn to smile. "You are right in that. And with you I have an option I do not have with these gods. With you I can always say, 'Prove it.'"

"Indeed, you can, and I will, but now comes the favor. When my spirit is absent from my body, my body is helpless. That is why I have not used the power before to enter the temple. I must ask you to guard me…to see that no harm comes to me while I am absent."

Bai blinked, and tried to decide whether or not he believed so wild a story. "What harm could come to you, Javi? Could some demon, or one of the old gods come to steal your body away?"

Now it was Javi's turn to be astonished. He did not think his brother would have been worried about demons or old gods when the foot of the new gods stood so firmly upon the necks of all.

"So far as I know there are no demons, and the old gods were never real. They were only priestly tricks. The dangers I speak of are real. Death by accident or by purpose at the hand of men, or of the new gods, or by cold or fire or earthquake. The same things that threaten all men. But I will not be able to defend against these things since the part of me which would recognize them as dangers will be absent."

Bai stared at his brother for a long time, unsure of whether the man was mad, or serious. He did not know what to do. He had never been faced with anything like this before.

Javi did not try to talk Bai into helping him. He kept quiet and waited for the Designer to work out what must be worked out. Hoping, but trying not to exercise his own will.

At last Bai said, "I am not sure if you are mad or sane, brother, but I will do as you ask, and pray that you are not touched in the mind by your study or your time of begging."

"Good," Javi said, smiling in triumph.

Bai began to regret saying yes, even as the words were leaving his lips.

"When will we do this thing?"

"Tonight. After everyone else is abed."

Bai shivered at the thought. "Spells at midnight," he said.

Javi laughed.

~ * ~

"Your part is very simple Bai," Javi explained. They sat beside the fire which burned low. No sound of life came from the house or the city. "All you need do is sit here drinking tea."

Bai examined his brother's face. It was bronzed by the firelight. There was a depth to it that he had not seen before; and there was a tiny glint of fear in his eyes.

"I will appear dead."

"For how long?"

"Perhaps an hour or a bit more. Longer than that I do not want to think what might happen."

"What might happen, Javi?"

Javi drew a long breath. "Those who have tried to stay separated for too long become sick when they re-united. It was as though they no longer fit together, physical and spiritual. One of them never recovered. He died in great pain, screaming about the prison of the flesh. It was horrible."

"But what will I do if something goes wrong and you cannot get back."

"Then you are free to do what must be done. Get rid of my body. Burn it, bury it, take it out to some alley and leave it. Just one more dead beggar."

"But how will I know?" he said worriedly.

"If I am not back before morning, I will not be back. Then do what you must…"

"There is more," Bai prodded him.

"No. Only, I would ask…if something goes wrong, please send word to Keep Holis. They will commend my spirit to the Maker of All."

Bai nodded, short and jerky. "I will, but now, can we get on with this?"

Javi smiled and patted his brother's hand. "Do not worry. All is in the Design. I will be back as soon as I can."

"The Design?" Bai said. "I do not believe in this Design."

"Doesn't matter. You are part of it, believe or not. Now be quiet. I must concentrate."

With that the servant of the Design lay down upon a mat before the low burning fire and closed his eyes. He brought the Mandala of The Fire before his mind's eye and began to feel the fire of it lick at the kettle of his body.

The process did not take long. Javi and others had perfected the techniques of meditation to the point of making it a simple chore. His spirit began to lift.

Bai felt the sudden chill of the room the instant Javi's essence separated itself from his body. Nausea rose and threatened to make Bai vomit, but the urge left him when Javi's essence departed, leaving only the husk of flesh behind.

Javi passed quickly through the streets and into the temple. He did not meet any gods and saw only one human there, as he passed through the public part of the temple in a bee-line for the forbidden part. He did not stop at the wall but passed directly through it—and thought he was once again outside in the pitch dark of some alley—or some dungeon.

A flash of pearly gray light blinked, driving the darkness away for a moment. Dark returned for a moment before the light came on and stayed on. The light came from a thing that looked like nothing so much as a gigantic doorway. It was taller than ten men and twice that wide, and as Javi looked around he saw that the room was larger than all of the public part of the temple and had many such doors.

Javi had come through the wall and his essence was hanging at the same level as he had entered, but the room was dug into the ground so that it went down about as far as it went up. That was why the forbidden part of the temple did not look to be any taller than the rest of the building.

Upon examination Javi decided these frames could not be doors. They seemed to be only free-standing frames. He could see through them to the wall of the chamber which was only a half-step or so away. Very odd. Doors to nowhere. He passed between the uprights, thinking something might happen there, but nothing did. Yet they must have some importance, or why would the gods have gone to so much trouble to keep the eyes of common Peshar from seeing them?

The pearly light which illuminated the room was coming from the other end of the hall and Javi moved toward it. He passed many of the doors to nowhere. Not all of them were finished. Many had only uprights with no cross beams.

The light proved to be coming from two of the doors to nowhere which were across from one another but not directly. Javi went closer and looked through one of the doors. He could see no source for the light, but he could not see the wall behind the door either. He moved closer and started to pass through the glowing door, but as he started through, a *Thing* stepped through into the Hall of Doors.

Javi was startled, and he retreated.

The *thing* was…a *THING*. It was so strange that Javi had nothing to use as a frame of reference. It was like a man, but different; far too tall and stretched. The arms were thin and long. They reached almost to what Javi would have called the knees. And the color of it, it was a pale green. Javi could not tell if this were some kind of machine or a living thing, but moments later he decided it must be a machine for it seemed naked yet showed no sexual characteristics. But as he watched he still was not sure whether or not it was alive.

After a little, the Thing turned back toward the glowing door and waved its arm. Two other Things stepped from the glowing door. One was like the first, but the other was a god, or at least he was dressed in the black armor of the gods. The three stood making sounds and gestures at one another, so Javi assumed they were talking. They separated after a little while and one of the green, stretched Things stepped through the glowing door, and the other two stepped toward the other glowing door.

Javi continued to watch and in a few heartbeats' time another Thing emerged from the first glowing door. It was not like the first Thing. It was huge. It could barely fit through the door and it seemed to be coming from nowhere. It reminded Javi of a jointed worm, like a caterpillar, and it inched forward like one, but no caterpillar had ever been so huge.

The Thing rumbled as it moved forward. Its head was going toward the other glowing door where the other two beings had taken positions at each side. Atop that insect-like head there was a clear bubble. Inside that bubble was the long green Thing which had stepped back through the door, or one who looked just like it. That one moved its head around as though looking for something. After a moment it spotted the other creature like itself standing beside the other glowing door. That one made gestures as though guiding the insect monster.

The Thing rumbled on and slowed as it came to the other door, but it did not stop. It continued through the door and disappeared, a segment at a time. The stretched Thing and the god turned and followed the giant caterpillar through the glowing door, disappearing like it had, and after a moment the lights in both the doors flickered and went out.

~ * ~

Time crept along for Bai. At first, he watched the body which lay by the hearth. It was as though Javi were in a deep sleep. His chest rose and fell in deep breaths, but there was something different about the movements from those of a sleeper. This body seemed too tense somehow, as though it were hard like stone. Bai rose and went closer to the body. He extended his hand to touch it, but drew his hand back without having done so. He feared that any touch might cause this *trick* to go wrong.

And what if it is just some trick, he thought. *Just some foolishness like a conjurer in Tapestry Plaza.* Bai had seen many such. He had even seen one who balanced a child on the point of a dagger, but that was to impress a crowd in hopes of gaining a few zari. What point could this trick have except what Javi had said? And there had been that moment of chill and sickness a few moments after Javi had lay down.

Bai studied the body again. It was still skinny to the point of emaciation, and the hair and beard were ragged and shot with gray, but it was in much better shape than when Bai had invited him to come and live again with his family.

The desire to touch his brother's body swept over Bai again and he reached out to it. It was as though the still body called to him and this time he did not resist. He put his finger upon the wrinkled brow. It felt cool and clammy, like a corpse must feel, but this was not a corpse. Corpses did not breath. Bai laid his finger upon the throat at the side of the chin and felt the heartbeat. It thumped steadily in counterpoint to the breathing.

Why am I doing this? Bai thought. *I have nothing to gain by this. I have no belief in this Designer. I have no need to antagonize these new gods. I do not care if they be gods or men or demons. I only know they are powerful and I do not want to antagonize them. And yet I am sitting with this almost-corpse while Javi spies on them. I am a fool. Fool!*

He backed away from Javi's body and slumped down upon the bench beside the fire and put his head in his hands. *I could call the temple guard,* he thought. *I could turn this body over to the gods. Perhaps I could gain something from them for it. Or I could pick up a piece of firewood and crack the skull. I could kill this thing and drag the body out into some alley. No one would know. Just another dead beggar, as Javi said.* That thought stopped him. He was not a violent man and he believed the corpse before him was his brother. Besides, he had no love for the new gods. He would do nothing for them unless compelled to do it.

The fire had burned even lower, throwing a flickering red light over the room. Bai watched the chest of the un-corpse rise and fall. It seemed that the rising and falling were not so pronounced now as they were before. How much time had passed? There was no time telling device in the house, not even an hour glass. House Ransis ran by the rise and fall of the sun. Hours were the demarcation of priests and kings, not weavers.

~ * ~

The cold insubstantiality of steam returning to water was upon Javi as he returned to House Ransis. He had waited and watched in the Hall of Doors, but no other door lighted. Then he had trouble finding his way out. He had to pass several times through walls before he re-oriented himself and headed home, and with each passing through the cold watery feeling increased. Javi feared he had been too long separated, but continued home, commending himself to the Designer of All.

~ * ~

A sudden, deep intake of breath by Javi's body pulled Bai from his thoughts. Javi's eyelids flickered and the presence of life was a feeling of fullness in the room.

Javi began to shiver and his teeth chattered; his legs drew up toward his chest as his body tried to conserve the tenuous heat of life even before the conscious part of Javi came to.

Bai took off his cloak and covered his brother, then he punched up the fire and added wood until the blaze lit the room like day.

Javi came conscious, but he could not move. "Help me," he whispered.

Bai picked up the body—it was remarkably light—and carried it to the hearth. He held his brother in his arms and began to rub his hands over Javi's body, trying to restore circulation.

After a long time Javi was able to sit up by himself and Bai poured tea from the pot which sat beside the fire.

Javi, still shaking with cold, managed to get it down and when Bai offered brandy in a small earthenware cup, he took it and slugged it down. The warming effect of the tea and the brandy helped. The shaking eased and Javi was able to stretch himself toward the fire a little more.

"Are you all right Javi?"

"I will be, I think."

Bai hesitated to ask about what had happened, but he had to know.

Javi tried to explain what he had seen, but he simply had no words to make it any more clear to Bai than it was to himself.

"And this caterpillar thing came from nowhere, and went through the other door to nowhere again?" Bai asked, his eyes narrow with doubt.

"Yes. I know it seems impossible. It seemed impossible to me even as I was watching."

"To see such a thing…" Bai whispered. "Surely these are truly gods. Who else could make such a thing? Surely no man who ever lived in Peshar."

Javi shook his head. "You are right about that, but these are not gods. They are far above us, but they are not creators of worlds. These things I saw were built of different stuff than the stuff of trees, or stones. These were things of metal, and they were made with hands. Would gods need hands? Would gods need slaves to build temples?"

Bai rose in anger and paced about the room. "Who are you to know what gods need, or what gods can do!" he snapped. He was at first astounded by what his brother had told him, but now fear was welling up again.

The depth of his brother's fear was clear to Javi. He could see that the power of the gods had stolen Bai's strength, and it made him sad.

"These are not gods, Bai. They were made by the Maker of All and for some purpose. They are not gods. Their power is only physical."

"And the power of this Maker of All, what is it? Surely not physical," Bai said bitterly. "This Designer shows his power through skinny old men who almost die in the exercise of them."

It was like a slap from brother to brother.

"I am sorry, Bai," Javi said. "I have brought more trouble on House Ransis. I did not want to do that. You gave me shelter, and I repay you with fear. I will go and leave you in peace, whatever peace you can find under these new gods."

The Patriarch of House Ransis looked deep into his brother's face, and saw that he was serious. He intended to leave and Bai, after a moment of consideration, decided to let him go…but not tonight.

~ * ~

Javi stayed ten days more. His re-integration was not completed easily. His body resisted what it felt was an invasion by his spirit. His spirit seemed ready to drift free of the prison of flesh at any second during the first several hours, but, by an effort of will, a joining was finally completed, but it was an uncomfortable joining. Javi had very little control over his body, and for a time he feared he would not be able to walk. It took until well after dawn for him to be able to stand and hobble around the room.

When the rest of the family came to get something warm to eat before going about the day's duties, Bai told them that Javi had suffered some sort of attack in the night, but that the effects of it seemed to be fading now. They accepted the explanation and helped with massaging Javi's arms and legs until he could walk with more ease around the room. But all the effects of the separation could not be driven away with hot tea, massages, and movement. Something which felt like a ball of ice was frozen around his spine and it refused to thaw. It made him hobble like an ancient, but even so, Javi was glad for that little. He still remembered the Servants of the Design at Keep Holis trying to ease the suffering of him for whom his own body had become a prison. That suffering had gone on for weeks, with the student screaming out of his mind most of the time.

After the first few hours of re-integration Javi felt well enough to go to bed. He slept the day and night away and when he rose, he ate a huge meal then went back to sleep. The next day his muscle control was better, but the ball of ice was still clenched tight around his lower spine. At best he could only manage a fast hobble. Even so he made ready to leave after three days, but Bai forbade it. "You must rest longer," Bai said. "You can leave, but not until you are stronger. I want you to leave, but not this way."

Javi agreed, but after a few more days he forced Bai to let him go.

Bai gathered some hard bread and dried fruit and meat for him, then gave him a few hundred zari. "I'm sorry it cannot be more, Javi," he said.

"It is enough. It is much more than I brought to Peshar."

"And I found this," Bai said. He handed him a tall staff with a carving of the House Ransis seal at the top. "You can lean on this. Perhaps it will help you to walk better."

The Servant of the Design accepted the staff with thanks. "I am sorry to have brought more trouble to this house, Bai." he said.

"I almost regret your going, Javi…Indi… It has been good to have you here," he answered, then thought how insane it sounded and blushed. A moment later he said, "I thought I had lost my brother forever, then I found him begging on the street. Now I send him back to beg again."

Javi smiled and patted Bai's hand. "Do not feel bad, brother. I go to carry out the will of the Great Designer."

"And how do you know what that will is, brother?"

Javi shrugged. "It will be revealed as time passes. The Design will be worked out no matter what. All is in the hands of the Designer, and whether I know what the pattern is or not, the Design will be worked out according to that will."

Four

2 A.C.G

Javi began begging in the streets again, but he did not limit his life to that. He placed his begging bowl in front of him and forgot about it. Instead he began using the power of The Ear to know the thoughts of those who passed him. It was difficult at first because the jumble of minds moving past set up such a babbling it almost deafened his mental ear; but, with practice, he learned to focus upon one mind at a time. After a little, he found he could even hear and understand more than one mind at a time. It was difficult and used up his strength rapidly, but it could be done if need be. Mostly he listened to only one mind at a time. That was quite racking enough to his spirit. Fear and despair were in almost every mind, but worse, in many minds was the firm belief that the gods were indeed Gods. There were some who believed the creatures from the sky were just men, albeit men with great magic at their beck and call. There were even a few believers in the Design, but most of them were confused and afraid. They saw this invasion as an overthrowing of the Design. Javi took special note of these and after some days of observation he sought out ten of these believers.

They feared the old man at first, thinking he was some agent of the new gods come to seek and find unbelievers so as to stamp out any opposition to the new temple which was rising steadily. But at last Javi convinced a few of them that he was truly a Servant of the Design. These he began teaching the use of the five powers.

The teaching was slow. Javi had nothing except his memory to lean on as a teaching aid. He tried drawing out some of the Mandalai, but he had no skill with pen and ink. The drawings were more of a hindrance than a help in many cases. Javi even tried placing his mental pictures of the Mandalai in the minds of his students, but this seldom worked. The receiving minds were not used to being manipulated in such a way and mostly they rejected the invasion of the master's mind. But four did learn and these went out to find other believers. When they found them, they tried to teach them the powers, but it was difficult, and most of the teaching fell back onto Javi.

Soon the teaching became too big a job. It would have been too big a job for a young healthy man, and Javi was not healthy. He was not old, but sometimes he seemed to fall into the maladies of the old. He found himself rambling as he tried to teach and it made him angry. And the tendency to fall asleep anytime he sat quietly for a few moments made him even angrier.

If only one or two of them could learn as I learned, Javi thought. *If only I had the Great Book.*

But The Book was far away in Keep Holis, and Javi was not sure he truly wished the book was in Peshar. What might happen if it fell into the hands of the sky creatures? Still, having the Mandalai of Power would have made the teaching much easier. He expressed this one evening when sitting with Sartin Fex, the strongest of the students he had taught.

"But Master," Sartin said. "Can we not bring the book here?"

Javi rubbed his bony hands over his face. "I have thought of that a thousand times, Sartin, but I am not sure bringing it would be a good idea. It might fall into the hands of the gods, and that would be a disaster. Besides, it is far away; a long and difficult journey even for a strong healthy person, and I am neither of those."

"Could not some other Servant of the Design go in your place Master?" Sartin asked.

Javi shook his head. "I doubt it. The Great Book is guarded closely. The Masters' Council would not release it to a stranger."

"Even to one who could demonstrate the five powers?" Sartin asked, unable to leave the idea alone.

"I doubt it. I doubt they would release it to me, even if I could make the journey." Javi fell silent for a time, still considering. No matter how he looked at it such a journey seemed impossible. "Besides," he continued at last, "the gods make it all the harder with their travel passes and constant watch on the roads. And if the book fell into the gods' hands? Even if they could not use the powers, they might destroy the book. If they feared the power of it enough, they might decide to destroy all of Peshar to be rid of us who can use the powers."

Sartin looked sour, but knew Master Javi was right. The gods already feared the people. There had been three uprisings, all put down with great brutality and little effort. After each the gods had clamped tighter controls on Peshar.

"Then we are stopped," Sartin said dispiritedly.

Javi stroked his beard thoughtfully. "Let me think on this, Sartin. Perhaps The Maker of All will present some solution that escapes us now."

Javi thought silently for several days. There was no escaping the conclusion that The Book of the Design was needed in Peshar now. With the knowledge of the powers open to any who would learn them the gods might be defeated, and belief in the Maker of All might become widespread. But he felt so weary, so unable to make the journey! Was this some sign from the Designer that the idea was not a good one?

Yet there seemed to be no other solution. Somehow, he had to go to Keep Holis and bring back the Great Book, dangers and difficulties notwithstanding.

He began discussing it with others in the small community of believers.

"I am sure the servants at Keep Holis will not turn The Book over to a stranger," he said. "Therefore, I must go, but I do not feel up to making the trip."

"Would it make you more inclined to try the journey if someone went with you?"

Javi had thought of this, but had reached no conclusion.

"Perhaps. It would be easier to bring back The Book if someone was there to help me."

"Then I will go with you," Sartin said.

"No, no, that cannot be. You are the lynch pin of the community of believers in Peshar, Sartin. You must remain here and continue to teach. You have the best grasp of the powers. You must teach others. I do not want to risk you in this."

"But Master, you cannot go alone," the younger man said flatly.

"That is true. But who can be spared from the work here?"

Sartin began throwing out names, but each was rejected in turn. All had too many others who depended on them. After hours of consideration they found themselves no better off than when they started.

"Please, enough," Javi said. "I am so weary my mind will no longer focus. Let us have some rest and some food. Maybe the mind will work better if the growls of the belly do not distract it."

Sartin laughed and agreed.

House Fex, Sartin's family, had taken Javi in after they found that this Master of the Design was begging to stay alive and sleeping in the streets. They were not a major house of Peshar, like House Ransis, but they were well established in the making of pottery.

The rest of the family had eaten hours earlier, but Sartin and his younger sister Mara, were always ready to serve Master Javi. Mara brought forth a plate of cold meats, fruit and tea as though they had been ready and waiting.

Mara was more than a servant to her brother and Master Javi, though that was mostly what she did. She was eighteen and would have been pretty except that the hard life of Peshar left her little time for herself. Her hair was a lustrous chestnut which few people knew for she kept it modestly covered with a dark green head scarf. Her eyes were deep green with golden flecks. She had studied the Mandalai with the others, but she had little talent in that direction. She could communicate a little with the mental voice, but the other powers were beyond her. She did not feel bad or lessened because of this as she was not alone. She hoped to be able to learn the skills with time and practice. She also hoped that seeing the Mandalai of the Great Book would help her. Meantime she did what she could to be of service to Master Javi, and the rest of the community of believers.

After they ate Mara went out to prepare more tea and when they were alone again the men resumed their discussion. They had come to the same conclusion as before when Mara returned with a steaming tea pot. She poured tea and stepped back to quietly await any further instructions. She listened to the men talk and considered their problem. She did not truly intend to participate in the discussion, but an obvious solution came to her and she felt she had to share it with them.

"Master," she said so softly that neither man heard her, so she said again, "Master."

Javi turned to her. "Yes, Mara," he said.

"I could go with you," Mara said, then blushed as she heard how bold she sounded.

Neither man said anything for a moment, then her brother said, "You?"

"Yes. I could go. We could travel as an old man and his granddaughter. We could even get real passes from the temple. We could tell them that my grandfather is very ill and wishes to return to the home of his ancestors before he dies," she said, then blushed again at her boldness and cast her eyes down.

The men looked at her in silence for several seconds before Sartin waved his hand as if to wave away a bothersome insect. "No, no. That is impossible…" he began but Javi cut him off.

"I think Mara has given us the solution. Even the gods would not refuse an old man going home to die, I think. Besides, this feels right."

"But Master, she is only a child."

"I am no child," Mara answered her brother. "I am old enough to marry, if there were any suitors. Mother was already heavy with you at my age, Sartin."

The firmness of her answer surprised her brother. She did not drop her eyes this time, but looked defiantly at him, then switched her gaze to Master Javi.

Javi found himself being drawn into the depths of her eyes, and for the first time in many days he laughed with real joy.

"It shall be so," he said. "We leave as soon as we get permission from the temple."

~ * ~

The process of getting proper documents went without a hitch. Mara was afraid the temple servants would question her closely, trying to catch her in a lie, but the hardest question she was asked was where her old grandfather wished to go. She named a village near Keep Holis and held her breath waiting for them to question her further, but they did not. Instead the temple servant drew, with an unskilled hand, the marks in the Divine Language that meant Ecrus, the village name she had given, then stamped his chop beside the scribble.

Mara took the paper and looked at the inky trail and the chop. She could not read the Divine Language and could barely speak it, but she was not about to question the functionary. She paid the two zari and took the paper home. She and Master Javi departed before daylight the next day.

"If you tire of carrying the pack Mara, I can take it for a while," Javi said. They had been walking for many hours.

"No, Master Javi, it would not be seemly for my grandfather who is ill to carry anything except his staff."

Javi agreed with her good sense. "That is true enough," he said, "but to go a step farther, I think it would not be proper for a grandchild to call her grandfather 'Master.'"

Mara looked from the side of her eye at the old man and saw that he was smiling. She grinned back and said, "I am sorry…grandfather. I did not mean to be so know-it-all."

"Not to worry, Mara. I occasionally have the same problem. We will both learn our parts, and perhaps a little humility as we go along."

"Perhaps so, grandfather," she said.

Javi winced at the sound of it. "I find it burdensome to be thought of as your grandfather though. I am not really old enough."

Mara glanced over at the old man, thinking that he seemed a thousand years older than the oldest person she had ever met.

The travelers planned to stay at hostels and inns, but they discovered that many inns which had been along the road when Javi had come to Peshar, were no longer open. Many were no longer standing. Javi thanked the Maker of All daily that the weather was warm, but he knew that could change in a few hours as they moved north and climbed higher, so they sought out a seller of clothing and bought heavy cloaks. The cost used up a large portion of their zari, and drew some strange looks since the day was steamy hot, but less than a week later they were glad of the cloaks. They were caught by darkness and forced to sleep on the ground beside the road.

Some days later they stopped to buy food and gather news of the road ahead. Until that time, they had not been molested by anyone, though their papers had been examined many times. But as they sat in the public house eating and resting, three local servants of the sky gods entered and began rousting the customers. They were dressed in red robes and had the shaven heads of temple servants, but Javi doubted that any of them had ever been to the temple. Two were armed with swords and lances. The third was armed with a wand of office —a ceremonial wooden rod — which the man used to poke and bludgeon those he questioned if they dared to look at him.

Javi assumed the guise of an addled old man. The ruse had worked well before, but this temple servant was enjoying his power too much to let a doddering old man and his granddaughter escape.

"You are strangers here," he said.

"Yes, my Lord," Mara answered, keeping her eyes on the floor. "We travel to Ecrus, my Lord. My grandfather is ill. He wishes to return to the home of his childhood one last time."

"And you, old one? Speak up. Have you no respect for the Servants of the Gods?" the red robe said and poked Javi with his wand.

Javi acted as though he did not understand.

"Please, my Lord," Mara said. "He is old and addled." She offered the dog-eared travel permit. "Often he cannot even remember my name."

The other took the paper from her. He squinted at the marks but it was obvious he could not read. "If he is so addled," he said, "how does he know where he is going?"

"I know the way," she said, careful not to look up. "And he has moments when all is clear."

"But this is not one of them," the servant laughed, playing to the other two red robes.

"No, my Lord."

The man looked back at Mara, then ran his eyes over her more closely. He put his wand of office beneath her chin and lifted her face. "You are far too pretty to be burdened with this old stick," he said.

Mara turned her head and slipped the wand from beneath her chin. She cast her eyes down quickly. "I was the only one of the family who could be spared to help him," she said.

The man lifted her face with his wand again, and saw a hint of fear in her eyes. "Do not be afraid, pretty one. I would not hurt you. In fact, far from it."

The others laughed and he glanced at them appreciatively, then looked back at Mara—just in time to see loathing replace fear in her eyes.

"Ah," he said. "Saucy as well as pretty. Perhaps I should take you to the store room and relieve you of some of your sauciness." He grinned wolfishly.

"Beg pardon, my Lord," Mara said, once more slipping the wand from beneath her chin and looking down. "I did not mean to seem saucy. It is only that the journey has been long and will be longer yet. Please forgive your servant."

"Perhaps I should relieve you of your burden, pretty one. I could have one of these shorten the old man, then you could come and keep me warm this winter."

Mara tried to shrink into the floor, but this only made the man feel more powerful. He reached down, grasped Mara by the upper arm and hauled her to her feet. He pulled her tight against him and put the hand which held the wand upon her bottom.

This was too much. Mara pulled free of him and slapped his face as hard as she could.

Javi had continued to play the part of the dotard, but as the situation deteriorated, he called upon the Mandala of the Enfolding Arms. He could feel the radiant calm flowing out to touch the two guards who were watching, but, as the other's lust increased, the calm could not penetrate. When Mara slapped him, the lust changed to rage, and that was more amenable to influence by the Enfolding Arms.

He felt the sudden drain on him as the power of the Mandala

grasped the temple servant. It almost tore his breath away, but he held on to the mental picture of the Mandala, and continued to radiate calm.

Mara felt the man's grip loosen, and she glanced at Javi. She understood in an instant what he was doing, and knew she could help him. She began to cry, softly at first, but with rising sobs which shook her frame and contorted her face with grief and fear.

Javi understood what Mara was doing and added his help. He changed his mental picture to The Whisper and placed a feeling of shame and fear in the red robed servant's mind.

The man suddenly looked away from Mara as though someone had called his name. He released her and she collapsed to the floor in a sobbing heap.

He stepped back half a step and drew a deep breath, then looked around the room. No one moved to help either the woman or the servant of the gods. He stood alone and felt the shame and fear Javi continued to put into his mind. He looked around again, then looked down at the sobbing woman at his feet. Suddenly he turned and stalked out of the room.

The other two did not know what to do for a moment, but at last turned and hurried after their leader.

Mara remained where she was for a few moments. No one came to help her at first, but then a serving girl hurried from behind the bar to help her to her feet.

"Are you all right?" the serving girl asked. "Did he hurt you?"

"No," Mara said, wiping her hand across her eyes and nose. "I am all right. He did not hurt me, only scared me."

"You are lucky," the girl said. "That one has let the power of the gods go to his loins."

Mara turned to Javi. "Are you all right, Grandfather?" she asked, and began examining him with care.

Javi continued to play the senile old man, and when Mara was satisfied that he was not hurt she hugged him with relief. He could not help but return the hug, and when Mara's ear was near his lips he whispered, "Well played, granddaughter."

Mara drew back to look into his face. There was a merry and

triumphant twinkle in his eyes, and Mara could not stop herself from laughing with delight. For the first time she saw beneath the crumpled body and gray hair to the man beneath Master Javi Holis. For the first time she believed that he truly was not as old as she had thought.

The serving girl looked on for a few moments with a warm smile, but soon she said, "Perhaps you had better get your grandfather out of here before that—Servant of the Gods decides he has made a mistake and returns."

~ * ~

The days grew colder as Javi and Mara climbed higher and the season progressed. Soon there was frost in the mornings, and the cold made the never ending ache in Javi's lower back worse. Their pace slowed to a crawl and many days they made only a mile or two. Then a day dawned bright and warm and clear, with the sky such a transparent blue it seemed there would never be another cloud in it. Both travelers unrolled from their cloaks feeling renewed, buoyed up with a sense of joy and well-being. Despite the chill of the preceding night, the ice around Javi's spine seemed easier.

Mara noticed the difference. "Grandfather," she had become used to calling Javi by that name and did it now without thought. "You seem changed today. Less stiff. Did you sleep well?"

Javi laughed. "Yes, indeed. It was a wonderfully comfortable rock I slept on."

The answer and the laughter startled Mara. It sounded so youthful.

"We should make miles today," Javi said. "Perhaps we can even find an inn for tonight. A hot meal and tea would be wonderful. Perhaps even a cup of hot spiced wine" he smacked his lips.

"Master Javi, may I ask you something personal?"

Javi laughed again. "For weeks we have tramped along together, slept wrapped together in the same cloaks, eaten the same food, or not eaten at all. What could possibly be so personal that you do not yet know it?"

Mara shrugged. "When I first saw you," she began, "I thought you perhaps the oldest man I had ever met, but I have changed my mind. I think you are not so old as I thought. What is your age, Master Javi?"

Javi lifted his left eyebrow so comically that Mara could not help but laugh.

"Why, I am a mere child, Mara. Much younger than the mountains. Even younger than the trees, but old enough to be your father."

"That is no answer," she said.

"Ah, you mean in years."

"Yes, in years."

"In years I am forty-five."

Mara was surprised. Forty-five was old to an eighteen-year-old, but not nearly so old as she had thought. "You seem more ancient than that," she said, then blushed at how it sounded.

Javi grabbed his heart as though Mara had stabbed him there. "I am considered an Ancient by young girls. My life is over."

"I mean forty-five is not old," she said. "Why do you seem so much older sometimes?" She blushed again, but the question was out already.

"Hm," Javi said, turning more serious. "If you had seen me before the coming of the gods…" he shook his head. "During the months since they came, I have gained an eon of age. I have used the powers much, and such use takes its toll. For a time, I slept on the streets and ate only what came from my begging. That used me hard." He shrugged. "But all things are in the Design. I am as I am because the Maker of All has used me to His ends. For that I am happy."

Mara stared at Master Javi for a long time, digesting what he had said.

"Come, Granddaughter. Let us not waste any of this glorious day," Javi said and linked his arm with hers.

Later in the day they stopped to rest and eat of their meager trail rations. Mara had been quieter than usual, mulling over what she had learned. "Master," she began. "Have you ever been in love?"

A sadness passed over his face in a flicker and was gone. "Once, when I was a child, I thought I was in love, but it was not so. The girl…ah well. It doesn't matter. She was not in the Design of my life. And, looking back, I am glad, for what might have become of her when the gods came?"

Mara nodded her understanding. "What did become of her?"

"She died long ago."

"Is that why you began to study the Design?"

"No, no. It was after I began to serve the Design that I learned of her death. She married another after I left Peshar. She died in childbirth. I was sad for her husband. He was a friend. I wish there had been something better for them in the Design, but…" he shrugged.

"Sometimes I think the Designer is cruel," Mara said feelingly.

"Sometimes I think that too," Javi agreed, "but then, I remember that the Designer made me. I did not make him. I remember then that what may seem cruel to me may not be cruel at all, as it is not cruel for a father to spank the hands of his child to teach that child that fire is hot and dangerous. Leah, the girl, lived and felt the joy of life for her time. She had her part and she played it. It is always that way. We have parts to play. It is all in the Design."

They were silent for a time, then Javi asked, "And you, my sweet Mara? Have you ever been in love?"

She shook her head. "I have not lived long enough," she said. "I hardly knew anyone with whom to fall in love. Before the gods came, I was too young to do more than notice the difference between girls and boys. My parents guarded me well. I think they had made a marriage for me, but…" she shrugged. "the gods came and all those things were lost against simply staying alive. If I had stayed in Peshar I might have fallen in love or married or perhaps both, but now—" she shrugged again.

"It sounds as though you believe this journey will be the end of your life. If it is in the Design, you and I will return to Peshar, and you will take up your life again. Perhaps you will yet marry and bear children."

Mara was silent for a time, then shook her head doubtfully. "Perhaps, but I think not. I have a feeling there is something else in the Design for me. Besides, I am not sure I want to bring children into a world ruled by the new gods."

~ * ~

They found an inn as dusk fell and slept in beds and ate fresh, hot food for the first time in days. They also re-supplied themselves with trail rations and gathered news of the road ahead of them.

"The way is easy," they were told, "but now is not the time to travel. Snow can whip up between eye blinks and trap you. In the spring we send patrols to bury the fools who disregarded our warnings and froze to death in a sudden snow." The innkeeper who warned them thus seemed to relish the thought of all those frozen travelers, but he only shrugged when they left the next morning.

Mara and Javi traveled under clear skies and warm sun for two more days. They were not far from Keep Holis now. Javi figured they would reach it in a week if the weather held, but it didn't. The evening of the second day the sky changed from soft blue-white to sharp-edged sapphire, and the wind became cruel. They found no inn or building of any kind, and as dark thickened they made what shelter they could of a deep niche in a cliff face. They pulled branches from the fir trees to help protect them from the wind and the happiness of three days ago seemed far away indeed.

"Perhaps we should have listened to that innkeeper," Mara said through chattering teeth.

"Perhaps so, but it seems a little late to think what might have been. Besides we are so close now, if only the snow will hold off."

But it did not.

They woke to lowering gray skies and the nose-stinging smell of snow coming. Near midday the first flakes fell. By dark the flakes had clenched themselves into tiny stinging pellets which blew directly into the faces of the travelers.

No convenient niche presented itself this night. They had to make do with the scratchy, low hanging branches of a cedar tree. Even so it was not a bad shelter. It kept most of the icy pellets from reaching them and, after a little while, their body heat and their tiny fire caused some of the ice on the branches to melt into a glaze which kept out most of the wind.

Mara and Javi were jammed tight together in the confined space.

Javi could feel the girl shivering. He wondered that he was not shivering himself, but he did not.

"Are we going to die here, Master Javi?" she asked as the sound of the wind and the hiss of the snow pellets increased against their makeshift shelter.

Javi did not answer for a long time but finally was forced to say, "I do not know, but whatever comes, do not be afraid, Mara." He lifted his hand and stroked her wind raw cheek. "All is in the Design."

Mara took Javi's hand from her cheek and kissed it, then she pressed her face against it again. She found that despite the probability they would freeze to death during the night she was not afraid. There was a warm, content feeling in the center of her being.

"I am not afraid," she said.

They held one another for hours, and the first hesitant comforting of one another became tenderness.

"Mara, I am too old to feel toward you what I am feeling now, and you are too young."

"I do not care, Master Javi. This is right. I feel it. I wish it."

He stroked her hair and her face again. "But our lives are not our own, and they are so uncertain."

"You are all the certainty I need now," she said. "Remember, all is in the Design."

Five

2 A.C.G.

Keep Holis was almost deserted when Javi and Mara arrived. What had once been a hive of students and masters now housed only a handful of people, most of them old.

"Like you, Javi," Master Aram said, "most have gone to see the new gods."

The old man was bed ridden and could do little for himself, but his mind was clear, and his speech, though soft and dry as centuries of dust, was firm.

"Some have taken to preaching against the new gods," he continued. "I fear they do not live long enough to do much good."

"Open preaching against them is useless," Javi agreed. "They are powerful and ruthless. The only way to resist them is quiet endurance. We can only resist by not seeming to resist. That is what I have told those who serve the Design in Peshar."

Master Aram's faded eyes blazed. "Then there are still Servants in Peshar?"

"They are few, but growing, and that is why I am here. I have been able to teach the use of the Mandalai to some, but I have nothing save memory to rely on. In my mind I can see the Mandalai, but, though I have tried, I cannot copy my mental images onto paper. I even tried to transfer my images directly to my students, but that was almost useless. A few could accept the transfer, but most…" he shrugged. "Their minds rebelled against the invasion. So, I am here to take The Book of the Design to Peshar. With those images before their eyes I am sure they can learn use of the powers so that the Design may be more widely known."

Silence thickened in the room.

Master Aram took a labored breath and closed his eyes. "I fear that cannot be, Javi," he said.

"But without it, knowledge of the Design cannot be spread."

"You said there were a few."

"Too few!" Javi said vehemently. "So few that these sky gods might destroy them in the time between two breaths. They may already be destroyed."

"If that is the will of the Maker of All," the old master said.

"I cannot believe it is. Otherwise why would the idea of taking the book to Peshar have come to me? With The Book of the Design at hand, knowledge can spread and that is the only way to preserve it. Make it so widespread that these sky gods can never stamp it out."

"Do you remember our talk before you set out for Peshar, Javi?" Master Aram asked.

Javi's face reddened. "Yes Master, I remember. The Design moves us, we do not move it, but I have also seen much that makes me believe what I wish is within the will of the Designer."

"Perhaps. Perhaps it is, but think on this: What if the Book fell into the wrong hands? Even into the hands of the sky gods? They might discover the power of it, or even if they did not, they might destroy it. Then knowledge of the Design could not be spread at all."

"But, is not your argument now something to use against such a thought. Is not all within the Design? Would not the Maker of All protect the book?" Desperation echoed in Javi's tone.

"Javi, we cannot so much as read the hearts of men. How can we begin to understand the heart of the Designer? How can we be so arrogant as to believe our desires are his will?"

"But are you not doing the same thing by refusing, Master Aram?"

The old man drew a ragged breath, strain showing on his face. "Perhaps, but I think the book should stay here where it is safe."

Javi bowed his head. "Master Aram, you are wrong," he said. A moment later he was sorry.

"Forgive me, Master Aram, I did not mean to be…"

The old man lifted a skinny hand. "Your passion was always hot, and it has led you to discover many things. Let me think upon this and speak with the others. Perhaps it is time to bring the book into the open."

Javi looked deep into the face of his beloved Master and saw that the old man would indeed think on it and talk to others, but there was little chance that anything would change.

Later Javi said to Mara, "I fear we have journeyed for nothing."

Mara put her arms around him. "No Javi, not for nothing."

~ * ~

Snow began to fall in huge, heavy flakes a few days after the travelers arrived at Keep Holis. Winter was truly on them and any thoughts of a quick return to Peshar, with or without the book, disappeared. Mara and Javi were fretted by the inactivity at first, but soon they began to enjoy their time together.

But this rejoicing in one another did not fill up all the hours. They also studied the Design in their own way. Javi took The Great Book from its resting place to study the Mandalai anew, and to feel the power of them drum through his nerves.

Mara studied the Mandalai which were everywhere throughout the keep. They fascinated her in ways she could not fathom. Even those called "minor" Mandalai radiated into her soul; then Javi opened the Great Book.

The power of the first Mandala, The Fire, was like a blast of heat that seared into her memory. Each line, each daub of color, each angle once seen was unforgettable. "Please," she said. "Enough. Close it."

Javi did so. "Now perhaps you can use the power of The Fire," he said.

Mara shook her head. "No. I will never be able to use any of the Mandalai. They would consume me."

Javi did not understand.

"All the Mandalai in the keep are powerful, Javi, and even those called Minor draw me into them. I have found myself seated before some of them for so long my muscles ache from immobility, yet I did not even notice time passing. I cannot use these powers. They would consume me."

Javi reached out to her, devastated that she should be so bereft, but Mara did not let him continue. "You do not understand," she said. "I have other powers. Powers which you do not have."

"Powers?"

"Yes. Knowledge of them came to me as I looked at the Mandala there," she indicated the book.

"But what other powers are there?"

"I must speak with Master Ekas" she said, leaving him with his mouth open. Then he closed it and looked even more puzzled. Ekas was the Librarian.

Master Ekas was more than the Librarian. He had been Master Scribe to Keep Holis for many years, teaching the Students of the Design the skill of the pen and brush. He was almost forgotten now when there were no students. He spent his days meditating on the great Design and compiling a history of Keep Holis. He also found joy in copying the Mandalai of the keep.

Ekas Holis had come to the Design late in life. He had been a scribe and fair witness of some reputation in Peshar. He had been caught up in the preaching of a Servant of the Design and became more caught up when that servant spoke of the Mandalai and of masters who taught the use of paint and brush. Soon after that, Ekas abandoned his shop and made his way to Keep Holis.

Ekas had been a student when the Mandalai of Power had been copied and bound into The Book of the Design, but he had not worked on the copying. He had always regretted that, but he had been a lowly apprentice then, and his hands had not been skillful enough.

When Mara came to him, he was surprised. He had not had a student for a long time. "But surely you know how to write, child," he protested when she told him she wished to learn.

"Yes, Master Ekas, but I want to know more. You are a master of pen and brush, and you know color. I must learn these."

"I am no creator of Mandalai child, if that is what you wish to learn. I only copy."

"I know Master. That is what I wish to learn."

The old man narrowed his eyes and looked closely into the young woman's face. "Very well then," he said after a moment. "We will begin."

Much to the delight of Master Ekas, Mara was an excellent student. She had an intuitive grasp of color and line, and her eyes were extraordinary. She could detect even faint differences in tone and shade, and she learned with a speed that was breathtaking. Ekas would no more than show her how to shade blue to purple without leaving a visible line than Mara was able to do it better than her teacher. In only a few weeks she could copy anything set before her with such dexterity that Ekas could hardly tell the copy from the original.

Mara was ecstatic. She felt truly useful for the first time in her life. It had been a source of pain to her that she could not use the five powers. Now that pain diminished to the tiniest ache at the back of her mind, and as she absorbed the knowledge and honed her skill, that ache grew smaller and smaller. Each day she worked until her eyes could hardly focus, then she would return to Javi bubbling with delight and love. When she showed him some of her practice copies he was impressed.

"These are magnificent," he said.

Mara could not suppress a giggle of delight. "I never thought to be able to do such a thing. I thought I was slow-witted when I could not learn the powers, but now…"

"There is nothing slow about your wits, my sweet Mara," Javi said and hugged her. "They only work differently from others."

Mara pulled herself tighter to him. She could not even fathom how she could ever have thought this man ancient. "I am so glad you brought me here," she whispered.

Javi smiled at that. "Who brought whom?" he asked, laughing. "I almost turned down your idea of coming along and Sartin fought it until the last moment before we departed. But the Maker of All knew better."

"Yes," she said and leaned back to look up into Javi's face. "And there is something else."

"Indeed, there is. I have been thinking that we do not need to take The Book of the Design back to Peshar. You can copy the five Mandalai."

Mara let out her breath in a gust. She had known what was about to be asked, and she was daunted by the prospect. She was aware of how skillful and talented she was, but to make copies of the Mandalai that could teach use of the powers?

But she knew she must try. In her heart of hearts, she knew that was why she had come to Keep Holis.

"Will Master Aram and the others allow it?" she asked.

"I do not know," Javi answered. "I can but ask."

~ * ~

"Mara has become an expert copyist, Master Aram," Javi said, pride showing in his smile. "Her work is perfect in every detail."

The old master was feeling the effects of the winter. He sat propped in his bed covered with blankets, and wrapped in a cured bear hide, but the cold still made his joints ache. He was in pain much of the time, and movement was agony.

"Ekas has told me the same thing. He is as proud as if Mara were his daughter. It is always good to have a student, and one so talented makes a master's life worth living."

"And that brings me to the reason for my visit, Master Aram."

The master's faded blue eyes twinkled. "You mean you have not come just to keep an old man company?"

Javi smiled at the jab. "Of course, I have come to keep you company. I have always delighted in the presence of Master Aram Holis, my teacher."

"But there is another reason as well," the old man finished for him. "Yes."

Again, Javi could not finish before being interrupted. "You want permission to copy The Book of the Design."

"Why have I bothered to come when you already know my every wish and desire, Master Aram?" Javi said laughing. "Have you been listening in on my thoughts?"

"There has been no need. Word of Mara's progress has echoed through these halls as though the very stones speak."

"But they have not told all," Javi said.

"No?"

"No. Because I do not wish permission to copy the whole of The Book of the Design, only the five Mandalai that are no longer dark. That way the book itself is protected and the tools of teaching are brought to Peshar also."

"I have been considering what you wished since we first talked," he said. "I have meditated upon it and sought the will of the Designer. I know the Mandalai of Power could help to spread knowledge of the Design, but I also know that there is danger."

"That is why I would have Mara copy only the five. You are right to worry about the danger, but this would minimize it."

The old man looked down at his traitorous hands which would no longer do his bidding without pain. They were bony, crooked claws, blue-veined, lumpy, and useless.

"And what if one of the Mandalai fall into the hands of the sky gods? Or, worse yet, what if a student who knows all five powers should fall into their hands? There could be no secret kept from them. The sky gods would know where to find the rest of the book then."

"I have thought of that too, Master, and I believe the book should be removed from the Keep and hidden. The location should be known to very few, and passed on only in the strictest confidence. That would protect it even as the Servants in Peshar study the powers."

Master Aram moved only his eyes. "I hate the thought of having the book anywhere but in the Keep, but perhaps we could move it from the library; hide it elsewhere within the walls."

"No Master Aram, if the sky gods discover there is such a book, they will not hesitate to take Keep Holis apart stone by stone until they find it.

"That could be a long process Javi. It took almost fifty years to build the keep, and it has never fallen to any besieger."

"Master Aram, you do not understand the power of the sky gods. They are like no besiegers ever before. Their power is beyond description. The journey which took Mara and I weeks, they could accomplish in moments. The walls of Keep Holis would be as nothing to them. They could carve them up like a well-cooked roast if that was their desire. No, Master Aram, these sky gods may only be another kind of men, but they are powerful men, and they are ruthless."

Amazement came into the old man's eyes. "With such power it is no wonder so many believe them to be gods."

"Truly, the Design is marvelous beyond all thought to contain such creatures, Master Aram, and such other creatures, or perhaps machines, as I saw in the great hall of doors within the temple the sky gods are building," Javi said.

"Tell me more, Javi," the old man said.

"May I tell Mara to begin her work, Master?"

The old man stared silently at his student for several moments, then said, "Yes. Let her begin. And when the weather eases find someone from the village who knows the mountains. There are many caves known to the shepherds. Seek out a safe place to hide the book."

~ * ~

Mara began her work the next day. With Master Ekas help, she moved the reading desk and the book so as to catch the light of one of the high windows of the library. Then she moved a lower, flatter desk, beside the tall reading desk so that she had her work surface. Satisfied, she asked Master Ekas, "Where shall we set your desk?"

"My desk?" the old man asked. "Why should I need a desk?"

Mara looked at her master and a feeling of dread came over her. "Yes, Master, your desk. You will help me with the copying, won't you?"

It was a chance the old man had wished for all his life; the chance to make true, important, copies of the Mandalai of The Book of the Design; and he found he could not do it. There was a quaking fear in the depths of him that made him tremble as though palsied.

"I cannot child," he breathed, almost weeping. "I am afraid. My hands shake at the very thought of it."

"But, Master, I cannot do this alone! I am only a student," she wailed.

"You are more than that, Mara. You are the best I have ever seen. You can do it. You must."

"But…"

"I cannot help you," he said and turned away.

Mara watched her retreating master's back, and she cried. It was like the feeling she remembered when her parents had died. She had never felt so alone in her life, but she knew what she must do.

She reached up to open the cover, which was half the size of a door, and her hand trembled. She drew back. The first time she had looked beneath that cover the Mandalai had almost consumed her. But she had been looking at it with different eyes then. Now she was possessed of knowledge she had not had at that first look. Now she knew at least a little of her part of the Design.

Mara opened the cover.

The simple act of opening the heavy cover made her head light, and the power of the first Mandala rushed over her like a tide of fire. So disturbing was it that she closed her eyes against it, but after a moment she opened them again and looked full and long upon the Mandala. After a time of looking she felt herself more comfortable with it, then she turned to the next, experienced the awe of it, waited to become used to it and turned to the next. This she did through the whole of the Book, not just through those she intended to copy. Those still called dark did not feel as powerful as the five known powers, or rather they were powerful in a different way. It was like the difference between an egg and a chicken. The one was the other, but the chicken was the fully realized egg. That was the way the dark Mandalai felt. Their potential was great but not yet ripe to use.

When Mara had studied each of the thick pages, she turned back to the first. The very arrogance of what she was about to attempt struck her. Her hands began to shake. She felt alone. Abandoned. How can I even consider attempting such a thing? she thought. Yet she knew she must make the attempt.

She picked up a fine-pointed quill made from the wing feather of a robin, dipped it into the ink pot, wiped off the excess and moved it toward the heavy vellum sheet which lay, cocked to the left, upon the work surface. But she could not touch the quill to the page.

"How can I do this?" she asked aloud, though there was no one in the library to hear her. "How can I do this?"

She sat in a paroxysm of doubt for near an hour before anything changed. Light streamed through the high slash window. Wind moaned around the corners of the Keep. Cold seeped through the ancient stone walls and she shivered. When she shivered it was as though the acknowledgement of the cold sharpened her mind and the fear left her. Her hand became steady, and she dipped the quill again. Without hesitation she touched quill to vellum and made the first mark in the center of the sheet.

~ * ~

The wind was full of icy razors and no cloak ever made could keep it out. The ice which clenched Javi's spine reacted in harmony with the bitterness of the wind. It bowed him down. His shoulders hunched and his legs ached. He leaned heavily on the staff his brother Bai had given him.

"How much farther to this cave, child?" he asked.

"A little farther Holy One," the boy said.

Javi flinched at the appellation. He had tried to tell the child he was not any more holy than any other creation of the Maker of All, but the boy only nodded and continued to call him Holy One.

"Let us find a place out of this wind and rest for a moment," Javi said. "I fear my legs are not as fleet as yours."

The boy, whose name was Deko, grinned. He admired the old man's courage. Even in good weather this was not an easy climb. But, admiration aside, the boy wondered what this foolishness was all about. Sane people stayed close to home and hearth when the wind blew and the snow flew. But this old one wandered far and wide over the mountains looking into caves and cracks as though hunting for bats and worms.

A few more steps up the trail brought them to a niche in the hillside where a little of the cutting wind was fended off.

"Holy One," Deko began after they had seated themselves on a thin ledge inside the niche, "have you truly seen the new gods?"

Javi did not answer for a moment, then said, "I have seen the travelers from the sky, if that is what you mean. But they are not gods,

Deko. They are mortal beings as we are. The Master of the Design has seen fit to give them powers which we do not have, but they are mortals like us, not gods."

"Did the Maker of All send them?" the boy asked, wide eyed.

"Of course. Everything is in the hands of the Designer. How could it be otherwise?"

The child looked at his feet. There was clearly more on his mind, but Javi did not press. After a while the boy asked, "These travelers, they are very cruel, aren't they?"

Javi shrugged his skinny shoulders. "Are we cruel when we shear a sheep to make warm clothes? Are we cruel when we slaughter a goat to roast for food?"

Deko frowned. "But those are animals," he said. "We must shear them and kill them and eat them so that we may be warm and not hungry."

"But does not the sheep think it cruel?"

"I had never thought of it that way before," Deko said. "Are we animals then, that these travelers shear us for their warmth?"

Javi was surprised that the child made such connections with such ease. Many adults would not have understood. "That is the way they see it," he said. "I do not."

"They are cruel then," the boy said positively. "They do not see us as we are."

"That is true."

"Then why did the Maker of All send these cruel travelers to us? Have we done something that deserves punishment? Are these travelers like a spanking from the Designer?"

Javi almost laughed. After a time, he said, "I think they are not. I think they are a part of the great Design which leaves nothing to chance. They have come here for reasons they do not know themselves. But the Maker of All knows why."

The boy and the man sat quietly together for a time. Then Javi said, "Time is passing, Deko. Let us go on. I do not want to be caught out here in the darkness."

Deko nodded and lead off into the icy wind.

The cave Deko showed Javi was perfect. The entrance was

invisible. It was only a slight widening of a crack in the mountain, and that widening was screened with a rank growth of mountain laurel. Javi did not even recognize the opening as a cave entrance until Deko disappeared from view then reappeared from the bush to wave him on.

The bush was thorny and it made the already tight entrance even tighter. Javi had to turn side-ways to squeeze even his skinny frame into the mountain. After a few steps the entrance widened so that boy and man could walk side by side.

The gray light that seeped through the narrow entrance was quickly overcome by the immense dark of the bowels of the earth, but Deko was prepared. He took a tallow dipped torch from the bag which hung across his shoulder and kindled it with his tinder box. The flickering light showed a large room with a slightly tilted sandy floor. There were no stalactites or other limestone growths and there did not seem to be any seeping water. The air was dry and, to Javi's aching bones, it felt warmer, but that might have been just being out of the wind.

"There are many passages deeper in the mountain, Holy One."

"Have you explored them all, Deko?"

"No, Holy One," The boy scoffed. "There are so many it would take a lifetime, but I know many of them."

"Good. Then tell me this. Is there a room, this size or smaller, deeper in the mountain?"

Deko shrugged. "There are many of all sizes."

"Good. Please take me to one."

The child looked surprised at the request, but after a moment turned and led on.

The pair looked at four different chambers and Javi rejected each of them as too damp, too large, too small, too close to the outside entrance; but in reality, he did not know why he was rejecting them. They just did not seem right for some reason.

An hour later and deep in the mountain they crawled through a low passage into a chamber which made a catch come in Javi's breathing. It was square, about twenty steps long and wide, with a flat sandy floor. Opposite the entrance was a huge stone flattened on top and about waist high. On each side was a stalactite as big around as a man which reached up into the dark vault of the ceiling. They had the look of columns set purposely to mark off the stone table.

Javi went to this altar of the earth and lay his hands upon it. It was cold, but dry and when he touched the columns, they too were dry.

"Does this room stay dry year-round, Deko?"

"I think so, Holy One. I have never found water here. The nearest water is a pool down one of the other passages, back there." He pointed back through the entrance.

"Animals? Bats? Rats?" Javi asked.

"I do not think so. I have never seen anything here. The bats are in another chamber. I do not go there. The stink is awful. It made me sick. I think the bats go and come only from there. They do not hunt in this part of the cavern because there is nothing to hunt."

"Excellent. Wonderful."

Deko beamed at the praise.

Javi looked in all the corners of the chamber and scuffed the sandy floor with his boot. "Excellent," he said again and again. Then, "Let's go, Deko. I do not want to be caught by darkness."

The boy agreed and started toward the entrance, but Javi called him back. "You must not tell anyone about this place, Deko. And that means, NO ONE."

The boy frowned at this. "Not even my father, Holy One?"

"Not even your father."

Deko chewed at his lip and looked doubtful. "He will ask, Holy One, and I cannot lie to him."

Javi scratched at his neck beneath his beard and thought about that for a little. "True enough," he said. "Sons should not lie to fathers. So, tell him that Master Javi Holis asked you to keep this secret. Will that satisfy him?"

Deko considered it a moment then nodded. He turned and led the way out.

~ * ~

At first, Master Ekas was ashamed and afraid to return to the library. He felt as though he had abandoned his own child in a dark forest. He was afraid to return to face the condemnation of Mara's eyes, or worse, her pity. But the pull of the great work being done in what he thought of as his library was beyond resistance. He could not stay away, so after a week's absence he crept back to check on Mara. The young copyist did not even notice Ekas' presence, her concentration was so intense. She was near completion of the first of the five Mandalai.

She is so young. He thought. *And she looks so fragile. I wonder when she last ate?*

Ekas talked to the cook. That one could not remember when he had last seen Mara. He asked Javi if she was eating.

"I force her to eat something in the evening, but it is difficult," he said.

Ekas had heard enough. He went to the kitchen, had hot tea and food prepared, and carried it to the library. Never had such a thing been allowed before. Ekas had protected the volumes there with his very life, but now it was clear that Mara would starve if food was not brought to her. The librarian felt it was the least he could do since he could not help Mara with her labor. Even so Ekas often returned to find the food barely touched, the tea gone cold, and Mara still hunched over her copy, straining to see through the gathering gloom of evening. More than once he forced her to lay down her pen and go to bed.

"I fear she will ruin those good eyes," he said to Javi and anyone else who would listen. "She works so intently she does not notice the growing dark."

Javi shared the older man's concerns. He remembered how Mara had said she feared that the Mandalai would consume her. Now Javi feared for her. He asked himself and Master Aram if the Maker of All could be so cruel as to use her up as those in Keep Holis might use up a candle.

"I cannot answer you," Master Aram said. "Once I would have said not, but so many things have changed."

"She feared she was stupid because she could not use the powers. I told her the Designer had given her gifts and would show her the use of them. Now I wonder if those talents might not use her up."

Mara was well into copying the third Mandala when Javi told her a hiding place had been found. She nodded her understanding, but that was all. The Mandalai had taken control of her mind to the exclusion of almost everything else. She would work on the copy before her until daylight was gone, and return to the task at the first light of morning. She worked from exhaustion to collapse. During the day she did not leave her desk.

Master Ekas watched Mara's progress with a mixture of awe and envy. She was so young. And her copies were perfect. "She is truly gifted," he said to Javi. "I wish she could stay to study more. She might even bring forth some new Mandalaya. Perhaps even add to The Great Book. But I know that is not possible, is it?"

"I do not think so, Ekas. When she is finished, we must return to Peshar. Each day we linger here I feel that the danger grows for those in Peshar. The Servants of the Design are in peril, and the powers can help them, I think."

Ekas sighed. "Such a shame that one so talented cannot stay and develop her skill. She has done nothing yet save copy the ancient masters, but there are great works in her, I am sure. She is not like me, not simply a copyist. She could be a great master."

Spring pushed the snow and ice from the mountain country inch by inch. The razor wind eased and became gentle breezes, and mountain flowers pried their way up through the rocks.

Mara hunched over her copy of the last of the five Mandalai. Her eyes burned from hours of work and her back ached from days of immobility. She had lost weight. Her wrists, slender, strong and shapely when she first came to Keep Holis, were now only bones covered by tight pallid skin, but her hands were steady and sure. Her quill never wavered and her brushes never smeared the tiniest drop of color from its rightful place.

In the late afternoon of the sixtieth day of work Mara laid the tiny brush—only half a dozen hairs—aside. She lifted her head and turned it from side to side to loosen the stiffness of her neck; then she put her hands to her lower back and stretched until the vertebrae cracked.

After a moment of rest, she picked up the brush again and looked for the place she had been applying color, but she could not find it. She glanced over the copy and compared it with the original, a seed of panic growing in her. She could not find the place where she had left off. She searched and searched and began to cry when she could not find the place, but as suddenly as the panic had come it was gone. She realized that she could not find the place to continue because there was no such place. There was nothing more to do. She was finished.

Mara put the brush aside and looked over her copy again, just to be sure. She could not believe she was finished, but she was.

At last the truth of it came flooding over her with a sense of joy and relief. She jumped up from the desk and began dancing around the library singing with all her might.

Master Ekas heard the noise and rushed in. He stopped short just inside the door and watched open-mouthed as Mara danced. He feared that strain had broken her mind and sadness almost overwhelmed him until Mara ran to him and hugged him so hard it made his old bones crackle.

"Finished," she cried. "The last one is finished." Then she laughed like a delighted little child. "Look- look- look!" She pulled at Master Ekas' hand. "Come see. It is finished."

Ekas looked at the copy on the desk, then up at the original. It was breath-taking. He could hardly believe what was before his eyes. He brought one of the candles that had been adding its feeble light to that of the sun nearer, and sat down to examine the work more closely.

After a long time, he sat back shaking his head in disbelief. "It is perfect," he whispered. "I have never seen a copy so perfect. Even the fading of the paint and ink has been matched. You could not tell them apart."

Mara had stopped her dancing and singing when Ekas began his examination. Now she heaved a sigh of satisfaction.

"Now you will leave," Ekas said.

Suddenly, all the joy fled; replaced by a feeling of desolation such as Mara had never felt before.

Mara's days of work and deprivation had taken their toll. She ate a huge meal and fell asleep sitting beside the fire. Javi saw that she was put to bed and looked in on her from time to time. She slept all night, all day, and all the next night, and when she woke, she ate another huge meal—larger than anyone could believe—and went back to bed for another day and night.

While Mara slept, Javi and Master Ekas prepared The Book of the Design for storage. Master Aram even rose painfully from his bed and tried to help, but ended only watching as the book was sealed in layers of cloth and oiled leather. They stitched the leather tight shut and sealed the seams with wax, then wrapped another layer of oiled leather around the book and sealed it too. Finally, they placed the considerably larger bundle into an oiled wood box, nailed it shut and sealed the cracks with wax.

"I think it will be safe even from a flood now," Master Aram said. "We can only trust to the Maker of All now."

"I wish I had taken time to have the casket decorated with carvings or paint," Master Ekas said. "It seems like sacrilege to hide the magnificence of The Great Book in a plain box."

Javi smiled at the master of the library. "Plainness is just another protection," he said. "Even if the box is found, who would think that so precious a thing would be hidden in so plain a box."

"When will you take it?" Master Aram asked.

"Tomorrow. The boy and I will take it."

"Are you sure you can trust this child, Javi?" Aram asked.

He had not been told Deko's name or the location of the hiding place, and he did not ask.

"He is trustworthy," Javi said.

"Someone other than you and a child from the village must know where this is located," Ekas said, and patted the box. "You are returning to Peshar. If you are lost the hiding place is lost with you, perhaps forever."

Javi nodded. "I have written out the location and drawn a map." He took out a folded sheet of paper. "I will seal it in leather and wax and wood, like the book. I will leave it with you, Master Aram. Hide it away and never look at it until the travelers from the sky are gone."

"That may be many years," Ekas protested.

Javi nodded. "This must be passed on to your successors, and perhaps to theirs until the gods leave this world."

The next day, while Mara prepared a travel kit for them, Javi and Deko tied the bulky, heavy box on the back of a sure-footed donkey and went up the mountain trail and into the cave. The trip was difficult and they could not take the donkey into the narrow opening. Javi and the boy took the box off the animal's back and with Deko pushing as Javi tugged they moved it into the cave. At one-point Javi feared they would not be able to shove and drag the box through a low passage, but, with much sweat and pushing and pulling, they did it.

When they reached the chamber of the stone altar, Javi was used up by the labor, but he and Deko hoisted the box up into the middle of the stone before he sat down to rest.

"Why is the box so important, Holy one?" Deko asked.

"Better that you do not know."

The boy frowned, unhappy with the answer. "But why not?" he asked.

Javi patted the boy's shoulder. "Someday someone may ask you what is in the box and you will be able to tell them truly that you do not know."

Deko's frown deepened, but he did not pursue it. "Holy One, we must go soon. I am almost out of torches, and I could not find the way out in the dark."

Javi took a deep breath, dreading the long journey out, but then he stood. "Lead on, Deko," he said.

When they walked out of the cavern the sun was very low in the sky. Even so Javi had to rest in the niche they had used upon the first exploration to the cave. He looked back up the mountain. "Forget what we have just done, Deko," he said.

The boy nodded. He could see that Master Javi was used up with the labor they had just finished. "I think you should ride the donkey back down, Holy One."

Javi nodded. "I am weary and can hardly see in this gloom." After a little, he swung onto the little donkey's back, and they started down the narrow ledge trail.

Six

3 A.C.G.

Peshar was a much-changed city when Javi and Mara returned. The Servants of the Gods had multiplied a -hundred-fold. Red robes were everywhere, and most of them were armed and belligerent.

Sartin Fex welcomed his sister and Javi with joy, but that was soon pushed aside by worry. "The winter was horrible, Master Javi," he said. "Many starved to death and many have turned to worship of the new gods to stay alive."

"And the students? How many have joined the red robes?" Javi asked.

Sartin covered his face with his hands to hide his shame. "Some. Mostly those who have been unable to learn the powers, but even some of those who can use the powers have turned to the new gods."

"Do they truly worship, or have they joined only to avoid hunger?"

Sartin shrugged. "Perhaps some are still serving the Design."

"All is in the Design, Sartin," Javi said quietly, putting his hand on the younger man's shoulder.

Sartin looked into Javi's eyes and suddenly smiled with relief. "I had forgotten that Master. Everything is in the hands of the Designer, even those things which seem to be against the Design."

"Sometimes it is a hard thing to remember when you are hungry and cold. That is why we Servants of the Design are only a few threads in the great tapestry. Now tell me the rest. I would not think that the new gods would place much trust in hungry people."

"There is not much trust, or was not at first. Now…" he shrugged. "When food dwindled the gods decreed a temple tax increase. They intended to starve out those still resisting and, I think, to precipitate rioting so that the truly rebellious could be identified and culled. Hundreds were killed. The gods brought forth their machines and mowed down the crowds as though they were wheat. While the city was still cringing, the red robes began the work of finding out who did not serve the gods. The choice was to become a worshiper of the new gods or to die."

"How did you escape?" Mara asked her brother.

Sartin grinned, but there was no mirth in it. "We became loyal worshipers of the new gods. We do the minimum necessary to keep the red robes happy and stay out of sight as much as possible. Those who had food shared it with those who didn't, and we continued to study the Design."

Mara looked at her brother and suddenly began to sob. "If only I could have copied faster. Perhaps more could have learned. Perhaps they could have helped those who were wavering to stand strong."

Javi pulled Mara to him and embraced her. "You could not have worked any faster," he assured her. "Remember—All is in the Design, even those who serve the new gods."

Mara's copies were put to use immediately. Many who had not been able to learn the powers before, now understood with ease, but there were still those who, like Mara, could not use the powers. These Mara took to her heart. "There are other talents than the use of the powers," she told them. "I cannot use the powers, but the Mandalai use me. When I copied, my hand was guided by them. I do not remember some of the days I worked. So powerful were the Mandalai that my mind could not comprehend them, so the Designer took control of my hands and eyes, and I copied them, even though I did not understand them."

"But, Mistress Mara," one of the students protested. "You were surrounded by the Mandalai. We have only these five. How can we be seized by the power of the Design with so few?"

Mara smiled a smile which had been released at the end of her work at Keep Holis. "The Designer works through everything. The power can reach you through anything, even the smallest thing in the world.

Therefore, we will begin with pen and ink to learn our part of the Design."

~ * ~

Mara laughed at herself and could not think how she had once considered Javi Holis old. Now he was friend, teacher, lover, and it seemed that he had never been anything else.

Everyone in House Fex knew Mara and Master Javi were living as husband and wife, and there was no disapproval or scandal attached to the knowledge. It was simply a fact of life – except to Javi.

Javi worried about it, but when he approached Sartin about legitimizing the union Sartin only lifted an eyebrow and asked, "What does Mara say about it?"

Javi Holis, Servant of the Design, and Master of the five Powers, blushed at the question. "She laughed," he said. "She said I should stop worrying about such nonsense and that All was in the Design."

Now Sartin laughed. Javi blushed deeper scarlet and found himself forced to chuckle along with him. After a while Javi said, "I found it disconcerting to be reprimanded for my unbelief by your sister."

"No doubt," Sartin agreed.

"Still, I do worry about it Sartin. What if Mara becomes pregnant? The child would be a bastard, having no claim on House Ransis or any other house. He would have no name."

"He would have the name of Javi Holis as father, and he could claim anything or everything from House Fex," Sartin snorted "though that is little enough at the moment."

"But…"

Sartin lifted his hand to stop Javi. "Do not trouble yourself more about this, Master Javi. It means nothing anyway. The only marriage and inheritance rights recognized by the new gods are those registered in the temple, and to claim those you and Mara would have to show yourselves to the temple clerks and ask for permission to marry. They would not grant that, but they would be happy to grant you new sets of chains and secure lodging in the dungeons."

Javi knew Sartin was right, but it still bothered him.

Mara knew Javi was bothered by their wed/unwed position, and that bothered her all the more when it became clear that she was with child. Mara was as torn as Javi about the child he did not yet know about, but for different reasons. One moment she was ecstatic, thinking of the baby as a continuation of herself and Javi, and of the wonder of the Design that it would let a thing as wonderful as making love result in a thing as wonderful as a baby. But she also feared for the child. She boiled with anger and shame at having ever allowed the child to be conceived, not because of the act or shame, but because she could see nothing in the future but pain and cold and hunger and perhaps death at the hands of the new gods for any child born now. What kind of a mother would bring a child into such a world?

Now she sat on her low stool beside the fire and looked toward Javi as he taught the students sitting at his feet. She could not put off telling him too much longer. Soon her middle would begin to swell.

"Mara?" Javi called. She did not answer though she was only a step away, so he called her name again.

Javi's voice pierced her brooding thoughts at last, and she answered.

Javi left his students, came to her, and knelt beside her. "There was such a look of sadness on your face," he said, stroking a strand of hair back from her forehead.

There was so much tender concern in his voice, and the gesture, that Mara's heart ached. She took his hand in her own and kissed it. "I am all right. I was just thinking sad thoughts for a moment."

"Sad thoughts come easily these days, but all will be well. We are in the hands of the Designer."

"Of course, it will," she said, and believed, but she could not forget all the dead children from the first contact with the new gods. They were part of the Design too.

~ * ~

General Itar, Cadeki Military Governor of Archlea, who was called the God-Resident, sat at his desk and stared at the scraps of paper and parchment before him. On them were crude drawings in lumpy black ink. Most of the drawings seemed like the scratchings of a child, but some of them were good copies of designs he knew. That bothered him.

"They were brought in by an Archlean, General," Major Rainek, the general's aide said. "He wanted to trade them, and some information, for food."

"What information?"

"It was not anything worthwhile, my Lord. Things we already knew. Plots and such connected with these," Rainek gestured at the drawings. "They are supposed to be some means to power. Magic talismans whereby the new gods may be cursed and defeated." He chuckled, but cut it off short when Itar glared at him.

"And what did you do with the one who brought this information?" The general asked.

"We took his papers, fed him, and put him back on the street, Sir. As per your instruction."

The general nodded.

There were many of these copies floating around and Itar felt that many were being brought to the temple only because it was known that they could be traded for food. That would have to end soon. It would not be good practice to let these people believe they could fool the gods by bringing in any more of these drawings. General Itar had several renderings of those on the desk before him. Some of them were quite beautiful. They were all rendered in paint and ink with such delicacy and precision that they pulled one's eye and mind into them. Itar had even had the set of five which he considered the best framed. They now decorated the walls of his private quarters.

The drawings were not dangerous in themselves, Itar thought. He gave no credence to magic or curses, but he knew that belief in magic and curses could be as dangerous as if they were real. A man convinced of his powers could convince others of them, and that could be dangerous. Very dangerous indeed. Such belief might kill many more Archleans, and Itar, though a soldier through and through, was tired of bloodshed, especially that which accomplished nothing.

Itar looked up to find Maj. Rainek still standing before his desk trying not to fidget.

"Find me someone who knows more about these," the general said. "I want to know all there is to know, lest we suddenly find ourselves in the midst of another uprising."

Rainek saluted and left, thinking that his general must be cracking under the pressure of command to take these animal scratchings so seriously. So what if the whole planet rose up in revolt? Thus far there had been not one Cadeki casualty in all the uprisings. Better the Empire should simply cleanse this mud ball of all vermin and get on with operation of the Gates. After all, there was nothing else here of any worth. If not for the Multi-Terminus on this miserable dust mote the Empire would not have ever bothered with it. There was not even anything worth taking! Even the tapestries that so fascinated some of the officers were nothing but crude rugs so far as he was concerned. And what else could be expected from creatures which had not developed enough technology to print with movable type, much less use laser disks? They were hardly more than intelligent animals!

Rainek shoved these thoughts aside, falling back on the soldierly philosophy that all high-ranking men were insane, but that orders were orders. Within hours Rainek rounded up a dozen Archleans and had their minds peeled. He reported to the general. "There are only a few involved, Lord Itar. They call themselves Servants of the Design. They do not seem dangerous. They do not preach uprising now, though some of them used to. They spread dissent by saying we are not gods."

Itar grunted. "Perceptive these..." he looked to Rainek for the right word.

"...Servants of the Design," the Major supplied.

"Yes, Servants of the Design. Strange that a people so underdeveloped technologically could be advanced enough intellectually..." Itar shook his head in honest confusion, then rubbed his forehead. He had an on-going headache. "Is there more?"

"The center of the...Cult, I suppose you could call it, is a man called Javi Holis. He is some sort of holy man the rabble look to as a leader."

"And what have you done about this Holis?"

"He is being sought now, my Lord. He should be in custody soon."

"Very well. When you have him bring him to me."

"Before he is mind peeled, my Lord?" Rainek asked, carefully keeping any hint of disapproval out of his voice.

"He would be of little use afterward, now wouldn't he, Rainek?"

"Yes, my Lord. That is true."

"Make it so then. Meanwhile spread the word that any Archlean found in possession of material connected with the Servants of the Design will be sent into slavery or executed at the discretion of the God-Resident."

"Yes, my Lord," Rainek said. He saluted and got out.

~ * ~

Javi watched Mara more in the next days. The brooding, sad look was often on her face, but as soon as she felt his eyes upon her the look would change to a smile. It might have fooled him if he had not seen what came before. At last he went to Sartin again.

"She is trying to make me think she is well and happy and content, Sartin, but it is not true. What is wrong? Is she ill?"

Sartin thought on that for a moment then said, "I don't know, but I have never seen her look healthier."

"But she seems so unhappy sometimes."

"Perhaps she is feeling trapped. I feel it myself sometimes. She has hardly left the house since your return, nor have you. All we ever do is work and eat and sleep, any of us."

Javi pulled at his beard, "Perhaps. But what can we do? It is dangerous to go out. Red robes are everywhere."

Sartin shrugged. "Is she any less safe on the streets than here? Those using the powers to keep track in the temple say that the God-Resident does not seem overly concerned with us. If he were, we could all be taken to the temple in chains at their whim."

"But what about the edicts against the Mandalai?"

"What of them? If Mara goes out, she will not be carrying copies of the Mandalai. Even if she is stopped, why would they do more than question her. They have done that to many. Most all have been released."

The idea did have appeal. High summer was upon Peshar, and with the hot bright days came the tapestry displays in the plaza. Mara would enjoy that. *In fact*, Javi thought, *I would enjoy it. I would very much enjoy sitting in a cafe upon the plaza with a cup of cool wine in my hand and the great tapestries of Peshar spread out before me.*

"Perhaps you are right, Sartin. And I believe I will go with her."

The younger man looked uncomfortable with that idea, but he didn't object aloud. So, the plan was made.

When Javi told Mara, her eyes lost the clouds that had been in them. For the first time in days her smile was genuine. "What a wonderful idea," she said, but then she frowned. "But won't that be dangerous for you?"

He shrugged. "No more dangerous than here, I think. If the gods want me, they could find me without much trouble."

Mara had to agree. She smiled and suddenly hugged Javi. "We will go. Like members of one of the great houses of Peshar. We will idle the day away sipping tea and eating dainties as we look at the wares in the plaza."

They woke before dawn and were on their way through the winding, narrow streets at first light. Sartin gave them each one zari and grinned like a proud father as he told them to be careful of thieves, and not to eat too many sweets. His heart was joyful as he watched them hold hands. They were like two happy children.

Sellers were setting up their booths with the coming of the light. There were not many tapestries yet, it was still too early, so Mara and Javi went to a table outside the establishment of Ramer Tul. A serving man was at their side instantly asking their pleasure.

They ordered a pot of tea and a ration of effas, sugared bread dough fried in sweet oil then sprinkled with cinnamon to make them sting the tongue deliciously. They sat and watched Tapestry Plaza come alive with shoppers and sellers. Skeletal tapestry racks began to rise on the west side of the plaza. Javi told Mara about the first time he had seen the tapestries of the plaza. He was only a child the first time he came to help his father stretch a Ransis tapestry on a display rack. He could still remember the crush of the crowds, the smell of fresh fruit and spices mixed with the smell of dye coming from the tapestry. The plaza had been a sea of pleasure to the young Indi Ransis.

The crowds were smaller now, the vendors fewer, and the tapestries were not so dazzling, but there was still an inescapable excitement and joy in the plaza which lifted the spirit.

When the tea and effas were finished the two began wandering among the booths and display racks. They held hands. Sometimes they stopped before one of the tapestries and examined it more closely.

"I wonder if House Ransis has anything out yet?" Mara said, thinking out loud.

The weaver before whose tapestry they were standing suddenly looked sour. "House Ransis," he growled. "They display rugs, not tapestries. If you want rugs you should not waste your time with works of art such as this," he indicated his tapestry.

Javi was surprised at the vehemence of the man. He looked more closely at the work, and after a few moments he could see that this master work was of poor quality. It was woven of bleached four strand yard with the design daubed on after it was woven. A fine quality tapestry used six or even eight strand yarn, and the colors were dyed into the yarn before it was woven into the design. Also, this work before them was completely flat. There was no sculpture work in it at all. Sculpting was a sign of true artistry. It took great patience and time to weave in and sew in thicker yarns to produce the illusion of depth. Such artistry was expensive, and drove the price of tapestries up and up.

After a moment Javi said, "Truly this is a master work."

The weaver smiled.

"It is far above our poor pockets. Don't you think so, Mara?"

Mara smiled, and her eyes twinkled. "Very true, husband," she sighed. "Never could we afford such a wonderful thing as this. Perhaps we should lower our hopes and see what we might find at the rug merchant Ransis. If you would be so kind as to direct us, Master Weaver?"

The man's eyes flickered between Javi and Mara. He was sure he was being mocked, but did not quite understand how. After a moment he said, "Be off with you then! If you want a Ransis rug you will have to wait until afternoon. I do not have time to natter with beggars." He turned his back on them.

Javi and Mara waited until they were out of ear shot before they laughed.

They wandered like children, drinking in the colors and the warm sun and the throngs in the plaza. They were lost in one another, and they failed to notice the number of red robes at the edge of the crowd, but after a little Javi felt a chill in the pit of his stomach. He looked around and suddenly knew the red robes were after the two of them.

He did not want to frighten Mara so he said, "Let's go get something cool to drink," and began pushing her toward the nearest street leading from the plaza.

Mara frowned at the sudden change and glanced around for herself. It took only a moment to see the red robes. They were forming a line at the east side of the plaza.

The two had not advanced more than a few steps when they saw that the exit street, they had been aiming for was blocked by an armed servant of the new gods.

The crowd was not aware of what was happening at first, but when the already crowded plaza began to shrink, a half-panicky buzz rose. Vendors and artists started packing their goods, but the moving red line did not give them time to finish. They continued to close in, herding people before them and allowed no one to get past them.

Some of the crowd protested and tried to push through, but this was met with jabs and clouts with the staffs the temple servants carried. They forced the crowd into an ever-tightening corral which, in turn, forced the people into an ever-narrowing corridor like water pouring down a funnel. The funnel emptied into a single broad street. There a group of priests scrutinized each person who squeezed past them. They allowed most to pass, but some they held and shoved against a wall where they were guarded by other servants of the new gods. These had swords drawn.

A hand gripped Javi's upper arm and his insides turned to water. He tried to pull away from the grip, but it tightened.

Javi turned, prepared to fight, but before he could raise his fist, he recognized his brother, Bai.

"They are looking for you, aren't they, Indi?" he asked, but it wasn't really a question.

"Yes," he answered.

"Come," Bai said. "Stay close. If we are separated, we are finished." He pulled Javi sideways across the stream of people. It was so quick that Javi barely had time to grab Mara's hand and pull her along.

"What …?" she asked. There was fear in her eyes.

"It is my brother," he said. "Stay close."

Bai continued to shove and elbow his way across the stream of people, earning many curses and not a few punches and kicks until the three of them were against a blank wall at one side of the plaza. They could go no farther to the side, and the crowd carried them forward a few paces toward a door in the wall. Several who were shoved passed the door pounded upon it with no result. Everyone knew it had been locked and barred for years.

Bai stopped beside the door and held against the stream of people. He pulled a key from somewhere in his robe and unlocked it. It was hard to push, but Bai and Javi forced it open. When it inched open others of the panicky mob tried to enter it, but Bai did not let them. He shoved Javi and Mara through, rolled round the edge of the door and all three put their weight against it to push it shut. Bai lifted a wooden bar from beside the door and dropped it into the hasps. Those who had seen the door open and close pounded on it. Their pleas to be let in came piteously to the three and wrung their hearts, but they knew they could not let anyone else through.

Bai turned and shoved the other two ahead of him down the dark corridor. After a few steps they came to another door which opened as hard as the one leading from the plaza, but this one led to a room. Its dimness was broken by sunlight which seeped in around another door. Bai closed the door they had come through then pressed his ear against the exit door. Satisfied with what he heard, he opened it and the three stepped into a small, well-tended courtyard garden. The room they came from was a tool room.

The courtyard was partly roofed over with grape vines twined into an arbor. Here they stopped for a moment to catch their breaths.

"How did you know?" Javi asked his brother.

The other shook his head. "I came and unbarred that door weeks ago, and have been carrying the key with me ever since. I did not know why. Now I do."

"The Maker of All moved you to do it," Javi said.

Bai shrugged. "Perhaps so. Come." He went across the garden and out a barred gate which let onto a quiet side street. He looked up and down, then motioned Javi and Mara to follow him.

The Patriarch of House Ransis led them through winding back streets and alleys for a half hour. At last they stopped before a door, and Bai knocked. The door opened and suddenly Javi knew where he was. The office of House Ransis' warehouse.

Bai told the servant who had opened the door to bring tea, and the man departed. "We can rest here for a bit," Bai said.

Javi looked at his brother for a long time. "Thank you, Bai," he said at last. "You took a terrible chance. They were almost certainly looking for us."

Bai rubbed his hand over his face. It was slick with perspiration. "For the life of me I cannot think why I did it. I unbarred that door—and then, today, I just knew they were looking for you. Before I even saw you, I knew; then I saw you, and I had to do something to help you."

Bai looked at the two of them for a moment. "Why were they after you, Indi?"

Mara looked questioningly at Javi.

"My birth name," he said in answer. "I am Indi Ransis, eldest son of House Ransis. I became Javi when I chose to serve the Design. This is my brother, Bai."

She is pretty, Bai thought, *or rather she would be if she were not so pale and thin.*

"This is Mara," Javi continued. Bai nodded his welcome.

"But why were they after you, Indi?"

"I don't know."

"There have been rumors that the Servants of the Design are plotting against the gods. Could that be it? Are you plotting some revolt?"

Javi shook his head. "The Servants of the Design are not plotters of revolutions. We believe everything is in the hands of the Designer, even these new gods who rule over us now. How could we plot against them? They are instruments of the Designer. To plot against them would be to plot against the very purposes of the Designer."

Bai stared at his brother for a long time, trying to determine the truth of what he had just heard. It sounded like the truth, and Bai had become very familiar with the difference between truth and lies. His daily life had become full of lies. He lied to clients about delivery dates, he lied to the red robes about how many zari he took in and how many people worked for him. One did not live as an honest man in Peshar.

The servant brought the tea and departed.

"If you are not plotting against the gods, why are they after you?"

Javi shrugged. "Because they are afraid of us. We serve the Design and do not worship in their temple. We are not plotting against them, but by not worshipping them we resist. They perceive us as a threat, and they are cruel enough to stamp out even the perception of threat."

Mara handed out tea and returned to her seat beside Javi.

Bai watched her as she served and then as she sat.

"We will leave soon," Javi said.

Bai took the time to sip his tea before agreeing. "I wish it could be otherwise, Indi, but I do not wish to bring trouble on House Ransis. Papa is very ill, and Mama is not much better. We are keeping House Ransis alive by cooperating with the gods and the temple. They take most of our work and pay us almost nothing for it, but what other choice is there? It has come to a choice of life or death, and I will not let House Ransis die."

"I understand," Javi said. "You have done well. Keep it alive if you can. I pray that such is in the Design."

Javi rose, and Mara followed, but Bai said, "Wait. Have some more tea, have some food. Wait until it is dark. That will give you a better chance to dodge the temple servants, and it will give us more chance to talk."

Bai had a simple meal prepared and brought to the office. The brothers talked as they ate. Mara said little but heard everything and stored away everything she learned.

There was love between the brothers, but there was also enmity.

"Papa has been growing steadily worse since you left a year ago, Javi. He does not even recognize me most of the time now. Sometimes he thinks that I am you and it is the time you chose to study the Design. He rages and pleads with you to stay. When he realizes that I am not you, he quiets and just stares into the fire, sometimes for hours. Then he suddenly begins to cry."

Javi's eyes closed for a moment, and when they opened again an impenetrable curtain had been drawn behind them. It was meant to keep everyone out; to shield others from the pain he was enduring. "I am sorry, Bai," he said. "If only there was something I could do."

The other sighed. "I almost wish you were plotting a revolt. It might be futile, but I am almost ready to attempt something futile. It would be better than simply enduring. But of course, enduring is something you believe in, isn't it?"

Javi did not answer the jab. Instead he asked, "How is mother?"

Bai shrugged. "As bad as Papa, but in a different way. Her hope is gone too, but it has not been kind enough to steal her mind as it has Papa's. She became sick after we were thrown out of the house when the gods came, but she stayed about the same as when you were with us. Now she is worse. She coughs all the time now. Sometimes she coughs up blood. She is so weak she can hardly get up from her bed. I doubt it she will live through another winter."

The weight of this litany of misery bore them down to silence. Mara could not see how House Ransis could survive. Almost everything had been taken from them. Her family had lost much, but nothing like what had been taken from House Ransis. She was angry at the gods for what they had done, and some of that anger spilled over onto the Designer, but that did not last long. Mara accepted the Design, even when it held pain for her and for those she loved.

"But that is enough of gloom," Bai said. He reached for the jug of wine that had been brought with the food and poured three cups. He lifted his and said, "Let us drink to escapes and endurance."

They lifted their cups and drank, but when Javi and Mara lowered theirs they saw that Bai had lowered his only halfway. He had an enigmatic smile on his lips and a lifted eyebrow that said he was very pleased with himself.

"Well, what else?" Javi prodded his brother. "You look like a well-fed fox."

Bai's smile widened and it infected them so that they smiled in answer. "I am getting married," Bai said.

"What?" Javi exclaimed and jumped to his feet. "When? Who?"

"Next month. It will be a union between House Ransis and House Lowel. I will marry Dirani, widow of Atham Lowel."

"Dirani Lowel, a widow?" Mara gasped, and was sorry as soon as the words were out.

The smile disappeared from Bai's face. He blinked a few times and his happy triumphant smile was replaced with a look of sorrow.

"Yes, Mara, she is widowed. Atham died in a riot a few months ago. It was an accident. He wasn't even involved in the fight, just caught up in the mob when the gods…"

He broke off, sorrow and anger mingling to choke his voice. After a time, he went on. "Hundreds were killed. Most were like Atham. They had nothing to do with the riot. For a time, it looked like House Lowel would be confiscated, but Dirani managed to avoid that. It cost a great deal, mostly in bribes. Even that was probably a waste. We heard later that the gods did confiscate property from most of those killed. Still, she did avoid losing it all, and now we will marry."

"I'm sorry," Mara said. "I did not mean to be so blunt."

Bai shrugged. "There is no way to avoid bluntness since the gods came."

"In any case," Javi said, "Congratulations to you, brother." He went to Bai and embraced him. "May you be blessed with many children."

"Many sons to carry on House Ransis," Bai said and once more lifted his cup. Javi and Mara hurried to lift theirs.

Afterward they sat in warm quiet comradeship sipping their wine and picking at the remains of the meal. Bai told them about the wedding plans and about the nuisance involved in getting a temple license. "Most contracts can be done through a Fair Witness, but marriage is something else. The gods wish to make sure those who marry are members in good standing of the temple so that no temple tax will be lost."

"And to weed out any resisters," Javi said.

"I suppose," Bai agreed.

"Mara and I would like to marry, but we could never get a temple license, so that is impossible. Besides, I have nothing to pass to a next generation, should there be one."

Bai thought how young Mara looked to wish to marry a man as old as his brother, but he put the thought aside. "Ah well," he said. "Inheritance is the main reason Dirani and I have gone through this temple business rather than simply living together."

"That is almost the same thing Sartin, Mara's brother, said."

Bai glanced at Javi wondering whether or not he should speak his thoughts. At last he did. "You could lay some claim to House Ransis, Javi," he said. "You are the eldest son."

Javi did not hesitate in his answer. "No, Bai. Any inheritance of House Ransis should go to any child you have with Dirani. I have no claim. I gave it up long ago when I chose to study the Design."

Bai was relieved. "Thank you. I thought that was what you would say, but…"

"But I do have another inheritance I wish to protect," Javi said, fixing his brother's eyes with his own. "It is something a temple marriage could not protect, even if such a thing were possible."

Silence was suddenly thick as cold oil. Bai could feel the weight of what his brother was about to say, and he dreaded to hear it, for he knew it would endanger him and House Ransis, but there was no way to stop it.

"And what is this thing you would protect, Indi?"

Javi drew a deep breath and let it out slowly. He waited a moment, considering the rightness of what he was about to do, then said: "The Book of the Design."

The words meant little to Bai. No servant of the Design, he knew almost nothing of those who were. He knew nothing of this book. Nevertheless, he felt the weight of it and it made his mouth go dry. "What is it?" he asked.

"You do not need to know Bai. It is enough that you know it is important and that you know where it is."

"This is dangerous knowledge, is it not?"

"Yes. And because it is, I will not give it to you unless you are willing."

Bai looked down at the empty wine cup which was still in his hand. "What must I do with this knowledge, Indi?"

"Perhaps nothing save pass it down to the next Patriarch of House Ransis, who may not do anything more than pass it on yet again."

"For how long?"

"Perhaps until the new gods are old. A thousand years. A thousand lifetimes. Until the purpose of the Designer is worked out."

"And if there is more to be done? What will it be?"

Javi shook his head. "I do not know. If there is more to be done the Designer will make it happen as he made you unbar the door months ago in order to save us today."

"This is a heavy burden to lay on the shoulders of one who doesn't even believe in your Designer," Bai said.

"Whether or not you believe does not matter. The Designer believes in you."

Bai searched his brother's face for some sign of levity, but found none. "All right. I will take your word for that, and I will take your knowledge."

Seven

3 A.C.G.

It was dark when Mara and Javi left the tapestry factory. Peshar was not well lit at the best of times—those forced to be out after dark usually carried lanterns—but now, even those few streets that were usually lit were dark, and no one was abroad. A pall of fear was over the city. It made Javi and Mara travel like timid mice, constantly probing the murky night with eye, ear, and nose. They became lost in the dark for a short time, but they stumbled into a small plaza which had a street lamp burning and were able to re-orient themselves.

A few streets from House Fex they stopped. The smell of smoke was strong and it grew stronger as they inched through the black street. The smoky stench planted a chill in their chests which grew colder as the stink grew more choking.

House Fex and the houses which had been on either side of it still glowed and smoldered. The buildings had been smashed by something of unbelievable power. The force had projected such heat that many of the bricks were melted to glassy puddles.

Mara sobbed and tried to catch her breath, awe-struck at the destruction. "Truly they must be gods to possess such power," she whispered hoarsely.

"No," Javi hissed. "They are not gods. Only men. Evil, blood thirsty, heartless men." He pulled her too him and enfolded her with his skinny arms. "They are not gods. They are not. They are not," he repeated over and over, as much to convince himself and calm that part of him which wanted to believe these were truly gods, as to convince her.

"What are we going to do, Javi? Where are we going to go now? There is nothing left. Nothing."

For minutes they stood locked together, supporting one another. They were numb with shock, but at last Javi said, "We must go. We must leave here now. There may be watchers left behind to trap stragglers."

Still leaning upon one another, they pushed back into the darkness.

They staggered, directionless, through the dark streets at first, but soon Javi directed them toward the poor quarter of Peshar he had inhabited during his days as a beggar. There were hiding places by the hundred there. They were not clean or comfortable, but they were safe— more or less.

They ended their flight buried inside a stack of moldy hay which was inside an abandoned stable. The smell of mildew, rot, and ancient manure was almost overpowering, but Javi had spent many safe nights there.

At first, there was the silence of waning shock between them, then Mara began to weep softly. Javi wiped the tears from her cheeks, smearing them over her face and leaving smudges of dirt from his fingers. He envied her the ability to cry. He wanted to weep with her, but no tears would come. They were dammed up by utter despair. For the first time since he had given up the name Indi Ransis to become a student of the Design, he truly doubted the existence of the Design and the Designer. How could a creator allow his creations, his very children, to be so cruelly used by others whom he had also created? There was no sense to it. No creator could be so hard of heart, unless he were the very soul of sadism, and Javi could not bring himself to believe so horrific a being could exist. Therefore, there must not be a Creator. The Designer must be a convenient lie born in the mind of the first Holis.

But, even as Javi thought these thoughts, years of belief, and practice, and training would not let him throw away the conviction that the Designer did create all; did control all; was not cruel and uncaring. Javi's faith would not die, though during that bleak night he tried hard to kill it. The flickering spark of hope and trust in the Design would not be quenched, no matter how many tears Mara poured on it, or how much Javi tried to smother it.

~ * ~

General Itar, Cadeki military governor and God-Resident of Archlea was sore displeased with his aide, Major Rainek. "You have been seeking this Javi Holis for weeks," he shouted.

Major Rainek tried hard to stand at attention and not cower beneath the tongue lashing of his general, but he was not succeeding very well. He had never seen Itar so angry. The man was purple with rage. Rainek thought, half with fear and half with hope that the general was going to burst a blood vessel.

"You have not so much as brought me a body that might be his, Major. You have not even brought me a prisoner who might know his whereabouts. Why is that, Major?"

Itar paused for breath, but Major Rainek was not so foolish as to believe an answer was called for yet.

"You have all the power and technology of the Cadeki Empire at your disposal, and still you cannot bring me this ignorant – this barely sentient – witch doctor. Why is that, Major? Are you so incompetent that you cannot be trusted to de-louse slaves? Are you an idiot, Major?"

This time the silence stretched on long enough to require the Major to fill it with his voice. "Sir…" he began, but his voice squeaked so he stopped, cleared his throat, and started again. "Sir, this Holis was not in the house our informants said he would be in, and those taken alive including one called Sartin Fex, the owner of the house, told the same story. They all said that Holis and his…wife Mara, sister to this Sartin Fex, had gone to Tapestry Plaza for the day."

"But Tapestry Plaza was sifted like baking flour, and no Holis was found," the general finished mockingly. "I have read your report, Major. I do not want to know why you have not been able to catch this Holis. I want you to catch him."

Rainek swallowed hard and continued. "We left troopers in powered armor to watch the ruins of the house, and they spotted two people believed to be Holis and his wife, but the troopers lost them."

"Lost them? How could they lose them, Major? They had infrared snooper-scopes, did they not?"

"Yes, sir, but the smoldering of the ruins confused them and they..."

"Lost them," the general again finished for the Major.

Rainek swallowed hard again and continued. "It is believed that Holis is now hiding in the poor quarter of the city. He was once a beggar and probably knows that quarter well. Patrols of temple servants, backed by mechanized troops, are combing that sector inch by inch now. Holis should be in our hands in a matter of hours."

The general drew in a deep breath and looked maliciously doubtful as he let it out. "Major, if Holis is not in my hands within the next few hours, I will send your head home in a barrel. Do I make myself clear?"

Major Rainek paled noticeably, and the already plentiful beads of sweat on his forehead became rivulets trickling down to stain the collar of his uniform blouse. "Yes sir," he said and managed a salute.

The general noted the sweat ring under Rainek's arm as that one held the salute. Perhaps this chewing out had truly gotten through to Rainek. Itar hoped so. It would be a waste to have to shorten the man.

Negligently the general returned the salute, and the Major scuttled out.

Itar pushed the copies of the Archlean designs to the side of his desk and leaned back in his chair. What was so special about these damned things? The five drawings repeated over and over. What was so special about them? He pulled the stack back in front of him and riffled through them again. The drawings—even the crude ones—drew him; filled him with a yearning that he could not understand, but he could not get anything from them save that.

After a long time of staring at the drawings he shoved them aside once more and continued the endless paperwork generated by this outpost of the Empire.

~ * ~

Javi and Mara heard the noise even through the insulating hay.

Shouts, screams, much clattering. The sounds of panic. Above that was a screeching hum neither of them could identify. They held each other and listened with growing fear for minutes, until Javi could not stand the uncertainty any longer. "Stay quiet here, Mara. I am going to see what is happening."

"No," Mara said, panic in her voice.

"But we must know. We may need to run again."

"If you are caught, I will not run anymore. Please don't go."

Javi brushed his hand over her face and said, "I will not go in the flesh then. I will use the power. No one will catch me, or even see me." He patted her hand reassuringly and felt the trembling of it subside a little.

In truth Javi had not wanted to use the power. He was reluctant to separate spirit from body because of the toll it took on him. Since the night he had stretched out the separated time to inspect the Hall of Doors, the cost to his body seemed greater with each use, and he had more difficulty re-integrating. It was as though that part of him which could travel away from his body did not want to be again imprisoned within the fleshly shell, and was always on the verge of breaking free without his willing it.

But there was no help for it now, so Javi began the exercises of breathing and concentration necessary to achieve the rising steam feeling of separating.

In moments Javi felt himself separate from his flesh, and when he opened his eyes, he found himself hovering a little above the moldy haystack. He moved forward through the wall and into the alley, then up the alley toward the source of the noises.

The street into which the alley emptied was full of red robes. These were herding hundreds of people who had been shaken from sleep into several god-machines. When each machine was filled, the door slid shut, the machine lifted into the sky, and another dropped from the sky to take its place.

At the far end of the street a Warrior-God in black armor called out in a voice too huge to be human, "This building will be destroyed in one minute. Come out now or die."

The promised minute passed. No one came out. The Warrior-God pointed a tube at the building which burst into blue flames. The fire stayed blue so long as the tube continued to point at the building, but changed to red orange when the tube was turned away.

Javi lifted himself high above the scene and scanned the area. A full third of Peshar was either in flame or in ashes. A thick cloud of acrid smoke hung over the whole city.

Javi hurried back to his waiting body, and Mara was startled when the quiet body suddenly gasped and tried to sit up. She put her arms around him. He was cold as death.

"They are burning everything Mara," Javi gasped. "They are looking for us, and they are burning everything to try and find us."

"Then we must go," Mara said and began to burrow out of the hay.

Javi stopped her. He was utterly calm within himself for the first time since they had escaped Tapestry Plaza. "I cannot go, Mara," he said. "My time is ended. My part of the Design is fulfilled. I don't think I can walk. The power has taken its payment."

Mara's eyes opened wide in fear and horror. "I didn't know…" she said. "But we must go. We cannot stay here!"

"I cannot, but you must. You must go and save yourself and our child."

Mara gasped. "How did you…"

Javi smiled. "I am not so lost in contemplation of the Design that I do not see the world around me," he said.

"But I cannot leave you, Javi. I love you. I want you to see the baby. I want you to name him," she pleaded.

"It cannot be, my love. Now go, or they will catch you. Your part of the Design is not yet worked out. Go."

"But where? Where will I go? Everyone is dead or captured. My family… I have nowhere to go," she wailed.

There was a chill more deep than Javi had ever felt before in him. It was growing and creeping up his legs into his hips. He knew he did not have long. "Go to Bai. Ask him for help. He will hide you, at least for a little while. Now go. The red robes will be here soon. You must go."

Mara hesitated a moment longer, then she kissed Javi and caressed his cold cheek. "I love you, husband," she said.

"And I you, wife. Now go, and be careful."

Mara blinked back tears, and took several breaths to strengthen herself, then pushed her way out of the haystack.

The coldness was midway up Javi's chest. He didn't really notice it anymore. The smell of burning overpowered even the smell of rot in the stable. Javi could not tell if the building was on fire or not. His senses were failing.

Mysterious, he thought. *Mysterious. The Design is so mysterious. I wonder if there is more beyond life? Strange, I have never thought of that before. Never considered it. But there must be more. After all, the Designer is beyond life and death. There must be more.*

Mysterious.

The giant voice rattled the dust loose from the old stable. He could feel the vibration of it. He smiled, thinking how angry the God-Resident would be when a few charred bones were presented to him as Javi Holis.

"You do not even know that you are a part of the Design, do you?" Javi said to the God-Resident. "How mysterious it all is."

"It will not seem so mysterious soon, my child," the voice of the Maker of All said.

Javi was not sure if he heard it with his fleshly ears or with his mind.

"My Lord, I am ready. My part in your Design is finished."

"Not so, child. The Design is much larger than that. There is yet another part for you."

Javi felt joy at that. "I am yours, my Lord."

"Then come to me child. Leave your flesh behind. Your next part in the Design awaits."

~ * ~

Mara did not look back once she squeezed through the broken board in the back wall of the stable. She wanted to, but she knew if she looked, she would turn back. She wanted to die with Javi. There was nothing left for her. Sartin was dead or a prisoner. If he lived through the questioning he would probably be sent into slavery. One way or another he was lost forever. All those she had taught to copy the Mandalai were gone—scattered or dead. The Design seemed more like chaos than Design, but there was the child. Javi's child.

Though it was midday, the streets of Peshar were empty. People huddled together indoors, fearing that to go out was to be swept into one of the god-machines that crisscrossed the sky. The sky ships ferried load after load of hapless people to the temple where they disappeared forever.

Mara's nerves were raw and her mind was flaming. She started at the slightest sound and ducked into doorways at each moving shadow. Her muscles carried her through the streets toward House Ransis by their own volition, for later she could not remember the journey at all. The entire time between leaving Javi and pounding on the office door of the tapestry factory was a blank.

The time of pounding on the door seemed forever. She began to think no one would answer, that they had been taken like Sartin and the others, but at last the servant from the night before – was it only the night before? – opened the door.

The servant looked over the beggar woman pounding on the door for several heartbeats before he recognized her with a gasp. He pulled her inside, looked up and down the street, saw no one, then glanced at the empty blue afternoon sky and closed the door. He locked it.

"Wait here," he commanded and ran off to find his master.

The Patriarch of House Ransis rushed to the office and found Mara, dirty and hollow eyed, leaning against the closed door.

"By the gods, Loura," he swore at the servant. "You could have let her sit down!"

"I am sorry, Master. I didn't think…" He hurried to help the woman. He could feel her trembling as he touched her shoulder.

"What happened?" Bai asked. "Where is Indi?"

"Dead. Burned up by the gods," Mara said, her voice flat, lifeless. "He said, 'go to my brother. He will hide you, at least for a little while.'"

Bai felt Mara's words like blows. Indi dead? This woman running from the gods? "Did anyone see you come here?" he asked anxiously.

She did not answer.

"No one was in the street, Master," Loura answered for her. "And there were no god-machines in the sky."

Bai nodded and pulled at his beard nervously for a few moments. "Take her to Mother's room," he said at last. "Have her bathed and dressed—like a servant. Burn her clothes, and I mean make sure they are nothing but ash when you are finished. Do you understand?"

"Yes, Master."

"And forget that you have seen her—ever."

Loura nodded and reached out toward the woman.

Mara submitted to all without protest. She was more like a doll than a living being. She did not speak. She did not move except in response to command. She hardly blinked her eyes. Semi-catatonia brought on by loss gripped her. She could not even mourn her dead yet.

When she was bathed and dressed, Bai and Loura took her into the wine cellar. They brought a table, a lamp, a chair, and a cot and placed them behind one of the tall racks at the back of the cellar.

Bai's heart was squeezed with pain for this woman whom he had only met a few hours before. She was so young and yet so ill used by life. *Indi's Design has been no kindness to you has it?* he thought. *Nor to any of us. Oh Indi, Indi,* he mourned.

"Stay here and rest, Mara," Bai said. "I will bring some food later. When the city has calmed you can come out."

Mara did not answer, but Bai was sure she would not come out until he told her it was safe. She sat on the cot as though it were made of stone.

Hours later Bai brought food and found her still in the same position. He touched her shoulder, but there was no response. He touched her forehead and found her cold. That, and the unchanged position, worried him. It was not natural for a human being to sit so still, but there did not seem to be anything to do except leave her alone. He dared not call a physician, assuming one could be found alive in Peshar. Anything which might draw attention to House Ransis was to be avoided at all costs.

After a little while Bai forced some warm broth down her and made her lie down upon the cot. It was like handling stiff clay. He covered her and carefully tucked the blanket under her chin then he sat down and watched her. The flickering light from the lamp made her seem by turns skeletal and little girlish. Her eyes held the same dead stare for hours, but at last they closed and some of the rigidity went out of her.

Poor child, Bai thought. *Poor Indi. Poor Peshar.*

Bai and the servant Loura took turns sitting with Mara for the next three days. She appeared to sleep most of the time, but it was not peaceful sleep. Dreams troubled her, and she called for Javi, then cried. Bai stood it as long as he could then went to her and touched her hair. "Javi?" She asked, still sleeping.

"I am here," Bai said.

Mara opened her eyes but did not see. She grabbed Bai's hand and squeezed it as though she would never let go. After a little she calmed but did not wake, nor did she release Bai's hand. When Loura came to take over from his master she still gripped it. They pried it loose so Bai could go.

When she woke, Mara was still hollow-eyed and haggard, but she was less rigid. She would not eat however. Bai and Loura forced broth and wine down her but they could get nothing else. Mara had gone deep into herself and become lost in the corridors of her misery. She wandered, lost and alone in her own mind, and could not find the way out.

More days passed, and Mara did not change. Bai began to think that she would never recover. She would lie on the cot until she joined his brother in whatever place was beyond life, but after a week she woke truly. The hollow deadness of her eyes was gone, replaced by a fevered, obsessed glare.

"Paper," she demanded. "Bring me paper and pens and ink."

Bai tried to get her to take some broth or some wine but she would have none of it. "Paper, pens and ink," she said.

Bai had the things brought and when they were laid upon the table Mara sat down and began to draw. Her lines were sure and straight where called for and sinuously, or subtly curved in their places; boldly angular at need. They were alive and vivid. Magnetic to the eye. First came repeated patterns that were rejected in turn; then came perfect line copies of the pictures in her mind. The Mandalai of power. When these were completed, she commanded, "Bring paint, brushes and colored inks."

Bai was beyond refusing. He had the things brought, and when

Loura came to relieve his master, Bai told him, "Whatever she wants bring it."

Loura, wide-eyed at the litter of paper on the floor, and at the array of paint and ink, could only nod.

"Another lamp," she commanded hours later. "No. Two more."

They were brought without question.

The drawings grew and, though Bai could not think how they might become more alive than before, they did. The five drawings Mara had finally settled upon, and was now coloring, were vibrant. They were living things which reached out and gripped the eyes with such strength that looking away was a major effort. They shook the heart!

Mara worked steadily for five days. She only rested a few moments at a time and took food and drink in tiny snatches, but at the end there were copies of the five Mandalai of Power worthy of the Book of the Design. When they were finished Mara collapsed upon her cot and slept, deep and peaceful; untroubled by dreams. The grooves of concentration which had become deep scars in her forehead smoothed and a young woman, hardly more than a child, emerged from the obsessed hag shell it had worn for days. When she woke she ate ravenously then fell asleep again. The blasted thinness of her frame began to ease and the angularity of her bones began to sink back into the soft curves of a woman in the early stages of pregnancy. The pale chill of her forehead and cheeks warmed.

Bai came to visit the sleeping girl often. He watched as she changed and was amazed that she was so young. The night she and Indi had hidden with him he had noticed that she was much younger than his brother, but he did not realize how much younger until the pain and stress of the last days began to disappear. She was a child. But a child who had seen much, learned much, and experienced much. And so talented. Bai looked again at the Mandalai and was still astonished at them. And this was not even the work of a mature talent. Just think of what she could do with a few years of seasoning.

The Patriarch of House Ransis put the drawings down and closed his eyes with weariness. He was surprised to find that the Mandalai were there, behind his eyes. He had unconsciously memorized the complex designs. They had stuck to his mind of their own volition. No human will had been needed.

"They draw the eye and will not let it rest," Mara said.

Bai was startled by her voice. "How did you know...?"

Mara smiled. "In the presence of the Mandalai there is nothing else."

"Truly they are powerful. They seem to suck the will out of me while, at the same time, pouring some new will into me. I do not understand."

"And these are only five. The known powers. The others in the great book..." words failed her. There was no describing the ecstasy of gazing at the others; of being caught up in them; of knowing to the very core of being, that power rested in each one if only it could be unlocked.

"Are they magic?" Bai asked.

Mara shook her head. "No. There is no magic in them. They are only ink and paint. Javi said they are focus points for the mind. They allow the mind to slip free of the bonds of flesh and bone."

There was a sad yearning in her voice, and Bai asked about it.

"I have never been able to use them to slip free," she answered. "I can only reproduce them."

"I saw Indi – Javi – slip free once, but he had nothing like these," Bai indicated the drawings on the table.

"Javi did not need to have the Mandalai before his eyes. When he needed the powers, he could call up the Mandala he needed and have it before his mind's eye."

Bai understood, for he could close his eyes and see any of these drawings he chose, but he did not know how to use the powers. "When I...guarded his body that one time, these powers almost killed him. He was never the same after that. He was crippled."

Mara nodded. "There is a cost, especially if the power is used for too long a time."

"I thought he had gone mad when he came back to himself. While he was...gone, his body was like those who have the dropping sickness, except that he did not shake or foam at his mouth. But when he woke, he was raving. I thought he had lost his mind. He went on and on about a hall of doors which went nowhere, and about machines that appeared and disappeared, and beings which were neither gods nor humans."

"He told me about the hall of doors. He did not understand what he had seen, but it was not madness. It is a real place. It is inside the temple of the new gods. A hall of doors, or gates, that do not lead anywhere, but which let huge machines appear and disappear."

"What could such a thing mean?" Bai asked.

"I do not know. Perhaps I will never know. It is not yet in the Design to understand that. Someday we may know."

Bai turned his eyes from her face back to the Mandalai. "I would like to use these in tapestries," he said. "Each could make a tapestry worth thousands of zari."

Mara gripped his wrist. "That you must never do, Bai. These are very dangerous. Just to possess these copies could mean your life."

"Then why did you make them," he cried, torn between fear and longing to re-create them.

"Because they must be preserved. I made them for you to keep. You must protect them as you protect the knowledge of the Great Book. But you must never tell anyone of them or of their power. Even now the priests are torturing those caught with copies to find out the meaning of them. I don't think the Maker of All will let the true meanings be revealed to the priests, but I do not know. The ways of the Design are beyond my understanding."

"But I do not even know what these powers are," Bai said.

"That is good. What you do not know you cannot tell."

Bai looked at the young woman and saw that she was much older than her years.

Mara rested five more days then began gathering a travel pack. A change of clothes, some hard trail biscuits, dried meat and cheese. Bai was both saddened and relieved that she was going. "Where are you bound, Mara?" He asked, but she just smiled.

"As before, what you do not know you cannot tell," she said.

"You could stay here."

"No. The gods may be still searching. Better that they have nothing to find in House Ransis."

"But the city is quiet. Almost normal."

"That may not last. They may only be waiting to finish questioning those they caught. If they decide to search house to house, I cannot stay and endanger this house. You are the guardian of The Great Book and I must not do anything to threaten its preservation."

"I have been thinking about that," Bai said. "It is not enough that I know. I must find some way to leave a key to the location. As uncertain as life is, I might not be able to tell the next Patriarch. With no further key, the knowledge could be lost forever."

"That is true," Mara said.

"I am glad that you agree. Now give me your opinion about this. What better way for House Ransis to pass on information than with a tapestry. Who would suspect that anything so open as a tapestry could be a secret message?"

Mara considered this for several moments as she pulled at her lower lip. "Yes. I think you are right."

"And I will give it as a gift to the new gods," Bai said with a bitter chuckle. "We will let them be the guardians."

Mara was not subtle of mind, and the irony of this escaped her, but she knew instinctively that Bai's idea was a good one.

"Do you have a design in mind?" She asked.

"Oh yes," Bai said and drew a folded sheet of paper from inside his robe. He unfolded it and laid it on the table. "I will call it *The Gods Show Mercy*," and again he laughed the mirthless, bitter laugh. "And the key will be so subtle that only those who know what to look for will find it. It will be a key as fragile and unnoticed as a thread."

When it was dark, Mara took her leave. "Where will you go?" Bai asked again.

Again, Mara only smiled. "Where the Design takes me —to fulfill my part of it." Her eyes became misty and unfocused for a moment. "That was the last thing Javi said to me before I left him. He said his part of the Design was complete, but mine was not." Her eyes took a long time to re-focus on Bai's face, and when they did, she smiled sadly. "You resemble your brother a great deal Bai Ransis," she said, and turned away.

Eight

3 A.C.G.

The second trek to Keep Holis Mara made was not as difficult as the first had been. This time, though she was hunted, she was not encumbered with the crippled Javi. Nor was the weather a hindrance. The worst thing about the trip was the first few hours of each morning in the first week. She was nauseous when she first woke. A few times she vomited, but after that first week her stomach decided that there was little enough sustenance coming in so it had best stay inside, and the vomiting stopped. The morning unease continued though.

Mara was not worried about her touchy stomach. She knew it was because of the baby. She was not sick, only pregnant, and often as she trudged along, she smiled at the thought of Javi's son growing within her. In her mind she knew she should be sad that the child would not know his father, but she could not be. She knew with positivity she had never felt before that she and the child were in the very hollow of the Great Designer's hand. That no matter what happened, she would be allowed to bring the child alive into the world. She would teach him the ways of the Design. She would teach him the powers in so far as she was able, and would let the masters at Keep Holis teach him more. And in all this she would rejoice as the child worked out his part in the Great Design.

The journey took nearly three months for Mara did not try to hurry. She reasoned that if anyone were looking for her, they would be more likely to stop someone who seemed in a hurry or furtive. Instead she went boldly. Several times she caught rides with carters. With them she was careful to say little. She left the impression that she was going only a short way to see her mother. She was not molested by anyone. Her closest brush with trouble came from a group of men who were probably road bandits. They stopped her, but only detained her long enough to see that she had nothing to steal. They might have raped her, but she smiled at the man who appeared to be the leader and melted his heart. He told her to go ahead.

"Be careful in the future, little one," he said. "All those abroad are not as kind to travelers as are we."

Mara smiled at him again. "All will be kind to me if it is in the Design," she answered him.

"Humph," he snorted, then he and his band disappeared back into the mountains.

Keep Holis' remaining students welcomed her with food and wine and the first clean bed she had slept in for weeks, and when she told them she was pregnant with Javi's child they began to treat her more like a goddess than a mortal woman. A midwife was called up from the village below the keep to examine her. The verdict was that Mara was as healthy as could be expected for one who had been deprived of food as much as she had been. The midwife left instructions that Mara should rest and eat, and nothing else until the baby was delivered.

Those in the Keep did everything they could to see that the midwife's instructions were carried out. They would not let Mara do anything for herself. Indeed, they probably would have fed her like an infant, but she drew the line at that. "I am quite capable of feeding myself and taking care of my personal needs," she said.

"But the child of Master Javi..." they protested.

"The child of Master Javi is fine. He will stay right where he belongs until time to come out, just as the Maker of All wills." But she smiled her charming smile to take the sting out of the reprimand.

One of the Servants of the Design celebrated Mara's return more than any of the others —Master Ekas. He had taught her the use of pen and paint brush and he felt a consuming joy for that, but guilt at not having been able to help her in the copying of the five Mandalai weighed him down. He could hardly contain his joy at her return; yet he hid himself from her. Never in his life as student or teacher had he met such a person as Mara. Never had there been one so talented or so willing to learn. Master Ekas's happiness at having such a student had been boundless, and his sadness at having abandoned her in her hour of need was deep and dark as a well. When she left, he had been glad in a way. He would never have to see her again and be reminded of his failure. But his sadness at losing her had been equally boundless. Now her return was a source of torment to the old man and such joy that he felt himself about to float away with the wonder of it. The mere knowledge that she was once again within the walls of the Keep pared years off him. He no longer even dreaded the cold of the coming winter. Yet he could not bring himself to see her, he felt such shame.

Mara asked after Master Ekas but, at first, no one would tell her anything. At last she threatened to rise from her bed and go seeking him on her own. That was when the others told her why Ekas was hiding himself from her.

"Bring him to me," Mara said. Her nurses started to protest that she should not upset herself, but she merely threw back the covers and started to get out of bed, and they relented.

Ekas came, but not easily. The others had to drag him, protesting and fighting, into Mara's presence. In an instant she sprang from the bed and threw her arms around the old man's neck. "I am so glad to see you, Master," she laughed.

"But," he said. "I did not think you would ever want to see me again after the way I abandoned you."

"Abandoned me? You brought food and tea and were there to keep away any who would bother me as I worked. How is this abandonment?"

"But I could not help with the copying," he cried.

"I know, and I am sorry that you could not have the joy of that work, but it was not in the Design Master, and we are all creatures of the Design. We submit ourselves to the will of the Maker of All, even when that will seems bitter to us."

The old man's eyes filled with tears. "I am glad that you have come back to us, Mara," he said. "It is good to be reminded that all is in the Design."

Master Ekas visited his student every day after that. At first, he did nothing more than make polite conversation and bask in her presence, but as the days passed, he took over most of the duties of serving her. He brought her meals and kept the fire burning rosy and warm. He wanted to talk to her about returning to her studies, but he knew she was under strict orders to do nothing but rest and eat, so he said nothing.

Mara enjoyed the quiet and the rest and the food for a time. She was more tired from her trek than she had known, but after a couple of weeks her life of enforced quiet and rest began to pall. She wanted to be free to move around, and, more than anything, her fingers itched to once again take pen and paintbrush and continue the studies she had started with Master Ekas.

At last she could stand it no longer. "Master Ekas," she asked, "could you bring me ink and pens and a lap board. I feel trapped in this room. I need something to occupy my hands and my mind."

Ekas was overjoyed. "I think I can do that," he said. "But you must be careful not to tire yourself."

Mara's smile dazzled him. "I only want to doodle."

"Yes. I understand." He studied her a moment then asked, "Will you continue your studies after the baby is born?" He held his breath waiting for her answer.

"Yes, I will," she answered enthusiastically. "I want nothing else so much. If you are willing to teach me that is."

Ekas let out his breath, happy to hear her answer, but afraid too. "Mara, I fear I did not make myself clear. I have nothing more to teach you. You know all that I know. I had hoped to study with you. Perhaps learn from you."

Mara blinked then stared at him for some moments, trying to fit her mind around this new picture. "How can I teach you anything, dear Master Ekas? You have studied the Mandalai and the writings about the Design for more years than I have been alive."

He shook his head. "All my years of study have not brought me to the level of art and skill you achieved in a few weeks. I would never have attempted what you accomplished and even if I were so bold, I could never have done it in so short a time. Even when my eyes were young, I could not see the line and color the way you do."

"But it was not my skill, master. I was only an instrument, like a pen or a brush. The Maker of All used my hands. I could never have done the copies otherwise."

Ekas saw that his pupil was telling the truth, but it was a truth that could be looked at more than one way. The Maker of All had used her hands, but her hands were skillful, no matter what her protest. And she had another ability which he had never mastered: the ability to open herself to the Designer. This was a skill he had tried to sharpen his whole life, but had never succeeded. Now he hoped that this young woman might teach him.

But Ekas could not explain this to her. He did not have a full grasp of it himself so he said, "Perhaps we can teach one another. I will seek what little I know that you do not, and perhaps you can teach me to open myself to the Maker of All."

"We will study the Design together," she said and patted the old man's hand.

~ * ~

General Itar was as good as his word. When Major Rainek failed to produce Javi Holis the general had the Major shortened and sent his head home to his family pickled in a barrel of brine. The act was wasteful in one way for, truth be told, Rainek had been a good and faithful soldier, but failure was not a thing the Cadeki Empire could live with. And the act did have its uses. It was a reminder to all the officer corps that General Itar's orders were to be carried out, no matter what and that Itar was a man of his word.

But shortening Major Rainek did not stop the proliferation of copies of the five designs. Those continued to circulate freely, ban notwithstanding and the name Javi Holis continued to crop up. The man was spoken of in terms more suited to a god than a man. Itar almost believed the wretched holy man did have some magic power, or at least some vast reserve of luck. Raids, traps, sweeps of the city, all were vain. Nothing turned the man up or held him down. And now, besides the designs, pamphlets calling for resistance and uprising against the gods were circulating. Worse, these pamphlets promoted the idea that the gods from the sky were not gods at all. This was worrisome. The divinity of the Cadeki forces had given them an edge in dealing with these primitive people, but if that divinity was widely questioned it might become a liability.

The pamphlets, like the designs, were hand copied, but there were so many of them circulating that Itar could hardly believe they had been done by hand. The general picked up yet another copy of one of the five designs which lay on his desk. It was a beautiful thing. So moving. So incomprehensible, but so moving.

Not for the first time the general considered simply withdrawing to ships in orbit and cleansing the entire mud ball of all life. Construction of the gates had not progressed far, and in any case, they would not be hurt if a short half-life radiation blanket were dropped over the planet. It would delay construction only a few weeks and there would be no more bother with resistance. Still…

Itar discarded the thought yet again. These Archleans were primitive, but they were still living creatures and the general's conscience would not let him destroy a whole race simply because some of them were fractious. And there were also the tapestries. The art of them was akin to the art of the designs, and between the two they almost made this dust mote worth all the trouble—those and the gate loci.

The general thought a while longer then decided on his course. He lifted his head and spoke to the air. "Record the following…

"Proclamation. Hence forward until forevermore, all written languages of Archlea are outlawed. Any teaching of written language other than the Divine language is forbidden. All books, scrolls, broadsides, certificates, or other document set forth in any Archlean tongue will be surrendered to servants of the Temple within ten days. Thereafter possession of any book, scroll, broadside, certificate, or other document set forth in any Archlean tongue—even so much as a scrap of paper, parchment, wood, cloth, or other material with one letter or character of any Archlean tongue upon it, will be cause for summary execution. By order of Itar, God-Resident of Archlea."

The general was quiet for a time thinking over the proclamation.

Then he said, "Give me a hard copy of that."

The copy emerged from the printer slot on the general's desk, and Itar took it, read it over twice, and nodded his head with satisfaction. "Very well. Translate that into every language of the planet and print a million of them for distribution," he said to the computer.

The computer beeped acknowledgment and General Itar turned to the designs stacked upon his desk. He picked them up again and looked through all five, marveling at them. Then he dropped them into the converter and turned back to his other work.

~ * ~

Doodling did not satisfy Mara for long. As her strength returned, she began to feel confined by all the luxury of Keep Holis. Never in the years of her life would she have believed that plentiful food and hands willing to prepare and serve it to her could become burdensome, but they did.

"I am fine," She protested. "I can get up and move around without help, if you will just let me —please!"

Master Ekas could not disagree. Mara glowed with health. She had fleshed out under the enforced rest and was looking more like the young mother-to-be than the stringy hag her trek had made of her.

"Perhaps you could be allowed to come to the library for a little while each day," he said. "But you must not tire yourself. We must protect Master Javi's child."

Mara giggled like a little girl. "I felt him kick a little while ago," she said, and suddenly she was out of bed with her arms around Ekas. "He is alive, Master Ekas. Alive," she cried, so full of joy and wonder that it brought tears to the old man's eyes.

"And we must see that he remains alive, by keeping his mother well," he said hugging her in return.

A chill passed over the old man, and suddenly his joy fled. Deep inside himself he knew beyond doubt that he would not live to see the child born. In that moment Ekas tasted resentment for the first time in years. In earlier days when he first studied the Design and found that his talent was great, but not singular, he had felt it. When he saw others less talented with pen and brush create original work, brilliant work, he had tasted it, but those times were long gone. He had resigned himself to a portion of the Design that taught others and did not create for itself. He had learned to enjoy his place, but now he tasted resentment again when he knew he would not see the child born.

Mara felt the change in the old man and pulled back to look into his face. "What is it, Master Ekas?" she asked.

He shook his head. "Nothing. Age. Now, I must go child. I must discuss your coming to the library with the others. I am sure they will agree, but it is only right that they have a say."

"Yes," Mara said. She was afraid her enthusiasm had dredged up some sorrow from Ekas' past, and she was sorry, but she did not pry.

I know so little about him, she thought. *I must find out more.*

~ * ~

General Itar's new aid, Lt. Col. Toly, heaved an internal sigh of relief when the general smiled at the information Toly had brought him. Toly did not show his fear of General Itar with cold sweat or trembling as Major Rainek had, but the fear was there all the same. Already he had ulcers which burned all the time, and since becoming the general's aide he had barely been able to keep even soft, bland food down. Now, with Itar's smile, Toly's stomach felt better than it had in days.

"Yes, sir. This place, Keep Holis, appears to be the center of the resistance. Almost all of those calling themselves Servants or Students of the Design have knowledge of it. I don't understand why Rainek didn't spot it. The mind peel data all made reference to the place."

"Rainek tended to be short-sighted about many things," Itar said.

"Yes sir," Toly agreed.

"Send a force up to this keep and bring this Holis back."

"I have already assembled them my Lord. We wait only for your permission," Toly said and snapped a stiff bow toward the general.

Itar looked at the bowed head and thought, *this one bears watching. He is ambitious and clever and just a little insolent, and that makes him dangerous.*

"Well done, Toly," he said. "My permission is given. Bring me this Holis—alive if possible—but alive or dead, bring him. If necessary, I will use his head as a teaching tool for these animals."

"Very well, my Lord," Toly said and bowed again, then he got out.

No need to stay in the general's presence any longer than necessary, he thought. *It might prove fatal, and I have no desire for my wife to receive a small cask of pickling brine with my head in it like Rainek's wife.*

Echoes of her screams were still bouncing around the upper halls of the military establishment. Those reverberations might cost General Itar dearly yet. Lady Rainek could trace her ancestry back to purest Cadeki blood, and it was almost never politic to behead anyone having ties, no matter how tenuous to the Cadeki Emperor.

Ah well, thought Toly. *Court politics are not my look out. I will bring this Holis to the general tied up in a red ribbon and my future will be made…at least until Itar falls out of favor.*

Suddenly Toly's ulcer burned again.

~ * ~

Mara studied the scroll she had found lying on the copy desk. The color of it was bright and vibrant and alive. She could almost feel the heat of the reds and the coolness of the blues. It was a Mandala worthy of the Great Book, though it was not one of those thirty three. But it was clearly a Mandala of import. The central drawing to which all lines and colors drew the eye was obscure. It seemed to be a box sitting upon a larger box with huge pillars standing on either side. All else was swirls and curlicues which made the eye believe the design moved and wavered.

"Marvelous, isn't it?"

Master Ekas' voice startled her. She did not realize how deep her concentration had been.

"Where did it come from?" she asked.

The old man held out his hands, palms up and wiggled his fingers with a dexterity that belied the gnarled appearance of them.

"But when? How?" Mara asked.

"It began to come to me in dreams. I didn't understand it at first. I still don't, but it is an answer to prayers. And so are you." He put his hand upon her shoulder. The bitterness of his knowledge that he would not live to see Javi's child born was softened by the touch of the Designer. Never before had he felt himself the conduit for creation.

"It is truly worthy to be called a Mandala, Master Ekas," she said. "It is a great work."

"You told me that the copies you made were not yours. That you were only a channel through which the copies flowed. I did not understand what you meant then. I do now. I did not do this. It came to me in dreams, and I knew I must bring the dream to reality, but when I sat down to begin, it would not come clear. Then I opened myself as you did, and the picture cleared in my mind. My hands seemed to work without my volition."

Mara nodded her understanding. "Perhaps that is the way of all Mandalai. There are designs and pictures which flow from us, but such as these," she indicated the Mandala before them, "these come directly from the Maker of All to some purpose."

The old man agreed.

"What will you do with it now?" Mara asked.

"I have no idea," he answered. "For right now I am going to sit and look at it and try to understand how I have been the instrument of its creation. Mara," he hesitated, but then went on, "changes are coming upon us. I will not live to see the child born."

Mara felt the words like pin pricks upon her heart. "No," she denied. So many had been taken from her. Javi, her parents, Sartin her brother, and now Master Ekas. "You are well. You are strong," she protested. "You have made this beautiful thing!"

"Yes, but my part of the Design is almost finished. You have yet more to do. You must stay strong and continue."

Mara was crying now. "But I cannot. I am tired and my child cannot be born into a world without his father or you, or… He cannot be born into a world where the gods rule."

"But they do not rule, Mara," Ekas said pulling her to him, trying to comfort her. "All is in the Design. Even those who call themselves gods."

"But why? Why must we who serve the Maker of All be hurt? Why did Javi die? Why did the gods come and destroy so much?"

"I do not know, child, but all is in the Design."

Master Ekas did as he had told Mara he would. For hours he stared at the work of his hands examining it minutely. It was perfect. So perfect that it brought tears to his eyes. If only he could understand why the Design of the world was as it was, his life would be perfect.

"The Design is as it is because I have made it that way, child," a voice said.

Ekas looked around, seeking the owner of the voice. The library was growing dark, but there was still enough light to see that he was alone.

"Who calls me, an old man, '*child*'?" Ekas said.

"I do."

And the old man knew. The Maker of All had spoken to him.

Ekas slipped from his chair onto his knees and bowed his face to the floor. "I am unworthy, Great Creator, that you should speak to me."

"You are not unworthy, child."

"But I question and wonder and wish the Design were otherwise than it is."

"That does not make you unworthy child, it only makes you human. I have created you thus."

"I am your servant, oh Maker of All."

"Yes, child, I know. And now your time within this Design grows short. Soon your pains and questions will cease. You will know more. Not all, for that is beyond you, but you will know more. Rise now."

Ekas stood easily though he should have been stiff from all the hours of stillness, not to mention the kneeling.

"Roll the Mandala child."

"But it is not dry, Master." Ekas protested, but stopped after a moment, laughing at his own pretentiousness. He rolled the velum sheet.

"Take a ribbon from the box and tie it round the page."

Ekas did as he was told, and when he had finished, the Maker of All said, "Place the scroll beneath the floor stone. There." One particular stone in the floor seemed to glow, and Ekas carried the scroll to it. He bent, probed his fingers into the cracks around the stone, and when he had purchase, he lifted it. There was a hollow beneath it. He placed the scroll within the hollow and returned the stone to its place.

"Now it is time to rest, child. Go to your chamber and wait."

"Master...?" the old man asked.

The great Creator knew already what the old man wished to know. "All is well with Mara and with the child. They are in the very hollow of my hand. Nothing shall harm them. They will carry on my Design."

"Master, Mara is so sad and confused now. Please can you calm her mind and make her once again know that all is truly in the Design," said Ekas.

"Yes, child, I will. But her worry and doubt are needful for now. I am sorry that she must be afraid and worried, but it must be for a time yet. Now you must rest."

Ekas felt the calm assurance that he could rest now. He was finished with his tasks and had pleased The One who had caused him to live. He shuffled off toward his chamber to rest and sleep, knowing that tomorrow he would wake to a different world.

~ * ~

Mara saw the black ships coming from the south. At first, she thought they were birds migrating, but then knew that was wrong. They were going the wrong way. Birds should be going south, not coming north.

That morning Mara had risen early and walked down to the village below the Keep. The cook, who was the only one awake when she left, protested that she should rest and not strain herself with walking, but she smiled at him and told him she felt fine, and it was true. Her health was excellent. She could feel the glow of the living child in her womb, and that glow made her warm all over though there was a nip of frost in the air. But, though Mara was well and strong, she was sad because of what Master Ekas had told her. The sadness seemed to multiply during the night and in the morning, she felt she had to leave the Keep, at least for the day.

The ships—four of them—came from the south, but they swung far to the east and disappeared over the mountains for a little while. When they returned it was as though they were bursting from the sunrise mountains. They swooped low over the village and one of them dropped from formation to land in the village. The other three continued on to the Keep. The noise of them was not loud, but there was a penetrating hum that Mara could feel in her bones. Others from the village could feel the vibration too. They ran from their houses and looked toward the sky, then toward the Keep.

A woman grabbed Mara's sleeve and, with terror in her voice, asked, "What are those things?"

Mara put her arm around the frightened woman. "The sky gods have come to Keep Holis. Now I must go. Run, all of you," she said in a quiet, but firm voice. "The gods will take all of you they can catch, and you will never see this place again. Go. Run."

"But where? Where can we go?"

Others drawn by some calm magnetism radiating from Mara, gathered round her and added their voices to that of the woman. "Yes, where can we go?"

"There. Go to the mountains. Go quickly. Warrior-Gods will come from that ship soon," she pointed at the black transport ship settling at the edge of the village. "Go now. And remember, All is in the Design."

Mara was not sure why she had added that last, but it seemed the right thing to say. She stood a moment while the people of the village eddied around her, chattering like stirred up chickens. Then she set out for the path back up to the Keep.

Black-armored troops had landed and secured the Keep well before Mara reached it. There had been no fighting. What could a few old men and women have done against the power of the gods? She was glad to see that pride had not gotten in the way of good sense causing those living in the Keep to attempt some futile resistance.

"And where do you think you are going, my pretty?" one of the Warrior-Gods asked as Mara stepped through the main gate into the courtyard.

"My grandfather," she lied quickly. "Is he alright? What have you done with him?"

"And how am I supposed to know which of these dried sticks is your grandfather?"

Mara could only stare at the opaque face plate of the armored god and plead with her eyes.

After a few moments the Warrior-God sighed and said, "Oh very well, Guard-Corporal." He did not raise his voice, but in a moment another Warrior-God came to him from inside the Keep.

"This one wants to know where her grandfather is," the first Warrior-God said to the second. "Perhaps you had better take her to the sergeant."

The second Warrior-God did not answer, only gripped Mara by her upper arm and pulled her toward the door he had exited. Mara could feel the power of his grip. He could have easily crushed her bones had he desired it.

In moments Mara was delivered to the refectory. A fire still burned in the fireplace, but there were no sign of cooks or people ready to eat. A Warrior-God sat at the head of a row of stone tables using the table as a desk. His helmet was off, sitting by his elbow on the table. Mara had never seen a god in the flesh before. Always before the Warrior-Gods had been completely armored, faces hidden behind opaque face plates. This god looked very like a human being. He had no beard and his hair was cut close so that Mara could see the pink skin of his scalp. He looked tired.

"What now?" The god at the table growled.

"She wants her grandfather, sergeant." Mara's escort said.

"Oh God," he said. "How in hell's name am I supposed… Does she speak Cadeki?"

"I speak and understand, my Lord," Mara answered in slow, but understandable Cadeki.

The sergeant's eyes opened a bit wider. It was refreshing to find one of these creatures that actually spoke and understood his language. This one did not seem afraid either, and she was pretty. She made him think of his own daughter.

"Return to your post, trooper," the sergeant said.

The Warrior-God who had brought Mara said "Yes, sergeant," and got out.

The sergeant looked Mara over from head to foot. She stood quiet and did not fidget as he examined her. "You are looking for your grandfather?" He asked.

"Yes, my Lord. He is my only living kin."

The sergeant did not ask what had happened to the rest of her family. He was afraid the answer would be that they were dead at the hands of the Cadeki Empire.

"And who is your grandfather?"

"He is the Master of Drawing and Painting here in the Keep. Master Ekas, he is called."

He glanced down at a square, flat object that looked like a school slate, then ran his finger along the bottom of it and continued looking for several moments. "I find no Ekas among the prisoners," he said.

"But he must be here. He is an old man and very stiff in his joints. He moves slowly. He would probably have been in the library. He went there early each day."

The sergeant rubbed his hand over his face. "There was one old man found dead."

Mara's sharp intake of breath stopped him.

"We had nothing to do with it," he hurried to say. "Unless the shock of our coming—but no. The corpse was cold when we entered the room."

Mara's eyes filled with tears and she thought of the last conversation she and Ekas had. He had said a great change was coming, and he had been right.

The girl's tears moved the sergeant in spite of himself. He stood and came around the table to her. "I am sorry," he said, and helped her to a chair.

"I have seen your destruction," Mara began. "I have seen you kill hundreds whose only fault was being before your weapons, but I have never heard one of you say you were sorry until now. Javi was right. You are only men."

The sergeant's ears pricked up. "Did you say Javi? As in Javi Holis?"

Mara smiled through her tears. "All who serve the Design are called Holis," she said.

"But you know this Javi Holis by sight?"

"Yes. I knew him..." she almost said *he was my husband*, but something stopped the words in her throat.

"Knew him? Where is he then? No one here admits to being him."

"Of course not. Master Javi is not here. He is dead. He died when you gods burned half of Peshar."

The sergeant flinched under her gaze. He heard the bitterness in her voice and could hardly blame her for it. But the Imperial troopers had been only doing their jobs. They had nothing to apologize for. He pulled himself together and extinguished the pity he had been feeling for this creature. "Guard," he called.

An armored Warrior-God appeared.

"Take this one to the others. We will depart for Peshar as soon as the Keep and the village are secured."

The Cadeki Troopers were under strict orders to bring back everyone and everything that might relate to Javi Holis, so they brought every scrap of paper and every person, including the corpse of Master Ekas, back from Keep Holis. Lt. Col. Toly ordered the scrolls and books sorted and a detailed list of them delivered to the general.

Toly personally questioned several of those taken at the Keep and had some of the villagers mind-peeled seeking confirmation of what the Keep dwellers had told him. He got it. Those questioned all said Javi Holis was dead. There was some confusion at first, since all those taken from the Keep seemed to be named Holis, but that was sorted out and the mind-peel evidence from the village made Toly believe he had gotten all he could from the captives. He considered having them all mind-peeled, but decided it would be a waste of energy...and potential profit.

The data from the questioning and the mind peels was delivered to General Itar and when the general finished studying it all he summoned Toly.

"This is all that was taken from the Keep?" Itar asked.

"Yes, my Lord."

Itar rose from his desk and began to pace. He had examined the books and scrolls from the raid and was very pleased with it. As God-Resident of Archlea it all belonged to him, and he intended to ship it all home for storage. When he rotated home the books and scrolls would be the envy of the officer corps. But this Javi Holis was still a plague. Even dead, which all the captives said he was, he evoked shivers of fear in those Archleans who had become servants of the temple.

"And what of the woman?" He asked.

"Which woman, my Lord? We brought several."

"The one from the Keep. The one whose grandfather died before the troops arrived?"

"She was questioned, my Lord, like the others. Her story was about the same as the others."

"But there is something more about her Toly, is there not? She was the only woman taken from the Keep?"

No, my Lord. There were a few others, but I agree with you that she is different than any of the others. For one thing she is much younger, and she is pregnant."

"Ah," said the general and placed a finger over his lips. "Did you, by any chance, ask who the father of the child is, Toly?"

Toly blinked. "No, my Lord," he said.

"Perhaps you should have asked," Itar said, half smiling. *Dangerous.*

"I will have her mind-peeled at once, my Lord. We will soon know if the child is the whelp of this Javi Holis," he said and started to turn toward the task.

"Hold a moment. Save her for now. We can always do it later if it seems indicated. But my curiosity is aroused. Bring her here. I would speak with her myself."

Toly frowned, but quickly dropped the mask of neutrality back over his face. "Yes, my Lord," he said and got out.

Minutes later Mara was brought to the general. Toly stood beside her, prepared to assist Itar, but the general motioned him out.

Itar left the woman standing before his desk for minutes while he looked her over. This simple trick often did more than threats or even pain to loosen the tongues of captives.

There did not seem to be anything special about this Archlean. He had seen many in Peshar more beautiful, and many who smelled better. This one reeked of the holding pen's disinfectant and overcrowded cells, but she did not seem much affected by any of this. There was no fear in her eyes. Most Archleans Itar had personally interviewed had been barely in control of bodily functions, but this one looked back at him calmly. Waiting.

"What is your name, girl?" Itar asked finally. He was not harsh with her but firm.

"Mara Holis my Lord," she answered.

Itar stroked his chin with his fingers and leaned back in his chair. "You are the…wife of Javi Holis?"

Mara was surprised, but not over much. Any of those from the keep could have told. She was not afraid. The time of sadness and questioning was behind her. It might come again, but for now she had given herself over in body, mind and spirit to the will of the Maker of All. She had ceased hoping or desiring. She only waited upon the Design.

"Come, come, girl. Do not deny it. There is no point. I can have you mind-peeled to find the truth." Itar said.

"Yes, my Lord," she said. "I am."

"And he is dead?"

"Yes, my Lord."

"You are sure of this?"

"Yes, my Lord."

"And you would like revenge upon me and my troopers for his death," Itar said with a knowing smile.

He had seen others bent on revenge seem fearless too. It calmed his heart to understand her.

Mara shrugged. "My husband's part in the Design was complete. How can I wish revenge for the completion of the Design created by the Maker of All?"

She sounded so sincere that Itar believed her and was confused again.

"Design? What is this Design? Tell me of it," he commanded.

"My Lord, I will tell you all I know, but may I please sit down first. I carry Javi's child and, though I am well, I am tired from the last few days."

Itar looked for some impudence in the woman, but found nothing. It was a pure request. "Sit then."

Mara looked around the room for a chair or stool, but the only one there was occupied by the God-Resident. After a moment she sank gracefully to the floor and sat tailor fashion, with crossed legs modestly covered by her stained robe. General Itar could see nothing of her save the top of her head from his position behind the desk, but he could hardly command her to stand again after just giving her permission to sit. He stood and came around the desk; propped himself against it. "The Design…" he prompted.

"Yes. The Design," she began. "The Design is…everything. It is the way the clouds cross the sky. The way winter follows autumn. The way children are born and grow and become parents themselves and die. That is the Design. Everything."

"But how can one become a servant of everything?" Itar said with a snort.

Mara shrugged. "I only know that the Design is everything, and that those who serve it have peace in themselves. Those who do not serve the Design have no peace. They fight against the Design. They try to make their will supreme, and when that does not happen, they are in turmoil."

"And you have this peace?"

"Yes."

"Even though you are my prisoner?"

"Yes."

"And even this is part of this Design?"

"Yes."

Itar did not understand what she was talking about. So far as he could tell what she was saying was pathetic gibberish. He stood, went back behind his desk, and picked up five small copies of the designs which had puzzled him for so long. His bans had not succeeded in stopping their proliferation. He carried these copies back around the desk and pitched them toward Mara. She let them fall to the floor in front of her.

"And these? Are they part of the Design too?" Itar asked.

"Yes. Everything is a part of the Design. How could these not be?"

"And what part are they?"

Mara did not understand what the general wanted and said so.

"I want to know what these are." he said.

Mara smiled at that. "They are Mandalai."

"But what do they mean?"

Mara shrugged. "Different things to different people. They are a means to touch, and be touched, by the Great Designer."

Itar thought about that for a moment, then said, "I believe that is a lie. Those are more than some religious doodles. I can feel the power in them."

"That is the Designer reaching out to you through these bits of ink and paint. How can you not feel the power of the Creator of All?"

The God-Resident blinked at that. "Lying is useless you know. I remind you again, I can have you mind-peeled. All that is in your mind will be known to me. Your lies will gain you nothing."

"Use your god-machine if you wish," Mara said. "I am not lying."

"But you will die if I have you examined that way."

"Yes, I know."

"But you are not afraid?"

Mara thought about her response for a moment. "I am afraid of the pain, and the moment of death, but I know that will be over sooner or later, so I fear it only as a time I would rather not go through. I do not fear it the way you mean."

"But you will tell all. Every secret of this plot you call the Design."

Mara smiled. "I can tell you all that without your god-machine, though I know little enough. But you have not believed the little I have told you, so you would not believe anything else either."

Itar studied her again, looking deep into her eyes. Perhaps she was telling the truth. Perhaps she did not know any more about the drawings than she said.

"This Designer of yours is a cruel god…" He did not know what to call her. At last he let it drop and did not do her the courtesy of name or title. "A cruel god," he said again.

"Perhaps, but until you came with your god-machines, and your Warrior-Gods, there was much less cruelty."

Itar barked out a laugh that had nothing of humor in it. "But everything is in the Design," he said derisively. "That would mean that we gods, and our cruelty, are also a part of it.

"That is true."

"Then this god of the Design is cruel."

Mara shrugged. "If it is true, it is true. I do not know."

The general looked for some sign of mockery in the woman's answer, but did not find one. This was getting him nowhere. The question was still whether or not to have her mind-peeled.

"Tell me who made these designs?" Itar indicated the papers on the floor in front of Mara.

Without picking up the copies she smiled. "Ober did these. He is very talented…was talented. Since these are in your hands, I suppose he is dead."

"You can tell by glancing at the top one who made them?" Itar scoffed.

"Yes," she said.

Her certainty convinced him. "How can you tell?"

"The stroke of the pen, the mark of the brush. The way the colors are mixed. They are not quite perfect. Very close. He was a wonderful copyist, though young. He might have…" She fell silent.

"He is not dead."

Mara lifted her eyebrows in surprise. She peered into the God-Resident's face, trying to know if he was telling the truth or not, but she could not. He was too different from anyone she had ever known. "Where is he then?"

"Not here. I sent him to my wife as a gift."

"A gift?"

"Yes. I thought she would be amused by him. She is fascinated by the art of this world. I have sent her several copies like these—better than these. And tapestries. She especially liked the tapestries."

Mara brightened at the knowledge of Ober being yet alive. "I am glad that even you cruel gods have eyes for beauty and creation. That was one thing I could not understand about the Design. How could the Maker of All make creatures who could only destroy? Who had no feeling for beauty?"

Itar felt the cut of Mara's words, but chose to ignore them. "How do you know about pen and ink and paint, woman?" he asked.

"They are how I serve the Designer."

"You are a maker of these?" He tilted his chin toward the pages on the floor.

"Yes." Mara wondered if what she was about to say would be better left unsaid, but she continued anyway. "I am a copyist. I taught Ober."

"And these Mandalai are designs of power, are they not?" he asked, thinking to catch her in a lie of some sort.

"Yes. They are called that sometimes."

"But what power? What power can paper and ink and paint have, other than power to move the soul with beauty?"

"You know more of that than I, my Lord. I am only a copyist. Others know how to use the powers. I do not."

Itar gazed long at the woman, but did not really see her. His mind was turning over data from mind-peels; remembering information these primitives had revealed. They believed these designs of paint and paper could give power to those who knew how to use them. Power such as the ability to move objects without touching them, or to speak directly to the mind of another. But the data did not say how such things were possible; nor did any evidence outside the mind- peels and interviews exist. No one, other than these Archleans, had ever observed anyone using any such power. No Cadeki had observed or measured any such power, and those with whom he had discussed the data rejected such ideas. They all said this was just religious nonsense.

"And this *Book of the Design*?" Itar asked after minutes of silence, hoping to surprise the woman into some admission.

"Yes, my Lord? What about it?"

"Do not lie now woman. Remember the god-machine, which will

tell all if it is used upon you."

"Yes, my Lord, I know, and again, you may use your machine, but you will find I have told no lie. What is it you wish to know?"

"This *Book of the Design*... What is it?"

"It is a gathering of thirty-three Mandalai, including these five. I have studied it a little, but it is lost now."

"Lost?"

"Yes. My husband, Javi, hid it away somewhere. He told no one where he hid it. Supposedly he left a map with some master, but I have never seen such a map. I am not sure it really exists."

Itar thought about the list of parchments seized at the Keep. There had been one which might have been a map, but it was badly water damaged and rotted—unreadable. Unless Cadeki technology might—but probably not. Still, he would try. But there was another possibility.

"Could you re-create the other drawings from the book?" Itar asked.

Suddenly, Mara could read the face of the God-Resident. It was as clear as if he had told her. He was hungry to the very depths of his soul to possess the rest of the Mandalai. He did not understand that the Mandalai already possessed him. The five Mandalai of power had taken root in him and they would grow like a tree growing under a wall. Sooner or later the tree would push the wall out of its way.

Mara could see each and every page of the book in her mind's eye. She could again feel the weight of the pages; the texture of the velum. She could smell the odor of ancient ink and paint as they mixed upon the pages.

"I do not know my Lord," she said. "Perhaps I could, given enough time."

~ * ~

Itar called Lt. Col. Toly into his private quarters. Toly had never been into the private quarters before, and the possibility both worried and excited him. If whatever the general wanted was important enough, and personal enough, to require the privacy of personal quarters, then perhaps there was some advantage to be had.

"I am at your service, General," Toly said, saluting.

Itar returned the salute and said, "I hope that is true Toly, for I have a job for you that is very important."

"I will do my best, my Lord."

"Very well. Among the papers from Keep Holis there was something presumed to be a map. Very water damaged and rotted."

"Yes, my Lord. I remember it. It was unreadable. Really no more than fragments."

"That may be very important, Toly. It may be the map to the very soul of Archlea, for it gives directions to the hiding place of The Book of the Design. Find it Toly. Dig it out and bring it to me. We must read it. If it can bring The Book of the Design into our hands, this planet can be pacified in a few days."

Toly saw the light of avidity in the general's eyes, and it made the burning worry in his stomach fountain. Was it possible that Itar had lost his mind to think that possession of this book would be of any help?

"My Lord, may I ask how this book will help pacify Archlea? Not everyone was a believer in this Design before we arrived. How can possession of some book of Designer scratchings be of any use?"

Itar looked with astonishment at his aide. "Have you so little regard for your head that you would contradict your General, Toly?"

"No, my Lord. I am your loyal servant. That is why I feel compelled to ask these questions. I believe we must pacify this planet, but I believe your desire for this book has more of a personal wish than consideration of usefulness in it. If that is true, I fear that this desire could be your undoing, my Lord."

Itar swept his eyes over Toly. "I did not know you harbored such brother feeling—or such courage—Toly," he said at last. "Thank you for your concern. It is noted. Now, bring the map."

Toly kept his face stony and his eyes riveted to the wall behind the general. "My Lord, please forgive me if I have mis-spoken. I felt it was my duty. I will personally bring this map to you." He saluted and turned to leave, not waiting to be dismissed.

"Toly," the general called, and the other turned back.

"Yes, my Lord?"

"There is one more thing."

"Yes, my Lord?"

"The woman, Mara Holis. See that she is dispatched to my wife as soon as possible."

"Yes, my Lord. Will there be anything else?"

"No. That is all."

Toly chose not to salute again, but bowed deeply and got out. In moments he had given orders for the map to be dug out and brought to him, and within the hour he had dispatched the Archlean woman to General Itar's wife. Within a day he had written and dispatched a report to the Chief of Staff of the Cadeki forces detailing the aberrant behavior of the first God Resident of Archlea.

Cadeki technology managed to reconstruct the supposed map to the location of The Book of the Design, but were disappointed with what they found. The crumbled, water stained velum sheet had long since been washed blank.

During Itar's term as God-Resident many probes were sent to Keep Holis. Some of the Keep was destroyed in the search, and many of the honeycomb of caverns in the surrounding mountains were searched, but nothing resembling The Book of the Design was ever found.

~ * ~

Sure*ly the Design is strange and wonderful,* Mara thought as she sat in the house of General Itar's wife. This new world was a place of warm yellow sun, and sweet-smelling air, where god-machines were not destructive things, but useful things to make life easier. Already she was learning about lights that did not need oil, and heat that had no need of flame. Here there was no need of servants. Machines did everything. Yet, the house of her mistress had a hundred slaves from many worlds who served in a hundred ways. Mara's service was something she knew and loved. Before her were pots of ink and paint, and paper so fine she could not even see the grain of the press in it. *The Maker of All has rewarded me for my poor part in the Design* she thought. *He has sent me to a place* *to do what I most wanted to do in life.*

At that moment the child in her womb moved and a fountain of joy welled up in her. *And you, little one,* she thought. *You will learn all I can teach you about your father, and about the Design. Perhaps you will become a master, like Javi. Perhaps you will return to defeat the gods who are not gods. All is in the Design.*

PART II

Nine

603 ACG

The air was hot and sticky and there was no breath of wind in the auction yard. The bidder's floor was jammed tight with duster-clad people. They were the bidders who would stand directly below the auction block. The dusters were all of a uniform gray hiding the clothes, and therefore the social standing of people bidding on the slaves who would soon cross the block. Social standing meant nothing here. Each bidder possessed a temple license allowing them to buy slaves and nothing save the money to pay for the slave mattered.

Most of the bidders were agents for the nobles who did not wish to be elbowed by the common herd. The nobles hired the agents and then sat themselves in the high galleries which ran around three sides of the yard. There, safe from the stench of the crowd, they could be served cool wines and watch the parade of flesh as it crossed the block.

In the midst of the crowd of bidders stood a short stout fellow with a neatly trimmed beard. He wore a flat round cap of blue with a blue tassel hanging from it. Other than that, he looked like all the other duster-clad bidders, but he was not. He was Garith Balal, Scribe and Fair Witness to the business community of Peshar, and he hated being on the auction floor. He felt the sweat running from his armpits down his sides beneath the long gray duster and wished he could get a cup of wine, or even water. Garith knew the duster was to protect his clothes from any mischance of spilled blood or urine, and that knowledge made him more uncomfortable than the weather. He regretted wearing the fine blue robe that matched his cap to the auction. It made him look like the prosperous Scribe and Fair Witness he was, but no one could see it beneath the duster, and it only made him that much more miserable. He swore softly and silently called upon the gods to have mercy upon him—to deliver him from the sharp tongue of his wife who had sent him here. Merta, his wife of ten years, wanted a slave and that was that. She would have one. She said she needed the help around the house. A slave to scamper about and fetch and carry at her command. "Perhaps he could even help you in your shop, Garith," she had wheedled.

Garith had resisted as long as possible. He knew she did not need a slave, but Alsai Kruth, the next-door neighbor and fashion setter for the neighborhood had one, therefore Merta had to have one, and she was a skillful nag. She gave him no peace day or night for weeks until he finally lifted his hands to the gods in surrender. The price of some broken down house slave was worth it if it would restore peace in his home and let him get on with business.

The roar of the crowd increased as time for the auction drew near. More bidders jammed onto the floor and added their stench to the already gut-twisting miasma of the slave yard. Sweat, feces, vomit, and disinfectant mingled to make a brew that was almost visible.

I will never get this stink off me, Garith thought as the skinny auctioneer stepped to the desk upon the raised platform.

The man rapped his gavel and shouted "Hear yea, hear yea! All bidders approach. All sales must be consummated in money. No paper of promise is acceptable. A purchase license, duly stamped with temple authorization must be presented to the cashier or there can be no sale."

The crowd quieted as the charge was presented and when it was finished the auctioneer turned toward the pens behind the platform and called, "First Lot."

A young girl of perhaps twelve years with long stringy blond hair and an ankle chain was shoved onto the platform. Naked and frightened she tried to cover her loins and her young breasts with her hands, but the auctioneer lifted a long club which hung by a thong at the side of his desk and pushed her hands down.

Poor thing, Garith thought, looking at the way her ribs showed. *What could she have done to offend the gods enough to end up on the auction block?*

"Lot 4833." the auctioneer read from the list on his desk. "Female, pubescent, no physical defect. Guaranteed disease free. Do I hear a bid of one hundred Zari?"

"Is she a virgin?" the man beside Garith called out.

Garith turned to him, expecting to see some glint of lechery in his eyes, but there was none. He had asked purely for information.

The auctioneer glanced at the papers on his desk and said, "Not specified, therefore not guaranteed."

"One hundred Zari," came a bid, followed closely by "One fifty."

Bid followed bid and the price shot up to seven hundred Zari before slowing. Garith watched, in pity for the girl, and in awe of the price. The final bid was Seven hundred eighty. The gavel rapped down and the girl was taken away.

Seven hundred eighty Zari, Garith thought. *So much. But she was young and healthy. Perhaps some other will be less.* He was willing to spend up to five hundred, but only if forced to it.

Other lots came and went. All sold for more than Garith could believe. The price of human flesh was steep. So steep that Garith actually considered leaving, then the sound of Merta's voice came to his memory and he decided he might be willing to pay up to seven hundred. After all, he reasoned, I do have to sleep with her. All gods be merciful!

"Lot 8336" the auctioneer called and waited as a male chained at wrist and ankle was shoved onto the platform.

Garith felt a tingling at the back of his mind and looked closely at the new lot. The slave looked a little older than Garith, perhaps thirty-five. Lean, and strong looking with a soft glow of health about him that the slave pens had not dulled. He was no perfect specimen, being too long of limb, but his musculature showed strength. His long dark hair draped just below his shoulders and he was bearded. Hair and beard had a few streaks of gray, but they only added dignity not age. Like all the other lots he was naked save for his chains, but he made no attempt to cover his nakedness, and his unconcern added strength and calm to him. His eyes were a shocking blue, and each person upon whom his eyes fell got full attention for the moment of his gaze. When those eyes met Garith's, the scribe found himself unable to look away.

"What am I bid for this fine specimen, gentles," the auctioneer began. "He is strong and peaceful, as you can see. He can give many years of service."

"Five hundred."

Garith turned to see who had been the first bidder. It took him a moment to realize that the voice had been his own. He had opened his mouth and all the money he had intended to spend had come tumbling out.

Without so much as a moment's delay the auctioneer said "Five hundred is the bid. Do I hear six?"

A voice from the back called "Six."

Garith, feeling relieved to have been saved from his own folly by another bidder was determined to keep his mouth shut.

"Six hundred fifty," came another bid, closely followed by "Seven hundred."

Garith suddenly could not help himself. "Seven hundred fifty," he called.

A murmur of interest rose from the galleries. The bidding had not risen to outrageous heights, yet but there was something in the air that piqued the interest of the nobles.

Another bidder, thinking to end the bidding with one stroke shouted, "One Thousand," but his words had hardly finished echoing around the galleries before Garith upped it by a hundred.

The excited murmur of the crowd rose. What was so special about this slave that the bidding had become so heavy? Garith could not have answered them. He did not know himself why it was that he had to have this slave at any price.

"Twelve hundred," the other bidder shouted. He was beginning to doubt the worth of the slave and the wisdom of bidding against someone who was either rolling in money or mad.

"Twelve twenty-five," Garith shouted.

"Perhaps it is his son," some wit from the back of the crowd called out, and laughter rippled around the galleries.

The other bidder was not sure he should go on after the laughter, but he was not willing to let the slave go yet. "Twelve fifty," he shouted, but was not heartbroken when Garith answered "Thirteen."

There was a silence that stretched until the auctioneer called, "Thirteen hundred is the bid. Do I hear more? Thirteen hundred, going once…going twice…third and last time…sold to the gentle with the tassel on his hat for one thousand three hundred Zari." The gavel cracked down and the crowd applauded and laughed.

With the crack of the gavel against the block Garith's senses returned to him and the bottom dropped out of his stomach. *All gods have mercy* he thought, his hands shaking. *Merta will kill me. Thirteen hundred Zari.*

But there was no help for it now. He could not even worm out of the sale by saying it had been a mistake, he hadn't meant to bid, or that he did not have the money. That would only result in the slave going back to the pens for re-sale and Garith going along with him.

A sudden stab of panic shot through Garith and he grabbed the purse that was tied to his belt beneath the duster. Merta had made him take extra money when he had thought to take only five hundred and he was by turns grateful and disgusted that she had.

An auction guard brought the slave from the block to the cashier's desk. The leg chain had been removed but the guard fastened the chain that still dangled from the slave's wrist to an iron ring set in the stone floor

Garith presented his buyer's license and the man examined it. "You are Scribe Balal?"

Garith nodded and extended his family seal stamp, called a chop, as proof.

The cashier took the chop, inked it and stamped it upon a much-stamped piece of paper. He compared it with the stamp on the temple license and when he was satisfied of the match, he returned the chop to Garith. He stamped the license with the sale yards chop and handed it back to Garith, who began digging his purse out from beneath the duster. The cashier said, "Let me help you with that Gentle," and eased Garith out of the duster so that he could more easily reach his money.

"Shackles?" the cashier asked.

Garith was so distracted with counting out his money and mourning its loss that he failed to understand what the cashier said. "Beg pardon?" he asked

"Shackles. Do you need shackles to transport your purchase or have you brought your own?"

"Oh, no. I have no shackles."

"A robe?"

"A robe?"

"Yes, gentle one. A robe. Something to cover the slave's nakedness. It is not permitted to parade a naked slave through the streets of Peshar. He must have some sort of clothing."

Garith, looking woebegone, said "No, I have no robe, nor shackles."

The cashier grinned wolfishly. "Not a problem, gentle scribe. For a mere fifty Zari shackles and a robe can be provided."

Garith groaned. Another fifty Zari from an already thin purse.

The slave had been listening to the discussion and watched his new master fading under the battering of the cashier. "There is no need of shackles, Master," he said. "I will make no trouble."

Garith and the cashier both looked at the slave with open mouths. The Cashier was surprised that the slave could speak such perfect Peshari. Slaves usually came to the yard mind-peeled with only the most rudimentary language left to them.

There was such an aura of calm strength about the words that Garith suddenly felt calmed himself, and his business sense returned to him.

The cashier, realizing he was about to lose a fee hurried to say, "Gentle scribe, I would not recommend transporting a new slave without shackles. They are wild and cunning when first sold. Best to keep them chained for a month or two until they become used to your mastery. Some recommend gelding the males, but I say why ruin a perfectly good breeder if there is no need."

"I do not need shackles," Garith said. "But I will need a robe. How much?"

"But, gentle Scribe…"

Garith cut off the man's protests with a wave of his chubby hand. "The robe please."

Looking as if his stomach had suddenly turned sour the cashier stooped to the box beside the desk and brought out a ragged robe.

"Almost better to let him go naked than wear that," Garith said. "A very small breeze will blow that right off his back. Something a bit less – revealing if you please."

The false courtesy disappeared from the cashier's face, but he held his tongue and stooped back to the box for another robe. The second was not much better than the first, but Garith was satisfied with it. He reached for it, but the cashier snatched it back. "Ten Zari," he snarled.

"Ten Zari? For that rag? You should pay me to take it from you. I can get a fine robe in the bazaar for less than that."

The cashier changed from snarling to whining in an instant. "It is recoverable, gentle scribe. Recoverable. Return it within a week and all save a tenth will be returned to you."

"Must be cloth of gold to require such an earnest," Garith grumbled giving the man a ten Zari coin. "And I will have a receipt with your chop on it too. If my money is not returned to me, I will personally see the temple marshals haul you to the dungeons."

"Of course, gentle one, certainly it will be returned," the man sniveled. He snatched a readymade-receipt from the desk and stamped it with his chop. Then he unlocked the chain from the slave's wrist and dropped the sack-like robe over his head. "Beware of this one, good scribe. Remember that I warned you not to let him go unchained."

"You may be sure that I will not forget you, cashier," Garith said, making it sound like an insult.

He turned and stalked off toward the auction yard gate and had taken several steps before he remembered his new slave. He had not even gestured for the man to follow him.

Garith turned back in panic and found himself face to face with his new acquisition, and so close that the man bumped into him almost knocking him over. "Is everything all right, master?" he asked catching

Garith by the elbow and steadying him.

The slave was fully two hands taller than the master and Garith found himself looking up into the other's smiling face. After a moment he stammered, "I'm fine. Fine. Let go of me."

The slave released his grip and the two of them began to walk side by side toward the gate, Garith casting little glances from the corners of his eye at the other. If he thought to find hate, or despair, or malice he was disappointed. The man's face showed only a pleasant smile with steady eyes directed forward.

It was not much cooler in the streets of Peshar than it had been in the auction yard. The pink and gray brick of the city perspired with the humidity as though they were flesh and made the cobble stone streets damp and slimy. Many of the people in the teaming streets, the lower-class inhabitants, were dressed in unbleached muslin shirts and breach cloths with twisted multi-colored head bands to keep the perspiration from dripping into their eyes. Here and there in the streams of people more prosperous folk were dressed in long colorful robes and skull caps. They looked wilted and envious of those more lightly dressed.

Garith and his purchase worked through the traffic toward home, but Garith did not really notice what was going on around him. He was busily trying to think of something to tell Merta. *Perhaps I could just lie,* he thought, but discarded the idea almost before it formed. Merta would find out and make his life hell. Perhaps I can tell her that many of the lots were going for fifteen hundred or more. That would make this one look like a bargain. But again, he discarded the idea.

"Master you do not look well. Shall we stop for you to rest a moment? Perhaps a cool drink?"

Garith glanced at his new chattel. "If you could tell your mistress that your price was only three hundred Zari it might help."

The slave grinned showing even white teeth. "I fear I cannot do that, Master. I make it a practice not to lie to my masters. It makes for an easier life. You see, if I lied and my new mistress caught me in the lie, she would probably beat me. I do not like beatings."

"Very wise, I am sure," Garith said.

"On the other hand, if beatings fall within The Design then so be it, but I prefer to avoid them if I can."

"We may both get beaten when Merta finds out how much I paid for you."

"Perhaps, but I think not. I am truly valuable. You did not pay too much."

"You think? It was not *your* thirteen hundred Zari which crossed that thief of a cashier's palm."

"One thousand three hundred and ten master. Do not forget the price of my robe. And there was also the price of the temple license."

Garith groaned. "All right, all right," Garith shouted. "Clearly I am a fool. There is no need for you to continue pointing it out."

They trudged along in silence for a time until the slave said, "I speak five languages, Master. "

Garith stopped short in the midst of the mob. "Five languages?"

The slave smiled and nodded.

"And is one of them the Divine Tongue?"

"Of course."

"And write as well?"

"All of them master."

Garith blinked and studied the slaves face as the crowd moved around them. He did not care if the slave could write any but the Divine Tongue. All documents were by law written in the Divine Tongue. Written Peshari was illegal. Possession of even a scarp with that ancient language upon it was punishable by death. It had been so since the coming of the gods.

"In a fair and readable hand? No chicken tracks."

"Fair and readable, master."

Garith twisted a curl of his beard, considering.

"And I can cook. Not fancy, but quite edible. Some have even said delicious."

"Five languages and can cook," Garith said to himself.

Merta wanted a slave to keep up with Alsai Kruth and this one certainly did that. If presented in the right light thirteen hundred Zari might be quite a bargain pulled off by a clever scribe.

The morning suddenly became brighter and cooler. Garith nodded his head and the two men turned and pushed on through the bustle.

After a time Garith turned into a broad street that spilled down into Tapestry Plaza. The two stopped to look across the expanse and the slave smiled.

Garith always crossed Tapestry Plaza on his way home even if it took him out of his way. The place always made him feel better for some reason. It always calmed his worries and stimulated thoughts of the magnificence of life. It was a gathering place for more than those involved in the buying and selling of Tapestries. It was the center of life in Peshar. Buyers and sellers of all sorts came here and others came to wine shops and cafes around the porticos. Poets and artists and philosophers met and talked and argued. Singers, jugglers, clowns and conjurers moved about the plaza trying to entice a few coins from the crowds which formed around them. In the evening young men and women would walk arm in arm, heads close together, around the portico. All Peshar came to Tapestry Plaza to fall in love.

As they looked across the plaza at all the magnificent tapestries the smile suddenly fled from the slave's face. Garith saw where he was looking. The slave's eyes were fixed on a particular tapestry among the hundreds displayed. This one was a depiction of the coming of the gods. In the center was a black sky ship with its belly open. In the foreground stood a group of warrior-gods. Three more black ships hung in the sunset at the top of the work. These were aglow with blue and orange light. At each side of the landed ship were the familiar lines of Temple way. These lines looked wrong however because they did not frame the sky-puncturing spire of the temple which now stood at the end of that street.

"It is not a very good rendering," Garith said. "It has no fire. The sky ships should be so bright they stab the eye, and the warrior-gods should dominate the whole structure."

"It is very sad," the slave said.

Garith looked at the slave and saw the deep sadness of the man. "We take our tapestries seriously in Peshar," he said. "But not quite that seriously. It is mediocre, not tragic."

"I meant the subject, Master, not the rendering."

Garith frowned. "What do you know of the subject, slave?"

"I know it is the enslavement of Peshar, and all the world Archlea."

Garith looked as though he had been slapped, and he turned pale. "Never say such a thing," he sputtered. "Never, never say such a thing. You are only a slave and such blasphemy would only cost you your life. I would be held responsible. Everything I have would be forfeit and my whole family, including parents and in-laws would be sold into slavery across the sky."

In rage and fear he backhanded the slave across the face. "I am no brute, but if you do not hold your tongue, I will beat you until you learn how. We serve the gods, willingly. We are not enslaved by them." He suddenly looked around to see if anyone else had heard and was relieved when no one seemed to have noticed. He went on more quietly. "We serve the gods. They allow us life. They allowed us life because of our tapestries, and for that we thank and praise them. For that we offer each tapestry to them and are much up lifted when our gifts are taken across the sky."

The slave's face had become stony when Garith had struck him, and he had bowed his head under the verbal lashing, but there was no repentance in him. Garith could see that.

Looking around again, Garith said, "We have wasted enough time. We must be on our way. I must make Merta believe you are worth the price I paid, but I am beginning to think you are a danger sent from hell to trick me and swallow me up."

Merta was waiting in the shop when they arrived. Garith had hoped to avoid meeting her too soon, but there she was tapping her foot with impatience. Shorter than her husband and not as round, she had soft red hair and snapping green eyes which caught everything. She was wearing a simple robe belted at the waist and a silver circlet held her hair back from her forehead. She wrinkled up her nose with disgust when Master and Slave stepped through the bead curtain that was the front door of the shop.

"All gods," she swore. "What is that stink? Did you buy him from a sewer?"

Garith had intended to stop at the public baths on the way home, but the upset of the slave's blasphemy had driven from his head any idea save getting home. Now he stood sniffing the mixed reek of sweat and the disinfectant the slave had been doused with. The smell was quickly filling the small shop.

"Go quickly, Merta. Bring soap and a bucket and sponge into the court yard."

"How much did you pay for this...stink?" she asked.

"Never mind that now. I will tell you later. Now we must get him out of the shop or the smell of him will offend clients for days. Go! Go!"

Merta grumbled, but turned and went through the door that led into the depths of the house. Garith turned toward the third door of the room which lead out onto the central court of the house and dragged the slave out it. On the patio he pointed to the drain grate in the center of the brick floor. "Stand there and take off the robe. And if you have any mercy in you, do not abuse that rag. Nothing must give that thief of a cashier reason not to return my money."

The slave did as he was told, being careful to lay the rented robe on a bench beneath the eaves of the court yard.

Garith went to the fountain which was only a square trough knee high and arm span wide with a pipe no bigger than a finger trickling water into it. He picked up the dipping bucket that sat beside the fountain, dipped it full and carried it to the slave. "Dump this over yourself. It is cold so you may thank the gods it is a warm day."

The slave grinned crookedly. "I will thank you for the coolness of the water on such a hot day," he said it with such calm good humor that Garith could not help but smile in answer, ignoring the veiled contempt for the gods.

Merta came from the house with another bucket, a sponge and some soap. She stopped at the sight of the naked man pouring water over himself. "Well at least he looks healthy," she said and handed over the sponge and the soap. Garith took the other bucket, dipped it full, and put it within reach of the slave.

"And how much did you pay for this miserable specimen?"

"You just said he was healthy. Make up your mind."

"How much?"

"He speaks five languages."

She smiled a little at that. "Good. Did you hear them?"

"Well, no, but…"

"That's all right so long as the factor warranted it." She looked at Garith and saw by his face that something was wrong. "The factor did warrant it did he not?"

"Well, not exactly, but he…" Garith pointed at the slave who was now soaping himself with the sponge, "…he said…"

"He said? All gods witness. My husband is a fool. He takes the word of a slave."

Garith was stung in his pride and it made him snap back at her, "He cooks too. Not fancy but delicious."

"Again, by his own warrant?"

The slave went on washing himself and did not appear to pay much attention to the discussion.

With hands on hips and foot tapping Merta demanded, "How much?"

Garith looked sheepish and said, "Did I mention that he writes a fair hand and knows the Divine Tongue?"

"How much, Garith?"

There was no more avoiding the truth so he took a deep breath and said, "Thirteen hundred," but he did not say it very loud.

Merta blinked several times, stopped tapping, then shook her head and leaned toward her husband. "How much did you say?"

"Thirteen hundred Zari," he answered – louder.

Merta was stunned with disbelief. She worked her mouth as though trying to say something, but no words came out.

Garith quickly jumped into the silence with, "But think how much better than Alsai's slave he is. She has only a broken-down house servant that cost only five hundred Zari. And the man is more liability than help. I have heard Mael complain a hundred times that he eats them out of house and home and produces nothing. This slave is of real value. Look at him."

Merta looked from Garith to the dripping slave in the middle of the court yard. Her smooth complexion became mottle with unreleased rage. She opened her mouth and lifted her finger to point at her husband while she looked at the slave, and she was caught by the depths of his blue eyes. It was like cool calm water washing over her, washing away all the rage. It was as though the slave had seized her by the shoulders with his hands. There was such an aura of warm gentle strength radiating from him that Garith felt it too. All rage and fear and worry went out of the husband and wife like cessation of a great storm leaving only quiet tranquility behind.

The strange seizure of calm lasted only a moment, but when it was gone all rage and recrimination was gone with it, leaving the patio quiet.

"I know it is a lot of money Merta," Garith began reasonably. "But I think he is going to bring back every Zari I spent tenfold."

Merta took a deep breath and said, "Perhaps you are right. And he does speak and write five languages. Perhaps he will be worth the price."

"I am worth more than the price, Mistress. Much more. And I will more than prove my worth. Do not worry."

Merta smiled and turned toward the house. Before going in she turned back and said sweetly, "I will bring one of your old robes, Garith."

"Yes," he answered. His mind was whirling with what had just happened. He answered her only out of habit.

She turned and went in.

"You are a lucky man to have such a woman as that, Master," the slave said as he wrung the water from his long hair.

Garith stared at the slave, surprised at himself for not taking offense at such forwardness. "Yes," he answered. "I am very lucky. She is very precious to me. If only I could control her better."

The slave smiled and nodded his agreement, and the power covered by that smile made Garith shiver.

Ten

603 A.C.G.

Rain drizzled down and chill seeped in from the street to make the shop cold. It was late afternoon and there were few people about. Garith had sent his hired letter writers and reader home and in truth he was not unhappy that custom had been light that day. The slow time gave him and Alvis a little time to catch up on the backlog of copies.

The slave proved to be as good as his words. He did indeed speak five languages, including the Divine language, and he did write a fair and readable hand. His cooking was good too, though he was not left much time to practice those culinary skills. Garith put him to work copying documents and in a short time he proved to be worth his weight in ink stones. Garith forgot about the horrible price he had paid

Both men were bent over the writing desk when the shop door rattled and the beaded curtain covering it made a sibilant clatter which told them someone had come in. Garith stood and turned to see who it was, but even as he rose, the high, melodic voice of a Temple Castrati sang out, "Make way, all who serve the Gods," The young man was very fat and feminine. He was dressed in fine robes of yellow velvet.

"Lord Baroth Linser, Chief Servant of the Gods of Archlea, High Priest of the Temple of Peshar, approaches. To bow before him is to bow before the merciful Gods."

Announcement finished, the young man made a flourish with his arm and bowed deeply, then dropped to his knees and bowed his head to the floor.

Lord Baroth Linser, fronted by two more servants, entered. He was short and heavy with bowed legs which seemed too spindly to bear the bulk of his upper body. His face was babyish with large blue eyes, a button nose and pouting pink lips. The servants who fronted the Chief Priest had parted the bead curtain so that Linser might not soil his robes by brushing against anything in the mean shop of a common scribe. They let the curtain go and it clattered back into place.

Garith hurried forward and dropped to his knees, keeping his eyes down. He thought of Alvis' disdain for the Gods and a thrill of fear gripped his stomach. If the slave decided to be arrogant now it could cost Garith everything, but when Garith chanced a look to the side he was relieved to find Alvis bowing in the prescribed manner.

Lord Linser moved away from the door a minimum distance to allow the man who had been following him to step into the room. Garith glanced through his eye brows and gasped. The man who had followed Lord Linser needed no crier to announce him. He could command a crowded plaza simply by walking across it. This was Dimar Ransis, Patriarch of House Ransis, whose tapestries were the finest in Peshar. Perhaps the finest in all the universe. Legend had it that a Ransis Tapestry had stayed the hands of the Gods from destroying every living thing in Peshar when they first came from across the sky. Legend said that tapestry was so beautiful it had made the Gods weep, and so they had spared Peshar to preserve this thing of beauty.

Ransis was old and thin, but there was no feebleness in him, only an air of great power. His beard hung almost to his waist, and his robes were closely embroidered with a running vine pattern in rich magenta.

Garith's mind whirled. Which of these men of power should he address first? His respect was greater for Dimar Ransis, but Lord Linser commanded the Temple. In a moment he made his choice.

"Lord Linser, you honor my humble shop beyond my greatest dreams. How may so unworthy a one as I serve you?"

"You are the Scribe and Fair Witness Garith Balal?" the Priest asked, and sniffed as though he were smelling something faintly malodorous.

"Yes, my Lord. How may I serve you?"

"You may rise, Scribe. I will have tea."

Garith rose and, with a flip of his hand, sent Alvis to bring tea.

A moment after Alvis left, one of Lord Linser's servants produced an ornately carved wood and silk folding chair, placing it so that the Chief Priest did not have to move even the smallest step before sitting. Linser sat in full knowledge that the chair would be behind him. If it were not, the servant responsible would not see another sunrise.

Silence grew thick as they waited for the tea. Garith worried about how fast the tea could be made and brought, and whether it would be acceptable to so high a personage as Lord Linser. But worrying about that would not help, so he turned to worrying whether or not he should offer Lord Ransis a chair. After a little he decided that he should.

"May I offer you a chair, Lord Ransis?"

The old man smiled a tiny smile which had mockery in it for the pretensions of the Chief Priest. "A desk stool will serve very well, thank you," he said. "I have spent my life sitting on one. I find them quite comfortable."

Garith could not help but smile in answer. He brought forth the desk stool and Lord Ransis perched himself upon it.

Alvis returned at that moment bearing a tray containing a tea bowl – the finest in the house – and eight cups. Merta followed her slave bearing another tray laden with sweet cakes, nuts, and fruit. Garith felt himself relaxing. He glanced at his wife and saw satisfaction and pride upon her face that her husband should be so honored as to be visited by both the Chief Priest and the Patriarch of House Ransis. His heart melted with love and gratitude. How had she managed anything so elegant in such a short time?

Alvis looked to his master, silently asking if he should serve. Garith shook his head minutely and took over the duty himself. Alvis placed the tray upon the desk and Garith carefully dipped from the bowl into a cup. He presented it to the Chief Priest using both hands, and keeping his eyes down. He considered kneeling but was afraid he might bobble the cup and offend by his clumsiness, so he merely bowed deeply.

Merta presented the tray of cakes in the same way, but Linser waved her away without taking anything. Garith saw her stiffen and knew she was hurt by the curt dismissal. It irked him too, but his smile did not falter.

Garith turned to Lord Ransis and dipped him a cup of tea. Ransis took the cup with thanks, then he took a cake from Merta's tray and thanked her also. It seemed to Garith that the old man was using good manners to insult the Chief Priest.

After a few moments Merta dropped a deep curtsy and, pulling Alvis along with her eyes, went out the courtyard door.

Lord Linser sipped his tea and held the cup out. A servant took it and knelt beside the priest's chair, holding the cup in easy reach.

"You are said to be the most honest Fair Witness in Peshar," Linser began.

Garith began to stammer out his thanks for the compliment, but Linser waved him to silence. "It is no good thing that you are more trusted than the Fair Witnesses of the Temple, but I suppose you cannot help your reputation in this."

A deep rich laugh came from Lord Ransis. "The Chief Priest is offended that I would demand an impartial Fair Witness to our contract," he said.

The scribe shuddered to hear such a thing. He knew House Ransis was powerful, but mocking the servants of the Gods was dangerous.

Linser was not happy with Lord Ransis' tone either, but he said nothing. He sipped his tea and handed the cup back to the servant. "Bring paper and ink," he commanded.

Garith grabbed a sheet of pounded linen paper. This was the type of paper Garith used for final draft documents usually, but under the circumstances... He brought an ink pot and pens from beneath the desk top and sat down prepared to write.

"The contract will be thus..." the Priest began. "I, Lord Baroth Linser, Chief Servant of the Gods of Archlea, Chief Priest of the Temple of Peshar, agree to pay ten thousand Zari in gold for a reproduction of the Ransis tapestry known as The Gods Show Mercy. The reproduction will be one quarter the size of the original, and will be of the original materials."

Dimar Ransis interrupted. "Make that, 'original materials as they are available' if you please."

Linser cast a look of barely controlled rage at Ransis, but said nothing to countermand the request. "As they are available," he said through clenched teeth. "The reproduction is to be delivered to me, and accepted only at my delight, within one year of the execution of this contract. Is that to your satisfaction, Ransis?"

"Almost, my Lord," the old man said with a slight bow of his head. "It should also say that one third of the price is to be delivered before the work is begun, and that, satisfaction notwithstanding, that earnest will not be refundable."

The priest colored and began to sputter a denial, but before words formed, he thought better of it, and after a deep breath to calm his temper said, "amend it thus, scribe."

Ransis smiled his tiny smile and nodded to Garith.

The scribe added the amendment and waited a moment to see if anything more was to be added. Nothing more was said for several heartbeats so Garith asked, "When will you require the copies, my Lords?"

"Tomorrow morning," Linser snapped.

"Very well, my Lords. Shall I make the execution date tomorrow also?"

"Tomorrow will be fine," Lord Ransis answered mildly.

"The usual four copies, my Lords?"

Ransis said yes, but Linser said, "No! Three copies only. I want no public display of this contract in a rat hole like this."

The Priest referred to the custom of Scribes to place a copy of impressive or very well written contracts on display for the public to see. This sort of display was good advertising for a Scribe and Fair Witness and Garith was unhappy that he would not be able to reap that benefit from his distinguished clientele, but there were ways around the ban, so Garith bowed his assent.

"I will file the third copy in the Citadel myself," Linser said.

"I believe I would rather have the scribe file the official copy," Ransis said.

The priest glared at him, but jerked a nod of assent.

Garith waited to see if anything more would come to the minds of the Lords, but when nothing further was said, he spoke.

"If there is nothing more, my Lords, may I ask you to affix your chops to this paper and witness as I affix my own?"

The two agreed that there was nothing more, but neither made any move to comply with the scribe's request so he reached beneath the desk and took up a lap desk. This he carried to Lord Linser.

The Chief Priest stamped his ornate chop on the rough copy and glared at Ransis when he stepped forward to affix his chop.

Garith squatted between the men so they could both see when he affixed his own chop, signed his name and dated the copy. He had hardly finished when Lord Linser stood. The folding chair disappeared, and the half empty tea cup appeared upon the desk. The movements of the servants had been so swift as to be almost invisible.

"We will return tomorrow morning to execute the contract," Linser said. "See that the copies are ready. Clean copies. If they are not." he threw a withering glance at Ransis, "we will go to the temple scribes."

"The copies will be perfect, my Lords. I swear it," Garith said.

"They had better be, or your reputation will be only a memory — as will you." The priest said pleasantly then turned on his heel and strode out so fast his servants had to scramble to hold the curtain out of his way. He did not see Garith pale or bow.

Dimar Ransis stood up from his stool with dignity and bowed to Garith. "I thank you for the hospitality of your house, Gentle Scribe, and for the work you are doing for me."

The civility of the great Lord Ransis almost took Garith's breath, but he managed to sputter out his thanks and protest that he was only doing his job.

"Lord Linser seems to have left without asking the price of your services," Ransis said, showing his mocking smile again.

"I am more than well paid by the honor of serving both House Ransis and the Temple at the same time," Garith said.

Ransis continued smiling. "But honor buys no tea and cakes." His hand disappeared into his robe and reappeared holding two one hundred Zari coins. He placed them in Garith's hand.

Garith stared down at the coins in his hand, feeling the buttery softness of the gold and the weight of it.

"This is too much, Lord Ransis. My usual fee for a contract is twenty Zari and I would truly have witnessed and copied this contract merely for the honor," he extended the coins, but Ransis did not take them back.

"Twenty Zari for service then," Ransis said, "and the rest as a token of trust between us, and a balm against the bad manners of one for whom you do service."

Garith bowed deeply. "As you wish, my Lord," he said.

"And do not worry about the priest's threats. He wants the copy of *The Gods Show Mercy* very badly, and I will never accept any contract sworn to by a temple scribe."

Garith did not know what to make of this. Lord Ransis spoke blasphemy, or at least spoke dangerous rebellion, but common sense heard truth in what he said.

Lord Ransis nodded good-bye and went out.

The bead curtain over the door had not even stopped clacking before Merta and Alvis stepped in. They had been listening outside the courtyard door.

"How much did he give you?" Merta asked.

Her husband let the two coins drop from his hand onto the desk top. They gave back a satisfying ring.

Merta stared at the coins with her mouth hanging open. For a moment she could not catch her breath. Then she said, "Husband, our fortune is made. With the trust of House Ransis and of the temple we will be rich in no time."

Alvis lifted one eyebrow at that. "Riches may be in the Design Mistress, but dealing with the gods and their servants is likely to prove more trouble than they are worth."

~ * ~

Dimar Ransis returned to his tapestry factory, instructed his foreman to contact the dyers and begin setting up a loom for the new contract. Lord Ransis did not like working in such a way. He would have preferred to create a new work with which to uplift the name of House Ransis, but few people in Peshar had money to commission new work. For that matter few on all Archlea had money for such things.

"Besides," Ransis had said many times before, "if a truly great work were to be created, the gods would probably snatch it up as an offering."

To have a work claimed by the gods was a great honor for the artist, but, as he had said to scribe Balal, honor bought no tea and cakes, and when the gods claimed an artists' work it often meant the end of the artist, for even creators found it necessary to eat.

Tapestry was no different from any other art form save that it involved more than one artist. Weavers, dyers, spinners, needle crafters, even farmers who raised flax or sheep. Many people worked to carry out the design of a tapestry, and each had a belly which grew hungry daily. Many had more than one belly depending upon them, so a tapestry snatched up by the gods might honor House Ransis, but it made the soup grow extremely thin for all connected with the work.

House Ransis had, through good management and reproduction of its own classic works, continued to be financially healthy, but repeating and repeating sapped the creative energy from the artists.

Dimar Ransis had managed to turn a profit each year since becoming Patriarch, and with the profits he personally commissioned artists to develop designs for tapestries, but such personal patronage could only do so much to maintain the artistic community attached to House Ransis.

After instructing his foreman, Ransis went into the factory office to pull the drawings and stitch design for *The Gods Show Mercy* from the file of designs. He crossed the room to the expanse of wall covered with pigeon-hole shelving, rolled the movable ladder to the far left, and climbed to the top. From the pigeon-hole he pulled a leather folder which was almost too large for him to handle alone. He carried it down the ladder and lugged it to the high desk beneath the window in the south wall. Inside the folder were many drawings of different sections of the tapestry, a drawing of the whole tapestry, and swatches of cloth which had been dyed with the colors to be used. In the drawings each figure and dimension were carefully marked. On each cloth swatch was a label telling the particulars of the colors, their origin, and how they were to be applied.

Ransis laid all this out upon the desk, then took paper and pen and began listing materials in order of need. He did not notice the tall figure slip into the office.

Alvis stood just inside the door of the office and watched Lord Ransis work for a moment. He smiled at the old man's back; at the way it was industriously bent over the scarred desk.

"Lord Ransis," the slave said quietly.

Ransis, still immersed in his work looked up in confusion. He glanced out the window into the growing gloom of the street. It took a moment for him to realize the voice had come from behind him. He turned to see scribe Balal's slave, long haired and dressed in a gray robe which was much too short for him, standing just inside the door of the office.

Ransis frowned. "How may I help you?" he asked.

"Do you recognize me, Lord Ransis?" Alvis asked.

"I do not know your name, but you are the slave of scribe Balal – Yes? You bring some message for me?"

"Yes, Lord Ransis, but not from Master Garith."

The old man was confused. "Is there some problem with the contract? Will it not be ready tomorrow?"

"It will be done. The message I bring is from the mouth of Javi Holis, Servant of the Design."

The shock of the name showed on Lord Ransis' face, but he said "I know no man by that name. Why should he be sending me a message?"

"In the time before the coming of the gods Javi Holis lived in Peshar…"

"Then you are a fool," Ransis snapped. "No man could be alive to send messages from that time to this. The Gods came centuries ago."

"Nevertheless, I bring a message." It was said with such authority that there was no doubting the truth of it.

"And what is this message from a man long dead, slave?"

Alvis smiled at the sharpness of the tone. "First," he began, "The time of the gods is running out. The Master of the Design has nearly finished with them. They are beset on many sides by those who will continue the Design. Second, I am sent to help preserve Archlea and return it to the strength it had before the coming of the gods. The means to regain strength is preserved here and only waits discovering again. And third, do not give Baroth Linser a true copy of *The Gods Show Mercy."*

Ransis stared at the slave for a long time. The surety of the man was impressive, but Ransis understood little of what he said. Only the last seemed to make sense.

"You speak gibberish, slave. Gibberish and blasphemy. The gods are eternal, and if I do not fulfill my contract with the Chief Priest, I am in danger of the auction block, or worse."

The corner of the slave's mouth lifted in a half smile. "There is danger, and, if it is in the Design, there may be death or slavery, but you must not give a true copy of The Gods Show Mercy to Linser."

"That is foolishness. Why should I not? There are already hundreds of copies. Probably there are twenty in Peshar alone. The original is in the hands of the Gods. What difference will one more copy make?"

"The original no longer exists. It was destroyed years ago."

"Destroyed? How? It was in the hands of the Gods."

"I told you. The time of the gods is short, and it grows shorter by the day. Already the gods seldom travel through the Transit Gates of the temple. It is dangerous to be so far from home when the Transit Net might break down at any time, or one might be cut off by a Garin attack or a rebellion."

Ransis understood none of this. It was just more blasphemous gibberish —frightening gibberish. Ransis was a well-known critic of the clergy, especially of Baroth Linser, but he did not hold with blasphemy. Perhaps this slave had really been sent by Linser to trick him into blasphemy.

But there was another reason the old man was frightened by this slave. What if he was speaking the truth? What if the Gods' power was fading? What if they were about to be overcome by some other gods more frightful than themselves? What if this slave really did know something of Javi Holis?

"Take your blasphemy elsewhere, slave," Ransis growled. "Go

back to scribe Balal and do not speak of this ever again. I will let your blasphemy be forgotten this time since the scribe has done me good service. But if I ever hear such from you or Balal again, I will report you to the Temple."

Alvis laughed and bowed with mock humility. "Many thanks oh great Lord Ransis, but do not cover up blasphemy for my sake."

Ransis could not move. He could only stare at the slave. There did not seem to be any fear in the man.

Alvis stepped closer to the old man. "I could do this by force," he said, "but I would prefer not to control you. I wish you to know in the depths of your heart what the gods from across the sky are and controlling your mind will not allow true belief."

Ransis threw his hands up as if to fend off an attack. "I do not wish to hear any further blasphemy. I worship the Gods. I pay my taxes and am present in the Temple on all the Holy Days. I will not hear anything against the Merciful Gods."

"Are you so happy under the heel of Baroth Linser?" Alvis asked with a bitter chuckle. "Is he the one you would pick as a buffer between the gods and the people of Peshar? Is he a man to be trusted? Perhaps that is why you brought Master Garith into your dealings with that most trusted priest."

Ransis dropped his hands, a look of distaste passing over his face. Chief Priest Linser made his skin crawl. More than a few times he had wondered why the gods might have chosen him as their Chief Servant upon the world. Could they not have picked a man equally faithful, but less arrogant, less…coarse?

Ransis shook off the thought and said, "the ways of the Gods are mysterious and beyond human understanding." It was a quotation from the catechism children took in with their mother's milk.

Alvis shook his head at the old man's retreat into catechism. "In a way you are right, Lord Ransis. The ways of the Maker of All are mysterious, but the ways of the gods of Archlea are all too clear. Their ways are nothing more than Linser's ill-mannered arrogance amplified ten thousand times."

The old man caught his breath at such disdain for the gods, but he could not contradict what the slave said. Too many times he had thought the gods and their servants spoiled children who did not deserve what they demanded, but whose tantrums could be deadly if the demands were not met.

"And you are no true believer anyway," the slave went on. "A true believer would have either looked blank or called for Temple Proctors when I mentioned Javi Holis. You recognized the name, yet you did nothing."

"I recognized the name," Ransis said, defiance bolstering his shaky voice. "It is the name of a fool. The name of a heathen who called upon the name of false gods in the days before the Mercy of the True Gods. A fool who died for his blasphemy."

"Very good, Lord Ransis, except you forgot to say that the name was changed. Javi Holis was welcomed into service of the Design under the name Indi Ransis."

"No, it is a lie," the old man sprang at the slave, his hands clawing for the other's throat.

Alvis did not move, did not stop speaking, did not even blink at the suddenness of the attack. He did not seem to notice the old man's fingers which gripped the front of his robe. "Indi Ransis, who was eldest son of House Ransis thirty generations ago. But he did not choose the art of tapestry. He chose instead to study the Design and to serve the Maker of All."

"He is dead," the old man hissed, trying to shake the slave into silence. "He died long ago. The Gods destroyed him and all those of the old way. The Great Design was a lie and, Javi Holis paid for that lie with his life."

"Only with the life of his body. Javi Holis still lives within the Design, and his wish before he departed this life was that Peshar and belief in the Design be preserved. That the Maker of All and his Design not be forgotten when the false gods depart. That is why you must not let Linser have a true copy of the tapestry. He knows already that it shows where something is hidden. He does not know what, but he hopes to trade what is hidden for favors with the gods. You see, he is not even a true servant of the gods. He is only a parasite attached to them for what he can get from them."

Ransis let go of the slave's robe and slumped back against the desk. *How could this one know all?* he thought. Even that the tapestry was more than it appeared. He might even know more about it than Ransis did himself.

The old man rubbed his hand over his face and down his beard. He looked into the eyes of the slave. They seemed lighted from within. They were visible despite the growing dark. "I do not understand how you know these things. They are the darkest secrets of House Ransis."

"I know because the Master of the Design saw fit to allow Mara Holis, who was Mara Fex, wife of Javi Holis, to be sold into slavery rather than die with her husband. I know because Mara Holis lived a quiet life in slavery, never resisting the will of her masters, but quietly teaching her understanding of the Design to her children and other slaves. She taught the Mandalai, though she did not know how to use them herself. She taught everything she knew of the Design and waited with patience as those she taught taught others, until knowledge of the Design was spread throughout the Cadeki Empire, to all the worlds of those you call gods."

Ransis shook his head. "I do not understand what you speak of. I do not even know what message the tapestry contains. I do not even know if the message encompasses the whole work or some small part of it. I do not even know what to change in order to make the message not say what it is supposed to say."

"That is good. What you do not know you cannot tell."

"But how do I avoid making a true copy? I do not know what to change. And if Lord Linser discovers I have made some change he will take me into the Temple dungeon and make me tell what is changed."

Alvis smiled —the slightest lifting of his mouth corners. "Use only the finest silk and wool and bleached linen," he said. "Use no inferior Palatine wool yarn. It is such poor, badly made stuff that it would be a shame to put it into a work of such perfection. House Ransis would be ashamed to use such inferior stuff."

Ransis frowned through the darkness at the tall slave. "That is all?" he asked.

"That is all," Alvis answered.

Ransis dragged his teeth over his lower lip as he thought. After a moment he nodded a short nod of agreement. "House Ransis will not be ashamed of its materials this time. I will use no inferior yarn. This work will be worthy of notice by the very Gods because of its perfection."

"And House Ransis will be honored until the Design is worked out at the end of time for its attention to detail," Alvis said.

The old man looked at the slave for a long time, then that one softened and smiled as at a beloved grandfather. At last the slave bowed deeply to the old man and left without another word.

Eleven

604 A.C.G.

Lord Baroth Linser was in a vile mood and his servants were relieved when at last he shouted, "Get out. Leave me in peace."

They knew he was capable of having any or all of them flogged, tortured or executed solely because he was feeling disconsolate.

The private quarters of the Chief Priest were opulent, with thick carpets on the floor, costly hangings on the walls and furniture custom built with shortened legs to fit Linser's disproportionate body.

Linser slumped in a large chair which looked rather like a throne. That appearance was enhanced by the chair having been placed upon a dais raised three steps above floor level. This raising of the chair was for pretension and that Linser would always be taller than those who came to the private quarters on business.

Now he leaned his infantesque head upon his left hand, unconsciously gnawing at the fleshy heel of his hand. He did not notice that his teeth had already pierced the flesh and brought blood. His mind was on Dimar Ransis. The insults the Patriarch of House Ransis had dealt him were galling. The man was an affront by his very existence and only Linser's need of him kept the old man's head on his shoulders. Linser promised himself to see House Ransis destroyed as soon as the tapestry was in his hands. He would bring the old man to the temple dungeon and break his arms and legs, then parade each of his sons, daughters, brothers, sisters and servants before him. The old man would watch as each of them were disemboweled.

The priest smiled at the thought and for the first time noticed the taste of blood. He took his hand away from his mouth and looked at the scarred ruin where he had bitten himself before. He started to call his body servant, Morat, but thought better of it and went to his bath. He returned with a soft white towel, the cost of which would have fed a poor family in Peshar for a year. He held it tight against the bleeding wound and returned to his throne. His thoughts returned to House Ransis.

Perhaps I should only disembowel the blood kin of Ransis, he thought. *The servants I could sell across the sky at a profit...if the gods continue on Archlea.* Linser shoved that thought forcefully away. He did not want to think of this, but in the last year it had never been far from his mind.

When Linser had first been an acolyte in the great Temple at Peshar, the Gods had passed through the temple's Hall of Doors in their thousands. Some had even stopped for a time to study the planet Archlea. That was the Gods' name for the world, so Linser thought of it by that name too, but only when he was thinking of the Gods. Otherwise, it was simply the world.

Linser knew more about the world, by whatever name, than did most of the people upon it. He knew it was round like a ball. He had seen it from space when the Gods had initiated him into the priesthood. From that journey he knew the world was round and much larger than most people thought. Much larger.

Soon after his initiation he had been taken with a party of Gods to the far south. The journey would have taken a year by the conventional means of foot and pack animals, but the Gods did not wish to waste so much time. Instead they brought a thing which resembled a sky ship, but this machine was much smaller. Linser had been afraid when first put aboard, but soon he came to enjoy the wonder of skimming across the earth above the trees at such a speed it made the ground below blur. This ship had taken the party to the far south where steaming forests covered all.

Linser had accounted well for himself on that expedition. He had been brought along to translate the barbarous Southron tongue into the Divine Language and vice versa. This was not easy. The Southron language bore only the slightest resemblance to the Peshari he spoke, but

Linser did his best. Sometimes he had to guess what the Southrons were saying, but his translations seemed acceptable to the Gods and that was the important thing.

But now the flood of Gods through the Hall of Doors had slowed to a trickle. Seldom did any God, save those who maintained the Hall of Doors, ever stop now. Even the God-Resident was seldom seen. Linser was the only mortal allowed inside the holy apartments, and only then when he was summoned. In the last year he had been summoned only twice and both times he had felt the God-Resident's worry. There had been a quivering nervousness which was out of place. One who commanded the power of a god should not fear anything, but the God-Resident seemed consumed with fear. It was infectious and Linser caught it.

The fear became less nebulous when the Gods who maintained the Hall of Doors began placing FORBIDDEN signs and god-shields in places which had never been forbidden before. The signs and the god-shields did not stay long. A day or two. A week or two. When the signs and the god-shields disappeared, whatever had been behind them was no longer there.

Such was the case with the kitchen which had once served those Gods who stayed for a time in the temple. It had once been a bustling place with many cooks and lights bright as the sun, but the signs and the god-shields had gone up and in a few days the kitchen was gone. The whole room and all the mechanical servants in it were gone.

Linser had stood before the FORBIDDEN sign placed upon what had been the door to the kitchen, and knew what was happening. In the very pit of his stomach he knew the Gods were leaving Peshar. He was not sure if they were only leaving the Peshar temple, making it less important, or if they were withdrawing from Archlea itself. He tried to convince himself that they had only built a new temple somewhere else, perhaps far to the south, but even as he thought it Baroth Linser knew he was wrong. If this were true why would the God-Resident radiate such fear?

No, this was no simple move away from Peshar. The Gods were preparing to abandon Archlea, and that meant abandoning their servants as well. Linser was almost paralyzed at the thought of being left behind. To be left on Archlea without the power of the Gods was a death sentence. The Servants of the Gods might bluff the people for a while, but there was enough rebellion just beneath the surface to make bluffs wear thin quickly. Then the people would rise, not against the Gods, but against the Servants of the Gods. Linser, the Corps of Priests and the Temple Servants were hated, even as the Gods were feared. If word passed that Linser and the other temple servants were no longer favored by the Gods, there would be a blood bath.

The day Baroth Linser came to the conclusion the Gods were preparing to abandon Archlea he began seeking some way to get them to take him along. He began thinking of some way to bribe the God-Resident. There must be something, but it had to be something very special to tempt a god.

About that time fortune had turned Linser's way. An informant, one of the Chief Priest's network of spies, had overheard two men concluding an illicit transaction. One man had a manuscript written in the old tongue. The man could not read the manuscript. Few could. To possess anything written in ancient Peshari was illegal, and had been for centuries. The man had probably never seen more than a few letters of the old tongue written down, but he recognized the manuscript as both danger and fortune. Decree of the Gods notwithstanding, there was a thriving black market in ancient books, so the man was trying to sell the manuscript.

Those involved in the transaction were taken into custody and questioned until they were wrung dry, then they were sold across the sky. That manuscript and several others the men's information led to came into the priest's possession. He should have turned the cache over to the God-Resident, but when Linser came to the altar to request audience, no answer came. This was unheard of. The God-Resident always answered within seconds, or minutes at most. This time there was no answer.

The priest was sunk in terror. He was sure the end was upon them. For twenty days in a row he returned to the altar, but the God-Resident did not answer. The Gods had abandoned them without so much as a good-bye, but he could not let such knowledge go out of the temple. He stopped going to the altar and began desperately studying the manuscripts himself, hoping some return to the old gods might save him. He had the rudiments of the old tongue. He had been taught it as an acolyte, for a priest must know how to recognize what is forbidden.

In one of the manuscripts he found mention of a cache of things left by one Javi Holis before his death. This Holis had been a believer in some ancient god called the Designer at the time the first sky ships had brought the True Gods to rule Archlea. He was one man the Gods would have liked to bring into their presence, but he had slipped through their nets time after time. He had never been caught, and it was written that in his last days he had collected a huge treasure of art, including many pre-Gods tapestries and books. Among the books was supposed to be one called the Book of Designs or some such thing. This was supposed to contain representations of tapestries so ancient that their origins were lost in the dimness of time.

After forty more days the God-Resident returned. Linser was flooded with relief, but it was short-lived. The God-Resident called him in and required a report of what had happened in his absence.

"Some pages of the ancient language were discovered, my Lord," Linser said toward the end of his report.

The God-Resident's attention suddenly sharpened. "Really? How ancient?"

"Very old, my Lord. Some were completely unreadable."

"Drawings?"

"No, my Lord, only pages of scribbles."

Linser saw interest fade from the God-Resident's eyes.

"And how have you dealt with the matter, Linser?"

"As usual, my Lord," the Priest lied. "Those in possession were questioned then sent through the Hall of Doors to be sold. I requested an audience with you my Lord, to allow you to rule on the material, but there was no answer for such a long time I deemed it necessary to go ahead and deal with the cursed things in the usual way, rather than have them remain to perhaps contaminate the temple."

Linser bowed low to the ground at this, but he did not miss the look of annoyance which passed over the God-Resident's face.

"Very well, Linser. You have done well. But next time, if there is a next time, do not destroy the material until I give leave."

"Yes, my Lord," he answered.

After this Linser began an on-going search for ancient writings. Through this search he discovered the link between the tapestry *The Gods Show Mercy* and the cache.

The link was not clear, but everything pointed to the tapestry as some kind of guide so Linser bought a copy, but, study it as he would, he could make nothing of it. If it were a guide or a map, it was not clear even to one who knew what it was supposed to contain. He studied it and asked questions about it and in doing so he discovered his copy was not an exact copy. And he discovered, to his frustration, that no true copy of the tapestry existed. He bought up twenty and each one was slightly different from the others. Each artist who copied the great work added or subtracted or changed it to make it his own rather than simply a re-doing of the classic work.

All the copies had the same basic theme. Each showed Tapestry Plaza with a crowd of cowering Pesharis beside the major tapestry being displayed in the plaza. At the other side, facing the crowd, were three Gods in black armor. Sky ships floated above the plaza, and in the right background a Sky ship was landing. Beneath it a crowd of horrified people crouched, about to be crushed by the weight of the ship. The agony of each face was distinct and separate though the figures were very small. The tapestry commemorated the final victory of the Gods. Legend said the Gods had stopped short of total destruction because of the beauty of the tapestries in the plaza, and particularly because of the main work. This tapestry was central to the focus of *The Gods Show Mercy*. The eye was drawn away from the cunning detail of the faces of the crowd and the precise representation of the square, and was drawn to the tapestry which had stopped the destruction.

That tapestry was a stylized picture of a village set in a deep, purple-shadowed vale surrounded by mountains pointed and sharp as the teeth of a saw.

Linser at first thought the village in the picture was the location of the cache, but study showed that there were a thousand such villages. This could be any one of them. Apparently, that had been the intention of the artist.

But each of the copies was different! Sometimes the changes were small—a few faces changed, some body positions changed, but sometimes the changes were major. Sometimes the tapestry pictured within the tapestry was completely different; or there were more Gods, or more sky ships.

Finally, Linser decided to go directly to the source. He commissioned House Ransis to make him an exact copy of the original work. That was why Baroth Linser, Chief Priest of the Temple of Peshar, Chief Servant of the Gods on Archlea was willing to swallow the insults of Dimar Ransis. At least until he had the true copy in his hands.

~ * ~

Garith Balal's clientele increased in number and quality when word of the contract between House Ransis and the Chief Priest leaked out.

The leak was easily arranged. Merta was a very effective rumormonger. She told Alsai Kruth and a few others and begged them to keep the news quiet. This assured the spread. It began to pay dividends within days.

A servant from House Kushar came to inquire if this was indeed the place of business of one Garith Balal who had witnessed the contract between Lord Ransis and Lord Linser. He was assured with many bows and a pot of fresh tea and some of Merta's crusty-sweet anise cookies that this was that same Scribe. Shortly thereafter Lord Kushar asked if Garith would be so kind as to witness a contract for him. Garith happily agreed and witnessed, copied, and filed the contract between House Kushar and House Adnash for the joining of their two houses in marriage.

Word of this contract did not need to leak out. It was posted in the little shop and all concerned talked of nothing else for days. Customers began to flood the little shop. So many wanted fair copies that Alvis was busy from first light until his eyes blurred with darkness. Garith was so busy witnessing and filing contracts he could seldom help his slave with the copying. This flood of clients was quickly turning into a curse of wealth. Both master and slave were always on the ragged edge of exhaustion and sometimes snapped at one another or at Merta.

But ill tempers did not take the shine off the new wealth so far as Merta was concerned. She was in paradise. She used the new money well and never let go of so much as a tenth Zari without receiving good value for it. She had the shop decorated as much as Garith would allow, which was not much. He allowed her to have the inside white washed and to replace the old lamps with new, and even to add a few more for the sake of his and Alvis' eyes, but he drew the line when she tried to replace his tall desk.

"Those seeking my skills see this solid old desk and the old but well cared for cabinets and think, 'Here is a man to be trusted.'"

"But new furniture would make you look prosperous," Merta argued.

"It would make me look like a marketplace letter writer trying to impress his clients with fancy lap desk and colored inks rather than proper work."

Merta lifted a hand toward the sky as if to say, witness all Gods, my husband is a fool, but she said nothing. She went on spending money on finer clothes, finer food, and new furniture for the little house. She spent all the extra that came into the shop and kept doing it day after day. House Balal was never in debt, but seemed always to be on the edge of slipping over into it.

One evening Garith and Alvis were bent over the shop desk when Merta brought them tea and told them food would be ready soon.

"Bring it to us," Garith said without looking up from his work.

"Again? You have not eaten at the table for days. I cannot remember the last time we actually went to bed at the same time," she complained.

Garith looked up and his heart melted at the look she was giving him. But then he remembered the stack of contracts which must be finished before the morning and the cost of the new wall hanging Merta had purchased for the dining room and the melting froze again.

"Just bring the food, Merta," he snapped. "I cannot take time to be civil and eat in the dining room."

"Then I wish we were as we were before the Chief Priest came to us," she blurted.

It was a remark of anger. She did not mean it. She would not have gone back to the old ways if she *could* have.

"Really?" Garith answered, drawing the word out to a sarcastic point.

"Yes, really," she snapped back. "How can I impress neighbors— how can *we* rise in social standing, when my husband is seen as no better than his slave? You never do anything but work. Social standing is built on being seen at the temple and in the wine shops and tea houses of Tapestry Plaza, and in company with others of great houses."

"I cannot be in two places at once. Alvis cannot keep up with the work alone. Every day more people want me to witness their contracts. I do not have time to sip tea in Tapestry Plaza. Now will you PLEASE bring the food?"

"Then why not go back to the auction and bring home another Alvis?"

Garith threw down his pen and ink spattered from it to blot the copy he had been working on. He drew a deep breath and held his temper only by force of will.

"That is ridiculous," he said with a softness belied by the veins standing out on his neck. "Finding Alvis was purest luck. A blessing from the Gods. If you'll remember, I went to buy a house drudge. It was only through the grace of the Gods that Alvis came to the block, and only through my astuteness that I paid what you thought an outrageous price for him. To have such luck twice in one lifetime is impossible."

"But we must do something," she said plaintively. "I miss you,"

Alvis had not looked up from his work, but he had been listening. Now he looked up and said, "If the Master and Mistress will allow me?"

"Oh, do be quiet Alvis," Merta cried. "This is not a matter for you. You are only a slave."

"Alvis is no common slave, wife," Garith growled. "He has much to do with the silken rags on your back and I will not have you abuse him because you are piqued at me. Alvis is my friend as well as my slave. I might almost say he is more family than slave."

Merta's face reddened. "Family? FAMILY? HOW DARE YOU? How dare you say such a thing. How dare you even think it? I am Merta Balal, owner of slaves. Not kin to them."

Garith's temper snapped. He stood and raised his hand to strike his wife.

A look of horror came across her face and seeing it Garith stopped his hand even as it was moving down to strike. He dropped his hand, but the anger still in him made him shout, "Silence! I will have no further insult to Alvis, and no more back talk from you about anything."

"Master, please," Alvis said quietly. "I thank you for your defense, but Mistress Merta is right. I am a slave and I regret that I forgot my place for a moment."

Garith and Merta both stared, open-mouthed at Alvis, whose head was once more lowered to work. After a moment Merta said, "You see, husband. Alvis knows his place. He is happy in his place. You should be grateful lest you go about calling him brother in public and embarrass yourself."

Garith twisted his mouth to contain the words in it and raised his eyebrows at Alvis. He saw what the slave was doing and it did not make him happy. Alvis had learned quickly to control his mistress through her vanity and hunger for position. All he needed do was bow and scrape a little, and his deference translated to easy management of her. Garith did not like to see his wife manipulated, but, in this case, it was to his advantage to keep quiet about it. Still, he wondered what means Alvis had devised to manipulate him.

"Please explain to your master what alternative we have to the slave market?" Merta purred.

Alvis put down his pen. "There are two choices, actually. The first is to hire another man to copy, as you hired the men to take over the letter writing."

Garith began to say something, but Alvis continued before he could get it out.

"And this might be worthwhile if you can find a trustworthy man soon enough. On the other hand, I have knowledge of a slave who might be had at a good price. To purchase him will not cost too much and he will be an investment against the future, rather than a constant drain upon the profit of the shop."

"And this one reads and writes like you?" Garith asked, interested.

"His hand is more fair than mine, though he is somewhat slower."

"And he can be had at a decent price?" Merta asked.

Alvis shrugged. "What is decent? He will cost what I cost, probably, but perhaps you can bargain for him. He belongs to Lord Fithian, and House Fithian is in need of coin."

"The temple license on such a purchase is cheaper than one issued to buy at the auction," Merta said, forefinger stroking her chin.

"And we will know what we are buying." Garith said, thinking out loud.

"Such a slave will sell quickly, Garith," Merta said.

"Yes. Therefore, you will go to House Fithian tomorrow at first light while I go to the temple for the license. Gods," Garith stopped short, struck by a terrible thought. "Have we enough ready Zari for such a purchase?"

"That is the least of our worries, my Lord Husband," Merta said grinning.

Garith was puzzled by this, but said nothing.

"I will strike a bargain which will be the stuff of legend," Merta said.

"Do not be too sharp, wife, or Lord Fithian will sell to someone less parsimonious."

"He will sell to no one else. I will see to that," she smiled.

"Very well. Now, may we please have something to eat?" Garith picked up his pen and frowned at the blotted copy before him.

"I will bring it quickly, husband," Merta said. Her smile changed from predatory to tender. "Perhaps tomorrow might see us at the table together while two slaves work for us."

Garith grunted, already immersed in the copy before him.

It did not occur to him until much later to wonder how Alvis, who seldom left the shop, knew of the slave or of House Fithian's need of coin.

Twelve

604 A.C.G.

The new slave was called Lakis, and he was everything Alvis had promised. He could read, and he wrote a fair hand, and he was not averse to helping Merta with the drudge work of the house.

Garith had suffered through the bureaucratic nightmare of obtaining the license, standing in lines most of the day to get the necessary stamps of permission. Even so, it was better than what he had gone through to get the license to buy Alvis. That had taken a half dozen more stamps and cost an equivalent amount more – plus cumshaw.

Lakis and Alvis seemed to be well acquainted, though Garith could not imagine how they might have met. Alvis never spent much time anywhere except the shop. But, as with many other things about Alvis, Garith wondered about it only a short while. The odd things he should have wondered about didn't seem to matter after a little while. Nor did the fact that Lakis and Alvis shared belief in the Design and disdain for the gods. That should have made Garith nervous, but it didn't.

With the coming of Lakis the burden of work eased. Garith even had time to frequent the tea shops on Tapestry Plaza, though still not enough to satisfy Merta. She nagged him unmercifully about being seen with people of quality. "That is the only way House Balal will rise to its rightful place," she insisted.

"House Balal?" Garith snorted. "There is no House Balal. And we do not have a son to carry on the name even if there was. House Balal indeed. I am a poor Fair Witness and Scribe. Such a one is not called House Balal."

"There will be a son…" Merta began.

"You mean…" excitement thrilled up Garith's spine.

"No, no, no," she said waving her hand at him. "Not yet. But it will happen soon if only you will take your nose out of your ink pots long enough to come to bed."

"Well, there is the afternoon."

Merta looked first incensed, then embarrassed.

"But no," Garith went on. "You do not want that. You would rather have me sitting in a tea shop, pretending to be House Balal."

Merta blushed and worked her mouth, but no sound came out.

Garith caught himself before he laughed, but Merta saw and stormed out of the shop. Then Garith did laugh, though he felt bad about it a moment later.

"If she had her way, I would never work at all," he said to no one in particular. "But I must admit, it is pleasant to sit in the presence of so many learned and talented men and be considered almost their equal."

"Almost, Master?" Alvis asked, not looking up from his work.

"Yes, almost. I could never be an equal of these men, no matter what the Matriarch of House Balal says. They are much better than I. I am only a simple tradesman. Hardly better than a market square letter writer."

Lakis, sitting at a new, smaller desk, looked up from his work. "I should think you their superior, Master. After all you have the confidence of the clergy."

Garith shivered with revulsion. "Please," he said, "the very thought of Lord Linser and his thousand grasping minions makes my flesh creep."

The words were barely out of his mouth before he was looking around in fear that he had been overheard.

The two slaves laughed. Alvis said, "Perhaps we are having some influence on the Pious Scribe after all, Lakis."

Garith whirled upon Alvis. "Do not mock me, slave," he growled. "I am a servant of the Gods and a respecter of the clergy. I will not have you speaking blasphemy under my roof. Now get back to work."

The two ducked their heads and applied their eyes to their work.

Garith glared at their bowed heads, then stormed out the door into the street. He was more angry at himself than at what the slaves had said. He was annoyed that they had gotten to him so easily. He knew he should ignore them and go back to work, but it was difficult. In their presence a small voice at the back of his mind kept whispering that the Gods were not Gods at all.

When this thought crept from the back to the front of the scribe's mind, he tried to shove it back under cover, but it would not go. *What if the Gods were not Gods?* he thought. *What if they were only ruthless, heartless conquerors who were godlike in their power, but were not Gods at all?*

BAH, Garith thought. *What does it matter anyway? I do not care whether the Gods are Gods or not. All I want is to be left alone! I almost wish Lord Ransis and that accursed priest had never set foot in my shop.*

That thought brought him up short.

"Fool. Where would you be without them?" he said to no one in particular. "You'd still be scratching letters to grandmothers for a pittance, that's were. Now you are richer and busier…" He lifted his hand to the skies. "So, what am I doing here? I should be back at the shop working."

He suddenly realized he had been talking aloud and waving his arms around like a mad man.

That is all I need, he thought. *If someone sees me wandering around the streets talking to myself, and waving at some invisible birds fluttering around my head, all the trust built up in the last year will disappear like fog under a hot sun.*

But no one seemed to have noticed. Garith quietly thanked the Gods and walked on, his thoughts still full of Gods and slaves.

They had reached no resolution when he found himself at the edge of Tapestry Plaza. He hadn't even known he was headed that way, but was happy to find himself there.

The weather was fine: clear and cool and dry. Many artists were taking advantage of the fine weather to display their work. Painters, singers, jugglers, clowns, poets reciting their own work or classic work found only in the minds of the people of Peshar, for to possess them in anything but memory was against Divine Law. The cafes and tea shops were filled with people being entertained by the performers. It was a kaleidoscope which lifted the spirit and drove perplexity away.

And above all were the tapestries. The mixture of color and movement in the Plaza was breath taking and the tapestries were like magnets drawing the scribe in.

A sweet aroma of honey cakes and spice tea tickled Garith's nose and brought home the fact that he had not eaten since dawn. He lifted his nose into the gentle breeze like a hunting hound and drew in the aroma of chicken in wine sauce with its overtones of onion and pepper. There was only one cafe that produced such a wonderful dish. Garith turned toward the flapping yellow awning of Cafe Turca.

The Plaza tables of the cafe were jammed, and Garith was sad to see that. Nothing was better than to take a leisurely noon meal at one of the broad tables in the cool shade of Turca's awning, while watching the strolling players and listening to the hum of conversation. This was as near to paradise as Garith ever expected to come…but that dream was out of reach at the moment, so he wound through the tables and went inside.

The dining room was crowded too. Garith feared his stomach was destined to disappointment, but a voice called to him.

"Scribe Balal. Garith."

Garith spotted Lord Ransis gesturing to him.

"Would you honor me by taking this chair, Scribe Balal?" the Patriarch of House Ransis asked, smiling.

Flattered at such an offer Garith bowed his thanks and sat.

"Turca can always be sure of a crowd when he serves chicken in wine sauce," Ransis said, still smiling.

"The aroma of it is all over the Plaza," Garith agreed. "I might even say it reaches all the way to my shop, for I did not even know I was coming here until I found myself pulled along by my nose." Garith laughed. He was gratified when Lord Ransis chuckled too.

A servant hurried to the table and with great deference asked, "What is the pleasure of the Gentles this fine day?"

Garith let Lord Ransis order portions of the chicken and a pitcher of cooled wine and was overcome with respect for the man when this great Lord thanked the servant for his service. Then he turned back to Garith.

"I trust everything is well with House Balal," the old man said stroking his beard.

Garith almost laughed, remembering Merta's words. "Everything is very well indeed, Lord Ransis. Business is good. In fact, I have had to buy another slave to help me in the shop."

A shadow passed over the old man's face and was gone almost before it appeared. "That is wonderful," he said.

"I owe much of this success to you, Lord Ransis. Without your patronage I would still be a simple writer of letters."

"Permit me to doubt that, Scribe Balal. You had a reputation for honesty and speed before. That is why I chose you. And I am sure your reputation as an upright servant of the Gods influenced the Chief Priest."

"Perhaps, my Lord, but still, I thank you for your trust."

The waiter returned with wine and cups. Garith reached for the pitcher to pour for Lord Ransis, but he was too slow. The old man poured for them and shoved a cup toward Garith.

Both men sipped, and took a moment to savor the tartness of the wine.

"Is House Ransis making progress on *The Gods Show Mercy*?" Garith asked after a bit.

Again, the shadow passed over Ransis' face. Garith feared he had been too forward and offended the man, but Ransis erased that worry in a second.

"It is almost finished. We will be completed in time to display it here, if the weather holds."

"Wonderful, wonderful," the scribe said, then more quietly, "In truth, I feared for you, Lord Ransis. I have seen some copies of *The Gods Show Mercy*. It is so intricate and detailed. I feared a year might be too short a time. But I should have known you would never have entered into a contract you could not fulfill."

"Your fears were not much misplaced, Scribe Balal. Materials were difficult to find. Since the contract called for an exact replica of the original, that meant finding yarn of the exact type used in the original.

Some of those yarns have not been spun in a hundred or more years. Not to mention the dyeing. There was a particular blue which was near impossible to reproduce. The dyer mixed it more than a hundred times before finding the right match."

Lord Ransis sipped his wine and sighed like a man who was weary, but satisfied with his labor. "I am happy to have the thing near completion," he placed his cup back on the table but continued to toy with it, turning it and making wet rings with the bottom.

"It must have been a great labor," Garith said. "I wonder why Lord Linser wanted so exact a copy?"

Lords Ransis' eyes fixed upon the scribe's face, looking for some motive other than simple conversation—but he found nothing, only a man flattered to be in esteemed company and trying hard to make conversation worthy of the occasion. "Only the Gods know," Ransis said and sipped his wine.

The afternoon wound away in conversation and good food and Lord Ransis was well satisfied—even a little sorry—when the scribe took his leave. Ransis was satisfied that Balal either knew nothing of the tapestry, or was a much better actor than any scribe should be.

Ransis left Cafe Turca and went to the factory. His meeting with the scribe had not been planned, but Ransis was glad it had happened. It eased his mind in one way, but it still left him with questions about the slave, Alvis. Since the night the slave had visited him, he had worried that the secret of the tapestry was more common knowledge than he had been taught. In truth he did not know what the secret was, only that there was one. He had not lied to Alvis in any way. The knowledge that there was a secret had been passed to him by his father the day before the old man died. Dimar Ransis could not think of that day without a knot tying tight in his stomach.

Old Ransis, Dimar's father had been ill for a long time. At the end he had wasted away to nothing but sick yellow skin and brittle bones. He was in great pain, and most of the time he was out of his mind with it, but on the last day he had risen from the sea of agony with dreadful lucidity.

Old Ransis called for his eldest son then sent all others from the room. When they were gone, he took his son's hand. "Dimar, you must listen now and do not interrupt. I do not have much time left."

Young Ransis began to protest, but his father squeezed his hand with such strength that the protests died, and he said, "Yes, father."

"House Ransis is possessed of a great shame, which is in reality a great honor," the shrunken skeleton on the bed began. "You have heard the name Javi Holis." It was not a question.

Fear gripped Young Ransis' bowels, and he said, "No father, I have never heard the name," though he had heard it whispered many times. He knew it was a name which was deadly dangerous.

Old Ransis smiled horribly. "Yes, you have, and this is no time to play the protesting fool. I know very well that mention of that name could mean death if it fell into the wrong ear, therefore, you must never mention it again until the time comes to tell your own eldest son what I am about to tell you."

Dimar could not look at the skull-like face of the man on the bed. He only nodded his assent and listened as his father told him the story of Indi Ransis and Javi Holis, and how that man with two names had resisted the gods with all his might, even unto death.

"Before Indi Ransis died, he gathered many things together and hid them. They are the true treasures of Peshar, which have never fallen into the hands of the gods. And chief among these treasures is the Book of Design. It tells of the old ways and of the old Gods. The true Gods whose creations we are."

Young Ransis had shivered. Blasphemers were subject to death or slavery. "Stop this, Father," he begged. "You are delirious and you speak nonsense. Our Gods are the true Gods."

"No," The old man shouted and tried to sit up. He grabbed the front of Dimar's robe and pulled feebly. "No, these creatures are beings like us," he gasped and began coughing in deep racking spasms which brought blood speckled mucous to his lips.

Young Ransis dropped to his knees and tried to help the old man, but there was little he could do. He supported the old man in his arms until the coughing subsided. It took a long time.

"Before Javi Holis died," the old man continued, "he hid these treasures. The secret of them he left with us, with House Ransis. We must guard that secret until the old gods see fit to return the old ways to us."

Dimar Ransis swallowed hard, but made no more protests.

"The secret is hidden in the tapestry *The Gods Show Mercy*," the old man said. "The weaving, the material, the picture, I do not know. I believe all parts have some part of the secret, but I do not know. I do not know how to decipher the secret, but someday someone will come who does know. That one will bring the treasures forth and teach the people of the true gods again. That one will destroy these beasts who call themselves gods."

Old Ransis drew a painful wheezing breath and allowed his son to lay him back on his pillow.

"But Father, the gods have *The Gods Show Mercy*. We do not have it. The ancient patriarch who wove and stitched that work presented it to the temple and the Gods took it across the sky."

The old man breathed in short shallow gasps. "We have the detail work. The stitch pattern, the color, the weaving pattern. We do not need the tapestry."

"But…"

The old man lifted his hand a little above the coverlet and said, "That is all I know. Remember what I have told you. Speak it to no one else, ever, until time to tell the next Patriarch of House Ransis. Meanwhile, pray to the true gods, especially to mighty Pesh, that they may soon send the one for whom we wait."

Old Ransis had died within a few hours of passing this tale along. Dimar Ransis had thought it the delusions of a sick old man until Baroth Linser had contracted for an exact copy of the tapestry. He remembered the tale then, and when the slave Alvis came with dire warnings about not giving Linser an exact copy, the tale became more than a tale.

Ransis thought of this as he checked the progress of the copy. It was finished save the last few knots to secure it from unraveling. It was ready to be removed from the loom. He ran his hand over the back, which was the side the weaver always saw. Those who had added relief stitching to the picture saw the front, but the weaver, the true master creator of the tapestry, never saw the front until the work was finished, but Ransis did not need to see the front. His mind's eye could see the whole design as clearly as if he looked at the original.

Linser was not to be trusted. Lord Ransis knew that. He also knew in the depths of his heart that Linser knew more about the tapestry and its secret than was good. That was why the priest had demanded so perfect a copy. The real question was, could he decipher the secret?

Ransis doubted it. The possibility had not even given him any worries. What had given him sleepless nights as the tapestry came closer to completion was, when Linser received the work and was unable to decipher it, might he come back to House Ransis and try to force the secret from them? Such a thing could mean the end of House Ransis. They had nothing to tell, and all the pain Linser could inflict could not change that. But the Chief Priest would not believe it. The man would keep on until House Ransis was no more. But what could be done? What could be done to save House Ransis?

~ * ~

Baroth Linser sat at his desk in his private chambers. The desk was strewn with manuscripts written in the ancient tongue. Thus far none of them had been of any use. The few references made to the cache were oblique at best. Once, Linser had become excited because a phrase "For the Book of the Design says we always see only the back of the weaving. The true Design is forever out of understanding," but that had proved as useless as the rest. It was some mystical nonsense that made no reference to the hiding place of the cache or its contents.

A soft tapping at the chamber door brought the Priest out of the manuscript with a start. A thrill of stomach-churning fear crept over him. The manuscripts, thrown so carelessly on his desk, were contraband. They should have been handed over to the God-Resident the instant they were discovered, but Linser had stopped releasing manuscripts to the God-Resident unexamined.

After a moment Linser controlled his fear telling himself he was a fool. After all, the God-Resident would hardly be tapping on his door.

"Come," Linser growled.

Morat, Linser's body servant, slipped into the room. He bowed low and remained bent until Linser said, "Well, what is it?"

"Your pardon, Lord Linser, there is one who would speak with you."

"And who is this one, fool? Has he a name?"

"No, my Lord. That is, I mean, yes, my Lord. He has a name, my Lord, I suppose, but he would not give it. He said to introduce him as a servant of the Gods and an eye of Lord Linser."

The priest straightened. "I will see him in the audience chamber," he said, standing.

Morat bent and backed out of the room, never showing his face.

The spy was one who worked in the tapestry factory of House Ransis. Linser was quite happy to see him.

"My Lord," the man said. "*The Gods Show Mercy* is being taken off the loom at this moment. Lord Ransis said it should be taken to the Plaza tomorrow or the next day, depending on the weather."

Linser smiled, and the spy answered with a toady's grin.

"Very well," the priest said. He drew a one hundred Zari coin from the pouch which hung from his belt and threw it to the man. "See that you forget where you have been."

"I have already lost all memory, my Lord," he said bowing himself to the floor and backing out the door.

"Morat," Linser shouted as soon as the door closed behind the spy. The servant appeared as if by magic. "Send the Captain of the Guard."

"Yes, My Lord," he said and disappeared as swiftly as he had come.

The priest leaned his elbow upon the arm of his chair and stroked his smooth face, congratulating himself. He was still smiling the same self-satisfied smile when the Captain of the Guard came.

~ * ~

The bright light of twenty torches and the rattle of armor against itself caught Dimar Ransis in one of the shallow dozes his night's sleep had become. He woke, startled and disoriented. At first, he thought the red robed temple guards kicking in his door were part of a nightmare, but that evaporated when the brutal hands hauled him from bed and rained blows upon him before any word was spoken.

The guards bound and gagged him and marched him through the sleeping streets of Peshar in his night clothes. They took him and the others from the house to the temple, but not into the temple court yard. Instead they went to an iron-bound door guarded by two armed men. The door opened and the prisoners were prodded down a narrow winding stair which ended in a small room with dark corridors leading from it. The prisoners were separated and two guards pushed Ransis down one of the narrow corridors. They passed many doors before they opened one and shoved Ransis into a cell. His arms were still bound to his sides and a gag was still in his mouth. He lost his balance with the shove and fell flat on his face.

The door lock resisted the key, but, at last, turned with a grind. Lord Dimar Ransis was locked in a cell only slightly larger than a grave and just as dark. The guards clanked away down the corridor. He was left lying face down on the slimy floor of the cell, shaking so hard from fear and outrage that he lost control of his bowels and bladder. The only sound was the thump of his heart and the hum of blood in his ears. He knew he was a dead man and House Ransis with him, and there was nothing he could do about it. Had he not been bound he would have sought a way to end his life before Chief Priest Linser could do it for him, but the bonds were tight and strong. He could only lie on the floor and weep.

~ * ~

The tea shops were abuzz with rumor, but talk was furtive. Men talked, but did so with backs hunched away from those only a table away, as though that small increase of distance could make the words less dangerous. All were asking what had happened? All felt the need to express opinions, but also felt the sick mistrust of everyone else. Men who had been friends since childhood looked at each other from the sides of their eyes and wondered if the other was an informer for the Chief Priest; wondered if temple guards would kick in their doors in the middle of the night to march them off to doom.

Garith Balal had no opinion when he sat down. He wondered what all the buzz was about. Silence was an island around him, and a crawling feeling went along his neck. He could feel the eyes upon him, though he never caught anyone looking at him.

The furtive glances prodded the scribe to rise and go to the table of Makala Juris, another scribe of good repute, to find out what was happening.

Juris' eyes betrayed his unease when Garith bid him good morning.

"And to you, Master Balal," he answered. He did not extend an invitation to sit down.

"Why is everyone so quiet this morning?" Garith asked.

Juris' eyebrows rose in surprise. "Have you not heard? Temple guards took Dimar Ransis, his family, and several who are in his employ to the temple last night."

Garith's heart skipped. "But why?"

Juris looked around as though expecting to find a thousand ears cocked to hear, but finding none he said, "Who knows? Lord Ransis was a well-known scoffer at the clergy—especially the Chief Priest. Perhaps he let his mouth carry him into trouble."

"But what has that to do with me?"

With lowered voice Juris said, "It is well known that you and Ransis… Only yesterday you and he were sitting together at Cafe Turca. His patronage has been the making of your reputation."

Garith's anger flashed. "Lord Baroth Linser has been my patron also. Those two men sought me out to witness their contract. I did not solicit them," he said hotly, loud enough to cause heads to turn.

"Please, Master Balal – I did not mean offense. It is only that any" Juris looked like a mouse wary of cats, "that anyone seen with Lord Ransis is automatically to be feared."

"What?" Garith sputtered. "Why every man here would have been honored, would have paid a hundred—a thousand Zari to be seen in the company of Lord Ransis yesterday."

Makala Juris dropped his eyes to his tea cup, acknowledging what the scribe had said, but that was yesterday. Today Ransis was a prisoner and House Ransis was finished. Ancient and powerful as it had been, House Ransis was finished.

Garith straightened himself and turned away. He did not return to his table, and all eyes followed him as he walked out of the tea shop.

Outrage and fear mingled in Garith's mind as he walked toward his shop. He was a moving blot of silence in the teeming city. Everyone he brushed glanced furtively at him and fell quiet, as though his very presence might infect them.

He burst through the bead curtain of his front door and stood a moment, hearing the clack of the strings of beads behind him and feeling a little safer when they made a barrier between him and the outside world.

Alvis was alone in the shop. He saw Garith's trouble in his stance. "What is it, Master?" he asked, rising from the desk.

Garith drew a deep breath and choked back the urge to weep. He could see all that he had worked for crumbling and dread of the future was a corpse's hand squeezing his heart.

"Dimar Ransis was taken in chains to the temple last night," he said.

Alvis laid down his pen with great care, his face a mask. "I had hoped such a thing was not in the Design," he said.

Master and slave looked at one another for the length of several heartbeats.

"What is to be done now?" Garith asked the man who was more than his slave.

~ * ~

Temple guards surrounded the Ransis tapestry factory. They stopped and questioned anyone who came near the doors, even some who were simply walking past. Alvis observed them from the door of a cloth shop a hundred steps away. The cloth seller was a Servant of the Design. Alvis had met him through a sweeping use of the Mandala called The Ear. There were several such servants in Peshar. They had gone on believing and serving the Design generation after generation; keeping to themselves, waiting for they knew not what. But waiting with patience.

Now Alvis stood in the shop and observed, not calling attention to himself.

"They have been there since last night, Master Alvis," Icar the cloth merchant said. "I heard them come clanking along sometime after midnight."

Alvis considered simply walking up to the guards as though he were just an ignorant slave who had been dispatched to House Ransis' on some errand, but discarded the idea as too dangerous. If the guards decided to question him, he would have to reveal that his Master was Garith Balal, and Master Garith was already under suspicion—at least by the people on the street. Alvis was not so sure. Master Garith had the same connection with House Ransis that he had with Linser. If Linser began hauling in everyone who had such contact with House Ransis the streets of Peshar would be empty. The Chief Priest was thorough, but not foolish. Still, there was no need to cast more suspicion upon the scribe than might already be there.

Alvis looked up at the sky, praying that the dark clouds rolling in from the west would thicken and dump buckets of rain on Peshar. Rain would make the guards miserable and men in misery were less alert. He hoped.

"They have not searched inside yet?" Alvis asked again.

"Not that I have seen, Master Alvis," Icar answered. "I watched them all night. They have only stood guard."

Unless they came in from the dye yard side, the slave thought.

But there was no way to confirm that. No convenient Servant of the Design owned a shop on that side of the tapestry works. But perhaps Linser would not have the factory searched until he had wrung all he could from Lord Ransis. That would not take long. Ransis did not know much. Alvis could only hope that the old man would resist telling Linser about the connection between slave and tapestry. He probably would not resist answering any question for long, but perhaps if Linser did not ask the right questions.

In any case, Alvis felt he must try to get a look at the plans and drawings of *The Gods Show Mercy*. He did not know why, any more than he knew why the Designer had sent him to Archlea, but the feeling of need was there and the slave had long ago learned to be guided by feelings. His mother had said feelings were the way the Maker of All spoke to his children sometimes.

Deep in the night Alvis rose from his pallet among the ink stones and paper rolls. He was gratified to hear the pounding of the rain on the tiled roof of the shop.

"Take care, Alvis," Lakis said from his pallet across the room.

Alvis only grunted an answer and slipped out into the drenched streets.

The slave made his way to the doorway of Icar the cloth merchant, but he did not go in. Instead he turned down an alley directly across from the merchant's door. Near the end of the alley he climbed up onto a lean-to's roof then boosted himself onto the roof of the building. From there he made his way across the rooftops to a place where he could look down upon the guards around the factory.

The guards were as miserable as he had hoped. They were hunched into their cloaks and only watching the space before their faces. Alvis settled himself to consider his next move.

He could make the jump across the narrow street and land on the tile roof of the tapestry factory, but there were many things which could go wrong. If he landed wrong, he might slip and make a noise, or fall off the roof right into the lap of the guard below, or a tile might break, or a hundred other things.

Alvis raked his teeth over his bottom lip as he considered. He swallowed and wiped his hands over his face to clear the streaming water from his eyes and glanced over the parapet of the roof. The guard was still there, still hunched against the rain.

The jump was too dangerous to make. Too much chance of being caught, especially since there was a way to discover if what Alvis wanted to see was even in the factory still.

The slave drew in several breaths, holding each for a moment before letting them push out. He could feel the beginning of relaxation, and when he felt his mind focused enough, he lay down upon his back. The rain beat upon him, but it did not pull his mind away from the picture which was building there. A picture of a tea kettle hung on a pot hook, the fire licking at the bottom of it. And as the contents of the kettle warmed, Alvis could feel himself rise from the vessel of his body as steam would rise from the heating kettle.

Moments passed as deepening concentration made the steam of the Servant of the Design's spirit thicken and rise. Alvis opened his eyes to find himself separated body from spirit.

He moved forward across the roof then across the street and down through the roof of the factory. He felt the characteristic chill of passing through a solid object and hoped there would not be too many more.

There was no guard inside the factory door, and none in the office. That absence made Alvis uneasy.

A quick glance around showed him why there were no guards. A few empty papers were scattered around the office, and many cabinets' doors hung open. Alvis put his head through a few of the doors that were still closed, but he already knew what he would find. Lord Linser had sent troops through the dye works yard to search the factory. They had done a thorough job of it. There was nothing left. All the plans for every tapestry House Ransis had ever made were gone.

Thirteen

605 A.C.G.

Baroth Linser had *The Gods Show Mercy* laid over a rack in his quarters. The rack was such that Linser could see both the picture side of the tapestry and the woven side. He went over both sides minutely, looking at every stitch of the over sewing in the sculpted front portion, and every knot of the warp and woof as seen from the back. The tiniest dot of color did not escape his notice, but in the end, he found nothing that added to his knowledge. This copy was, for the most part, just like the other copies he had. The materials were better, the stitchery tighter, the colors purer, the weaving more uniform, but aside from the craftsmanship, it was the same as the cheapest copy.

Linser set clerks to sorting the recovered drawings and samples to separate the plans for *The Gods Show Mercy* from all the others taken from the factory. It was no small job. House Ransis had been creating tapestries for several hundred years and the factory records were voluminous, but after several days the drawings, stitch patterns, dye samples and material orders – both old and new – were gathered together and presented to Linser. Now they rested on his desk and they had told him nothing.

The priest leaned back in his throne and began to gnaw at the fleshy part of his palm. *Nothing, nothing, nothing!* He thought furiously. *There is nothing to be learned here! And nothing had been learned from the preliminary questioning of Ransis or the others taken in the night raid.*

Linser did not really expect to learn much from any of the prisoners save old Ransis, but he intended to enjoy the questioning all the same. And now it would be necessary to question old Ransis more vigorously. The priest smiled at the thought. He still nursed anger at the way Ransis had treated him before the Fair Witness and his slave.

The thought of avenging that slight lifted his spirit. He would have liked to prolong the questioning for weeks, but that was not possible. Linser felt pressure from the God-Resident. Time was growing short. The God-Resident seemed more harried each time Linser came into his presence, so the treasure of Javi Holis must be found quickly.

The Chief Priest shoved these thoughts away. They caused the acid that never seemed to leave his stomach to churn, a fiery reminder of his fears. Now was not the time for panic. Now was the time for action. The time for questioning Dimar Ransis.

When the guards returned the second time for Dimar Ransis he did not know how long he had been in the cell. The first time the guards returned he thought they had come to acknowledge that they had made some sort of error, for they cut his bonds and allowed him to stand up. They put some rough questions to him about *The Gods Show Mercy*, but the questions were such that he had no trouble answering them truthfully and still not give anything away about the message. But after that session the guards had bound him again and thrown him back to the floor of his dark cell.

Ransis had no way of knowing how long he lay on the slimy floor the second time. No sliver of light entered the cell. No creeping dot of sunlight told him of the passing hours. No sound of movement – human movement – filtered through the thick walls. Ransis might as well have been blind and deaf. He almost wished he were, for then he could not hear the squeak of rats or the clicking of the insects called death beetles.

After the second visit by the guards Ransis managed to gain some control of his fears. He managed to roll and push himself into a sitting position against a wall. It was no more comfortable than laying on the slimy floor, but it made him feel better. The bonds holding his arms against his sides were tight. They cut the circulation to his hands and restricted his breathing, but the two visits by the guards had given them some relief. Not so his thirst. It was torture, as was the indignity of not being able to relieve his bladder or bowels in any civilized way. These had reduced the old man to tears several times, but he strengthened himself with cursing Linser and all gods, both old and new, which had brought him to this. But most of all, after he knew not how long, Dimar Ransis cursed his luck at having been born into House Ransis. *Why could I not have been born a beggar in the streets of Peshar,* he thought. *Or better still, why could I have not been born at all.*

These thoughts tortured him like thirst and indignity and they drove him so deep into despair that he was even happy to hear the measured tread of the guards coming to question him for the third time.

Feeble torch light seemed bright as the sun to the old man. The guards did not speak this time and they did not release him completely as they had before. This time they cut only his ankle ties. They hauled him to his feet and kicked him repeatedly until he got the idea he was to go out of the cell and down the corridor.

They kicked and prodded him into a room which held a thing which resembled a tall saw horse. The cross piece of it was sharpened; not keen like a knife blade, but made into a thin edge. Without a word spoken the guards lifted the old man and sat him astride the device. The edge crushed his testicles sending twisting, pulsing pain through him. The guards did not seem to notice his cry of agony. They held him in place and dropped a noose around his neck. They did not pull it tight so it did not take any of the weight of his legs off the thin edge of the horse. It continued to jam his testicles hard between the edge and his pubic bone.

The guards knelt and attached weights to each of Ransis' ankles so that they pulled down yet harder, then they stepped back to view their handiwork. Ransis was left to balance himself on the thin edge of the horse with his legs dangling down, but not touching the floor. When the old man lost his balance and tipped over, the noose tightened to strangulation until he fought his way back to balance. When he was not able to right himself, the guards let him choke a while before they righted him. They threw cold water in his face to bring him back to full consciousness. During all this the guards did not speak a word, even to each other.

Time blurred into one long stretch of agony, which increased as the leg weights slowly separated the joints of his knees and hips and ankles.

Fleeting pictures of home and family passed through Ransis' mind as his senses fled the horror of reality to the more bearable world of delusion.

The noose suddenly began to choke Ransis as he lost his balance yet again. He fought to right himself, but could not. After a time, the guards lifted him back to the center.

"Good evening, Lord Ransis," a mocking voice said.

The old man blinked hard to clear his eyes and saw Baroth Linser standing before him.

"Are you quite comfortable?" the priest asked with a smirk.

A flash of rage passed through Ransis, charging him with new strength. He would have spit at Linser, but his thirst swollen tongue could find no moisture.

"Lord Ransis, I can end your suffering. All you need do is answer a few questions."

Ransis only stared at the priest.

"I want to know the secret of *The Gods Show Mercy*."

Ransis tried to speak, but could not. His mouth was too dry and his throat was swollen.

"Give him water," Linser ordered.

It was done.

Linser asked his question again.

"What secret?" Ransis croaked in answer.

"That is very foolish, Ransis. It will do you no good to resist. Sooner or later you will tell me. Why not save yourself pain and tell me now? Tell me the secret of *The Gods Show Mercy.*"

"I do not know any secret."

Linser hesitated a moment, then turned to the guards. "Heat irons," he commanded.

Fear welled up in Lord Ransis, but the rage was still there as well, and the memory of the scribe's slave. "All the hot irons you can use will not help me to remember a thing I know nothing of," he said, hoping to sound both defiant and pleading at the same time.

Linser drew a deep breath and let it out at a gust. "Ransis, do you take me for a fool? I know about the treasure. Where is the cache left by Javi Holis?"

Ransis' eyes opened a little wider in surprise, and Linser did not miss that. "So, you know the name Javi Holis," he paused waiting for some answer. None came. "I know about the cache. I know about the contents. I know about the Book of Designs. The only thing I do not know is the location. Tell me that, and you will be free…and all your people with you."

"I do not know what you are talking about," said Ransis.

He thought about his father's racking coughs and the bloody foam around his mouth as he passed the secret on to the next generation, and he cursed the memory. He cursed the old man for telling him anything —but even as the first of the hot irons was applied to the bottom of his foot, he knew these gods from the sky were truly beasts to have such a one as Baroth Linser as their chief servant.

The torture went on for hours and Linser was almost convinced that the old man knew nothing. After a time, he tired of watching, so he told the guards to continue the questioning and send for him if Ransis broke.

As the hours passed the old man fell into a pain-induced trance which could not be reduced by the use of cold water. He babbled about his father and his family and talked to his wife as though she were in the room with him. Linser would have been happy to produce Ransis' wife, but she was out of his reach, long dead and buried. The same was not true of his sons and daughters, so Linser had the youngest son, a man of twenty-five, brought and placed on a horse beside his father.

The old man looked at him as though he were a stranger.

At last Linser told the guards to take Ransis down. "Let him rest an hour, then we will begin again."

Ransis was dragged from his horse, dropped on the floor of the cell and doused repeatedly with cold water until he was semi-conscious, then the guards went out, taking the light with them and locking the door. Ransis was once more left in the dark, but now he had the groans of his son to keep him company.

Lord Linser returned to studying the tapestry, but gained nothing more. All was the same as the other copies except the workmanship. He laid out the drawings and the material lists of the original work and those for the copy before him. He read down the lists, comparing them line by line, word by word. They were the same. The only difference at all seemed to be in that one type of yarn had been substituted for another in a small part of the sculpture stitching. The color was the same; the number of filaments was the same; the tightness of the spinning was the same. The only difference was that the thread in the copy came from a spinnery in Peshar. The original yarn had come from a yarn maker in the Palatine Region, far to the north. Probably yarn from there had not been available, or had been too expensive.

And yet...

The contract had been for an exact copy, he thought.

An exact copy...or had it?

Linser dug out the contract and cursed as he read it. No, the copy did not have to be exact. It had to be as nearly exact as House Ransis could make it "Using the original materials if available."

The priest leaned back in his chair and stroked his chin with his pudgy hand. *Could this change be significant* he wondered, *or was it just that the old type yarn was not available?*

He leaned over the lists again and continued his comparison. After a little he leaned back again. That small change was the only change. Everything else was just like the original. And in the original the Palatine yarn seemed odd. All the other materials had been locally made. Only that bit of yarn was in the least exotic. Odd. Yes, odd.

Ransis was back on the horse. He had been there for an hour when Linser returned. The Chief Priest could see that life was flickering in the Patriarch of House Ransis, but there was clarity in the old man's eyes. He was no longer entranced by pain.

"Give him water," Linser commanded.

It was done.

"Perhaps I should let you rest again, Lord Ransis."

A spark of hope came into the old man's eyes. It was gratifying to the priest. He enjoyed holding out hope, then snatching it back.

"But no," he said. "You have given me nothing, so I can give you nothing. But of course, I could simply have you shortened. I have no need for your head if your mouth will not speak.

"Or perhaps I should shorten some of your children. This one perhaps?" he indicated Ransis' son who was still on the horse beside his father.

"Or the others? Perhaps their loss would loosen your tongue. Or maybe have them disemboweled.

"But no. It would give me great pleasure to do all of those things, but it would complicate my life, and right now I need no more complications. Instead, I think… Yes, yes." Linser turned to one of the guards. "Bring the daughter," he commanded. "The youngest one."

The guard bowed and left.

"You can stop this, Ransis," the priest said. "All you have to do is tell me what I wish to know."

Ransis understood what was about to happen, but he still could not bring himself to reveal the little he knew. A secret which had been passed from generation to generation for more than six hundred years was not something to be revealed lightly.

"I know nothing more than you know, Lord Linser," he begged. "Don't you think I would tell you to save my daughter?"

The priest looked into Ransis' face and considered. After a moment he said, "I am not sure. You might very well let your daughter be used and killed to keep the secret. After all, through all this you have not told me about the yarn."

The other's face was hard to read now. Hours of pain had made it drawn and gray, but mention of the yarn made Ransis flinch as though struck. Linser knew his ploy was about to pay off.

"Why didn't you tell me about the yarn, Ransis? It was such a small thing."

The old man's eyes filled with tears of defeat. He tried to speak but thirst and the noose made it impossible.

The guard returned with Nina Ransis, youngest daughter of House Ransis. She was twelve and beginning to bud into young womanhood. Her robes, expensive blue and green silk, were filthy rags now. They barely covered her, but she didn't notice. Her eyes were glassy, disconnected from reality.

Fear for his daughter showed in Dimar Ransis' eyes and Linser was pleased to see it. "Give Lord Ransis a drink of water," he commanded, "so that he may be refreshed as he watches the pain of his child."

It was done, and as Ransis swallowed the last drop from the gourd dipper Linser told the guards, "Amuse yourselves for a while before we get down to questions."

"Stop," Ransis croaked. "Stop, please. I will tell all I know, but spare her."

"Hold," Linser said as the guards ripped the rags from the girl's body. They stopped.

"Very well, Lord Ransis. Say on."

"You already know most of what I know. The tapestry is a map or chart leading to the cache. I do not know how to read it, but the Palatine yarn is a clue. I do not know what the clue means though. Perhaps the cache is in Palatine, I do not know," the old man stammered to a stop.

"But of what use is that to me, Ransis? I already know this. You must tell me something that I do not know."

"But there is nothing else," Ransis sobbed. "I don't know anything more."

Linser sighed and shook his head in mock regret. "Truly a shame," he said. Then to the guards, "Go ahead."

"Wait, Wait," Ransis cried. "The slave. The slave knows."

"Hold," Linser said and the guards stopped.

"What slave? One of your slaves?"

"No, not mine. The one called Alvis. The slave of Scribe Balal. He knows everything. He made me change the yarn. He knows everything."

Linser frowned. What could the slave of Scribe Balal know? It did not make sense.

…And yet…

"I think you are lying to me, Ransis. I think you are telling me this tale to gain a little more time."

"No, I swear by all the Gods. It is the truth. The slave knows. I do not know how he knows, but he knows."

Linser steepled his fingers again and laid them upon his lips. After a moment he said "Very well. We shall see. If this is not true, you and all from House Ransis will pay for it. Take them back to their cells."

~ * ~

Alvis returned to the shop after his scouting trip to House Ransis. He did not think there was anything to link him to *The Gods Show Mercy* except Ransis. But Ransis was in the hands of Linser who would surely wring him dry of everything. How long before Alvis was in danger was dependent upon the will to resist in old Ransis. But the old man could not resist more than a few days at most, and he might resist only a few moments —or not at all. That left only one conclusion. It was time to run.

But this conclusion, while best and safest for Alvis, did not satisfy him. He did not want to run and leave House Balal to the mercy of Baroth Linser. That was not a thing Alvis would allow if there was anything he could do about it.

Unless such a thing is in the Design, he thought, and did not like the thought.

The death of innocents was a thing to be loathed, not merely accepted. But all is in the Design. Perhaps even the death of innocents.

If it is in the Design, there is nothing I can do about it, the slave thought. *So, I will try to prevent it.* With that he walked into his master and mistress' bed chamber.

Garith, still heavy with sleep, could not understand why Alvis was waking him. Merta did not understand either, but she was more vocal about it.

"What do you mean Temple Proctors are coming to arrest us? We have done nothing," she said.

"That does not matter, Mistress. They are coming, and none of us must be here when they arrive," Alvis explained patiently.

"How do you know this," Garith demanded.

"They took Lord Ransis and his family." he began.

"Yes, yes, but what has that to do with us?"

"No doubt Lord Ransis is being put to the question now. Sooner or later he will admit the connection between this house and his own."

"Admit?" Merta said. "Of course, he will admit it, though it is not much of an admission since Lord Linser was here when that connection was forged."

Garith watched his slave's face and after a moment said, "Merta, be quiet."

She glared at him and started to scour him with her tongue, but something about him stopped her.

"What connection, Alvis?" Garith asked.

"I cannot explain it all now, Master. Our time may be short, but I will explain when we are safe."

The men stared at one another for three long breaths, then Garith rose from the bed and said, "Merta, pack a few things." He did not wait for an answer. He and Alvis strode out across the center court and into the shop to wake Lakis and pack a few things.

When Garith returned to the bed chamber Merta was still sitting with the coverlet wrapped around her.

"Don't just sit there Merta. We must move quickly," he said.

"But why? We have done nothing to anger Linser or the Gods. Nothing. We are honest people and servants of the Gods. You have written and witnessed contracts for the Chief Priest," she said reasonably. "Why should we suddenly abandon it all and run like thieves? On the word of a slave?"

"Merta, I do not know why, I only know we must."

"But why?"

"Because Alvis says so, and I believe him. So enough. Get up and get moving."

For a moment Merta looked like she would protest more, but she thought better of it, got up and began to dress.

Garith went out for a few moments. When he returned, he found Merta stacking expensive bronze oil lamps on the bed beside a tapestry she had just purchased a few days before.

"What are you doing?" Garith asked.

"Packing," she answered.

Garith's temper snapped. "Stupid woman. We are running for our lives. We have no need of lamps or tapestries," he shouted.

Merta blinked at him and almost cried. She knew what he was saying was true, but she was trying hard to resist that truth. She did not want to run. It was not that she did not think the Proctors were coming. She was sure in her heart that they were, but her mind said *THIS IS WRONG*. Everything she and Garith had labored to gain was evaporating and she could not understand why.

~ * ~

The four stood in the court yard of House Balal. They were ready, carrying a small bundle each.

"We must warn my parents," Merta said, not quite begging.

"She is right, Alvis," Garith agreed. "When we are missed Linser will certainly question them."

Alvis nodded. "Lakis," he said. "Go and warn them. Tell them nothing more than you must. Meet us outside the city gate on the road south."

Lakis looked as though he were going to protest, but thought better of it and went to do as he was told.

Garith thanked the Gods his parents were safely dead so they could not see the sorry pass their son had come to, then caught himself. *Why should I thank the Gods?* he thought. *They are the reason I am leaving my home like a thief in the night with what I can carry and the clothes on my back.*

Suddenly, rage was boiling up in him. Rage at gods and priests and slaves who had brought an end to his life just as it was beginning to be more than a struggle to survive.

"I should have had you whipped the first day I bought you," he said to Alvis, bitterness in his voice. "I should have had my stupid tongue cut out before I ever thought to buy a slave."

He wheeled on his wife. "And I should have beaten you for wanting a slave. All because you wanted to be better than Alsai Kruth."

He drew back his arm to strike her, but Alvis grabbed his wrist.

"Do not blame your wife, Master," he said. "It was not her fault. If you must blame someone, blame me. I am the reason for this trouble. I picked you from the crowd of buyers at the auction."

Astonishment crept over Garith's face and he stopped trying to pull loose of his slave's grip. "But why? How?"

"I knew I needed a place where writing and reading would not seem odd, and I saw that you were a scribe."

"But how could you know that?" Garith said.

Alvis let go of his wrist and Garith lowered his hand.

Alvis shrugged. "I knew by the stoop of your walk, the stains of ink on your hand."

Garith looked at his hand. The stains were easy to see even in the dim light of the moon.

"And no doubt the finger of the Master of the Design stirred in me, and I chose you."

"Master of the Design," Garith said disgustedly. "Master of Chaos. There is no Design, only an end of lives."

"Or the beginning of a greater Design," Alvis said. "Come. We have wasted enough time. They will be here soon."

Merta looked at the two men for a moment then cried, "Wait," and ran back into the house.

The men thought she had gone mad, and they ran after her. They found her in the kitchen prying a tile from the floor, and when they tried to lift her from the floor she slapped at their hands. "Leave me be for a moment," she commanded, and they did.

Merta tugged and pried at the tile and it suddenly lifted from the floor. She thrust her hand into the hollow space that had been hidden beneath the tile and brought out a large, leather draw string purse and tossed it at Alvis' feet. "This new Design will no doubt take money," she said and lifted her chin toward the bag. Alvis bent and picked it up.

"I was leaving it here against the day of our return, but I think that day may never come."

Alvis opened the purse. It was filled with gold Zari coins.

"Five thousand three hundred Zari," she said. "Perhaps that will be enough to keep us alive until this Design is painted, or whatever it must be."

~ * ~

Baroth Linser wasted no time in ordering Balal and anyone else in the house to be brought to him. He knew this might all be a lie, but it was worth the time to find out. The priest shook his head. *How could this be true?* he asked himself. *How could a slave know anything of Javi Holis, or any other part of Archlean history? The slaves had to be from other worlds, and all slaves arrived in Peshar with minds emptied of everything save the most basic knowledge of speech. Most had to be re-trained to do even the simplest of jobs. How could this slave know anything?*

At the back of his mind tickled the thought that this slave might be some sort of spy sent by the Gods for some reason of their own, but he discarded the idea as ridiculous.

Morat, Linser's body servant, crept into his chamber and bowed deeply.

"What is it?" the priest snapped.

"The Guard Captain, my Lord."

Linser sat up straight. "Well, bring him. bring him!"

"Yes, my Lord."

The Guard Captain who served as Chief Proctor stepped in, and Linser's fist clenched on the arm of his chair at the look on the man's face.

"My Lord Linser." he began, his voice quavering; his face gray with fear.

"Well, where are they?"

"My Lord, they were not in the shop. They were gone, my Lord."

The priest's eyes blazed with anger. "The neighbors...did you question the neighbors?"

"Yes, my Lord. Vigorously. They knew nothing. They said the shop had been closed all day yesterday. They feared for their lives, my Lord. They would not have lied."

Linser thought for a moment stroking his chin, his eyes unfocused. This confirmed Ransis' story. The slave, or the scribe, knew something.

Linser pulled himself out of his thoughts. "Find them, Captain," he said. "Comb Peshar until not a louse has escaped your notice. If you do not find them here, we will begin looking elsewhere. I will dispatch messengers to clergy all over to begin looking. They will be found, and when they are you will be rewarded, Captain. But if they are not found, I will have you shortened. Do I make myself clear?"

"Yes, my Lord. Very clear. They will be found."

Lakis met the other three just outside the gate as he had been told. "I told them," he said.

"Then where are they?" Merta asked, cutting off anything Lakis might have been going to say.

He shrugged. "They did not believe me. They said it was just some nonsense that their fool of a son-in-law had gotten himself into and had nothing to do with them."

Merta's mouth fell open at that, but no words came out.

"I am not surprised," Garith said.

Merta snapped her attention to her husband intending to deny what he said, but the look he gave her cut the words off unspoken.

"Now what?" Garith asked Alvis.

The slave thought a moment then said "Come," and started off.

The fugitives wound through the countryside until they came to a large farm. The house was a sprawling structure made of bricks the same color as the plowed fields that could be seen as they approached. Beside the house, across a wide yard was a barn. Alvis headed directly for it. He did not stop at the door or even call out. It was as though he owned the place.

A man was cleaning one of the stalls. He looked up at the sound of steps, and when he saw Alvis he smiled and dropped his shovel. He had never seen Alvis in the flesh, but had communicated with him many times through use of the Mandalai of Power. Now, seeing the slave for the first time was like seeing an old friend.

"Master Alvis," the farmer said, opening his arms in welcome.

"Jondrel, we are in need," Alvis began.

"I am at your service, Master Alvis," the one called Jondrel said.

"Before you commit yourself, understand that there may be

danger. We are pursued by Baroth Linser."

Jondrel did not even hesitate. "Whatever I can do, Master, I will do."

"Thank you," Alvis said. "We will need shelter for a night or perhaps two, depending on how quickly we can get horses and travel gear together."

Jondrel nodded his understanding and led them to the house without even asking who the others were.

Garith and Merta were given a room in the cellar. It was not exactly a secret room, but one probably would not find it unless he knew where to look.

Merta spent most of the night weeping and Garith spent the night comforting her and worrying that there would be a sudden knock on the door followed by a troop of Temple guards. Toward morning Merta quieted and slept. Garith tried to sleep too, but could not relax. At last he gave up and crept out of the hidden room.

In the kitchen Jondrel's wife, a short round woman with an infectious smile, greeted him. Her name was Noli.

"You are up early, Scribe Balal," she said. "Would you like some tea?"

"How do you know my name?" Garith said then thought how rude the question sounded.

She laughed. "All servants of the Design in Peshar know you, Scribe Balal."

"Servants of the Design?"

"Yes."

"So, that is how you know Alvis."

"Yes."

Garith sat himself upon a stool beside the kitchen table. "So far this Design has brought me nothing but pain and loss," he said.

"Sometimes it seems that the Designer has no heart for his creatures, but I think it is not so. I believe the Designer feels all the pains of his creatures and regrets what must be."

Garith shook his head. "I think this Designer, if there is such a thing, glories in pain. I think he glories in the cruelty he inflicts."

The woman shrugged and turned to the hearth where a tea pot sat. She took a bowl from the mantle and poured tea into it, then brought it to Garith.

"Perhaps you are right, Scribe Balal," she said. "But even if that is true, nothing we can do will change the Design, so why resist. Change yourself. That is something that you can change."

"Change myself? How?"

"Stop resisting the Design, Master Garith." Alvis said. He had been standing unnoticed beside the yard door to the kitchen for a while.

"How can I stop resisting?" Garith snapped. "Resisting is the only way I have remained alive. When I was young, I had to fight for enough room on the plaza to sit with my writing desk upon my lap. That was resistance. I had to fight to remain there. I could have done less. I could have allowed the others to push me out. I could have given up and taken some menial job, but I wanted to be a scribe. So, I resisted the weariness and those who would have pushed me out. How can I stop resisting?"

"In your mind, Master. Release your life into the hands of the Designer and peace will come into your mind. When you acknowledge the Design—when you truly believe—you will no longer need to resist. You will accept whatever part the Maker of All has for you in the universe."

Garith shook his head. "I cannot believe in your Design, Alvis. I think I do not believe in anything except purest chaos. The gods of my youth have proved false – or if not false then as cruel as your Designer. I have lost all. My life is forfeit if Lord Linser's temple guard takes me. My wife has probably lost her family because they do not trust their son-in-law, and she may lose her mind as well. How can you believe there is any design in any of this?"

"Because I have seen parts of it worked out," the slave said.

Garith snorted. "If your coming here is part of his Design, then I know this Designer is nothing but cruelty. And if it is part of this Design that you are to die under question, then why must you have come to Peshar to drag me into death with you."

Alvis smiled a small smile. "I should have spent my life as my father and his father before him. I should have spent my life teaching the sons and daughters of Lord Caron to read, write and cipher, and when they were old enough to marry and care for themselves. I should have helped Lord Caron to run his everyday affairs. Perhaps I might even have gone as Lord Caron's personal secretary when he served his term on the Imperial Council. I should have spent my life teaching my sons and daughters about the Design and the use of the five powers just as I was taught, but The Master of the Design had other plans."

"You have children?" Merta asked.

She had come up from the secret room looking for Garith. Her eyes were puffed, and black circles like bruises were beneath them, but she had cried herself out.

"How are you, Merta?" Garith asked.

She shrugged. "I am here, coming out of hiding in a cellar. How should I be? You did not answer my question, Alvis."

"No, Mistress, I did not answer. It is not a thing I like to think about. A part of the Design which has caused me pain as it causes you pain now."

Merta looked at the man who had been her slave and forgot her own losses for a moment in the face of his. "You do have children then?"

Alvis stepped away from the door and came to the table. He sat down and then nodded. "Yes," he said, "two sons and two daughters."

Merta came and sat beside the slave. "Where are they, Alvis?"

"I don't know. They were on Lord Caron's estate at Rashti, but I am sure they were sold."

"Sold?"

Alvis glanced at his mistress and one corner of his mouth turned up in a half smile. "It is the lot of slaves to be sold Mistress. Part of the Design."

Merta was outraged. "How can you be so...they are your children," she said.

Alvis looked down under her words, drew a deep breath and said, "Would my tears help them? Would my worry bring them again to my arms? All is in the Design, Mistress. I must leave behind worry about things I cannot help. I must believe that the Maker of All has done only what must be done to fulfill the Design. I must believe that the Maker of

All is good, even when bad things happen and I must believe that all things have a purpose."

"But what purpose could be served by your separation from your children?" Merta asked.

"And your coming has certainly not been good for us," Garith said bitterly.

"For that I am sorry, Master. Had I the power to do so I would restore all to you tenfold. I would grant you a long, fruitful, peaceful life. But I have no such power."

"Wonderful," Garith said, still holding tight to the regret of loss. "I have a powerless slave wishing me things he cannot grant. How wonderfully the Design has worked itself out for me."

Alvis shook his head and tried not to laugh at the bitter sarcasm in his master's voice, but it was difficult. Even Merta saw the humor of what her husband was saying, though she felt exactly the same way.

"How did you come to be here, Master Alvis?" Noli asked.

Alvis shrugged and tipped his head to one side. "As it turned out that was simply accomplished, or rather it seems simple from this end. At the beginning it seemed impossible. A little while ago I was the possession of Lord Caron, who was a very rich and powerful man in the Cadeki Empire. A member of the Imperial Peerage. A man whose fortune was near as old as the Imperium. Then I would never have thought— never even considered—that there was the faintest chance that Lord Caron would ever be reduced to selling even his house staff to meet his obligations. But that is what happened. Revolts on three worlds cut him off from his mines and fields and manufactories. Garin attacks on two or three outposts of the Empire destroyed trade goods Lord Caron had purchased to re-sell, and it was done. I was sold to a slave Factor for a very high price and slated to be re-sold to another lord of the Empire, but before that could happen, the Factor died. And it seems that he had forgotten to register my purchase or my intended sale. That probably would not have made any difference if the Factor had been an honest man, but he was not. He had lied and cheated and left his creditors unpaid, so there were many carrion birds hovering around his corpse. I was seized by a creditor and sold to another Factor as a common house slave. That

Factor shoved me through a transit gate leading to Peshar, and here I am. As simple as that. It only took a major re-arrangement of the financial and political alignment of the Imperium in general, and of six or eight worlds in particular to bring me to the auction block in time to be bought by you, Master Garith."

"I did not understand about half of what you said, Alvis," Garith said. "What is this Cadeki Empire?"

Alvis looked from Garith to Merta and then back to Garith. The slave was unsure whether these people, so lately believers in the gods of the temple, were ready to hear and understand truth. After a few moments of consideration, he decided they had a right to know.

"The Cadeki Empire is the name of those people you have known as the gods," he said.

Garith had heard both his slaves say that the gods were not gods before. He thought it was only a way of denying their power in favor of their own god, but this new name…

"The Cadeki Empire stretches over a large part of this galaxy."

A look of puzzlement crossed the faces of Garith and Merta, for Alvis had switched from Peshari to the Divine language.

Alvis noted the look and explained, still in the Divine Language. "There is no way to say what I must say to explain the Cadeki Empire in Peshari. The words do not exist." He waited for them to nod their comprehension, then went on. "A galaxy is a group of stars. Around these stars are worlds like this one. The Cadeki Empire rules many worlds in this group of stars. Six hundred years ago the Cadeki Empire came to this world, which they call Archlea. They did not come to conquer exactly. They had no use for a backward world…"

Garith's eyebrows drew down at the insult, but Alvis ignored it and continued.

"…full of people ignorant of even the existence of other worlds. What they needed was the location of this planet in space. Here a hundred folds of the universal fabric touch one another. Here, the distance between stars means nothing. Here, if one knows how to open the doors between worlds, a man—or ten thousand men—can step across the distance between stars more easily that I could step across the yard to the barn.

That is why the Cadeki Empire came. That is why they stay. When they came, they might have striped all life from Archlea, but that was not in the Design. Instead, they decided they could profit in other ways besides the transit gates. They decided Archlean slaves could decorate the great houses of the Empire as slaves had once decorated the houses of ancient empires. There was no real need for slaves. Machines do the work ancient slaves did, but Cadeki egos were not stroked by machines. A machine does not know, or care, who dominates it. But a slave, a slave knows he is a slave and that he is bound to a master. A slave can believe in a power greater than himself...can believe in a master."

"And after Archlea had been spared, the Cadekis found raw ores, dense woods, and heady perfumes which could fill the coffers of the Empire; jewels which could adorn Imperial garments and most of all, they discovered the tapestries of Peshar."

"The people of this dust mote were so uncivilized that they did not even have use of machines more complex than looms. They did not even use steel, only bronze and cast iron. These ignorant animals considered the Cadekis gods because they had come from the sky and could destroy cities and armies with the mere sweep of their hands."

"There was profit in this ignorance, too. What better way to rule this primitive planet than to let the people believe their conquerors were gods'?

"But Archlea was ignorant only of technology. The people might not have machines to cross the sky, but they had quick minds and histories of men who thought and reasoned and considered. Such men were dangerous, for it would not take them long to wonder if these conquerors were truly gods. Such a one was Javi Holis, a Servant of the Design. Those who served the Design believed that a single god had made all things, and that the hand of the Designer was in all things, including the coming of the gods."

"Javi Holis and others began to speak aloud what they had considered in secret—that the gods might not be gods at all. And when the Cadekis heard of this they became afraid. They became afraid of Javi Holis, an ignorant animal. The child of a weaver of tapestries. One man made the gods quake, because he spoke the truth."

"They tried to silence him and all the others, but truth is hard to silence. Holis continued to teach in secret. He taught about the Designer, and the gods feared him. They sought him and tried to destroy him and all trace of the Servants of the Design, but they failed. Javi Holis beat them and saved the knowledge he and other servants of the Design had discovered. He put it into a book called The Book of the Design, and he hid the book away from gods and men. He left only a clue to the location. It is in a tapestry woven by House Ransis..."

"*The Gods Show Mercy*," Garith breathed.

"*The Gods Show Mercy*," Alvis agreed and fell silent. He picked up the small bowl of tea that Noli had set before him.

"But how did Lord Linser find out?" Merta asked. "How could he know?"

"I do not know, but clearly he does."

"And now we are all caught up in this Design," Merta said quietly.

"Not only now, Mistress. We have always been parts of the Design. The difference between yesterday and today is that today you *know* you are a part of it."

Fourteen

605 A.C.G.

"But they must be somewhere," Lord Linser shouted, his face crimson.

The Chief Priest had been growing steadily more crimson over the last several minutes as the Guard Captain reported. The Captain had tried to make each of the reports seem like something worthwhile, but each really amounted to the same thing; Scribe Balal, his wife, and his two slaves had disappeared from Peshar.

"We will find them, my Lord," the Captain stammered. He was sweating profusely.

"I begin to think not, Captain," Linser growled "It has been days, and you have found not so much as a smell of them."

"But, my Lord..." the Captain was beginning to feel the keen edge of the executioner's sword tickle the back of his neck.

"Spare me the excuses Captain, and stop that shaking. The block won't get your neck – yet."

The captain swallowed hard and tried to get control of himself.

"It is clear," Linser continued, "that Scribe Balal and company have left Peshar. So, you must widen your search. Expand it to cover the whole province. Put every garrison to work seeking them."

The captain swallowed again. "Yes, my Lord."

"Dispatch messengers to every garrison. Give them descriptions and tell them to take anyone who even vaguely meets those descriptions into custody for questioning."

"Yes, my Lord. At once, my Lord," the captain said, bowing

himself out the door.

Linser looked at the closed door for a time. He was sure the captain had turned over every rock in Peshar, yet Linser was no wiser. Neither had he gotten anything more from Ransis. The old man had insisted the Palatine yarn was all that had been changed in *The Gods Show Mercy,* and Linser was convinced. Not that it mattered anymore. There would be no more information from the Patriarch of House Ransis. The old man had died under the last questioning. A feral smile crossed the Chief Priest's face. *No more insults from that quarter,* he thought. *House Ransis is no more.*

After a few more moments of self-congratulation Linser turned once more to studying his copy of *The Gods Show Mercy.* There had to be more than the Palatine yarn, no matter what Ransis said. The old man had simply not known anything more.

Linser examined the tapestry again. Several black armored Gods stood in Tapestry Plaza before a tapestry being displayed. A crowd of Pesharis drew back from the Gods, and one man knelt before them, his arms upraised in supplication. However, the Gods looked toward the tapestry being displayed, not toward the pleading man. Legend held that the beauty of the tapestry had moved the Gods so much that they were persuaded not to destroy Peshar.

The tapestry within the tapestry was perfect. It showed a ruined Keep perched upon a rugged cliff. Below the ruin, in a narrow valley, was a village. It was the very picture of a thousand mountain villages which existed by scratch farming and sheep raising; an idealized version of a perfectly righteous, perfectly happy place. A place far from the evils of the city and dripping with the virtues of peasant simplicity. The colors were deep-dyed in the warp and woof, and the artist had overstitched portions of it to emphasize them. There was an illusion of depth in the tapestry within the tapestry. Amazing in so small a section of the whole work. That area was no more than three or four hands breadths, and perhaps twice that in length, yet its detail was perfect. It could have been cut out of the whole and used as a wall hanging by itself. In fact, it called the eye to it. It was the first place an observer's eyes fell in this complex and beautiful work.

Why would the designer of *The Gods Show Mercy* go out of his way to draw the eye of the observer to that small part of the work, Linser wondered? There were other important parts, rendered with equal skill and art, yet the first thing the eye was drawn to was the tapestry within the tapestry. Why?

The mountain area shown was obviously the Palatine. The three-pointed peaks in the background were called the Palatine needles.

But House Ransis had never had anything to do with the Palatine, had they? They had been Peshari society forever. The very history of Peshar was the history of House Ransis, so why should the Memoria of a Patriarch of House Ransis show some obscure Palatine Village?

Linser's mind clicked over and made a connection. The ruined Keep in the tapestry had to be Keep Holis, ancient seat of the Servants of the Design. Of course. Where else would the cache of Javi Holis be?

"Morat," Linser shouted, and immediately began scribbling a note:

"Mighty God-Resident, I have come into possession of information which could be of great profit in these trying times. I would be most grateful for an opportunity to explain this information, and its potential value, to you at your earliest convenience."

Linser signed the note and sealed it with his personal chop, then handed it to his servant.

"Take this to the altar and hurry about it. Delay it by more than a breath and I will personally shorten you."

Morat began shaking, knowing that Lord Linser did not make idle threats. He took the folded, sealed paper and bowed himself out.

Linser was not sure what he was about to do would work, and he feared that the God-Resident would once again be away from the temple, or not deign to answer his request, but, with the power of the Gods to send messages over great distances in moments, Linser could dispatch troops to take Keep Holis, and the village below it, long before the scribe could arrive there; if indeed that was where they were going. Perhaps, with the power of the Gods, the legendary cache of Javi Holis could be found before the scribe or his slave could even get close to it.

~ * ~

The fugitives stayed three days at the farm of Jondrel and Noli. The morning of their departure the four sat around the table in Noli's kitchen eating porridge and drinking hot tea.

"I considered leaving you here," Alvis said to Garith and Merta. "Four are more easily caught than two, but for some reason I could not convince myself of the rightness of it. For some reason the Designer seems to want you with me."

"And how do you know this," Garith asked with only the slightest taint of sarcasm.

He was gradually coming to accept the loss of his old life and the danger of his new life, but there was still some bitterness in him.

"I do not know how I know," Alvis shrugged, "but I do know."

Garith and Merta stared at him for a long moment then turned to Jondrel and Noli.

"Thank you for the help you have given us, for hiding us," Garith began

"Yes," Merta agreed. "I wish you peace and prosperity in the future."

Lakis looked stricken as he heard his mistress' wish and the look did not go unnoticed.

"What is it, Lakis?" Garith asked.

The slave looked to Alvis who nodded and shrugged.

"I have news of your parents, Mistress Merta," he said.

Merta knew by the look of him that the news was not good. "Go on," she said, steeling herself.

"Temple guards came and questioned them yesterday. Your parents told them they knew nothing, but Lord Linser had given orders not to accept any such answer." He hesitated a moment then rushed through the rest. "They were taken to the temple dungeon."

Merta sagged against Garith, knowing what the news meant. Those who went to the temple dungeon almost never returned.

"I am sorry, Merta," Noli said, and put her hand on Merta's shoulder.

"I am sorry too, Mistress," Alvis said. "I wish there had been less pain in the Design for you, but…" he stopped, knowing that anything he could say now would be useless.

After a little, Jondrel said, "You had best be moving on, Master Alvis. It is almost daylight."

"Yes," he agreed. "Let us go now."

~ * ~

Linser waited impatiently for some answer to his request for an audience, but none came. He called Morat in and made sure the request had been delivered to the altar. The man swore he had done so, and Linser was sure enough of Morat's fear to know the request had been delivered.

Early the next morning, even before morning devotions, Linser was up and at the altar, presenting his own prayer, but no answer came.

Nor did any answer come the next day or the next. Linser became frantic, but decided the God-Resident was away as he had been before. The fear that the Gods had left Peshar which had shrunk to an icy seed after the God-Resident returned before, began to grow once again. But the priest knew he could not simply wait on the return of the God-Resident – if he returned. Linser called in the Guard Captain.

"Captain, dispatch a messenger to ride with all speed to the garrison at Macar. I would that the garrison take and hold the ruin of Keep Holis and the village below it."

"Yes, my Lord, but…the man stopped.

"But what, Captain?"

"Would it not be better, faster, to send such a message via the Divine Network?"

Linser glared daggers at the man, but he dared not say that the God-Resident was not answering his prayers. Such a thing might give others the idea that Linser no longer had the ear of the Gods. "Do you think me a fool, Captain?" he said, his voice rising.

"N-No, my Lord."

"Do you think I do not know that the Divine net would be faster?"

"N-No, my Lord."

"And do you make a habit of questioning my orders?"

"No, my Lord."

"Then do as you are ordered," Linser screamed.

"Yes, my Lord. At once, my Lord."

"Tell the messengers to ride with all haste. Take fresh horses at every opportunity. When the message is delivered and my orders carried out, have messengers dispatched to bring the news back to Peshar."

"Yes, my Lord," the captain said and bowed himself quickly out of the room.

Oh Gods, Linser's thoughts wailed. *Why have you chosen this time to turn a deaf ear to me?*

~ * ~

The fugitives traveled hard, pushing horses to the point of collapse. They rested only the time it took their mounts to recover their strength before pushing on. They changed horses as often as possible, but a few times they were reduced to abandoning worn out horses and walking.

Three weeks of running found the travelers paused beside a rivulet just off the road. The pause was for the horses, which stood with heads hung in weariness, to drink and rest. Any spirit which had been in them was long since ridden out.

The four took a stand-up meal of bread, cheese, and salty ham. Lakis watered the horses and brought them back to stand near their riders. Alvis handed Lakis a chunk of bread and some cheese. He offered some of the ham, but the other shook his head. "It is too salty. I stay thirsty enough without it," he said.

"How much farther, Alvis?" Garith asked.

"Three or four more days I think," Alvis answered.

"You think?" Merta snapped. She was more tired than she had ever been in her life and it made her temper even shorter than usual. "Why don't you know, slave? Have you brought us to ruin and running without even knowing where we are going?"

"Now, Merta," Garith began soothingly, but she cut him off.

"Do not 'Now Merta' me!" she shouted, a hysterical edge to her voice. "I have had enough of running as though Linser himself were an inch behind us. I am tired of riding dawn to dark and of sleeping in ditches and flea-ridden hovels. I am tired of salty ham and moldy cheese and water that tastes of mildewed water-skins. I am tired of being commanded by slaves which are my property."

Garith gripped his wife by the upper arm and shook her. "All your screaming will not make anything better," he said firmly. "Linser *is* an inch behind us and he will happily drag us back to his dungeon if he lays hands on us. Now be quiet and rest while we have a moment."

Alvis and Lakis kept their own counsel while Garith reasoned with his wife. They had seen this before from her, but the incidents were getting closer together and stronger. Soon Garith might not be able to quiet her. She might slip over into screaming madness next time, and that could be disaster.

"She needs some rest," Lakis said, not unsympathetically.

"We all need some rest," Alvis said sharply.

His nerves were frayed, too.

Lakis knew that the pressure on Alvis was terrible. Nevertheless, he felt that he had to continue. "Alvis, the horses are finished. If one of them does not drop dead beneath us before dark it will be a miracle. We need fresh ones. Now."

Garith and Merta had moved off a little and stood in a weary embrace. "Can we get fresh ones ahead?" Alvis asked.

He had come to rely on Lakis' knowledge of the road between Peshar and Keep Holis.

Lakis shrugged. "There is an inn ahead, or rather there was. We should be able to get horses there."

"How far?"

Again, Lakis shrugged. "If we push on now, we should reach it shortly after dark…if it is still there."

Alvis raked his teeth over his lower lip as he thought. "Very well. We will push for this inn, and we will rest the night there. I pray the Maker of All will favor us with fresh horses."

Lakis nodded. "Mean time I think Mistress Merta needs

something to ease her pain."

"Perhaps you're right," Alvis said and walked to his horse and untied the strings of a leathern bottle from his saddle bow. He took the bottle to Garith and unstopped it.

The scribe took the bottle and sniffed it. "Brandy, Master Garith. Take a swig and pass it to Mistress Merta. We will try to reach an inn tonight, but meanwhile the brandy may ease Mistress Merta's mind."

Garith nodded, "Thank you," he said.

He tipped the bottle up and drank. The liquor was raw and burned all the way down. It made him cough, but the heat of it radiated through him quickly. He passed the bottle to his wife. She sniffed at the mouth of the bottle and made a face.

"Swill," she said, and tried to hand it back to her husband, but he refused to take it.

"Drink some. It will help."

"Nothing will help," she said, acidly.

That was enough. Garith lost his temper. "I did not ask. I told you to drink, and by all the gods you will drink." He shoved the bottle back into her hands.

Merta looked as though he had slapped her. After a moment she took a sip from the bottle. Tears came to her eyes, but Garith could not tell if his words or the sting of the brandy had caused them.

The sun lowered, and a chill wind rose. The horses picked up their heads with the cold, and their steps lightened, but the chill added more misery to the riders. Thus far the days had been warm, but not too warm, and the nights had been cool, but not too cool. The travelers were higher in the mountains now though and autumn, which was only half over in the lowlands was well advanced here. The trees had gone from dusty green to multi-hued in only the days they had been traveling, and in the last few days the leaves had begun to fall thick upon the road.

Merta continued to pull at the brandy bottle through the afternoon. It helped to hold off the cold wind, but it added more melancholy to her already low spirits.

"Can we not stop for the night Alvis?" she begged.

"Tonight, we will sleep in a fine inn, Mistress," Lakis said, silently adding, *I hope*.

"But I am cold and tired and sore," she complained. "Can we not at least stop to rest for a moment?"

"The longer we rest, the longer it will take to reach the inn," Alvis said. He did not say he feared that if the horses stopped now they might not ever go on again. "Take a little more brandy, Mistress. We will be there soon."

Merta's body drooped with weariness. She lifted the bottle and sipped, then made a face at the raw burning of the liquor. She was taken with a fit of coughing from it and Garith gently pounded her back until she stopped. She held out the bottle to him. He took it and drank a little.

Merta began to cry softly as the brandy flowed through her. "Garith, Garith, what have we done to deserve this? We were good, prosperous people. We served the gods and turned an ill hand to no one. What happened? Why has this happened to us?"

Garith could not answer her. These were questions he had asked himself over and over with no answers coming to him. Alvis would have said that all, even the downfall of House Balal, was in the Design, but Garith did not believe in this Design. The gods he had once believed in were not gods, and the world he had always known was changed beyond all recognition. It had gone from being the center of the universe to being an insignificant dust mote among other dust motes in a universe so vast he could not begin to comprehend it.

"Oh, Mamma," Merta moaned through her tears. "Why didn't you listen?"

Garith felt a pang of responsibility that Merta's parents were in the dungeons and probably dead. There had never been any great love lost between him and his in-laws, but he had never wished them harm.

Garith's horse stumbled and the jounce brought him out of his thoughts and back to the cold road. He lifted his eyes and saw a light ahead.

There were horses in the paddock of the inn.

"Will they trade?" Alvis asked Lakis, who shrugged.

"If not, they may sell, but…" he shrugged again.

Alvis nodded. "Do the best you can. We have Mistress Merta's

Zari if we must use it. One way or another we must have fresh horses. Use the Enfolding Arms to ease the hostler's mind, but do not cheat him."

Lakis grinned crookedly. "Would I do that Master Alvis?"

"Yes, you would, but don't."

Lakis lifted his hands palm out to show his innocence and went to his horse-trading duties.

Merta was incoherent with brandy and woe when Alvis and Garith finally managed to get her into the room they had taken for the night. The innkeeper was not happy about having this strange band of people in his establishment, but after Zari changed hands, he let them pass.

"Just see to it that the woman…"

"My *wife* is ill," Garith said, cutting the man off.

"Of course, Gentle," the man said, all oil. "But please see to it that your ailing wife does not disturb my other guests."

"Certainly," Garith agreed, but not gently. "Send up hot food and mulled wine," he said, being only as civil as necessary.

"Of course, Gentles. And will you require water for bathing?" The man wrinkled his nose to make clear that the aroma of horse was strong about them.

"Yes," Garith said.

"I will take care of that, Master," Alvis said.

"Fine. Now help me with your Mistress."

When Garith and Merta were safely in their room and occupied with bathing and eating, Alvis took his own meal in the kitchen.

The help were mostly sitting around by this time. Dinner hour was passed, but, though this was an inn, travelers were not so frequent as once upon a time and a friendly face with a willingness to share a bottle of wine with the help was even rarer.

Alvis had found that a little wine and a willingness to listen were generally enough to get any news of the area without having to resort to questions. This was true in the Inn of Capani too, but the news was of no interest. At least there had been no word sent out to look for the four fugitives.

Lakis came into the kitchen as Alvis was preparing to leave.

"I have traded the horses for fresh ones," he said. "The deal was bad, but…"

"Just do not mention to Mistress Merta how many of her Zari you had to spend."

Lakis nodded.

"Food?" Alvis asked.

"Yes, and wine. I am starving and the taste of that cheese is still in my mouth." He made a face.

Alvis smiled and clapped his hand on the other's shoulder. "Then perhaps the cook's stew will taste better to you than it did to me."

"So long as it is hot."

Alvis laughed and called for food for his friend, but before it could be brought, there was a clattering of hooves and a man stomped into the common room of the inn.

"Inn keeper," he shouted. "Food and a fresh horse, in the name of the Gods and Lord Linser!"

Alvis stepped back into shadow and watched as the inn keeper scurried around trying to determine what was needed by this distinguished visitor.

After a bit, the rider sat himself at a table and a bowl of stew and a cup of wine were brought.

"Your saddle will be changed to a fresh horse, my Lord," the inn keeper said. "It will be ready to ride as soon as you have finished your food and rested a moment."

Alvis returned to Lakis' side. "That is bad news sitting there. Keep your ears open and your face hidden. I will see what I can find out."

"What are you going to do?"

"Probe that one's mind, I hope." Alvis said.

"I could deal with him," Lakis said with a feral glint in his eyes.

Alvis considered it for a moment before disregarding the thought. "There would be too many questions. It may still come to that, but let me try first."

Lakis nodded, and Alvis went upstairs.

Garith and Merta had bathed and eaten and were the better for both. The brandy was still warming Merta's blood, but the food had helped bring her from weeping despair to mere sadness. Garith put her to bed and thought about crawling in himself, but though he was more tired than he had ever been in his life, he knew sleep would not come soon, so he sat in the window seat staring out at the night. It was so black. There was nothing but emptiness and sorrow out there, and fear.

A soft knock on the door brought his mind back to the room. Alvis opened the door and slipped in.

"Merta is sleeping," Garith said.

"Good. I had hoped so," the slave said, urgency in his voice.

"What is it?"

"There is a messenger from Lord Linser in the common room."

Garith rose from the window seat, a tingle of fear going through him.

"He demanded a fresh horse and food. He is eating now and that does not give me much time."

"Time?"

Alvis drew a deep breath then let it out. "I did not want to find you asleep. I need your help"

Garith could hear the tension in his slave's voice and it made another jolt of fear shoot through him. "What would you have me do?" he asked

"It is very simple really. I want you to do nothing save sit in your window seat while I probe the mind of that messenger, and perhaps plant a seed of fear there."

"And how will you do this?"

Again, Alvis drew a deep breath and let it out. "I have spoken of the five powers."

"Yes,"

"Now I will exercise one of them. It will be disturbing for you and dangerous for me, unless you are truly willing to help."

"I do not understand." Garith said.

"Nor do I expect you to, Master. Even when you have seen I do not expect you to understand. All I ask is that you sit quietly and see that I am not disturbed for a time."

Garith's face showed his confusion. "And what will you be doing while I sit quietly?"

"It will appear that I am sleeping, or perhaps even dead, but that will not be the case. I will be in deep concentration and that must not be disturbed, but because of the depth of my trance, I will be unable to defend myself should someone attack me, so…I am putting myself in your hands."

Garith blinked at the man who had been his slave. "I still do not understand Alvis, but I will not disturb you, and I will try to protect you if need be."

"That is all I can ask, Master Garith," Alvis said, and with that he lay down upon his back on the floor beneath the window seat where Garith sat down again.

Alvis might have accomplished what he intended while sitting, but he thought it far better to lie down flat since this was going to be as deep a trance as if he were going to separate himself into body and spirit. This was going to entail keeping two of the Mandalai before his mind's eye at the same time.

The Mandala of The Ear was the Mandala Alvis kept uppermost in his mind as he cast his mental ear around the inn, seeking the mind of the messenger. A time of confused mental noise almost made Alvis give up, but suddenly he struck the right mind. He probed delicately.

The messenger had many jumbled thoughts in his mind, not the least of which was anger that what had started out as a simple task had become so complicated. At every turn of his journey things had gone wrong. Horses had pulled up lame; saddle-girths suddenly broke; flash floods washed out pieces of the road; and headaches, the like of which he had never experienced. Worse than the worst hangover he had ever had, though he had not taken more than a cup of wine in days. And the rider from whom he had taken the packet had told him much the same thing.

But all Gods be thanked, he was near the end of his leg. If there was no more trouble, he would pass the message packet along to the next rider in a few hours.

Alvis probed deeper for the contents of the message, but the man did not know it. It was in a water proof envelope which the messenger kept beside him all the time. That could be taken care of later. First the messenger must be dealt with.

Alvis moved the Mandala of The Ear to the back of his mind, still keeping a clear picture of it and brought the Mandala of The Whisper to the front of his mental vision. It was difficult. It took much deeper concentration than merely listening to the messenger's thoughts.

When the Mandala was clear enough, Alvis projected his own thoughts toward the messenger's mind. He formed a thought; dark, foreboding and full of dread, that left no doubt in the mind of the messenger that doom had come upon him.

~ * ~

Garith sat in the window seat, hardly breathing, watching Alvis. It was very strange to watch the man he had known as slave and co-worker become something else. Garith had seen Alvis asleep before. One could not live in as close quarters as the house and shop in Peshar without knowing a person intimately, but this was different from sleep.

Alvis' body seemed to relax to the point of death. His breathing slowed and slowed so that, at last, Garith could hardly see the movement of his chest. There was no sound of breath, no movement of nostrils or mouth, yet there was a radiant energy pouring from the inert body. He had felt the sweep of the other's mind as it touched his mind and he felt that touch move on after a moment. Then there was nothing save the living, yet unliving, body on the floor before him.

Minutes passed. The wind sighed and moaned around the eaves and corners of the building and thickened the silence of the room. Garith found that he was holding his breath, waiting for something. He didn't know what.

Merta turned on the bed, the rustle of bed clothes loud in the silent room. Garith started at the sound and looked toward his wife. Her eyes were open.

"Garith, are you all right?" she asked.

The body on the floor was out of her view so long as she was lying down.

"Yes," he answered, "I am fine."

"You looked strange, as if you were afraid. Has something

happened?"

"No, nothing has happened. Go back to sleep."

"Are you coming to bed?"

"Soon. Go back to sleep."

Merta pushed herself onto one elbow. She could feel the power that filled the room, but had no clue what it was. When she lifted herself, she saw Alvis and she gasped. "What is wrong? What is the matter with Alvis?"

"Nothing is wrong. Alvis is…" But Garith didn't know what Alvis was.

Merta shivered. "What is going on?" she asked.

Garith rose from the window seat and carefully stepped over the body on the floor. He went to Merta, sat beside her and held her tight against him. "It is all right, Merta. Alvis told me what was going to happen. I didn't understand. I still don't, but it is all right. Don't be afraid."

There was no one in the common room when the messenger stopped eating with a spoonful halfway to his mouth; but when the man screamed, the cook, a serving man and Lakis ran from the kitchen to see what was causing the commotion.

The messenger, hearing the foot-steps drew his short sword and turned to face, what he thought, were enemies come to kill him.

The three men stopped and looked at one another, then at the man with drawn sword.

"What is it, my Lord," the serving man asked. "Is something wrong?"

"Stay back," the messenger shouted. "I will kill you."

"Yes, my Lord," the cook said. "We will stay away."

The messenger waved his sword, then turned and ran out the front door of the inn.

The three men looked at one another then shrugged in confusion. The cook turned to the servant and with a shaking voice said, "Find Master Capini, at once."

The serving man turned to do as he was told. As he left Lakis went into the common room and scooped up the packet that had been beneath the elbow of the messenger. It had fallen on the floor in the commotion. Lakis stuck the packet beneath his tunic then said, "I must tell my master what has happened," and went.

Alvis drew a deep, noisy breath. The sound of it was startling—fearful—as though a statue had suddenly taken a breath. Then his eyes opened and blinked and opened wide again. His head turned, and what had been like something dead became Alvis again. A sheen of perspiration was on his face and his color was pale, but he was once again the living being, they had known.

"Are you well, Alvis?" Garith asked.

"Yes."

"You are very pale and your hands are shaking. Are you sure you are all right?"

"I am well," Alvis said. "Use of the powers has a cost. The concentration leaves little of the mind to maintain the body."

"Powers?" Merta asked.

"Powers of the Mandalai, Mistress." He saw that the words meant nothing to her and she was about to ask more, but he sat up and stopped her with a raised hand. "I am sorry I cannot explain more clearly right now. My mind is whirling and I am exhausted. I will explain tomorrow as we travel. Now we must sleep a little. We must go soon though. I think I have bought us some time, but the presence of this messenger shows that Lord Linser knows we are headed for Keep Holis. I will try to get the message from the packet he carried to find out exactly what he does know."

Alvis tried to rise, but his legs were shaking so much that he could only make it to his knees.

"You are in no condition to move yet," Garith said, going to steady him. "I will get this packet. Where is it?"

Alvis sat back down on the floor. "It is a waterproof leather pouch that the messenger had beside him at the table."

A knock on the door frightened the three of them. Without waiting for permission to enter, Lakis burst through the door. The wooden bolt had not been drawn to lock the door. He drew the packet from beneath his tunic and held it up. "I do not know what you did to him, Master Alvis, but he ran out of the inn as though it were on fire."

Alvis took the pouch and began opening it. "Did anyone see you take it?"

"No," Lakis said and smiled.

"Good." Alvis finished reading the message. "It is an order to take and hold Keep Holis and the village below it," he said. "It also gives descriptions of us all."

The four were silent for a long moment. "What do we do now?" Garith asked.

"Get some sleep and move on quickly, before too many questions are asked." Alvis answered.

The fugitives were up and moving when daylight was still half an hour away. They took tea and gruel together in the kitchen.

Slave and master sitting at the same table made the cooks eyebrows crawl up, but he said nothing. These guests were already grumbling about being disturbed by mad men, and wondering aloud if something in the stew had sent the man off into madness.

As they left the kitchen Garith said, "You may tell the innkeeper that I will let all my friends and associates hear about his inn. He began by insulting my wife, then let some crazy man disturb our rest. I only hope the horses we traded for prove better than the service."

But Garith's words proved prophetic. The horses Lakis had traded for were not as good as the tired ones. The only thing better about them was that they were fresh.

"How much?" Merta asked, looking critically at them.

"Far more than I would have wished, Mistress," Lakis said.

"Be happy we have horses and are away from here with nothing more than a bad trade to show for it," Alvis said crossly, still weary from use of the Mandalai.

The sun rose and warmed the frost out of the air, and as it did, Alvis sensed that he could not avoid the explanations he had promised. At last he edged his horse between their two and began.

"First, let me tell you that I cannot really explain what the powers are, or how they work," he began. "I only know that they work. There are many I do not know how to use. I only know the five which my father and mother taught me. To use them one must be able to remember the designs and hold them in the mind. These designs are called Mandalai. If I had skill to draw, I could show you, but I have no such skill.

"And you can use these powers to your own ends?" Merta asked.

"If you mean could I use the Mandalai to help myself become a rich man, or a god of some sort," he shrugged, "I don't know. I have never thought of that. Perhaps I could, but somehow, I don't think so. I do not think the Master of the Design would allow it." He paused to consider this for a time and at last said, "Still, everything is in the Design, so perhaps. I do not know. I am a Servant of the Design and, as such, I will not use the powers except to accomplish the fulfillment of the Design."

"And what is that fulfillment," Garith asked.

"I do not know. I did not know I had any more than the small part of a slave to the Cadeki Empire until I came here. Now I know I am here to protect The Book of the Design, but that was not clear at first. It is still not clear why, but the Maker of All will reveal his will to me as I need to know it."

"Revealed?" Merta asked. "How?" She could not believe she had asked such a question, yet she found that she truly did want to know.

"I cannot tell you," Alvis said.

"Is it a secret?"

"Perhaps it is, but not one I am keeping. It is secret even from me. I know only what I must do."

"It sounds like nonsense," Garith said. "and yet…"

"I agree, but it is only the truth. I only know at the moment what I need to know. I suddenly find myself possessed of knowledge that something must be done. For instance, that is how I picked you from the crowd that stood before the auction block."

"But you said it was by the stain on my hands and the stoop of my stance and other such things," Garith said defiantly.

"Those things only confirmed what I knew in my heart. I cast my eyes over the crowd, and I knew that you must buy me."

Garith remembered how Alvis' eyes had locked onto his own, and how, from that point on, his bidding had not been within his own power.

"You…influenced me," Garith said, understanding. "You caused me to bid more than I ever would have."

"Yes."

"But there was no time when you lay as you did last night," Garith said.

"It was not necessary for that. Last night I used more than one Mandala at once. It is very difficult. It takes much concentration. At the auction I had only to influence you to do what you already had come to do. And I could look into your eyes. That makes the task more simple."

"You have used this power on me too, haven't you?" Merta asked.

The slave smiled. "I have calmed you many times. It was not difficult for the same reasons it was not difficult to influence Master Garith. You did not truly want to rave and shout at those times. You are a much better person than you let those around you see."

Merta tried to be angry, but found she couldn't and wondered if Alvis was perhaps tampering with her now. She tried to feel around in her emotions, and decided he was not. She turned her attention back to Alvis and Garith.

"But this power—last night it drained you. You were pale as death, and so shaky you could not even stand for a long time."

"Small use demands a small price. Large use demands a large price, like last night."

"Where are we going, Alvis?" Merta suddenly asked.

"Keep Holis," Alvis said frowning. "I have told you that."

"But why? Why did you not use your power to change Lord Linser's mind, or to hide whatever you wish hidden by clouding his reason? Why did you not spare us all this? Why did you not? My parents…?" Merta's voice fell almost to a whisper. Tears were not far away from her eyes.

Alvis felt her pain and wondered himself why all had worked out as it had. "I do not know why, Mistress Merta. I would that it had not, but none of those things ever occurred to me. I did not think what I might do, only did what seemed right. I did not mean to involve you anymore than…but it was all done almost before I knew what was happening. The

Maker of All directs. I am only his tool. It must be that you both have a part of the Design, that is why you have been forced along the path with me. I do not understand why, but it must be so, else why are you here?"

Fifteen

605 A.C.G.

The news from the frontiers was bad, but then the news from the far reaches of the Empire was almost always bad. Still, the regularity of it did not make Cadek IX, four hundred fifth Emperor of Perus, Ruler of Ten Thousand Suns, Defender of the Faith, Preserver of the Races, any easier in his mind. The Empire was collapsing —imploding under pressure from a hundred planetary uprising and continual attack by Garins who coveted the Ten Thousand Suns. But more dangerous was the internal rot of the imperial government, and the rot of the infrastructure. Things as simple as bridges were on their last legs; and crumbling bridges and roads were only the dimmest reflections of other neglect. There were no new starships and old ships were falling out of service by the dozen. Those ancient, non-serviceable ships were being cannibalized to make repairs on ships still fit to travel, but those repairs were temporary and, for the most part, badly done. Without serviceable starships there could be no travel outside the Transit Net. No travel to set up new Transit Gates. No travel to attack the Garin hoards who carved off slices of the Empire almost at will.

But more important than the starships was the Transit Net.

It had once stretched from rim to rim of the Empire. Transit Gates were the means of intra-Empire travel, but more than that, they were the means to govern an Empire that included near half the galaxy. With a serviceable Transit Net Cadeki governors could step from Perus at the center of the Empire to Farstar at the edge of the Empire in minutes. An Emperor might personally take a hand in governance if he cared to. The last several Emperors had not cared to. This reluctance was part addiction to luxury and part self-preservation. There was a distinct chance that a traveling Emperor might be assassinated (few Emperors died of old age), but more to the point, the Emperors feared the questionable condition of the Transit Net. The Gates, when maintained, were as sure as anything in life could be, but the Gates were no longer well maintained. Now, one might step through a Gate to another world and not be able to step back; or step into the midst of a planetary revolt; or into the depths of outer space.

All these problems weighed upon the mind of Emperor Cadek IX as he heard the latest dismal assessment of the situation at the edges of the Empire. His attention kept drifting away from the reports of General Vembra Tretcher and Admiral Inted Perma.

"We cannot continue to hold all the Transit Gates, Majesty," Perma said. "We have neither ships nor troops enough."

General Tretcher agreed and added, "If every person in the Empire could bear arms, we could not hold all the gates, Majesty. We must pull back to a defensible perimeter."

"And relinquish part of the Empire?" Cadek asked, stunned. "No, absolutely not. We will not have it. We will not go down in history as the Emperor who gave away the Empire. We will not." The Emperor's voice rose in pitch and volume as he delivered this Imperial decree.

Perma swallowed hard at the thought of bucking an Imperial decree, but he had to do something. "Your Majesty, we would pull back only from those worlds for which we have no use and over which we no longer have control."

The Emperor narrowed his eyes at Admiral Perma's contradiction, but he was not fool enough to call guards to take the Admiral into custody for insubordination. Perma was popular, and worse, he might be right. Cadek drew a deep breath and puffed it out. "And if we do relinquish these worlds, could they be taken back later?"

Perma and Tretcher looked at each other, trying to read one another's minds. Both considered whether they should lie and say yes, or speak truth and risk everything including the lives of their families. Both knew there would be no re-taking from the Garins. The only chance to preserve any part of the Empire was to back away from them; to throw them a bone to gnaw while the Empire made itself strong enough to resist further invasion. Only sheerest luck had allowed the Empire to stave off the Garin invasion so far, and the largest part of that luck was that no functional Transit Gate had fallen into Garin hands. If a Gate, or worse a Multi-Terminus, should fall into their hands they could push troops through in their thousands right onto Perus, the very heart of the Empire.

In a second each man made his decision.

"We can re-take the worlds, Majesty," they agreed. "If we pull back now it will give us time to re-build the fleet and repair the Transit Net."

The Emperor leaned his elbows on the arms of his throne and massaged his temples, trying to drive away the pain of indecision. At last he said, "Very well, very well. You have our permission to withdraw, but only enough to give us time to prepare to recapture the Empire."

Perma and Tretcher both heaved sighs of relief and bowed their way out of the Imperial presence. They retired to a council room and ordered food and wine. Over the meal they discussed their options.

"We must set up a buffer," Perma said. "If we go out to the hundredth ring of the Transit Net and destroy all the Terminals it will break contact with the Garins. It could take them a thousand years to find us again."

"That will not make the Emperor happy," Tretcher said. "You are giving away almost a tenth of the Empire."

"Better to give away a tenth and preserve the rest than to lose it all."

"True enough."

"Besides, if God is merciful, we may have a new Emperor soon…" Perma said.

Tretcher lifted his hand to his mouth, holding a finger across his lips. He then pointed toward the ceiling and twirled the finger in a small circle.

Both men hoped for a strong emperor to replace Cadek IX, and they were not alone. Already odds makers were taking wagers that Cadek X would be on the throne within a year, but prudent men did not speak such things aloud.

"I have already drawn up plans and begun salvage operations on fifty worlds," Perma continued.

"You were so sure you could convince the Emperor?" Tretcher asked.

Perma shrugged. "I was sure withdrawal had to come whether I lived to see it or not."

"True enough. Have you a list of worlds in mind?"

Perma removed a single sheet of paper from the breast of his tunic and smiled with some bitterness. "This is the only copy. Naturally I will have more made now."

"Naturally," Tretcher said.

He could hardly believe the audacity of the Admiral. The man was ambitious. Perhaps he even had designs on the throne. He would bear watching. *It might be well to ally myself with him more firmly,* the general thought.

"Archlea," Tretcher said aloud as he read down the list. "A shame to lose that one. I have several tapestries. Such beautiful work!"

"I have never understood the fascination of them," Perma said. "They seem crude to me. It is a very primitive place."

"But that is their appeal, my dear Perma. They recall times when life was as simple as eating and sleeping."

"I suppose, but Archlea cannot be spared. It is a major Multi-terminus and we cannot let it fall into Garin hands, no matter what its bucolic charms."

"You are right of course. Still it is a shame."

~ * ~

Keep Holis looked like a ruin from the village in the valley below it. The towers and battlements appeared crumbled and decayed. The people of the village, which had no name save Village Beneath the Ruins, looked fearfully up at the ruin when they were asked about it.

"It is full of ghosts," they said. "No one from the village has been there for as long as forever. We are afraid the ghosts will kill us and make us ghosts too."

The travelers had come to the village in the midst of a driving autumnal rain storm and, though the villagers were mistrustful of strangers, they had been taken into the house of the village elder.

The old man could not, or would not, tell them anything except that the people of his village were servants of the gods—servants who seldom saw anything except their sheep and goats and the changing of the seasons. The Elder might even have forced the strangers to leave, rain or no rain, had it not been that Merta was burning with fever.

"You come to bring trouble on this village," he said, but his wife scolded him for thinking of turning out a sick woman to die in the rain. The old man grumbled, but gave the four a corner of his house and some sheep skin blankets to keep Merta warm. It did not hurt that Garith showed the old man some gold Zari and promised that they would be his if he helped Merta.

Alvis was anxious to begin searching for the book, so he left Garith and Lakis to watch over Merta and began questioning the villagers about the Keep. There was a burning fear in Alvis' middle and that fear grew each hour he did not have possession of the book.

The villagers were no help. All seemed truly fearful of the Keep. Alvis even mentioned the name Javi Holis, but received only blank stares. Either these people truly did not know anything about the book, or they were unbelievably good at concealing their connection. Alvis even probed a few minds, but that came to nothing.

At first light on the second day, Alvis set out to search the Keep himself. Tradition taught that *The Gods Show Mercy* told where the Great Book was hidden, but tradition did not tell how to read the hidden message in the tapestry. As he climbed through thorny brush and over crumbling shale a part of Alvis' mind went over and over the picture in the tapestry. The Palatine yarn had led him here, but that was all. The rest of the puzzle was in the picture…he hoped.

After an hour of climbing Alvis sat to rest. The air was still and chilly. Not cold enough to make breath turn to steam, but not far from that. The clear mountain air made the village below the Keep seem almost unreal in its clarity. Alvis could see every stone of every house even from this distance. Smoke rose in straight columns from chimneys colored with gray green lichen. It was a perfect picture of tranquility and peace.

It suddenly came to him that the central portion of *The Gods Show Mercy* was a picture of this village. He drew a deep breath of satisfaction. The knowledge didn't really help him much, but it did mean that he had not been wrong in coming here. The book was near, but he was no closer to finding it.

When Alvis reached the Keep, he found that it was not quite the ruin it appeared to be from the village. Most of the battlement walls had fallen, and the out-buildings were nothing but heaps of stone and dust, but the main Keep was mostly intact. Inside there was not much ruination. The stone floors were thick with dust and windblown leaves. Some had grass growing up through cracks, but the lack of sunlight in the depths of the building stymied the efforts of Archlea to call everything man-made back to its natural state. It had been a long time since anyone had set foot inside the Keep, but there was evidence that not everyone stayed completely away. Through the ruins outside the Keep there were footpaths worn. The heaps of stone which had been the battlement walls were threaded through with them. Probably some of the houses in the village below were built of stones scavenged from the fallen walls and buildings. Also, there were sheep droppings in the grassy meadow which had once been the commons of the Keep, and the grass was trimmed close to the ground. Some brave shepherd was using the Keep grounds as his own private pasture.

Alvis did not find sheep or shepherd before the hastening night made him head back to the village.

Merta was better. Her fever had broken and she was hungry, but more indicative of her recovery was that she expressed disgust with the hovel which the village elder called a house.

"The place is infested with fleas," she said. "And I have not seen that old woman wash so much as one dish since we have been here."

"Now, Merta," Garith began. "They were kind enough to take us in and share what little they had when we were in need."

Merta snorted at that. "They shared nothing. I heard you offer to pay and I saw you slip the old man a Zari this morning. I was fevered, not delirious."

Garith colored at being caught in this lie, but came back with, "No matter what you think you saw, we needed a place to take care of you and this was what came to hand. Don't make trouble. They could still throw us out."

"Perhaps it is time to leave anyway," she said. "I am much better."

"We have no need to move, Merta. We are here," Garith said.

"Yes, Mistress. This is Keep Holis, or rather the village below Keep Holis," Alvis said.

Merta wrinkled her nose. "But must we stay here? Is there no place else where we may get away from the fleas…and the stink?"

"There is no inn and no vacant house." Garith explained.

"Well, what about this Keep you have been on about, Alvis? Could we not go there?"

Alvis shrugged. "It is a ruin, Mistress. Full of dust and cobwebs and ghosts, if the people of the village are to be believed."

"All Gods be witness," Merta moaned. "I have been brought to the ends of the world to sleep on the floor of a stinking, flea-ridden hovel."

At that moment the elder's wife returned from the village well with a jar of water that seemed almost as large as she was. She looked sharply at Merta, and Merta gave the look back with more iron in it.

"There are some enclosed rooms in the Keep," Alvis hurried to say. "We could go there. It will not be as comfortable as this gracious house…" He used The Enfolding Arms on the old woman to calm the situation.

Leaping at the idea Garith said, "That would be wonderful."

"The Keep is full of ghosts," the old woman said, seeming to relish the news.

"We will take our chances with the ghosts," Merta said, smiling sweetly.

In the morning the travelers moved to the Keep. For the sake of the horses, they found it necessary to go a long way up the valley before cutting back along a faint trail.

They arrived at mid-morning and began looking for a room still tight enough to keep the wind out, and the heat of a fire in. They found it in a room off what had been the main hall of the Keep. It was not large, but there was a fire place with stone benches to the right and left of it.

Lakis set a fire and when it was blazing merrily, he made tea while the others explored.

The quiet was enough to make them believe in the ghosts of which the villagers had warned. The only sounds were the moaning of the wind and the flutter of the birds who roosted inside the ruin.

In one room they found many stone tables like those in a restaurant. Just off that room they found the kitchen. The huge kitchen fireplace still held swing arms and pot hooks of metal which told more truly how much the villagers feared this place than all they had said. One might take stone from the collapsed walls, but one dared not come inside the Keep, even for anything as precious as usable metal swing arms and pot hooks.

"This kitchen could have served a hundred people," Merta said.

"Once it served more than that," Alvis said. "My father told me that Keep Holis once housed a thousand Servants of the Design."

"And how did he know?" Merta asked sarcastically. "This place has not housed anyone from time out of mind."

"Legend, Mistress, passed from parent to child since time out of mind."

"Where did they all go, Alvis?" Garith asked.

The slave shrugged. "Again, all I know is legend. It says the Great Designer allowed the gods to find all these and send them across the sky to serve the Design there."

"And did they serve the Design?" Merta asked, trying to sound acid but failing.

A sense of awe blunted her sharpness in this place. Try as she might to disbelieve, in this place the Design had once been the rule, and she could not maintain her hostility toward belief. Perhaps it was because she was still reeling from all the blows of the last weeks, or because she was still weak from fever, but the idea of the Design did not seem impossible anymore.

"Yes, Mistress. They did. They still do."

Merta and Garith looked their doubt at the slave.

"Oh, I do not mean those same people. They have long finished their part of the Design and gone on to the next work the Maker of All has for us. I mean that those Servants of the Design fostered others who fostered others down the ages, and so the Design continues. In my former master's house, there was constant talk of the Servants of the Design. They are on many worlds. Those of the Cadeki Empire did not know whether to fear or help them, so, as with many things of the people you call the gods, nothing was done."

"But…" Garith began, but trailed off to begin again. "I do not understand, Alvis. Why has this Designer seen fit to destroy my life and cast me into danger? I am no Servant of the Design."

Alvis could only shrug. "The Maker of All works his will even through those who do not believe. You have some part to play, but I do not know what that part may be."

The exploration of Keep Holis gained the travelers nothing. They visited each part of the place, both those that were relatively whole and those that were complete ruin, but they found no sign that might lead them to the book. Alvis was discouraged and worried. Time was running out. He could feel the seconds slipping away, but there was nothing to do save continue to look and wait upon the will of the Designer.

After the first day of exploration the four prepared to bed down. They ate a meager supper of trail meat (dried strips of meat of unidentifiable source) and hard bread, then rolled themselves into their blankets to sleep.

The night wind moaned and wept its way through the ruins and made them uneasy in their sleep. Merta particularly felt the unease. Her dreams roiled about like a dust cloud and she half woke to see the fire burning low and the others bundled close in their blankets and cloaks against the cold.

Then she heard the voice of the Maker of All.

Merta dreamed of a room in the midst of the Keep. It was empty like all the others, but there was a smell which permeated the very walls of the room. It was an aroma she knew well. The aroma of paper and ink and paint. It smelled like Garith's shop in Peshar.

"Seek here, child," said the voice.

In her dream Merta looked around the room seeking the source of the voice but found no one.

"Who is it?" she called.

"It is the one who made you, child. The one who made all," the voice answered.

"But I am no servant of your Design, oh Maker of All," she said.

"You are a part of it, nevertheless."

"But I do not wish to be a part of it," Merta cried. "I wish to be back in Peshar, in the house of my husband."

"That time is past Child. All the universe changes, and you are a part of it."

"You are most cruel, Designer, to let your creatures be used up in this way. Why did you not make everything kind? Why did you make so much pain?"

The voice sounded sad when it said, "I cannot explain it to you, child. You would not understand, but it is like the goldsmith who burns his gold to take out that which is not gold."

"But people are not gold," Merta said bitterly. "We are living things."

"Yes, and I regret your pain, but it cannot be helped."

Merta bowed her head, knowing that the Maker of All spoke truth; the pain in the Design was not just the pain of the people, but of the Designer. Yet she could not bring herself to submit, though she knew the truth.

The fire crackled and popped and Merta sat up, wide awake. She spent the rest of the night thinking upon the dream and looking into the fire.

When there was light enough Merta left the others still sleeping and went to the room she had seen in her dream. High windows let light flood into the room, and it was like the room in the dream, but there was no smell of paper and ink. Dust was thick and soft, and the corners were tangled with cobweb, but there was no feeling of fear or worry as she looked around the room. The roof was mostly intact when she looked up, though she could see blue sky through a few holes. After a while Merta stretched out her arms and said, "Oh, Designer, I am here. What would you have me find?"

Alvis, Lakis, and Garith woke as if someone had called them from sleep. As one man they discovered that Merta was not among them.

A thrill of fear went through Garith. He was no believer in ghosts, but the ruined Keep was enough to rattle even the most stolid realist. "Where is she?" he cried. No one answered him, and he threw off his blanket and stood and began shouting "Merta? Where are you, Merta?"

"She cannot be far, Master Garith. It is barely light and she would not have wandered off in the dark," Alvis assured his master.

"How do you know?" Garith snapped, his voice rising with a note of panic.

"I will go look for her," Lakis said.

"I will go with you," Garith said.

"We will all go," Alvis said and rose. He brought the Mandala of The Enfolding Arms before his mind's eye and sent the radiant calm of it out toward Garith. The effect was almost immediate. Garith calmed and became more rational. After a moment Alvis let the Mandala fade and the three men went out the door.

Lakis scanned the dusty stone floors for foot prints, but there had been too much going and coming the day before. There were a thousand tracks and it was impossible to tell one from the other. "Perhaps we should look outside," he said. "Tracks should be less muddled there."

"I do not think she went outside," Alvis said. "She is somewhere close, I am sure."

"Well then, which way?" Garith said. He was not panicky now, but he was still barely in control.

"There," Alvis said pointing across the great hall toward a door at the other end. They went.

Inside the door they found a single set of tracks in the dust. The smallness of them told the men the tracks belonged to Merta.

After a few moments they entered the room where Merta was. She was kneeling in a spot of sunlight which slanted through a hole in the roof. Before her was a loose flagstone which had covered a small cavity beneath the floor. She held a scroll made of vellum and stared at it intently, her concentration so deep that she did not even look up when the men came to her side.

Garith put his hand upon her shoulder and she looked up at him and smiled. "I found it," she said. "Right here under the stone. The sun showed me where, and I lifted the stone and there it was. Isn't it beautiful?"

And it was beautiful. In the center of the vellum was a block with a post upon each side of it. A smaller block sat atop the larger block, and from that smaller block radiance seemed to pour in swords of light. Surrounding the central picture was an intricate pattern of lines which looked like a maze.

"It is a Mandala," Alvis said. "But one I have never seen before."

"I can feel it reaching into me," Merta said. "It is as though it is trying to tell me something, but I do not understand."

"May I see it?" Alvis asked.

Merta did not hesitate. She held it out to her slave. "It is brittle," she said. "But I do not think it will break."

Alvis took the scroll gently and examined it minutely. He could feel the power of it drawing him in, but he could not understand the meaning of it.

"How did you know to come here, Mistress?" Lakis asked.

"The Designer told me in a dream. He said I was his child and that I should look here," she lifted her arms to the room. "This is a place where people once worked with paper and ink. I could smell it in my dream. It smelled like the shop Garith."

"But you are not..." Garith began.

"A believer in this Design," Merta finished for him. "I said that to the Maker of All, but he said the same thing Alvis said. He said it didn't matter if I believe or not because we are all part of the Design whether we believe or not."

Lakis smile. "All is in the Design, Mistress."

Sixteen

605 A.C.G.

Alvis studied the Mandala for hours. He could feel the power of it, but the interpretation of it, the use of it, escaped him. Like all Mandalai this one was lines and patterns which led the eye into the center of the drawing. The colors of it were vividly, vibrantly alive. The center was strange, like nothing any of them had ever seen, yet it was not solely a pattern of color and line. It looked like a table, or perhaps an altar, with thick columns at each side of it. In the middle of the table, between the columns, sat something else, a box perhaps. But if it was a box there was no indication upon it, or anywhere else in the Mandala, what it might contain.

At last Alvis put the scroll down and rubbed his eyes. His head pounded because of the prolonged concentration. "I am too blind or stupid to understand," he said to Lakis who had been puttering around the fire preparing food.

"Perhaps if you sleep on it," Lakis said. "Here. Eat." He extended a steaming bowl of stew.

Alvis made a face at the bowl, but took it and began to eat. He expected the usual slightly musty taste of trail meat stew, but this time the taste was of fresh vegetables and meat that had been fresh killed. Alvis stopped chewing in surprise. "Where did this come from?"

"While you studied, I explored one of the trails leading from the grassy place outside. I found a flock of sheep. The shepherd boy sold me a haunch he swore he had just killed. Personally, I think the sheep died of old age, but even gamy mutton is better than stringy trail meat."

"You are not wrong my friend," Alvis said and shoveled more stew into his mouth. He continued to do so for quite a time, savoring the taste. After a time, he lowered the bowl and wiped his mouth with the back of his hand. "Where are Master Garith and Mistress Merta?" he asked.

"Where she found the Mandala."

"What are they doing there, searching for more loose stones?"

"They are sitting. They aren't even talking, not even Mistress. They are just sitting."

"Hm," Alvis grunted and frowned, but then shook his head and resumed eating. Too soon the bowl was empty and he put it down regretfully. "Not at all bad, Lakis. Not at all bad. Now if you could just come up with some kind of bread other than these trail biscuit stones."

Lakis laughed. "I asked the shepherd boy for some bread but he said he didn't have any."

Alvis grunted again. "Ah well. Whatever made you go exploring?"

"I thought the grass looked a little too short to have been left on its own, and then there was the pile of sheep dung I stepped in." He shrugged.

"And who is this brave shepherd that isn't afraid of the ghosts of the Keep?"

"Just a shepherd boy. He had his sheep penned into a little dell with a hollow in the cliff at the back. Said he closed his sheep into the hollow at night so he didn't have to worry about wolves."

"That is probably what happened to that fellow in the pot," Alvis nodded toward the still bubbling stew. "Probably wolf killed. The boy found the carcass abandoned on the hillside…"

"And sold it to us," Lakis finished for him and laughed. "Leave it to these mountain people not to waste anything."

The sun was still above the horizon, though not much above and Alvis felt he should study the scroll more, but his weariness and his pounding head, made him give up the idea and roll up in his robe beside the fire and go to sleep.

Sheep penned in hollows invaded his dreams. They milled around and around in a circle, keeping their heads toward the center of the group. As they moved, they seemed to change into the whorls of the Mandala he had been studying. The hollow full of sheep was now a circling whirlpool and at the vortex was a table with pillars on either side. On the table sat a box.

Alvis snapped awake and sat up. He struggled out of the folds of his robe and went to the scroll.

Lakis stared at Alvis in surprise. "What is it? You have hardly fallen asleep and here you are up again."

The other did not answer. His full concentration was on the Mandala. He allowed the Mandala to pull him into itself, and stopped trying to understand it. He allowed it to speak to him and in a moment he understood.

Alvis lowered the scroll and lifted his head. He closed his eyes and turned his head slowly from side to side. The scroll was clear in his mind and as he turned his head from side to side, the colors of it became more bright and alive when he faced in a particular direction. With his eyes still closed he took a step in the direction where the Mandala seemed brightest. Then he took another and another…and tripped over Lakis' outstretched legs.

"What are you doing?" Lakis demanded, rubbing the place on his shin where Alvis had kicked him.

"Stand up, stand up," Alvis commanded. "Take my hand and lead me."

"Lead you? To where?"

"Just do as I tell you. Take my hand and lead me where I point."

Lakis stood up and took the outstretched hand. Alvis pointed toward the blank wall across the room. Lakis thought his friend had lost his mind, but he led him to the wall and stopped.

"No, go on," Alvis said excitedly.

"We can't. We are at a wall."

Alvis opened his eyes, saw where they were, then turned and ran from the room. Lakis followed, wondering if the other really had gone mad.

Outside in the sheep meadow Alvis closed his eyes once again and turned in a slow circle until the Mandala was clear and bright before his mind's eye. When it was, he opened his eyes and ran on up the sheep trail before him. After a few dozen steps he stopped, closed his eyes again to assure himself he was indeed going in the right direction, then opened them and ran on up the trail.

Lakis followed at a distance. He watched Alvis run, stop, and turn with closed eyes before running on. He tried closing his own eyes thinking perhaps to see whatever it was Alvis was seeing, but there was nothing but dark behind his eyelids and nothing but dirt and brush and slowly darkening twilight before them. But he continued to follow and drew closer as the twilight thickened, fearing he might lose sight of Alvis. He was not sure he could find his way back to the Keep in the dark, but he feared to let Alvis go on alone in such an insane fashion for fear he might run off a cliff.

It was full dark when Alvis stopped. He had come hard up against a sheer rock wall. It was so dark that Lakis could hardly see the other, though they were only a pace apart.

"Alvis, what is it? We must go back. It is dangerous to be out here after dark. We could fall down a hole in the rocks or lose ourselves."

"It is here, Lakis. It is here. I can feel it."

"What? What is here?"

"The Book of the Design. It is here." He pointed to the sheer rock wall before him.

Lakis squinted, trying to see better through the darkness. But there was nothing save a solid wall of living stone. "I see nothing, Alvis. Only a wall."

"It is here nevertheless," Alvis said.

After another moment of squinting at the wall Lakis said, "If it is here, we will find it tomorrow. We will come back at first light. Now we must go back to the Keep. Master Garith will be worried."

Alvis looked again at the wall and said, "Tomorrow at first light."

Alvis and Lakis left the Keep when it was barely light enough to see the path before them. Garith and Merta stayed behind, glad to rest another day and go on with the talking and quietness of the day before. It was as though they were preparing for something, waiting for something, though neither could say what.

The rock wall was as solid in the daylight as it had appeared in the dark. There was no crack or hole or fissure, but when Alvis faced the wall and closed his eyes, he could see the Mandalaya more clearly than if he had the scroll in his hands.

"There must be a way up or around or through," Alvis said.

A reedy child's voice startled them when it said, "There is a path leading up, back that way." It was the shepherd boy who had sold Lakis the mutton. The slaves noticed that he had a withered arm, and that the left side of his face was slightly deformed.

"And where does this path lead?" Alvis asked with more sharpness than he had intended, but the boy did not seem to take offense.

"It goes to a small meadow where I sometimes graze my sheep."

"A meadow," Lakis said, disappointed. "Nowhere else?"

The boy shrugged. "There is a crack in the rocks that leads to a cave, but it is too small and too high up to be of any use."

"Where are your sheep, boy?" Lakis asked, noticing for the first time that they were not with the shepherd.

The boy tossed his head to indicate they were behind him somewhere. "The dogs watch them while I hunt," he said twirling the sling he carried.

"Will you show us this meadow, shepherd?" Alvis asked, trying to temper his eagerness.

The boy considered the proposition for a moment then said, "Perhaps I will find a fat rabbit along the way. Come."

Alvis and Lakis looked at one another, surprised at the tone of command in the child's voice, but they followed.

The shepherd led them along the path at a quick trot, as though daring them to notice the slight limp in his left leg.

Soon the slaves were panting with the exertion. The boy did not seem to notice, only went on trotting and leaping and weaving like one of the lambs from his flock at play.

Alvis had almost decided to ask the child to slow down when he stopped.

"Are you tired?" he asked, grinning.

Both men were breathing hard. "How much farther?" Lakis asked.

"A little way. You can see the crack from here." He pointed up the path. "Are you ready?"

"A little slower, if you don't mind," Alvis said, capitulating to the boy.

"Very well, a little slower," he answered and started.

A half hour of climbing brought them over a ridge and down into the shallow bowl of a meadow. "The cave is up there," their guide said, pointing toward what appeared to be a smooth cliff face.

"Where? I do not see it." Lakis said.

"There," Alvis said. "Behind that big bush."

The shepherd nodded.

The bush seemed to cling to an almost vertical rock face. A line of ledge so faint as to be almost invisible from the floor of the meadow to the bush.

"Are you sure, Alvis?" Lakis asked, swallowing hard. He did not like climbing even on wide paths, and this ledge looked exceedingly thin.

Alvis closed his eyes and faced the rock wall. The Mandala glowed so bright it was as though it were on fire.

"I am sure," he said.

"Have you been inside this cave," Lakis asked the shepherd.

"Yes, a little. There are many tunnels. You could get lost forever if you are not careful. Or the ghost of the old man might get you."

"Ghost? Like the ghosts in the Keep?" Alvis asked.

The boy grinned. "No. The ghosts in the Keep are only moaning wind and stirring dust. The old man is a true ghost. He is very bent and crippled and old. He reaches out toward anyone who comes near and tries to grab them."

"And you have seen him, this ghost?"

"Yes. I turned down a tunnel where I had never gone before and he reached out to grab me. I ran. That was the last time I went more than a few steps into any cave."

The men looked at one another, not knowing whether to smile at the boy's story or take it seriously, but something told them that this was another sign from the Maker of All.

"We would like to see this ghost," Alvis said. "Could you take us to where you saw him?"

The shepherd boy swallowed hard but did not answer directly. "The entrance is up there," he said, pointing toward the bush growing out of the cliff.

Alvis said, "I know," eager to be off all the same.

Lakis was not so sure. "Is there no other way?" he asked.

"Perhaps. Most caves have more than one entrance, but I do not know of another."

"Will you take us?" Alvis asked again.

"The opening is very small. You will have to crawl to get through."

"I can crawl if need be," Alvis said.

The boy still hesitated.

"You are afraid of this old man," Alvis said gently.

The boy hung his head. "Yes," he said.

"How is it that you are not afraid of the ghosts of the Keep, but you are afraid of this old man?" Lakis asked.

The boy shrugged; his head still sunk in shame. "If there are any ghosts in the Keep, they are my friends."

The men did not understand and the boy, glancing up, saw that they did not. "The ghosts of the Keep help me. All the boys from the village are afraid. They do not follow me there because they are afraid of the ghosts."

The men looked at the child's withered arm, deformed face, and limp, and understood the torture other children must have inflicted on him. No wonder the boy thought of the ghosts of the Keep as friends. They did not care if he limped.

An idea came to Alvis. "What is your name shepherd?" He asked.

"Javi," the boy said.

The men were so stunned for a moment they could not say anything. Surely this was a sign from the Maker of All!

"Javi, I think I know who the ghost of the old man is," Alvis said at last.

The boy studied the slave's face, thinking to find mockery there, but he did not. "Who is the old man?" he asked.

"His name is Javi, too. Like yours. He guards the Great Book and we must find that. You can take us there and I promise the old man will not hurt you. He has waited a long time and he will not hurt you."

Javi blinked at them several times, then nodded and led off up the ledge toward the opening.

The ledge proved somewhat wider than it appeared from the bottom, which made Lakis' knees less wobbly, but the climb was still steep, and the opening was as small as Javi had promised. And it was dark. Very dark. "We will never find anything in here," Lakis said. "I can't even see my hand in front of my face."

"I hadn't thought of this," Alvis said.

"There is light." Javi said. "I left a lamp and a jar of oil once. It is probably still there."

"Very well," Alvis said. "Go ahead."

They squirmed and crawled through the tight, black throat of the mountain for what seemed hours, but was really only minutes. At last they could no longer touch the sides of the cave with their out stretched arms and Javi said they could stand up.

"Wait," Javi said and they did.

After a moment there was a click of surface striking surface and a white spark jumped. It ignited a small flame which illuminated Javi's hands. He lifted the tender box above his head. The dim light was like a beacon, and in a moment the boy had found what he was looking for. A brighter flame rose from the oil lamp, illuminating the chamber. Several dark openings led from it.

Javi capped his tender box to put out the flame, then put it and his fire making stones in the pouch which hung at his waist.

"I left this oil and lamp last time I was here. I was too afraid to come back for it. Come," he said, again with that strange tone of command in his voice. There was no sign of fear there now.

After a time, the boy slowed. He had been moving with confidence, turning into openings and ducking beneath low overhangs as though he were walking along the village street, but now he crept along, then stopped. "Up there a little farther is where the old man is," he said.

Alvis had not closed his eyes to look for the Mandala since coming into the cave. Now he did and turned slowly around.

The Mandala was clearer than ever before. It was blinding in its brightness. He opened his eyes and found himself facing in the direction the boy had indicated. He was not surprised. "That is the direction we must go," he said.

Javi swallowed hard, his fear showing in his widening eyes. He looked down the tunnel then back at the men. "I am named for Javi Holis," the boy said. "He was a holy man from times before the gods. My mother told me always to remember that. This ghost is that holy man, isn't it?"

"I think so," Alvis said.

Javi looked down the tunnel again, took a deep breath and started forward.

No ghost appeared, but at the end of the passage Javi's lamp illuminated the stone altar with the stalagmites beside it. It looked just like the Mandala Alvis had been following, and in its center was the box containing The Book of the Design.

"Where is the ghost of the old man?" Javi asked.

"He is here," Alvis said. "He has showed us the way."

"But I did not see him," the boy said.

"It doesn't matter."

"Is this the book then?" Lakis asked.

"Yes."

There was a silence then, until Lakis asked, "We have the book. Now what?"

In truth Alvis had not thought about what to do next. Since it became clear to him that he had to retrieve the book, he had not thought of anything more than his next few moments. Now he had the book and no idea what to do next.

"Master Alvis?" Javi the shepherd boy said.

Both slaves looked at him. They had not known that the boy knew either of their names.

"We must do something soon," the boy went on. "The oil in my lamp is almost gone, and I have only a little left in the jar."

Alvis recognized that the boy was right. Something must be done, but somehow it did not seem right to take the book out of the cave. It had rested safely here for six hundred years. If he took it out that protection was ended. But why had he been brought here if not to bring the book out?

A gasp from Lakis and Javi caught Alvis' attention and he looked up. Standing before the altar stone was an old man, very stooped and gray. He leaned upon a staff. As the three watched he lifted his hand and smiled. "It is time," the old man said. "All is in the Design," and then he was gone.

The journey out of the cave was more difficult and time consuming than had been the journey in. The box was heavy and many narrow passages seemed to have become more narrow, but Javi the shepherd was relentless. He slowed only a little if the others fell behind and each slowing he would glance accusingly at the lamp flame then back at the struggling men, and the men would demand more of their aching muscles.

The last of the journey was made in darkness, for Javi's oil played out just as they entered the throat which lead out. They pushed and pulled and clawed their way down the black tunnel until they emerged from the womb of the earth into the bright light of afternoon.

Javi, the shepherd boy, did not accompany the two slaves back to the Keep. Somewhere along the paths through the brush and weeds he dropped off unnoticed. It was only when Alvis missed the boy that he wondered whether the shepherd had been real or some messenger from the Designer.

Merta and Garith waited with tea and trail biscuits when the other two returned with the box.

"Is that what has cost us everything?" Merta asked, but not sharply.

"The Great Book is in that box…I think," Alvis said.

"You think?" Garith said unbelieving. "You mean you have not opened it?"

"There was not time. The lamp oil was low."

"Then let us open it now," Garith and Merta commanded together. "I would know what the thing which has destroyed my world looks like,"

Garith added.

The opening proved to be more difficult than they had anticipated. The box was nailed shut with bronze nails and sealed with wax which had hardened until it was like glass. Inside was a package also sealed with wax. This wax made the package almost like a quartz boulder. This stopped them for a time. They tried cutting it with a bronze knife, but the sharp blade hardly scored the surface.

At last, Alvis took a loose floor stone and gently tapped a corner of the bundle. The ancient wax shattered into flesh-scoring shards. The four picked out the pieces of shattered wax, and the brittle leather pieces which had also cracked.

Several more layers of the packing were glassy and brittle, but in the final two layers the wax was still soft, and the leather wrapping pliable. Trembling with anticipation, they carefully peeled off and discarded the last protective layers which had guarded *The Book of the Design* for six centuries, but, before opening the book they cleaned and doctored their hands. None of them had managed to come away unscathed. Each had cuts from the wax shards.

When the book was opened, Alvis turned each and every page with reverence, the others sitting beside him. They felt themselves drawn into the vibrant colors and precise designs of the Mandalai of power, none more so than Garith.

Later, as he lay in the darkness trying to sleep, Garith could not close out the image of Alvis' hand slowly, reverently turning each of the heavy pages. The meanings of the Mandalai were beyond his ken, but the image of them was burned into his mind. He could see every line, every color, every curl and sweep. He could almost see the hands of those who had created them—hands of men and women long dead, who created, not knowing that centuries later a displaced scribe of Peshar would see them. They did not know what they were creating. They followed the dictates of the Maker of All to a purpose beyond them.

And now those creations were a part of Garith. So much a part that he could not understand how he had lived without them before. They were as essential as breath. As integral as blood. The Mandalai had taken possession of him. His life and his future were welded to them. His hands fairly itched to be at work making copies of them. He could feel his fingers curled about pens and brush handles with line and color flowing from them.

But this is nonsense, he thought. *I cannot do it now. I have no desk, no inkwell, no paint. And it is not time yet. It is not time.* He did not find these thoughts odd. Not in the least.

Merta's sleep was not troubled with images of the Mandalai of the Great Book, as her husband's was, or rather not with all of them. One page, though, had affected her from the first instant she laid eyes on it. When Alvis had turned to the twelfth of them, she had shivered with deep recognition. Now, in sleep, that page came to her not as ink and paint, but as a living thing.

A stream of water flowed from the center of the picture. It was a small stream which flowed from a deep spring and formed a peaceful brook from which people of the village drew water to drink and wash with. A young girl brought her kitchen jar to the water, filled it, and carried it home. The girl would heat the water until it bubbled and steamed, preparatory to making tea.

Then the seasons of the picture changed. The brook froze over and the people of the village had to break a hole in the ice to draw water. The ice was more than mere ice however. It was hardened water, but Merta did not understand what significance was in that.

Spring came to the Mandala. Trees budded and leafed. Grass grew, and the brook thawed and flowed away. All was well with the village and the world. Merta heard the voice of the Maker of All. "Thus, also flesh," the voice said.

Merta woke with a start and sat up. All was quiet in the Keep. The men slept and the fire burned low, throwing black, flickering shadows across the room. Merta listened for the voice of the Designer, but heard only the sighing of the night wind and the crackle of the fire. She lay down again and returned to sleep. The dream came a second time, and when it ended, she woke to find it was morning.

Alvis listened to Merta's dream, then took the Great Book from its box and opened it to the twelfth Mandala.

Indeed, it was a stream of water bubbling up from the ground, but there was no village, no girl drawing water.

"Thus, also flesh," Alvis muttered.

"That is what the voice of the Maker of All said."

"Flesh is water? Flesh is a stream?" Alvis muttered, then shook his head. "I do not understand, but I will think on it."

"It is a message from the Designer?" Merta asked.

"Yes."

"But why is it so…confusing? Why does the Designer not simply tell us what we need to know?"

Alvis shrugged. "Perhaps it is not time for this knowledge to be clear, but it will still be needed soon, and when it is, it will be there."

"But that is foolish," Merta said. "And why send this dream to me. I have no idea what it might mean. It should have come to you. You are the believer."

"I have no doubt that there is a reason, but I do not know what that reason might be. I only know that this is the way the Maker of All works. We are never told more than we need to know, and only those who must know will know."

Merta blinked at him several times and finally shook her head. "It seems a strange and cruel way to run a universe," she said.

Alvis laughed. He had thought the same thing many times, but felt that he was learning to accept that all was truly in the Design.

Still, the meaning of the Mandala did not come clear, though he thought about it as he had thought about the Mandala from beneath the floor stone. He could feel the power of the twelfth Mandala drawing him in. Understanding was on the edge of his consciousness, but he could not draw it forth. His mind could not interpret what his spirit seemed to know.

But the lack of understanding of the twelfth Mandala was not so worrisome to Alvis as the lack of any idea of what to do next. There was no feeling in his heart or any of their hearts. No further dreams came, no visions, no instruction of any kind. The Maker of All had moved heaven and earth, had destroyed the old lives of Garith and Merta, had set them running to the ruined Keep, and now there was nothing left to do save wait upon the fulfillment of the Design.

Seventeen

605 A.C.G.

Lord Linser was on the edge of nervous exhaustion. He paced his audience chamber, then sat upon his throne and chewed the heel of his hand bloody. Lord Nikali had returned and summoned him, but, before Linser could make his petition for use of the god-message network, Nikali had begun giving him orders.

"Within two days local many Warrior-Gods will arrive," the God-Resident said. "Most will continue through the Hall of Doors to other destinations, but twenty of them will stay here. Therefore, they will require quarters. Prepare to receive them, and give them any assistance they require."

He was then dismissed without any chance to put his petition to the God-Resident.

Linser had been given such orders before, but not in the last few years and there was something else this time, a tension in the God-Resident that had never been there before. *What could make a God tense?* Linser wondered, but did not take time to ponder the question.

The Chief Priest called the Chief Steward of the Temple and passed on the orders from the God-Resident.

"Prepare quarters for the arrival of one hundred Warrior-Gods," Linser commanded. "They will be here no later than tomorrow evening. All will be in readiness or I will have you shortened. Do I make myself clear?"

The steward stood stiff as a statue with his eyes bulging. There had not been so many Gods in the temple at one time for many years. At most his department had dealt with four or five at a time.

"Well, don't just stand there with your eyes popping out, man," Lord Linser shouted. "Get busy. Everything must be perfect. Do you understand? Perfect. If it is not, you will need a basket to carry your worthless head in before the echoes of complaint die away."

The Chief Steward got himself under control, bowed deeply and left.

When the Warrior-Gods arrived, they brought nothing but chaos. They did not even make a nod to the amenities. They did not wait to be greeted by the Chief Priest, nor did they present themselves to the God-Resident. They merely waved the priest aside and dispatched a servant of the Chief Steward to inform Lord Nikali that they were here.

The servant did not of course, attempt to deliver any such message to Lord Nikali. The Chief Priest was the only Archlean allowed into the audience chamber of the God-Resident, so the servant turned to Lord Linser with a frightened look.

Linser shooed the man out and congratulated himself on not having sent the man to the dungeon in a fit of pique. Linser did not like being reduced to the role of messenger boy. Nor did he like finding himself in the presence of the angry Lord Nikali when the message was delivered.

Lord Nikali did not like being treated as an afterthought by mere Warrior-Gods and he raged at Baroth Linser. Linser shook in the God's presence, fearing that Lord Nikali's wrath would fall on him as the messenger, but it did not. Instead, the God-Resident stormed out of the audience chamber and Linser was happy to slink out unnoticed.

Back in his own chambers Linser dispatched a servant to keep an eye on the Warrior-Gods.

Hours passed with nothing for Lord Linser to do but worry and pace and chew at the heel of his hand, which was already so scarred he could hardly close it.

At last the servant returned. He bowed himself to the floor and said, "The Warrior-Gods are carrying boxes about this big," the man lifted his arms and held his hands apart indicating a thing about twice the size of a man's head. "They are placing these boxes in the Hall of Doors. The

God-Resident," the man said in an awed voice, having never seen the God-Resident before, "the God-Resident came and raged at them, then he left and returned later to rage at them some more."

"And what did the Warrior-Gods have to say about Lord Nikali raging at them?" Linser asked.

"They did not seem too upset, my Lord. They said something about foolish protocol and that they did not have time for such nonsense, since the Garins were well on their way."

Garins, the Warrior-Gods had said. It was as he had thought. There was a war and the question was, would the Warrior-Gods defend this temple. If so, what were these boxes, and why were they being put in the Hall of Doors. These did not sound like defensive weapons. They did not sound like weapons at all.

Linser leaned back in his chair and stroked his cheek thoughtfully. "And what is in these boxes," he asked, more of himself than of the spy.

"I do not know, my Lord," the man said. "But even the Warrior-Gods handle the boxes carefully. They wear great shiny gloves upon their hands."

"Why did you not get close enough to hear more of their talk, fool?" Linser shouted, and regretted it almost instantly. The servant was already frightened—trembling and barely in control of himself.

"Do not soil my floor, fool," Linser warned, but more softly.

"Yes, my Lord Linser," the man said, still trembling, but more in control again.

"Now then, why did you not get close enough to hear?"

The man hesitated. "Because I fear them, my Lord. I fear them and their boxes. If Gods handle them with such care, an insignificant one such as I would be eaten up without a thought."

Linser pulled at his lower lip and looked at the man for a long time. "Yes," he said at last. "Perhaps you are not the fool you appear. Very well. Be gone." He waved his hand and the servant gratefully backed out of the audience chamber.

When Linser was again alone he thought on the reasons for this sudden visitation by Warrior-Gods after so many years. Rumor had come through the gates that the Gods were at war with other Gods. These other

Gods of the Sky were called Garins, and the war was apparently going well for these Garins. Therefore, these Warrior-Gods who were passing through the Peshar temple were going to the war and those staying behind in the temple were preparing a defense. . . unless…

The acid in the Chief Priest's stomach suddenly increased with the return of the thoughts of the Gods abandoning Archlea. If they decided to abandon the temple, they might wish that these Garins not be able to follow them. Perhaps these boxes were the means for the Gods to cover their tracks. And if they abandoned Archlea?

There had been no serious uprisings against the temple in many hundred years, but if the people discovered that the Gods were gone… The people of Archlea did not love the gods they worshipped, and they especially did not love the servants of those gods. When it was discovered that the power of the Gods no longer backed up the temple, the servants would be fair game.

Linser looked again at the tapestry. *If only I had the cache,* he thought, and with that thought came the reason for his most recent upset. Where could the garrison at Macar be? Why had he received no word that his orders were being carried out? Nearly a month had passed since he sent out the messenger.

Morat crept softly into the room and prostrated himself before Linser.

"Speak fool," Linser growled.

"My Lord, there is a messenger."

Linser jumped forward in his seat anxiously. "Well, send him in. Send him in!"

"Yes, my Lord," the servant said, and backed out as silently as he had entered. He returned a moment later leading an exceedingly fat man who was quivering from his greasy hair to his pudgy toes. Morat forced the fat man to his knees without much effort. The man seemed almost unable to contain himself. He was sweating profusely.

"You bring me news?" Linser asked skeptically, perching himself on the edge of his throne.

"Yes, my Lord. I bring news of a messenger of this temple, my Lord." The man stopped and did not seem as though he was going to continue until Linser said, "A temple messenger? Yes?"

"Yes, my Lord," the man swallowed and visibly took a deep breath to control himself. "I am Capani, innkeeper of a small, but reputable establishment north of Peshar. Temple messengers often stop at my inn on their way, and usually I am happy to have them, my Lord, but…"

Linser controlled his urge to scream at this fat innkeeper to get to the point and instead assumed an air of gentility. "Good man Capani, are you a loyal servant of the Gods?" he asked.

The quivering man lifted his eyes only enough to be sure he could be heard in his answer. "Yes, my Lord," he said.

"Good. It warms my heart to meet with faithfulness such as yours. Now, what is it you wish to tell me?"

"My Lord, the temple messenger who stopped at my inn has lost his mind. He went mad sitting in my common room, and ended by locking himself in an outbuilding where horse tack is stored. He screamed at any attempt to help him, my Lord, and finally burst forth swinging his sword, screaming that demons were after him. My Lord, he almost killed two of my hired men before we could subdue him."

"Subdue him?"

"Yes, my Lord," Capani said, his shaking increasing.

"And where is this messenger now?" Linser asked.

"He is here, my Lord. We thought it best to return him to you."

Linser had a terrible, sinking feeling in his stomach. "You have done well, good man Capani, and your service to the Gods will be rewarded."

Capani, unable to believe his good fortune said, "Thank you, my Lord."

"You said your inn is north of Peshar? Near Macar?" Linser asked offhandedly.

"Yes, my Lord. About a day's journey from Macar."

"Ah. And when did this messenger go mad there?"

"About two weeks ago, my Lord."

"Two weeks?" Linser said, his face going red with the effort to contain his anger and fear. "That is a long time."

"Yes, my Lord, but it took us three days to subdue the man, and the journey to Peshar is not an easy one, especially with a bound madman to look after," Capani said with only a tint of defensiveness.

"Of course, of course. And when did the man…go mad?"

"The night of his arrival, my Lord. He had stopped only to refresh himself with food and wine before going on, or so the serving girl heard. He was served food and wine and he went mad before he even finished it."

Linser listened and stroked his beardless face with his scarred hand. When Capani fell silent he asked, "Is that all?"

"Yes, my Lord."

"And did none of your other guests go mad after eating your food and drinking your wine?" Linser asked, barely controlling his temper.

Capani heard the strain in the priest's voice and was alerted by it. He had almost stopped shaking and begun thinking about the ache in his knees, unaccustomed to long periods of kneeling, but the shaking suddenly started again and the pain of his knees was forgotten. Lord Linser's changeable moods were known far and wide and Capani did not wish to become a victim of one of those changes. "My Lord, all who ate from my kitchen that evening ate from the same pot, and drank from the same wine cask. None of them went mad."

"Ah, you had other guests?"

"Yes, my Lord. Three other parties of travelers… No, four parties. I forgot the party that came a little before your messenger."

And suddenly Linser knew. "This party that came right before the messenger, was it four people, two of them slaves?"

"Why, yes, my Lord. I believe so. They said they were dye buyers. The woman —well, they said she was ill, but she reeked of brandy. But they paid in advance, so I did not question further. And they traded tired horses for fresh with a tidy profit."

"Names?" Linser snapped, leaning forward. "Did you get their names?"

"No, my Lord. There was no need. They paid in gold and they left at first light."

"Was the master a short fellow? Beard and hair shot with gray?"

Capani was surprised and more anxious than before. "Yes, my Lord, but how did you...?" He stopped himself, realizing how presumptuous such a question was.

Linser raised his voice, "Morat." The servant who knelt beside Capani was all attention. Capani began to shake again, fearing his head was about to roll from the headsman's block, but Linser said, "Take good man Capani and give him one hundred Zari for his trouble, then another hundred for any trouble the messenger who went mad in his inn caused."

"Yes, my Lord," Morat said, hauling Capani to his feet. The innkeeper began to stammer out his thanks, but Morat dragged him out before he could finish.

Linser slumped back in his throne. *So,* he thought. *That is why I have heard nothing. The message never reached Macar, and the scribe and his slaves have gone toward the Palatine. But why?*

Because that is where the treasure is, another part of his mind answered. *The treasure of Javi Holis is there and they are going to find the cache, —and if they do, I will have nothing to use as leverage against abandonment by the Gods.* The situation seemed hopeless, and Linser was on the verge of despair.

~ * ~

Lord Nikali had spent two weeks jumping from world to world through the gates of the Archlean Transit Net. He had called in political favors stretching back many years to find out what was in the mind of the Imperium, and, more especially, what was in the minds of General Vembra Tretcher and Admiral Anted Perma. Rumor said that these two were the real power now—that Cadek was only a figurehead.

Nikali had not liked what he found. Rumor said that Tretcher and Perma were pulling the Empire in on itself like a mole pulling its hole in after it. That had only been rumor until the demolition teams had showed up on Archlea. They had come to destroy the gates to prevent them from falling into Garin hands.

The technology of the gates was beyond the Garins thus far, but they had hyper-light drive to propel their warships and hyper-light drive was only a short step away from the technology of the gates. If a functional gate, or even a recognizable ruin of a gate, fell into their hands, it would be a disaster. Functional gates meant the Garins could march directly into the heart of the Empire in seconds, rather than be limited by the acceleration and deceleration times required for their ships.

But Lord Nikali did not want the gates of the Archlean locus destroyed—at least not yet. There was still considerable profit to be made on Archlea and the other worlds accessible through the gates he controlled, and Nikali intended to exploit them all for as long as he could. That was when Linser's message came to his mind. He sent for the priest.

"Baroth Linser," the computer voice, seeming to come from thin air, announced a few moments later.

"Admit him," the God-Resident said.

Linser came boldly into the presence of the God-Resident. A bit too boldly to suit Nikali. Linser was usually more deferential, entering with many deep bows and hesitant steps, but now Linser strode across the chamber almost as though he were in the presence of an equal. The only thing belying his boldness were the jewels of perspiration which stood upon his shaven skull and his upper lip.

When Linser was only a step from triggering the automatic protection of the throne of the God-Resident he stopped and bowed. It was a head bow only, not involving the body. It was barely within bounds of good manners and there was nothing of deference in it.

"Have you decided that it is time to depart this world for the next rather than continue your service to ourselves?" Nikali asked.

"It has been to my profit and pleasure to serve the Gods of the black ships all my life," Linser began, "and it would be my pleasure to continue that service, save that I believe the gods are preparing to leave this world and abandon their servants." The priest looked directly into the eyes of the God-Resident.

Lord Nikali was surprised by this. He had always thought these creatures more clever than they were given credit for, but this exceeded even his expectations. How could this priest have known?

"We would never abandon our children," Nikali said, menace in his voice.

"Especially if those children might show you a promise of profit."

"Is that profit to be the loss of your impudent head, Linser?"

"That would profit you not at all, my Lord Nikali."

The God-Resident lifted an eyebrow at this. "Nor you priest."

Linser shrugged. "It might profit me in that it would save me a great deal of suffering."

"Suffering?"

"Yes, oh great God-Resident. For suffering would be my lot if I were left here when the Gods of the black ships depart. You see, my Lord, though you have been the mighty Gods of Archlea for twenty-five generations, you are not beloved to your worshipers, nor are your servants. When you see fit to cast off the woes of this world, leaving me behind, I am doomed."

Nikali silently studied the priest for a time. "And what makes you believe that we Gods would abandon our children, priest?"

Linser smiled tightly and only with his lips. There was cold, hopeless calculation in his eyes. "The signs are all around us, my Lord. When I was young, the Hall of Doors was a busy place. Ten thousand times ten thousand creatures passed through each day. Now the gates are dark most of the time and those who step through do so quickly, as though pursued. Oh yes, my Lord. You Gods of the sky are preparing to leave. That is why the Warrior-Gods are here; to protect your retreat. And to see that none who wish to accompany you step through to other worlds without your leave."

Nikali leaned back and closed his eyes. There was no point in denying what Linser said. "And you would like to be one of those protected as they step through the gate to another world? Is that right, Linser?"

The priest bowed deeply and said, "That is my desire, oh mighty God-Resident. I would be honored above all men to be the servant of the great God Nikali in the world of the Gods."

"And why should I take you with me, Linser? I have a thousand servants."

"But none who can give you the treasure of Javi Holis in return for their servitude."

Nikali's interest was piqued, but he did not wish to let the priest see it. "The treasure of Javi Holis is a myth, Linser. Many have sought it; none have found it."

"They failed, my Lord, because they did not know where to look. I do."

"And how is it that you know so much of the blasphemer Holis, priest? Is it perhaps that you are a believer in his gods?"

Linser was not prepared for such an accusation, and he paled. He thought of himself as a disbeliever in any gods, but the teachings of a lifetime were planted deep within him and the shadow of possible belief in other gods made him nervous. "I am no believer in gods other than those I serve, mighty God-Resident. I know of this Holis for I have studied him for years."

"From proscribed books in the old language, no doubt," Nikali said, and was rewarded with another loss of color from Linser's face. The priest began to stutter out a denial, but the God-Resident cut him off.

"I care not at all about your breaking the law. I care about what knowledge you have gained from it. So far you have shown me nothing to change my mind about this fictitious treasure. If this is all, you may go back to your chambers."

Linser's voice suddenly took on a tint of desperation. "My Lord Nikali I have studied this Javi Holis for years, and I have discovered that the cache is real, and that it is hidden in the Palatine mountains. I know this is so because I have also questioned Dimar Ransis and he has confirmed my guesses with true knowledge."

"Ransis, eh? And what has that venerable man told you?"

Linser's eyes flickered over the face of the God-Resident, wondering if that one was playing with him. But he was in too deep now to pull away. "If I tell you that, you will have no need of me, my Lord," he said, and prepared himself to die for his impudence.

Nikali was quiet for a dozen heart beats. "Perhaps I should ask Patriarch Ransis myself," he said.

"That would be difficult, my Lord. Patriarch Ransis has gone to the next reality, as have all the members of his family."

"Well, well. Then I find myself left with you Linser. Perhaps I should have you mind-peeled, but there is not much left of one after a mind-peel. Of course, there is not much to you in the first place, is there priest?"

Linser smiled. He knew he had won when the God-Resident resorted to threats rather than simply having him seized and mind-peeled.

"But why go to so much trouble, my Lord Nikali, when a better result can be gained by lending me a god-machine to transport me and a few temple servants to the Palatine?"

"Perhaps so. Yes. And if you cannot produce the treasure, I can always have you shortened on your own block," Nikali smiled wolfishly.

"And if I do return with the treasure, my Lord?"

"I am always in need of loyal servants, Linser, even in the next world," Nikali said, smiling.

Eighteen

605 A.C.G.

Alvis awoke knowing some final part of the Design was about to be played out. It had been two days since he and Lakis and the shepherd boy had brought *The Book of the Design* from its hiding place. That done, the four travelers all knew there was nothing more to be done save wait upon the Design. But waiting did not sit well with Merta.

"Why did we have to run in the first place?" she demanded. "If we are going to sit and wait for Linser, why did we run at all? We could have saved much grief and pain by letting Linser take us back in Peshar."

"We had to come here, Mistress," Lakis said shrugging. "It was in the Design."

Merta snorted, but it did not hold the same conviction it had held the week before. Since finding the Mandala beneath the floor stone, much bitterness had gone from her. Now she half believed that all was controlled by hands of a power she could not understand. She had continued to question Alvis, but it had become questioning more for information than for contention.

"If all is controlled," she asked, "why can we not just sit and wait for it all to unfold before us?"

"Because we are creatures of the Design, whether or not we believe it," Alvis explained. "But we live our lives as though there is no Design. That too is part of the Design. All things are in the hands of the Designer, but we must live our lives as though the whole of the Design rests upon us. That is how the Design is carried out."

"But why?" Merta cried.

"Because it is the way of the Design. What is, is. We cannot change it one whit, no matter how we resist, so, we who acknowledge and serve the Designer, do not resist. We know that resistance will bring only grief."

"As though following this Design has brought me anything other than grief," Merta said bitterly. Her losses continued to be obstacles to her belief.

Alvis lifted his hands to the heavens in despair. There was no explaining to one who would not hear.

And now, this morning, when Alvis had heard the hum/whine of a sky car as it landed in the village below, he had simply punched up the fire and begun to make tea. There was nothing more to be done save wait upon the Design.

~ * ~

Baroth Linser had brought six temple servants. They were all that could fit into the god-machine Lord Nikali had given him. He would rather have brought a platoon, but these would have to serve.

Linser commanded the god-machine to land in the village below the Keep, then sent the Guard-Captain to bring him the village head man. So great was the old man's fear that he had to be carried.

"You know that I am the Chief Priest of the Temple in Peshar?" Linser asked the old stick of a man.

"Yes, my Lord," that one answered, just above a whisper.

"Answer me truthfully or you will die, and all in this pest hole you call home with you."

"Yes, my Lord."

"Have a scribe, a woman, and two slaves come here?"

"Yes, my Lord. They stayed in my house for a time. The woman was sick."

"Ah. And where are they now?"

The old man shook even harder, and the sound of his bowels loosening was plain to hear.

"Answer me," Linser demanded, but quietly, so as not to scare the old man more. "Truth will not hurt you," he promised. "But lies will find you shortened by a head."

"They are not here, my Lord."

"And, where are they?"

"I do not know, my Lord. They said they were going to the Keep. There." He barely lifted his arm to point at the mountain. "No one has seen them since."

Linser raked his eyes over the old man and decided he was too frightened to lie. "Very well," he said. "The Gods will reward your truthfulness." He flipped a gold Zari coin toward the old man, and turned into the god-machine.

The fugitives were awake and had finished hot tea and leftover stew when Linser's god-machine landed in the courtyard. They did not go out to meet Linser, nor did they try to run. They waited. The temple servants found them in the refectory and forced them outside into the sunlit morning.

"So, we meet again, Scribe," Linser began. "And this time there is no disdainful Ransis to taint the meeting."

Linser waited for some response, but got none. "Very well then," he said. "We shall come right to the point. You came here to find the treasure of Javi Holis. Have you found it?"

The scribe turned his eyes toward the tall slave and all other eyes followed his.

"There is no treasure," Alvis said.

"No treasure?" Linser asked in mock surprise. "Then what is this?" He indicated the box which the guards had brought out with the captives.

"It is *The Book of the Design*," Alvis answered.

"Is it not treasure?" Linser demanded, his voice rising a little.

Alvis shrugged.

"Open it," the priest commanded the Guard-Captain.

The man did as he was told and found that the box indeed contained only a large book which filled the box completely.

"Where is the rest?" Linser demanded.

"There is no treasure. Only The Great Book," Alvis said again.

The priest looked over the four of them, trying to determine if this was true. He could not decide so he turned from the slave and put his hand under the chin of the woman. "And what do you have to say?" he asked Merta, his voice soft and poisonous.

"If there is treasure, my Lord Linser, I do not know about it. This is all I have seen," she answered.

"Perhaps I should have you shortened to loosen the tongues of the others," he said.

Fear came into the eyes of the woman and her husband. It made the priest smile.

Garith took half a step forward, but was restrained by a temple servant. It wasn't necessary. Garith had no violence in him. He could not have killed Linser if the priest had been at his mercy. He had only stepped forward to plead for his wife. "She knows nothing, my Lord Linser," he begged. "Alvis spoke the truth. There is no treasure, only the book."

Linser half believed the Scribe. He turned from the woman to the book. "Take it from the box," he commanded, and two guards did so. They held it up so that Linser could see it.

The power of the volume radiated even though the closed wood and leather covers. Linser stretched forth his hands and opened the heavy cover. Instantly his eyes and his mind were drawn into the first Mandala. The Fire. Moments passed, but they could have been hours.

The Guard-Captain, watching the prisoners, glanced at Lord Linser and was so disturbed by the stillness of the priest that he asked, "Are you well, my Lord?"

Linser pulled his eyes away and, realizing how the book had pulled his mind into itself, he closed the cover and motioned the two guards holding it to step back. Then he took several deep breaths to recover himself and turned again to the prisoners.

"Perhaps I should shorten *you*, Scribe. You have been in the midst of this from the beginning. The slaves and the woman belong to you and Ransis insisted we bring our contract to you to be witnessed and copied. Yes. Perhaps I should have you shortened." Linser's eyes took on a faraway look of cold consideration, and after a moment he nodded to himself. "Yes," he said. "Yes. Captain, take the scribe over there and shorten him. We have no further need for him."

Garith's knees gave way and he fell down, fear undoing his mind and body for a moment, but when the Guard-Captain and another jerked him up to drag him away, his courage returned a little. "You may kill me, Lord Linser, you may kill us all, but there is still no treasure save the book," he said.

"Then one less of you will make no difference, will it?" Linser said.

Merta screamed "No." And sprang to her husband, throwing her arms around him. One guard threw her grasping hands off and another pulled her away.

They dragged Garith a little farther and forced him to his knees. The Captain drew sword and lifted it above his head with both hands and paused before the down stroke.

"Hold," Linser said.

The sword stopped and lowered. "The treasure?" Linser asked Alvis again.

"There is no treasure," Merta begged, weeping. "Would I not tell you to save my husband? Please. Please."

Alvis had been trying to use the Mandala of The Enfolding Arms during all this, but it did not seem to be working. The situation was beyond control. He could only watch and wait upon the Design now.

Linser looked at the three prisoners in their little group. The slaves stood passively watching; the woman was on the ground with her arms up, pleading. "Bring the Scribe back," he said.

"Oh, thank you, my Lord, thank you." Merta cried and rose to her knees, holding her hands toward the priest. "Thank you, thank you," she said over and over still sobbing.

The guards brought Garith back. He was stunned. His mind had fled, refusing to believe what was happening.

Merta scrambled up and threw her arms about her husband and kissed him. He did not react.

Linser looked at them, then at the two slaves. *There is no treasure,* he thought, *only the Book.* "Captain bring them and all they had with them. We are leaving," he said.

"Yes, my Lord," the Guard-Captain said, then hesitantly, "my Lord, there was only room for those who came from Peshar."

Linser's face reddened with frustration and rage and the Guard-Captain feared for his life. "You have your orders, Captain," Linser said through clenched teeth.

The Guard-Captain bowed quickly and said, "Yes, my Lord," then scuttled away. In moments the prisoners, all their goods, and *The Book of the Design* were in the Sky car.

"Home," Linser commanded the machine, and it lifted leaving all the Temple servants save the Guard Captain standing in the courtyard looking up at the departing God-Machine.

Linser was not sure why he decided to bring the four back to Peshar with him. Some vague idea of asking Lord Nikali to mind-peel them passed his mind, but he was sure beyond doubt that the book was the only treasure. The logical thing to have done would have been to leave their corpses cooling on the grass of the courtyard; yet he hadn't. It puzzled him.

Evening was thickening toward night when the sky car arrived in Peshar and there was something wrong. The lights which usually burned at the gates of the Temple were out as were the lights in the quarters of the temple servants. Ordinarily the temple blazed with lamps.

Toward the city there were a few lights, but not nearly as many as usual. No street lamps had been lit at dusk.

There was a flash of light, blue-white like lightning, but no rumble of thunder followed. All in the sky car turned toward the flash, trying to see what was happening. The Guard-Captain looked from the direction of the flash toward the sky and his gasp pulled the attention of the others.

Hundreds of new stars speckled the sky. And these stars moved in strange patterns—zigzagging, looping about, and moving back and forth. One of the stars grew brighter before their eyes, then was gone like a suddenly extinguished cinder floating upon a breeze.

Linser understood. Those stars were not stars. They were ships. Those whom the Gods feared most were here and a battle of unimaginable forces was being fought above Archlea.

"Land in the courtyard of the Temple," Linser commanded the car.

The car's computer accepted the order and landed.

When they were grounded, temple servants swarmed over the car. They were on the edge of panic and relieved to have Linser back to tell them what to do.

"Be calm, fools. Are the Gods not still the Gods?" Linser shouted over the babble of voices. "Go about your business. Light the lamps and torches lest the people think that something is amiss."

"But, my Lord," a young priest said. "Lord Nikali himself ordered us not to light them."

Linser rounded on the young man set to scour him with sharp words, but he thought better of it. "Very well then," he said. "Go about your other business—and take these to the dungeon. But not too deep. I may have need of them soon."

"Yes, my Lord," several answered at once.

"You two," Linser said, grabbing two of the crowd by their arms and holding them. "Bring the box with the book from the god-machine and follow me. And be careful with it. It is worth more than a thousand of you."

They did as they were told.

Inside the Temple there was more panic. Linser commanded those who ran up to him to go on as though nothing were wrong. All were relieved to have someone to tell them what to do.

The priest went directly to the door of Lord Nikali's audience chamber, but two black armored Warrior-Gods stopped him entering. Linser almost began ranting at them that he must see Nikali, but managed to contain himself and went back to the Altar in the center of the Temple. The book bearers followed him. At the Altar he knelt on the largest cushion, lifted his hands in the prescribed manner, and said "Oh, great God-Resident, I have the treasure of Javi Holis." Then he waited.

Seconds ticked away into minutes and fear gripped the priest's bowels. Sweat ran from his body in rivers. He was just about to give up and go back to the audience chamber to confront the Warrior-Gods, when the voice of Lord Nikali came from the Altar.

"Come to my chambers Linser, quickly," Nikali said.

"Yes, my Lord," Linser said, and rose from his knees.

He gestured the book bearers to follow him. But he did not go directly to the audience chamber.

Lord Nikali stood before his desk. Every fiber of him looked as though it were ready to bolt, but was held back by sheer will.

Linser bowed himself to the floor. "My Lord I have the treasure of Javi Holis," he said.

"And where is it?"

"Safe, my Lord."

"You do not trust me, Linser? After all the years you have served me in this temple. There is little time for your games."

Linser, shaking, his stomach burning and aching with fear, lifted himself to look directly into Nikali's face. "I trust the God-Resident," he said, "but I also know that all treasures of Archlea belong to the Gods, so I worry about the Warrior-Gods. Can they be trusted as can the God-Resident?"

"They will not know anything until *we*..." Nikali gestured from Linser to himself to make sure the priest understood the *WE* "...are safely on the other side of a closed gate."

"Then I will have the treasure brought."

"Good."

Linser backed out of the chamber and returned in moments accompanied by the two book bearers.

"Put it there," Nikali indicated a table.

The servants did as they were told and got out without waiting to be dismissed.

Nikali knew the instant his eyes fell upon the ancient leather-bound book that it was a treasure beyond price. He felt the power of it before he even touched it. He stretched out his hand and touched the cover. The vibrant life of it shot through his hand like electricity. He opened it and the beauty and radiance of the first Mandala, The Fire, washed over him. He was speechless, almost breathless in the presence of so great a work of art. He turned the page and felt the commanding calm of the Enfolding Arms reach from the book to still his heart, which had a moment ago been wracked with fear.

Linser stepped forward and, keeping his eyes turned away from the Mandala with great effort, slammed the cover shut.

"Why did you do that?" Nikali demanded, fury rising. "I want to see the rest."

"Yes, my Lord, I know. And you can look to your heart's content when we are safely away from here."

The God-Resident recalled where he was and the situation with a jolt of returning fear. "Yes, you are right. Come. Let us go to…a quieter place."

Linser looked at the huge book, hoping he could lift it. He stepped forward to try, but Nikali waved him back.

"Tractor field," the God-Resident said, and touched the cover of the book. When he removed his hand, the book rose and followed him as he strode away. Linser stood with open mouth for a moment, watching the book float along behind the God-Resident, before he remembered to follow himself.

They hurried down corridors Linser had never seen before, and in only a short time they stepped into the Hall of Doors. Only one of the gates glowed with life. The others were empty frames standing a little away from the walls. Beside each gate was a black box installed by the Warrior-Gods.

Nikali and Linser came to the lighted gate. Two Warrior Gods, Cadeki demolitions techs, stood beside it. "Can we blow this place now?" one of them said, not giving Lord Nikali even the barest courtesy. They were jumpy. They knew that Nikali should have taken what little he could carry and let them finish their job long ago, but he had delayed and delayed until it was almost too late.

"Have you some desire to lose your stripes sergeant?" the God-Resident snapped. "I am the Imperial governor of this terminal and you will address me with respect."

The sergeant did not look much impressed by Nikali's display of temper, but he did come to attention and say, "Yes, my Lord."

"Step through sergeant," Nikali commanded. "Send a small grav-truck back to carry this," he pointed at the book which floated between him and Linser.

"No, my Lord," the sergeant said. "My orders are not to leave this post until the timing devices are activated."

Nikali glared at the trooper, but the other did not flinch. He had his orders and nothing Nikali could do would change that. Probably it was the same with the other trooper so, rather than lose more face, he turned to Linser and said, "Wait here. I will get a grav-truck." He did not wait for any answer. He turned and stepped through the glowing gate.

~ * ~

The prisoners were shoved down the stairs into the dungeon, then down a corridor to a cell. They were shoved into the cell and the door was locked, closing out the light of the guard's torches. All was blackness.

"What is happening?" Lakis asked.

Alvis answered, "The time of the gods is at an end my friend. Those new stars we could see were ships of the Garin Confederation."

Garith and Merta could hear the satisfaction in their slave's voice. Garith was still not recovered from the fear of his close brush with death, and flight in the god-machine had done nothing to help calm his fluttering heart. But now the barely-covered joy in Alvis helped to calm him.

"This too is a part of the Design?" Merta asked.

"Yes," Alvis said.

"But our part is finished, isn't it?" Garith asked, his voice sinking. It had just come to him that the four of them would probably die of hunger and thirst in the dark of the temple dungeon.

Merta reached out in the dark and found her husband's hand.

Alvis turned his eyes toward his master's voice. He felt sad and bitter for Garith and Merta. Not for the first time, he asked himself and the Maker of All why the Design was so cruel.

"The Design is exceeding strange, isn't it, Alvis?" Lakis said from the other side of the cell. "To have come all this way—to have gone through all this—only to die here even as the gods are defeated. Exceedingly strange."

With nothing else to do, the four fell quiet. After a time, Alvis felt his way to a wall and leaned back. In moments he was asleep.

The dream came to him just as it had to Merta in the Keep. The stream, the village, the girl, and finally the voice declaring "Thus also flesh." It almost made sense to him. The water and the ice and the steam which no doubt rose from the cook pots of the village. It almost made sense.

"Mistress," he called quietly so as not to disturb anyone if they were sleeping.

"Shhhh," Merta whispered back. "Garith is asleep."

"The dream came to me," he went on.

"What dream?" She asked.

"Your dream. Of the stream of water. The Mandala."

"Don't talk of water. I thirst already and it will only get worse. We are forgotten down here."

"Do you remember anything else from the dream Mistress?"

"No, only what I told you. The stream and the girl and the voice. That is all. And who cares anyway. It means nothing."

"It was the twelfth Mandalaya."

"Yes. The twelfth. It was so beautiful," she said, her voice taking on a dreamy quality. "I looked at it the first time and felt myself become weak in the knees. I had to sit down. Felt as though my legs had turned to water."

Alvis came wide awake. "Say that again," he said.

"What?"

"About the watery feeling."

"I just said my legs felt weak and I had to sit down."

"No. You said watery."

Yes, yes. But so what? It is just an expression. Watery in the knees or in the head. It just means you feel strange or weak or sick…"

"I understand."

"Good. Now be quiet. You'll wake Garith."

"No, I mean I understand the dream. I understand the Mandala."

"Wonderful," she answered bitterly. "Now shut up before you wake Garith."

Alvis stood up from his corner and felt his way around the wall to the door. He examined it by touch and found that it did not fit well. There was a crack beneath it wide enough for him to put his fingers through. He nodded his head with satisfaction and lay down across the door with his right shoulder almost against it. He brought the twelfth Mandala before his mind's eye and examined it closely. He pictured his own flesh flowing like the stream of water. Flesh was like ice frozen to a certain shape, but when warmth came, when spring came to warm the earth and cause the seeds to grow the solid ice became liquid. It did not change its basic self. It was still water even when it was ice, or when the girl with her water jar carried it to her house to warm for tea. Alvis allowed himself to be dipped up by the girl and carried to the waiting fire to be heated. To be turned into steam which rose and expanded and billowed. Then it began to cool and become liquid again. With the cold it solidified.

Alvis opened his eyes and found the thick darkness was just as thick as before. He lifted his right hand and tried to touch the door. He found nothing but empty darkness. He sat up and reached out with his left hand. An inch away was the rough wood of the cell door. He was outside the cell in the corridor.

Alvis could hardly contain his joy. He blinked his eyes, trying to clear them of darkness, but when he opened them, it was still black. *Now what?* he thought. *I am out, but now what?*

He closed his eyes again and found the Mandala from beneath the floor which had led him to the book's hiding place was before his mind's eye. He turned himself as he had then and found the Mandala was brightest in one direction. He moved with closed eyes in that direction.

At first Alvis put his hand out to guide himself by touching the wall at his side, but soon found it was not necessary. So long as he kept the vision of the book bright behind his closed eyes, he could not go wrong.

Torch light glowed red through his closed eyelids as he approached a corridor crossing. He opened his eyes and looked for guards down both corridors. There were none. The same was true at the junction where stairs led up. There were no guards anywhere. Alvis whispered thanks to the Maker of All and went up the stairs.

~ * ~

Baroth Linser felt the eyes of the Warrior-Gods bore into him. He wanted to run from them, but he dared not. Lord Nikali had said he would be right back, but several minutes had passed and the God-Resident had not returned. Linser did not fear that Lord Nikali would not come back. *The Book of the Design* still floated on its magical field beside the glowing gate. The God-Resident would come back for the book, Linser was sure. He had seen the longing in Nikali's eyes when they first touched the book, and the sorrow and desire which had overflowed when Linser had closed it. Lord Nikali would return, but the time he had been gone was worrisome.

More minutes trickled by. Linser paced before the gate, trying to see through, but he could not see anything to make him wiser. There was only a small room with white walls and a door with a square window. Linser stepped closer to the gate. He almost stepped through into the room beyond, but the hand of the Warrior-God who was anxious to destroy the gates pushed him back.

"Not for you, priest," he growled.

Linser felt the blood of anger come to his face, but he dared not explode for this Warrior-God would not think twice about killing him. Gods were Gods, and priests were priests.

But where was Lord Nikali?

A suspicion came into Linser's mind. What if Nikali had left instructions with these Warrior-Gods to kill him. Then the book would belong to Nikali without encumbrance of priest. But if that were so, why had they not killed him already and gotten on with whatever business they had yet to do?

They are toying with me, he thought. *Playing. They are enjoying my pacing and looking and worrying.*

He pushed the thought from his mind. There was nothing he could do now but wait on the will of the Gods, whatever that might be. *Strange,* he thought. *The will of the Gods.* It was almost like what he had heard about the Design. *We have no choice but to wait upon the Gods, so relax and accept their will since we cannot change it.*

~ * ~

Alvis followed the bright Mandala behind his closed eyes. He was out of the dungeon and across the main floor of the temple going toward that section reserved for priests and the God-Resident. He did not hesitate, but went through the door before him, the Mandala still brighter.

The corridors changed from worked stone to smooth metallic tubes which glowed blue-white. The light was not bright, but it made Alvis's eyes water when he opened them. Then he realized it was not the light. There was smoke in the air, acrid and eye stinging. He looked back toward the entrance. Thickening smoke was rolling toward him. He turned again to the direction of the Mandala and ran toward it.

The sound of another coming into the Hall of Doors called the eyes of the priest and the Warrior-Gods. Linser gasped when he recognized the tall slave.

"How did you…?" Linser began

"Halt," commanded the Warrior-Gods. "This is not a place for you. This is a place for Gods and the priest-servants of the Gods."

"This is a place of transit for Cadeki citizens and Imperial troops," Alvis said. "The only God is the Maker of All, The Designer, and I am his servant. I have come to take back what belongs to the Designer and the Servants of the Design."

Alvis continued walking toward where *The Book of the Design* floated.

"Stop, slave," the Warrior-God who was a sergeant said, drawing his side arm. "When Gods speak, you should listen."

"When God speaks, I do listen," Alvis answered, not stopping. "I have listened to the Maker of All and he has told me the Cadeki Empire is finished. Your part of the Design is worked out."

The Cadeki trooper did not know what to make of the bold slave, but such talk was dangerous and the cure for it was death. He prepared to fire.

Lord Nikali burst through the gate. "Do it," he screamed. "Destroy the gates. Do it. Garins!"

The sergeant was caught by surprise. He swung toward Nikali and saw that the ante room door on the other side of the gate was standing open. Armed Garin troops were storming toward him from where no troops but Cadeki Troops should have been. He raised his weapon and fired through the door.

The advancing troops from the other side of the universe returned fire and the sergeant flared to a smoking cinder.

Baroth Linser ducked back from the gate and the confusion of shouts and sizzling weapons fire. He looked for Lord Nikali, but did not at first find the God-Resident. Smoke was thickening the air, and a stench of burned flesh gripped his throat and roiled his stomach.

The book, Linser thought. *I must find the book.* But the thought drew up short amid the thundering feet of the advancing Garin troops.

Lord Nikali saw the demolitions sergeant go down and knew the Archlean Terminal was lost. He would have blown the gates himself had he been able to find the detonator, but he did not even know what it looked like, and, with both the demolitions troopers dead, the first functional transit gates would fall into Garin hands.

Because of me, Nikali thought. *Because of me, and the priest, and the book.*

Nikali was lying flat on the floor a little out of the angle of sight from the other side of the gate. He looked around and located the priest. Linser crouched in terror against the wall on the other side of the gate entrance. The book still floated on its tractor field before the gate. Miraculously, none of the shots fired had touched it.

A dozen Garin troops ran through the gate from the far side; the side where Lord Nikali had gone looking for the grav-truck. Almost as their feet touched the Archlean side of the gate, a crash that rattled the whole temple came from above them.

"They're down." A Garin officer shouted. "Fan out and hold these gates. You, Strelich! Go back through. Tell Commander Vechtar that we have the transit terminal in our hands and that landing craft from the Third Battalion are on the roof. We should be able to link up soon. Go!"

"Yes Sir," the trooper called Strelich answered and loped back through the glowing gate.

Lord Nikali, still unnoticed, slowly drew the tiny personal weapon he had carried for the last year. His focus was not on the troopers, but on the priest. There was nothing left now. His life was forfeit, even if the Garins left him alive. He could not return to the Cadeki Empire and he would not be a slave to these Garins. All was lost. When he had the weapon in his hand he jumped to his feet, knowing that it would be his last act. "Priest," he shouted.

Baroth Linser looked up and knew ultimate betrayal by the gods he had served.

Nikali pressed the firing stud, and Baroth Linser, Chief Priest of the Temple of Peshar, became a charred heap of smoking flesh.

The movement and the sizzle of Nikali's weapon grabbed the attention of every trooper in the Hall of Doors. At that moment the lights in the Hall of Doors blinked out, and the tractor field holding the Book of the Design let go. Only the light which still poured through the transit gate lit the scene. A heartbeat later each Garin trooper fired at the movement and sound of Nikali's weapon. The God-Resident was hit by so many beams there was nothing left of him save ashes.

Alert troopers swept the gloom for any other enemy. They found only Alvis. He was lying on the floor, atop The Book of the Design, protecting it with his body.

When the Garin troopers had turned toward the sound of Nikali's weapon, the book, still floating on its tractor field, had been between the God-Resident and many of them; but, just as they turned their weapons, the power in the temple had been cut by the troops on the roof and the book had fallen to the floor. Alvis had been lying almost under it, and when it fell, he threw himself over it. He knew the troopers would char him as they had Nikali, but he would die protecting The Great Book. He squeezed his eyes shut and waited for the burning of death. The flicker of a thought passed his mind—What part of the Design comes next...? but then it was gone.

No shots came. Instead Alvis was hauled to his feet and shoved against a wall beside another of the transit gates.

"No move," a trooper shouted in bad Peshari. "No move." He waved his weapon at Alvis.

Alvis lifted his hands, palms out, to show he had no weapon and no hostile intention. "Please," he said. "The Book. Do not hurt the Book."

The trooper looked at the slave with wide eyes. He had not expected a peasant of a Cadeki world to speak Lutor, a widely used trade language in the Garin Confederation. He did not take his eyes, or weapon, off the man, but called, "Lieutenant!"

In a moment another trooper came up through the gloom. "Yeah, what?" He growled, still sweeping his eyes around the Hall of Doors.

"I think maybe you better have a look at that Book down there," the trooper pointed with his chin, still not taking eyes or weapon off Alvis. "This guy seems to think it's pretty important.

Nineteen

605 A.C.G. (Year 1 of Garin Rule)

General Arlen Gaiter, short, stocky and dark, with quick black eyes that could instill fear or calm in his troops at will, read through the last few paragraphs of his after-action report.

"The attacks were perfectly timed so that UGC forces took both sides of the interstellar transit gates at the same time, avoiding destruction of either terminal. The transit gates upon Arkalia..." he pronounced it with hard K sound, "were prepared for destruction, but perfect execution of the battle plan caught the engineers left to destroy the gates completely by surprise. The gates upon Rindia were not prepared in any way."

"The Arkalian Terminal has been given a preliminary look over by the exo-spatial engineers from the fleet, but they have not discovered anything more than how to turn the gates on and off. Those gates, not active at the time of our invasion, have been of no use to us and probably will not be. Word must have passed within the Empire that we have taken Arkalia intact, and all planetary connections from this terminal except that to Rindia are no doubt destroyed. What is needed is a group of exo-spatial theorists. My engineers have neither the equipment nor the expertise to understand these gates and I believe it is imperative that we understand them as soon as possible. If we learn to use them, we can carry the war into the heart of the Cadeki Empire."

General Gaiter slouched in the throne of Lord Nikali. He was tired almost beyond thought. He hadn't been to bed in more than seventy-two hours, having caught only short catnaps in that time. But now the terminal was secure, and his troops were rounding up the last of those who called themselves Servants of the Gods. Mopping up was going on in other parts of Arkalia, but the Cadeki troops were not putting up much resistance. Soon he could get some real sleep.

The general pushed himself straighter in the chair. *Gods,* he thought with disgust. *How could the Cadekis have had the arrogance to call themselves gods?* He shook his head in disbelief and stood, heading for the door. As he was about to leave the room, he glanced at the huge leather-bound book lying upon the table at the right side of the throne room. He stopped.

Gaiter had looked through the book before, when the lieutenant had brought it to him, and he had to admit it was an impressive thing. These primitive people had a flare for art the like of which he had never seen before. Of course, he was no great art lover, but he knew what he liked, and he liked this book. He opened the heavy leather cover and looked at the first painting—or whatever one called such a combination of ink and paint. It was like nothing he had ever seen before. It drew him into its center as though it had a hold on the front of his tunic.

"Amazing," he said aloud. "Truly amazing." He continued to touch the heavy page thinking; I'm going to have a talk with that fellow the lieutenant said was so worried about it.

A yawn caught him, and he remembered how tired he was. He closed the cover of the book and headed toward a bath and bed.

There had not been much resistance when the UGC troops had grounded. The fight had mostly been a navy thing. Lots of ships maneuvering in and out of exo-space, firing at places where enemy ships were going to be in two seconds. That didn't matter to drop-troopers. All they cared about was resistance on the ground, and there hadn't been much. That did not mean everything was safe and clear, so everyone having anything to do with the temple (and that meant everyone including prisoners) was tagged so they could be found at a moment's notice. UGC troopers injected trackers into the thigh muscles of each person found in the dungeons and released them.

~ * ~

Garith and Merta and Lakis were stunned by their sudden freedom. They had given themselves up for dead and were confused by Alvis' absence when the Garin troopers opened the door and shined lights into the cell. They were so confused they simply sat down in the temple courtyard when they were released.

Alvis found them sitting with their backs against the wall of the temple when he was released. They looked at him as though they thought he was a ghost.

"What now, Alvis?" Lakis asked.

"Yes, what now?" added Merta and Garith. "Everything, including the old gods, are gone. Now what?"

"I think we should go home," Alvis said.

Garith perked up a little at that. "Do you think the shop is still there?"

"We might as well go see. We cannot keep sitting here," Merta said.

The shop was not a ruin, which surprised them, but it had been looted, as had the house. Nothing was left except some copies of contracts Garith had witnessed. No one had thought them valuable enough to steal.

"I suppose they were right," Garith said. "Those concerned are probably dead or out of business."

"Perhaps not, Master Garith," Alvis said, trying to ease the scribe's pain.

"The Designer has certainly left us with a bleak part of the Design," Merta said disgustedly.

"Perhaps it is the beginning of a new and richer part, Mistress," Lakis said.

"What I do not understand..." Garith began, then stopped and amended himself. "First among the thousands of things I do not understand, is that we worked, and suffered, and lived in danger to get the book. And now we do not have it at all. It is in the hands of the new gods."

"True enough, Master Garith," Alvis answered him. "I do not understand either, but all is in the Design. We can only accept and continue."

Garith managed to scrounge some paper and ink and a few pens.

With these meager tools, and the remains of the money Merta had stashed, they set themselves up in business once more. He sat himself down before his shop in the place he had once allowed his hired letter writers to sit. He sent his slaves out into the city to look for work of any kind that might bring a little money into the house so that they might starve a little more slowly. Garith Balal, once Scribe and Fair Witness to the powerful of Peshar, was reduced to what he had been as a young man: a writer and reader of letters for illiterates.

Days passed and those needing contracts written and witnessed began to come to Garith again. The Zari did not flood in, but, between the fees for his services, and what Alvis and Lakis brought in from day labor, they did not starve.

One morning Garith was seated in his accustomed place beside his door, copy desk in his lap, when a man stopped before him. "Scribe Balal, I am happy to see you alive," the man said heartily. "I have need of your services."

Garith looked up at the man. He was vaguely familiar. "How may I serve you, gentle," the scribe asked in his best professional manner.

"I wish you to witness a contract between me and the new gods. They have need of fresh vegetables, and would have me deliver them."

Now Garith recognized the man. He was Ackar Martan, the seller of fruit and vegetables. But he had never been a man of means, only a small vendor. Still, Garith was not one to look askance at a gift from the gods.

Even as he thought this, Garith's mind lurched. The old new new gods were not gods at all. And now these Garins who replaced the old new gods were the new gods. So which gods did one thank for the mercy of a client when one was needed?

The Designer, of course, he thought then. *All things are in the Design. Even a small-time seller of vegetables now become a supplier to the new new gods.*

"Have these new invaders begun calling themselves gods now?" Garith asked his client.

Martan shrugged. "Not that I have heard, but what else would you call them? They come from the sky like the old gods, and they drove out

Lord Linser and the old gods, so they must be gods too."

"But the old gods were not gods," Garith said. "They were only men of great power."

The other looked a long time at Garith, as if making up his mind. "Will you witness my contract or not?" he asked at last.

"But of course, gentle Martan. I am in the business of bearing witness, and I do not care if the contract is between men and men or gods and men or even gods and gods. Tell me what you wish the contract to include, and where and when to present it to the other party, and I will do it."

"After payment of a proper fee," came Merta's voice from the depths of the shop.

"Yes, my dear, when the proper fee has been paid," Garith agreed and dipped his pen into his ink pot.

~ * ~

General Gaiter was completely surprised by the visit of Nyle Atzen, Holy Father of the Church Universal. The general could think of no reason the exalted churchman should come to this dangerous center of conflict between the UGC and the Cadeki Empire.

Gaiter received the Holy Father in what had once been the audience chamber of the God-Resident. He did not sit upon the throne at the end of the long hall, but in a folding chair beside the steps of the dais the throne rested upon. He had an ornate chair, the legs of which were really too short for comfortable sitting, brought from what had been the quarters of the chief priest of the temple. Gaiter placed it so that a strong light would be upon the Holy Father, but not so that the light would be in the churchman's eyes. General Gaiter sat in a softer light. He wanted the advantage of bright light on a potential adversary, but did not want to be too obvious about it.

When Nyle Atzen, dressed in simple but elegant black and white silk, entered, Gaiter knelt and kissed the ring on the cleric's left hand. "I am honored beyond words, Revered Father," he said.

"But you are wondering what so useless a one as I am doing here, getting in the way of good Garin troopers, and wasting the time of their good general," Atzen said with a laugh as he helped Gaiter to his feet.

Gaiter could not help but smile at the sharpness of the man. Atzen was a tall bony fellow with thinning white hair. There was an aura of power about him, but his ever-smiling face said the power would be wielded with wisdom and kindness—if possible.

"I would not have been so crass as to put it in those terms, Revered Father, but you are right. It is not often that troops of the line receive visits from a Prince of the Church."

"That is true, I suppose and shameful. Did you know, General, that once upon a time, a man could not become a churchman unless he had served time in the military?"

"Yes, Holy Father, I did know that."

"But of course, you did. How foolish of me to think you would not. But I must plead distraction. Other matters than small talk occupy my mind."

The general waited for the cleric to go on, but when he did not Gaiter asked, "What is it that distracts you, Revered Father? Is there some trouble with…?" but he could not think of anything troubling that would bring the Holy Father to distraction or to journey halfway across the galaxy.

Atzen took no notice of what Gaiter had said, or even that he had stopped speaking. Instead the cleric drew his lower lip up between his teeth and raked over it thoughtfully for several moments. At last he said, "General, I am no believer in miracles, or dreams, or auguries. I do not believe, nor does the church teach, that God works through such fripperies. We believe that God is an orderly creator and ruler of the universe, who has designs and plans beyond our understanding. The God of the Church Universal is not some primitive magician who impresses and awes painted savages with trickery…but…those beliefs do not exclude the possibility of wider reality than we have thus far perceived. If that were not so, we, in our ignorance, would be able to deny the very existence of such things as exo-spatial drives for starships, and now these exo-spatial gates which the Empire has used for centuries, but which we have yet to unravel."

"We will understand them, Holy Father." Gaiter said. "There are technicians and theoreticians working right now in the transit terminal. Our capturing this planet and Rindia at the same time and having the transit gates functional, was a great piece of luck."

"Yes. Luck." Atzen smiled impishly. "But of course, the Church teaches that there is no such thing as luck. All things are functions of God's creation."

"Yes, of course," the general hurried to say. He felt like a school boy caught in error, and he was still puzzled as to why the Holy Father had come. The reason had gotten no clearer with this conversation.

"Calm yourself, general," the churchman said. "The Church Militant has not punished anyone for straying from the proper patterns of speech for several hundred years."

Gaiter smiled sheepishly. "I am a product of Church education, Revered Father. I still have lumps from misspeaking."

The other laughed. "I still have a few lumps for that myself," he said.

General Gaiter found himself liking this man.

"But, of course, you are still wondering what I am doing here," Atzen continued.

"I must admit, Holy Father," Gaiter nodded agreement, "I have no idea what you are doing here."

Atzen drew in a deep breath as though he was about to start a sprint. "In your reports you have mentioned a peculiar book which has fallen into your possession. It was in the transit hall when your troops first landed, I believe?"

Gaiter was surprised by the question. How had a churchman, albeit the Holy Father, gained access to military reports? Those were supposed to be strictly top secret. He wondered if he should acknowledge the truth of what Atzen said. Would it be a breach of security? But the churchman was a loyal Garin in a position of political as well as spiritual power.

"Yes," the general answered carefully. "But I am not going to ask how you came by such knowledge."

"Perhaps that is better," Atzen said. "Just take it for granted that such knowledge will never be used in any way that will endanger the Confederation."

"Of course, Holy Father. There was never any doubt in my mind."

"Thank you for that, now if you will tell me…this book. It was…protected, for want of a better word, by a man who was a slave to the Empire?"

Gaiter was uncomfortable with this. Security was still security, but he could hardly tell the Holy Father of the Church Universal, one of the most powerful men in the Confederation that he was a security risk. After another moment of worry the general said, "Yes. Actually, it seems the man was a slave belonging to a man who is something like a Notary Public."

"But this slave was not a native of Arkalia, correct?"

"I believe that is correct, yes. I did not personally question him, but those who did kept records of the sessions I am sure."

"Ah," the cleric said and visibly relaxed, but a second later his tension returned. "The book? It has been preserved?"

"Yes, Revered Father."

"And the slave, the book's protector?"

"He was tagged and released. He can be called back in a matter of moments."

"Wonderful, wonderful," Atzen said rubbing his hands together gleefully. "I would like to question him if you don't mind."

Gaiter's mouth fell open at the audacity of the request. It assumed that he would comply without so much as a protest.

"But first I would like to see the Book," the cleric continued.

The general was in deep now. How could he deny the request when he had already breached security as far as he had?

"Of course, Holy Father," Gaiter said. "It is in my quarters."

Atzen's eyebrows rose. "You keep the Book in your quarters general?"

"Yes, Revered Father. It seemed the safest place. Besides," Gaiter smiled suddenly—wistfully. "It is very beautiful."

The general realized what he had said a moment after it left his lips, and hurried to add, "I am no great lover of art, but there is such power in this book that…I could hardly bare to think of letting it out of my possession."

It was as though Gaiter's mouth were running of its own volition. He should never have said any of this, yet he was sure that he could not have stopped himself.

Atzen took his time looking over the general upon hearing this. "And if the Church discovers the need to take this Book into its possession, how will you feel about that, general?"

Gaiter returned the calculating look of the Holy Father. "In all honesty, Revered Father, I will be sad to see the Book in other hands than mine, but if the Church finds need of it, I could let it go."

"And if the Church finds need to…secret this Book away because it is dangerous to the faith?"

Again, the general found his mouth hanging open with no words coming out. He pulled it closed and looked deep into the eyes of the churchman, trying to fathom that one's true motives. After a moment he feared he knew what the Holy Father was asking.

"You cannot destroy this Book, Revered Father," Gaiter blurted out, horror in his voice.

"I did not say destroy, general."

"No, you did not, but that is what you meant." It was a bold thing for Gaiter to say. A believer in the Church Universal did not usually accuse the Holy Father of duplicity.

Atzen was surprised and uncomfortable at being so transparent, but he could not deny what the general said. "Is this Book truly so beautiful?" he asked.

Gaiter delayed his answer for several heartbeats before he nodded. "Beautiful—and much more," he said.

Nyle Atzen sat on the edge of the desk chair with *The Book of the Design* upon the desk before him. He had turned through the pages of it ten times in the last few hours, considering what to do with it. The power of it was obvious and enormous. Everyone who had contact with the Book felt it. But, aside from that, the drawings—called Mandalai according to the slave Alvis in the recorded interviews Atzen had watched—were of such breathtaking beauty that they were worthy of being called art and protected through the ages.

And yet, this Book, this collection of magic charms —but Atzen put that thought aside. These Mandalai were not magic. There was no such thing as magic. But Atzen did not know what else to call them.

The question that went continually through his mind as he caressed each page with his eyes was, should the Church suppress this book? After all it was just a book of primitive scratchings.

But then again there were also legends and prophesies in the ancient Scriptures. Scholars thought the references to a book which would reveal the very mind of God was reference to the assembling of the Scriptures into one book. This had been accomplished at the hands of the early church fathers more than two millennia past. But when passing reference to this Book was made in General Gaiter's reports, it had sent shock waves through the church all the way up to his own throne.

What would this book do to the Church? What would it do to the throne of power at the top of the Church? Already there were those who said the Church Universal held too much sway in the Confederation. There were those who said the Church no longer served those it was intended to serve. That it had become aloof from the people, that it was a living Church no longer. There were rumblings of schism, and calls for reform. Even calls for his own removal from the throne.

Atzen did not worry about being removed from power. He told himself he did not serve the Church for the sake of power and under his rule the riches of the Church were once more being used to help those in need. Hospitals were again being built and staffed, and no one was being turned away because they could not pay. Atzen took pride in this.

And now appeared this book of scratchings to threaten what he had rebuilt!

But why did it threaten anything, he thought. *It is only a book. And not even a widely distributed book. Can it be that I am over reacting? Am I so emotionally ill that I am suddenly chilled, or perhaps thrilled at the existence of this?* He caressed the edge of the heavy page. *Strange,* he thought. *President Alleneck sees references to this Book in Gaiter's reports and suddenly thinks it necessary to send those reports to me. Through all the campaigns against the Cadeki Empire Alleneck has never so much as consulted me, then he sends me those reports. Why?*

The Holy Father turned through the pages yet again, taking in each line and stroke. Some were moving and uplifting to the soul. Others were frightening and made him want to slam the book shut and never open it again.

Atzen looked up. The room was empty. He cleared his throat and asked, "Is anyone monitoring me?"

"Yes, Holy Father," a voice from thin air answered.

"Ah, good. Could I ask that you have the man who was captured in the assault on the transit hall brought to me?"

"Of course, Holy Father. At once," the voice said, then asked, "Would the Holy Father like to rest, or have something to eat before you interview that one?"

Atzen wondered at the question. It wasn't something that a servant usually asked out of the blue. "Why do you ask?" He said.

"It is just that the Revered Father has been here two days and has neither eaten nor drunk anything to our knowledge. Nor have you slept," the voice sounded apologetic. "General Gaiter was concerned."

Two days? thought Atzen. He glanced down at the Mandala beneath his hand. *Had he been absorbed in the Book all that time?*

"Perhaps I should have something to eat and a nap before I talk with this man. Thank the general for his concern," he said and firmly closed the Book of the Design.

~ * ~

Garith and Merta had stopped thinking of Alvis and Lakis as slaves. They were more like friends now. Even protectors of sorts. Merta seldom forgot that contact with Alvis was what had stripped them of a budding fortune, but she was much less sharp-tongued than before the end of the Cadeki Empire. Hardship and loss had mellowed rather than embittered her. Now she valued Alvis and Lakis in more than the monetary way. The slaves were still legally the property of House Balal, but neither Garith nor Merta thought much about that anymore. But when the messenger of the new gods, or whatever they were calling themselves, came for Alvis, Garith surprised himself and his wife by stepping between Alvis and the messenger and saying, "Alvis is my slave. I am the responsible one, not him. If anyone is to go to the new gods it should be me."

"I have no instructions to bring anyone save the man called Alvis," the Garin trooper said.

"But he has done nothing," Merta protested. "We are only poor people who wish to be left in peace. We will serve you new gods if that is what you wish, but please leave our slave."

The Garin took a deep breath and contained his impatience. "First off," the trooper said, not unkindly, "No one of the UGC claims to be a god. Second, none of the republics in the UGC allows slavery, no one can own another human as property anywhere in the UGC—though that may not be enforced here for a time… until you can be brought some civilization; and lastly, the man Alvis will not be harmed."

This last was not precisely the truth. The trooper had no way of knowing whether Alvis would be harmed or not, but it seemed the proper thing to say in order to accomplish his mission.

"Then Alvis will be allowed to return to us?" Merta asked.

"When General Gaiter is finished with him," the trooper said.

Merta and Garith were surprised that a general wanted to talk with Alvis. "Very well then," Garith said. "May we have a few moments with Alvis before you take him?"

The trooper, after a moment, shrugged. "I will wait outside. Make it short. General Gaiter is not a patient man. Therefore, I cannot afford to be. And don't bother trying to run." He held up a small round thing that looked like a pen. "This will track you anywhere on the planet within minutes, and the next time I will not ask. I will just take you by force." He looked at them for a moment to make sure they understood, then he turned and went out.

"What could a general want with you, Alvis?" Garith asked.

"The Book," Merta said. "It must concern the Book. Design."

Alvis nodded. "Even Garins are a part of the Design."

"Yes, yes, but, Design notwithstanding, can we trust these Garins?" Merta asked. "Will they truly let you come back to us?"

Alvis shrugged. "I serve The Maker of All. I will go, or come, live, or die according to the Design."

"We cannot seem to get away from that, can we?" Garith said. "We all live or die by the Design, whether or not we know it."

Merta ignored her husband and hugged Alvis.

After a moment Alvis broke from her. "If I do not return," he said, "do not worry. It is the Design. You two have some great part yet to work out. I do not know what it is, but whatever it is, serve the Designer gladly. It will give you strength to do what must be done."

"Strength," Merta said with a little of her old acidity. "May I never again need more strength than necessary to lift a spoon to my mouth." Then she smiled.

The Garin trooper put his head back through the bead curtain covering the door.

"I am coming," Alvis said and turned from his master and mistress.

~ * ~

Nyle Atzen did not rise from his chair when Alvis was escorted into the room, but he only stayed seated with some effort. His eagerness made him want to leap from his chair, grab the slave, and shake information out of him, but he did not move. Instead he took time to look over the man. He saw a tall man with long dark hair and beard streaked with gray. The face was tanned from exposure to sun and wind, but the tan was fading. There was a grayness under it and a thinness to the body that said this man had suffered privation in the not too distant past, but there was a tranquil fire in the blue eyes that reached out to the Holy Father.

"You are called Alvis?" Atzen asked, just to make sure.

"Yes."

"Please sit down and be comfortable. Would you like something to drink, or to eat?"

Alvis had brought the Mandala of The Ear to the top of his mind the instant he entered the room. He tried to listen to the thoughts of the other, but there was too much other mental noise in the temple around them. He might have been able to hear more had he been able to close his eyes and concentrate, but he could not do that and still listen with his physical ears. He did get a feeling of sincerity from the man, but he did not trust the feeling. It might be only because he was in the presence of the book again. It lay, closed, upon a table near the elbow of the other man. That alone made Alvis feel that all was right in the universe.

"Could I have a cup of water?" Alvis asked.

"Certainly. Is that all? I can order tea if you wish."

"Perhaps tea would be better."

Atzen spoke to the air. "Bring tea and cakes right away."

"At once, Holy Father," a voice answered.

Atzen glanced at Alvis, expecting to see some awed reaction to this magical voice from nowhere, but there was no reaction, not even surprise.

Alvis needed no Mandala to see the puzzlement in this one called Holy Father.

"I am not of this world," Alvis volunteered. "I was born on a world which had all the technology of the Empire."

"Ah. Then how did you come to be here? I would have thought the Empire more circumspect in sending people to this little world. Letting you wander free in Pcshar would be equal to telling these people that their gods were not gods."

"That is true. Usually memory is scrubbed before a slave was sent to a primitive world. Mine was not. I have long since stopped questioning. So many things have happened that should not have, or could not have. It has all been in the hands of the Designer."

"Yes. The Designer. You made reference to this Designer in your questioning by the UGC troops."

A trooper, one of General Gaiters personal staff, came in laden with a tray bearing tea, cups and several covered plates.

"Just put it over there," Atzen said, indicating a table at the side of the room.

"Shall I pour, Revered Father?" The trooper asked.

Atzen almost barked an impatient NO, but contained himself and said, "Yes."

The trooper poured and placed the cups beside each man. He placed milk and sugar on the table beside *The Book of the Design*. "Will there be anything else, Revered Father?"

"No thank you. That will be all. And, if you please, do not monitor this room." The request was clearly an order though it was couched in polite terms.

"Yes, Revered Farther," the trooper said and got out.

Alvis sipped the steaming tea and was glad he had asked for it. Atzen waited until the other lowered his cup then asked, "You are a Servant of the Design?"

Alvis nodded.

"And what does that mean?"

"A Servant of the Design submits himself to the will of the Designer completely, so that he may be used as a tool in the working out of the Design of the universe."

"But in your interview, you said, All is in the Design. How can your submission or non-submission make any difference?"

Alvis shrugged. "I am sure The Maker of All would work out the Design with or without my submission, but through history, from the time of the first Holis through the time of Javi Holis and his wife Mara, the Designer has called people and used them when they submitted to his will."

"And could this Designer call me to be a tool of his will?" Atzen asked, leaning forward.

"Yes."

"But I am not a believer in your Design."

"Macar Holis was a worshiper of Pesh who was called the Father of All the Gods in ancient Archlea. The Designer spoke to him as he sat in the Temple of Pesh."

"Then why submit if this Designer speaks to whomever he wants?"

"Submission brings harmony with the universe. It gives you peace," Alvis answered.

"Ah. Peace. Does it give you anything more? Wealth? Power? An easier life? Eternal life perhaps?"

Alvis thought of the Mandalai of Power, then of Garith and Merta and Lakis. He thought of Javi Holis and Mara Holis and of how the Design had used them up, yet he could think of no other way to have lived his life save in submission to the Design. "Perhaps there is life after this life," he said. "But I have not heard of it."

The Holy Father of the Church Universal found it hard to believe anyone would enlist in such a religion. Yet, peace of spirit…

"I still do not understand why you serve this Design. Peace is all very well, but there must be more," Atzen said.

"Why do you serve your god?" Alvis asked. "Are you like Baroth Linser who was Chief Priest of the Cadeki gods? He served for the sake of power and reward."

Atzen winced. "I serve God in order to help people," he said. "As years pass, I find myself more surrounded by wealth and power, but I have very little of my own."

"That is a lie," Alvis said quietly.

"How dare you call me a liar," Atzen flared angrily.

Alvis lifted a hand and said, "You are rich and powerful, and a priest of a rich and powerful people. I could see it in the eyes of the man who brought our tea, and hear it in the voice of the man who was monitoring this room. How could I not call you a liar?"

Atzen's mouth was a taut line, his lips white with anger. "You must be very sure your Designer will protect you," he snapped.

Alvis laughed and it was like a blow to the cleric. "I live and die within the Design," the slave said. "The Designer does not protect those whose part of the Design is worked out, nor could any power of yours destroy me if the Designer did not will it."

"There is no arguing with that," Atzen said, still angry. "No matter what happens, it is in the Design. Therefore, there is no arguing with you."

Alvis shrugged. "That is true, and if that is the only reason you have brought me here," he made as if to stand, "I may as well return to the shop of my master, for we are finished."

"Sit down," Atzen commanded. "You will leave here by my will."

Alvis subsided into his chair.

The Holy Father glared at the slave for some minutes, gathering control of himself then said, "I called you here to ask you about this." He indicated *The Book of the Design*.

Alvis suddenly got a clear thought from the man. He feared the Book. He wanted to suppress it, or destroy it. "It would be a great shame not to let knowledge of the Design go out within your empire," he said.

"We are no Empire," the cleric began, but then cut off sharply. "How did you…?" He cut himself off again.

"But even if you do suppress it, knowledge of the Design will go on as it has for centuries. The power of the Book and the Servants of the Design cannot be stopped. They will continue no matter what."

"I could destroy it," Atzen slammed his hand down on the cover.

"Yes, if that is the will of the Designer."

"And what of my will? Have I nothing to say in this matter?"

Alvis examined the Garin's face with his physical eyes, and his thoughts by means of the Mandala of The Ear. "You have looked at all the Mandalai. Could you really destroy a thing so full of beauty and power?" he asked.

Atzen could not look away from the calm blue eyes. "My own Holy Book has prophesied that a new testament will arise and change all that is. I think this," he touched The Book of the Design without moving his eyes from the slave's gaze, "this may be that testament. It will destroy all that has been my life—my church's life for more than two millennia— and you ask if I could destroy it?"

A jolt hard enough to rattle the bones of the men shook the temple.

"Revered Father," fear was apparent in the voice which came from the air.

"I am here," Atzen answered. "What is happening."

"Holy Father, please come to the shuttle in the courtyard. This is an emergency evacuation order. We are under attack."

Atzen sprang to his feet. Two more jolts, one overlapping the other, shook the temple. The violence of them threw the cleric to the floor. Concussion from the blasts and the shock of being thrown to the floor dazed him, fogged his mind.

~ * ~

Alvis was thrown hard against the back of his chair, and it tumbled over backward. The slave's head bounced off the stone floor with a sickening crunch. Gray slivers of pain drove through his skull and out his eyes, blinding him for the moment.

Dust and stone chips sifted from the ceiling with another wall-jarring blast. The room filled with choking dust. Smoke, eye-stinging and acrid, billowed from a hole blown in the wall opposite the door. Black armored Imperial troopers poured through the breach firing their weapons and tossing anti-personnel explosives ahead of them. The explosions rocked the two unarmored men. Alvis was somewhat protected from the concussions by the chair which was on top of him, but shock and confusion kept him disoriented. One thought was in his mind. *THE BOOK!* Where was it? He had to find it. He had to protect it. He pushed the chair off him and tried to stand, but could not. His legs were like wet rags, and his vision was spotted gray with concussion. It faded in and out. He managed to get to his hands and knees, and that was all.

~ * ~

Atzen had been thrown around like a doll by the explosions. He was bleeding from his nose, mouth, and ears. He had landed on his left arm and it was broken. He lay face down, not unconscious, but so dazed he did not know where he was. He tried to push himself up and failed.

Troopers of the assault force did not even try to open the door. They slapped magnetic charges against it and turned their backs to get full protection from their armor before detonating the charges. The door blew out and the troopers bumped and jostled each other shoving their way through. They did not pay any further attention to the two men they had passed. They were moving fast, trying to retake the terminal—at least long enough to destroy the gates.

Atzen's head cleared a little, enough to recognize the pain. He groaned and tried to push himself up again. Fear and pain injected adrenalin to give him strength to save himself. He rose to his hands and knees and crawled toward the door. After a few feet his hand struck something heavy. He could not tell what it was. It was square and dust-covered and in the way of his retreat. *The Book of the Design.*

~ * ~

Alvis shook his head, trying to clear the spots from his vision and make his mind work. Blood matted the back of his head. He lifted his eyes and saw Atzen beside the book. The other seemed puzzled by what his hand was against. He looked at it first with one eye and then the other, then sat back on his haunches as if to begin climbing over the obstacle.

An Imperial trooper came through the hole in the wall. He was in the sweep position, cleaning up anything necessary behind the first wave assault. He saw Atzen raise himself and fired more by instinct than because of any threat.

The beam weapon had no power to throw the Holy Father forward. It merely burned through his body leaving a smoking ruin behind. The cleric was dead even as he looked down at the cavity where his chest had been. There was a look of utter astonishment on his face. He lifted his arms the least bit, as though he would embrace *The Book of the Design,* and collapsed over it.

The trooper swung his weapon toward the other man on his hands and knees, but he did not fire. He saw that the man was bleeding profusely from a cracked skull. *Won't live long. No threat,* the trooper thought, and trotted on through the opening where the door had been, looking for serious threats.

Alvis' arms and legs began to tremble. Sweat burst from his pores. He was soaked in a moment, and the floor rushed up to crash against his face.

Twenty

Year 1 of Garin Rule

"They came through the transit gates we thought were destroyed at the other end, General," Colonel Barge explained. "Apparently there is a way to activate the receiving gate from the sending gate. If we had only known how ourselves... Well, it makes no difference now. They very nearly caught us with our pants around our ankles."

"It is as much my fault as anyone's, Barge," General Gaiter said. "I was so busy congratulating myself on having taken both ends of the one gate that I managed to forget that the Cadekis still held the rest of the net."

"Yes indeed. It was both fortunate and unfortunate for them was it not?" The colonel said, smiling and bouncing on his toes with pride. This counter attack had been a stroke of luck for him that was sure to lift his stock with the promotion board. There might even be a brigadier's star in it for him.

"Hm," Gaiter grunted. "Fortunate and unfortunate. I do not understand why they did not simply come through into the transit hall, hold it long enough to destroy it, and get out. Why did they try to take the whole temple with such a small force? They had to know we were here in strength. If they were going to try to take the whole planet back, they should have done a coordinated strike from ships and through the gates. That might have worked but this... It was madness."

Barge shrugged. "'I do not ask the why of fortune,'" the colonel quoted. "'I only revel in her grace.'"

"Hm," Gaiter grunted again.

Barge saw a glint of what might have been either sadness or

triumph in the general's eye. He could not tell which it was—not that it mattered. "We should have everything wrapped up in a day or two, sir. We are stretched a little thin as far as occupation troops here, what with shoving every man we could through the gates to hold other terminals, but more transports should be here in a few days."

This did not make the general ecstatic. He was on the verge of committing the same tactical error the Cadekis had committed, but there did not seem to be any help for it. He had a huge prize in the capture of three other functional gates, if he could only hold them for a few more days.

"Fortune…" Gaiter said again.

"Yes, sir," Barge said. "They say it favors the bold."

"That depends on who is telling the story Colonel."

"Yes, sir, I suppose it does."

"Let me have your after-action report ASAP. Don't worry about making it pretty, just make it quick and accurate."

"Yes, sir," Barge said. He saluted, and when the salute was returned, he got out.

Gaiter stood, stretched, and sat back down. He was at the large work table in what had been the chief priest's quarters of the temple. Upon the table beside his right elbow was *The Book of the Design*. The dust and stone chips had been cleaned from its cover, but some blood stains, dried hard and brown, were still visible.

This was what had brought Nyle Atzen here, Gaiter thought. *This was the proximate cause of his death. But why? Was this really such an important thing? It was a relic of a primitive, backward, subject world of the Cadeki Empire. What made it so important?*

The last conversation between general and cleric had led Gaiter to believe the Church might wish this relic destroyed. That would be a shame. It was a beautiful thing, and it had a way of seizing the heart which was…interesting.

If I were to package this thing and send it home, Gaiter thought, *who would be the wiser? Who would care? Atzen is dead.*

But what of those that had let him know about the Book in the first place. They will ask about it and the new Holy Father will probably know about it and will probably ask.

He scratched beneath his chin. He had not removed his beard in two days, too busy with life and death to worry about grooming.

I could just plead ignorance, he thought. *After all I am ignorant. I know almost nothing of this Book.*

Perhaps it was destroyed when the Holy Father was killed? Perhaps. Yes.

Gaiter's mind lurched. There was another who knew the truth. The slave. What of him?

He might die, the general thought. *He is in the hospital with a cracked skull.*

UGC soldiers had entered the audience chamber where the Holy Father had last been, but they were too late by hours. His body had been draped over the book, dead. The slave that the Revered Father had been interviewing lay nearby, not dead but close. A corpsman had gone to work on him moments after he had been found, but no one thought he had a chance. Field medical facilities were almost as good as any hospital, but the slave's skull was caved in from the back.

"Orderly," Gaiter said.

"Sir," a voice from the air answered.

"I told the hospital to let me know about the condition of the slave that was found with the Holy Father."

"Yes, sir," the voice answered the general's question before it was asked. "I got something a few minutes ago. I would have told you before sir, but you were with Colonel Barge."

Gaiter lifted his eyebrows at the quick excuse. When a man made an excuse without need, it was time to find someone else to do his job. He had grown too fond of it for the good of the service.

"And what did this report say, if I may be so bold," Gaiter said with frost in his voice.

"Sir, the slave is hanging in. Seems he was not as bad as was first thought. He may live."

The general waited for more, but there was none. "Is that it?"

"Yes, sir. That is all."

"Very well," he said and leaned back in his chair. He looked at the

Book for a long time before sitting forward again and putting his hand upon it.

"Orderly," he called again.

"Sir?"

"I am going out for a look around. I'll be back in an hour. Should anything urgent arise call me on the note-net."

"Yes, sir."

"But only if it is urgent. Understand?"

"Yes, sir," the orderly said.

~ * ~

Alvis opened his eyes to find a uniformed man standing beside his bed. He did not recognize the insignia on the uniform, but it was different from any other he had seen thus far. He tried to bring the Mandala of The Ear to the front of his mind, but there was still confusion and pain when he tried to concentrate, so he left off.

"Do you understand me?" The uniformed man asked. He had a not unpleasant accent when he spoke Cadeki.

"Yes," Alvis answered.

"Do you know who I am?"

Alvis looked harder at the face and the uniform for a moment, but recognized neither. "I do not think so, but my memory is fuzzy about some things."

"Ah," the man said. He stopped talking and just looked at Alvis for a time, speculation in his eyes.

"Do you know *me* then, my Lord?" Alvis asked, falling back on his slave manners.

"Yes, I know you. You were with the Holy Father when the Cadekis attacked."

Alvis blinked. "Yes," he said. "I saw the Cadeki trooper blast away his chest. He fell…"

"Onto the book you were discussing," Gaiter finished for the slave.

Alvis tried to read the man's face, but could not. Clearly this was a man of some rank. The discussion with the one called Holy Father had led Alvis to believe knowledge of *The Book of the Design* was held by very few. "Is the Book safe, my Lord?" he asked.

"Yes, for now."

"You have it, then?"

"Why is it so important to you? You were trying to protect it when my troops first landed, and I have a feeling you were trying to protect it when the Cadekis blasted into that audience chamber. Is it really so precious to you that you would risk your life for it?"

"You have possession of the Book, and you can ask that?"

Gaiter's tongue tip licked the corner of his mouth as he studied the slave lying in the hospital bed.

"What is it really?" he asked after a while.

"It is *The Book of the Design*, my Lord."

"And what does that mean?"

Alvis locked eyes with the man and held tight to them. They did not try to shift or pull away. "My Lord, why have you come to see me? I am only a slave. You have the Book. You can see what it is. You can feel its power, see its beauty. Why ask me what it is? It is what it is: *The Book of the Design.*"

"Mumbo jumbo," Gaiter said. "What is it really?"

"It is a glimpse into the very mind of the Designer, the Maker of All."

"More mumbo jumbo."

Alvis shrugged and regretted it. "I can only tell you what I know, and that is what I know."

Gaiter studied the slave silently for a moment, then said, "Atzen wanted it suppressed, or maybe destroyed. A man as powerful as the Holy Father of the Church Universal does not feel threatened enough to want to destroy a book that is only some pretty religious pictures. What is it really?"

"My Lord, I cannot explain more than I have. What more do you want of me?"

"There is more, I can tell, but…" The general fell silent, staring at the slave.

"Perhaps if you understood more about the Design." Alvis began, but Gaiter lifted his hand and shook his head to stop him.

"I am considering whether or not you should die of your wounds," Gaiter said. He got no reaction from the man on the bed. "Did you understand what I said?" he asked.

"Yes, my Lord."

"And you are not frightened?"

Alvis almost shrugged again, but thought better of it. "I live or die at the will of the Designer. If you are the means to end my life, so be it."

"Hm," Gaiter grunted, not quite able to believe the slave could truly be so phlegmatic about death. As he stared into the man's face looking for some sign of a lie he was taken by an inspiration. "Would you like to continue as protector of the Book?" he asked.

Alvis' breath caught in his throat, and he had to swallow hard before risking speech. "If that is the will of the Designer," he said.

"It could take you from this world to another. Perhaps many others."

"I have seen other worlds, my Lord. If it is in the Design, I will see others yet."

"I think perhaps it is," Gaiter said and started to turn away, but he stopped and turned back. "Should anyone else ask you about the Book you are the most ignorant man in the universe. Do you understand me?"

"I believe so, my Lord. If asked, I know nothing of books or Holy Fathers or you, whoever you are." Alvis said.

Gaiter smiled crookedly. "You will know me soon enough," he said. "Meanwhile, heal quickly."

"If it is in the Design, my Lord."

"Yes, the Design. You must tell me more about this Design when you are well and I have more time."

"Yes, my Lord," Alvis answered.

Gaiter turned and left.

After a while a little an orderly came to Alvis' bedside. "You should feel honored," the man said. "General Gaiter doesn't often visit the hospital."

"General Gaiter?" Alvis asked.

"Why, yes." the orderly said, astonished. "You did not know who that was?"

"No."

"But you talked for a long time."

"Yes. He seemed a very kind man."

The orderly's eyes widened. "I don't believe anyone has ever described General Gaiter as kind."

"Perhaps not, but I think they should, for I believe he is."

"If you say so," the orderly said and left.

~ * ~

Garith Balal leaned back from his high copy desk and rubbed his eyes. It was growing dark. Soon he would have to light a lamp if he was to continue his work. The thought did not distress him now as it would have a few months before. Lamp oil was still expensive, but Scribe Balal could afford it better since the gentles of trade were once again paying him to write and witness their contracts. If business continued to increase, he would have to find a letter writer to take over that business. As it was, he and Lakis were barely keeping up with the demand.

And the five thousand Zari that had come from General Gaiter had helped too. It had given Garith capital to re-establish his shop. With it he had bought furniture and ink and paper and paints. The money had come a month after the UGC trooper had come for Alvis—that is, a month after the gods had tried to take back the temple of Peshar from the new gods.

No, Garith corrected himself. They were not gods. They made no claim to being gods. In fact, they seemed to get upset if a Peshari slipped and addressed them as such. They had even announced that the people of Peshar could worship whomever they pleased, including the Cadeki gods if they wished, so long as they did not try to worship Garins as gods.

Whatever they were, they had fended off the attack of the Cadeki gods and now, almost a year later, life had settled into a more regular pattern.

Still, Garith wondered from time to time what had happened to Alvis. The notice which came with the money had not been much help. It was basically a bill of sale for the purchase of one male slave called Alvis. The trooper who had brought it and the money had waited while Garith read the paper, signed it, and affixed his chop. Then he left Garith with a copy of the paper and went. He either could not or would not answer Garith and Merta's questions.

Merta had snorted at the money. Not that she was now opposed to money, but she said, "I thought these Garins were against slavery. They seem easy enough with it when it comes to a slave as valuable as Alvis."

Garith had said, "Now Merta, we do not know what is in the Design. Besides, they did send five thousand Zari."

"Yes, and cheap at twice the price," she had answered, but without any real heat.

Garith leaned forward over his desk again and dipped his pen in the ink pot.

Merta watched a moment then went out. She returned to the shop half an hour later. "Food will be ready soon, husband," she said.

"Ah. Good. I am hungry."

"It is very dim in here," she said. "You should light a lamp. You will hurt your eyes."

"I was just thinking to do that."

"In the market there was a man, a Garin I suppose. He was selling lamps which use no oil. They light with a touch and go out with a touch."

"What?" Garith said skeptically.

"Truly," Merta said, her voice taking on a tint of awe. "Alsai Kruth bought one. She paid one hundred fifty Zari for it. But it does give good light, and the seller promised that it will continue to do so for years. It is from the UGC."

"Ah, yes. They have brought many things never before dreamed of."

"Perhaps I should buy such a light for you, to save your eyes," she said.

"A hundred and fifty Zari?" Garith asked.

"It is not so much if it really will give light for many years. We could save a fortune on lamp oil."

"True enough, I suppose," Garith bit at the end of his pen. "And my eyes are not growing younger. Well, if you think we can afford it, buy one of these magic lamps."

Merta smiled, satisfied. House Kruth would not be able to lord it over House Balal for long.

"Come and eat," she said after a moment.

"Now?" Her husband asked, not looking up from the letter on his desk.

"In a little while. I will call you."

"Is Lakis back with the ink stone?"

"Yes, he came a little while ago."

Good," Garith said, delighted, and went back to his copy, squinting through the thickening gloom.

Merta frowned and almost told him to light a lamp, but stopped herself. *He will light a lamp after supper,* she thought. *And I will get him the light from the UGC soon.*

She went out.

"Child," A voice spoke.

Garith looked up, thinking that child was a strange way for Merta to call him to supper, but when he looked around, he saw no one. "Who calls me child?" he asked

"The Book of the Design is in you, child," the voice of the Maker of All said. "Bring it forth."

Garith smiled at remembrance of the lines and colors of the great Book from Keep Holis. He had dreamed about it often in the last year, and with only the least mental effort he could call each of the thirty-three Mandalai to mind. He could see every brush stroke and dot of paint in each of them, and his hands itched to recreate them.

So, this is the next part of the Design that I am to work out, he thought, not at all surprised or worried. But a question did bother him. "Oh, Maker of All, why has all this happened? And where is the Great Book?" he asked, unafraid.

"The Great Book is safe," the voice said, "and all has happened because it was in the Design."

Garith thought on this for a time. These were not very satisfying answers, but he knew he would have to be satisfied with them for now.

"As you command, oh Maker of All," Garith said.

About the Author
ghelm1109@earthlink.net

G. Lloyd Helm is a ne'er-do-well scribbler who has been scratching away for fifty years through the support of his long-suffering wife. He has many books on the market of which this is one. He has traveled the world seeking adventure and has found that most "adventures are cold, hungry, painful things best avoided."

Also by G. Lloyd Helm
at
Rogue Phoenix Press

Serpents and Doves

The title "Serpents and Doves" comes from the warning Jesus gave to his disciples as he sent them out to preach the gospel, knowing the dangers they were going into. He said "Be wise as serpents and harmless as doves." Stephen Mitchell learns first-hand what that warning means when he goes to a Tennessee church college in the midst of the turbulent sixties. He learns about friendship, war, protest, the sexual revolution, and civil rights.

Chapter One

The bunk creaked and groaned as Stephen Mitchell rolled onto his back, but he hardly heard the sound. Years of sleeping on the upper bunk with his younger brother Mike on the lower bunk made him immune to the noises of the California night. Mike's soft breathing, the moans from the bedstead, the musical chirring of the crickets in the ivy and the calm hum of the breeze were all the mixture of silence to him.

Stephen didn't usually have trouble falling asleep, but this was a special night, the night before the day he had been thirsting for and dreading his whole senior year of high school, and especially this past summer. College, but not just a trip over to Valley State or even to UCLA to continue school, to continue life as it had always been with Mother,

Father, Grandmother, brother, and friends. College was far away in Tennessee. Two thousand miles, give or take a few, and that whole journey began tomorrow at seven minutes after ten AM. Stephen pushed a leg out from under the covers. His feet hung over the end of the bed. They had been hanging over that way since he was fourteen. He'd gained a few inches since he first noticed he was too long for the bunk, but they had crept up on him in such a way they made no difference. He had been long and skinny since he could remember. A kid named Dennis Conover had called him 'Stork' on the first day of first grade and the name stuck. It bothered him a lot at first. He hoped to lose it when he transferred from public school to Hardtwick Christian Academy in sixth grade, but he couldn't shed the name even then. His new classmates looked him over like he was some strange animal and Lance Stanley, the class wise guy, said, "He looks like a potato with pencils stuck in for legs."

"Mr. Potato Head, only walking," Joey Cushing, Stanley's best friend agreed.

"Betcha he stands on one leg when he sleeps like one of those pink birds at the zoo," Stanley said.

Stephen was almost mad enough to fight, but he bit back the urge. Fighting on his first day would get him sent right back to public school and that was something he didn't even want to consider. He hated that place much more passionately than he wanted to mash Lance Stanley's slightly hooked nose all over his smirking face.

"They are called flamingos," Stephen began with a light contempt in his voice. He'd used this tactic before—a sort of verbal jujitsu. See where the other guy is going and give him a strong pull in that direction. "I'm no flamingo, I'm a stork. Storks build big nests in chimneys. Dutch people think they are good luck." He ran his eyes up and down Stanley's form and, with a good deal more contempt than before said, "You probably think they bring babies," then turned back to the book which was open on his desk.

Stanley didn't quite know how to cope with this kind of verbal jiggery-pokery. He thought maybe he had been insulted, but he wasn't sure and he didn't have time to come up with a riposte because Mrs. Hudson, the steely eyed, steely haired teacher, stepped into the room.

Stephen was pleased with having shut Stanley's mouth but the outcome of it wasn't much to his liking. He wound up with the nick-name he had hoped to leave behind. *Consequences. There were always consequences,* he told himself as he lay awake. He closed his eyes, tried to force sleep to come, but he found himself staring at the reddish haze inside his eyelids. That was dull. At least with eyes open there were less dull shadowy lines in the ceiling and walls.

He reached into his underwear and scratched his groin. The itch went away but Stephen felt a thickening in his loins. Blood was trickling into him, making him harden. He hadn't wanted that to happen, but there was hardly any way he could touch himself anymore without the stirrings. Sometimes when he went to pee the very act of opening his fly and taking himself out to do what must be done caused his penis to harden.

It embarrassed and shamed him, though he mostly covered it well. There was a knot of guiltiness about it that he hated, but that was with him almost constantly. It intensified when he tried to ignore it and the desire to satisfy that hunger was almost unbearable. It wasn't so much the act of stroking and fondling himself that had guilt with it as it was the pictures; like movies which unreeled behind his eyes as he did it. Naked girls who wanted him, who touched him, who offered themselves to him. Sometimes they were blank-faced strangers who conformed to the idea of voluptuousness he had formed. "Dirty Magazine" women with large breasts and legs coyly closed. There was never any hint of pubic triangle hair in those pictures. Some artist with an airbrush erased any such hint of humanity from them. Other times his fantasies were more specific. Girls from school whom he slowly undressed before making savage thrusting love to them. In ways these girls were like the others. Somehow, he could never picture the reality of what a female human looked like between her legs. A mental airbrush wiped out the detailing.

This time Stephen's mental movie was Sherry Kinert. She was a junior when Stephen was a senior. She was pretty, but not beautiful. Her long brown hair hung fetchingly down before her breast all the time. He had taken her out to a movie a couple of weeks before.

The date came about rather strangely. During all the summers since Stephen was fourteen he had worked for the school he attended during the winter. Hardtwick Christian Academy was constantly building on land acquired through gifts. It was being built by those most concerned with it, the students and their parents. Stephen started working by donating his labor. After a month of coming in every day five days a week, Harry Elton, the school supervisor, hired him at below minimum wage.

This summer was different from all the previous summers. This summer, for the first time, a girl was hired on. Sherry Kinert. Stephen found himself working with her, painting the inside of new classrooms. They talked as they worked and after hours of painting and talking they began to talk very intimately. Stephen found himself admitting to his desires and fantasies and hearing Sherry's admissions. Her admissions brought the question, "What would you do if a guy tried to put his hand down your pants, Sherry?" The question caused his loins to thicken, but he didn't even try to hide the growing lump in his faded, paint-spattered jeans.

"What do you mean, Steve?" she asked, not put off by the question and apparently not noticing the rising in his groin.

"I mean, would you let him?" Stephen asked. His mouth was dry and there was a burning at the back of his throat.

Sherry stroked paint on the wall for a moment then said, "It would depend on the guy. If I liked him a lot and was pretty sure he wasn't going to hurt me or go telling his friends—maybe."

She looked over at him and the serious consideration she had given the question showed in her clear golden eyes. She didn't give any other indication, neither a "come along" nor a "hold it buster," just the thoughtful, considering look.

They stopped painting for a moment and stared at each other, embarrassed to have been so frank. Both blushed under the speckles of light green paint on their faces, then went back to brushing paint on the wall with a little more vigor than a few moments before. They painted quietly for the rest of the afternoon, only speaking in short non-committal sentences.

~ * ~

Stephen thought a lot about that conversation over the next few days, but didn't do anything about it until the following Thursday. At the end of the day Stephen and Sherry were side by side laving their hands and arms with paint thinner to get the green off when he said, "Would you like to go to the movies with me?"

She looked at him and he saw remembrance of their conversation flicker through her golden eyes. No answer more firm than she had given him Monday showed in the shadowed remembrance, but the conversation danced there for a moment and then was gone. "What's playing?" she asked.

He shrugged. "*The Bible* is over at the Cathay Circle."

Stephen considered carefully which movie because he knew Sherry's parents were very strict about movies and such things. He knew she would have to clear it with them and if the rating was anything but G or PG they wouldn't let her go.

"Long way to go," she said. "Clear over on Wilshire."

He shrugged again. "Doesn't matter."

She began wiping her hands and arms on a big rag that used to be a shirt. "Okay," she said at last. "But not tonight. I gotta go with Jane Curtis to a prayer circle tonight. I promised."

"I figured tomorrow night anyway." With a sudden sinking feeling he asked, "You weren't going with the youth group to Disneyland, were you?"

The trip had been the talk of the young people's Sunday school group for weeks. Stephen had considered going but decided the twenty bucks could be better spent elsewhere.

"No. I just didn't feel like going."

"Me neither," he said, relieved.

She offered the paint rag to him. "When does it start?"

"Seven-thirty, I think. I'll have to look in the paper and tell you tomorrow."

"Okay," she said, nodding. Her hair, which had been tied up in a red bandana, was now loose. It shimmered in the afternoon sun. Reddish sparkles winked at him.

Stephen didn't know exactly what he had in mind when he picked Sherry up Friday night. All night Thursday and all day Friday mental pictures flashed behind his eyes—Sherry lying naked, beckoning. Sherry in a high necked, long sleeved floor-brushing white dress that might have been a bridal gown. The shimmering of the sun on her hair. The speckles of green paint on her pretty face with one large dot on the end of her small, well-shaped nose. Her legs, shinning as she sat at a school desk, her skirt ridding up just a little more than was decorous. He had, once accidentally, looked up her dress at Sunday school and seen the satiny blue panties she wore. That picture skipped in and out of his mind more than any of the others.

Sherry didn't say much on the drive over Laurel Canyon from the Valley to the Wilshire district. She didn't sit close to him, but she didn't hug the other door either. There was no feeling of apprehension or coldness between them. She simply sat looking out the windows and glancing at him occasionally. She wore a burnt orange skirt and a white short-sleeved blouse and she carried a light beige sweater against the cool of the Los Angeles evening. Her hair was brushed smooth and shining, tied away from her face with a velvety ribbon not quite the same color as her skirt.

"Do your folks put an eleven o'clock curfew on you?" Stephen asked, as they crossed Hollywood Blvd.

"On weekends," she said. He voice was a melodious low soprano. "School nights I have to be in by nine."

"My folks used to be pretty strict about it too," Stephen said. "Midnight and no later or there was some serious explaining to do, but they've let up on me some this summer. Guess it's because I'm going off to school. I still try to come in on time though. No need causing problems if it can be avoided."

"When are you going?"

"Couple of weeks."

They drove in silence until he turned onto Wilshire, then she said, "Tennessee is a long way off."

"Couple thousand miles."

"I've never been out of California. I can't really feel how far that is," she paused. "Is it exciting to be going away like this?"

He shrugged, maintaining an exterior off-handedness he didn't really feel. "It isn't like I'm going someplace completely strange. My uncle is Dean of Students and my mom graduated from Mason. I know people there."

"I'd still be so excited I couldn't stand it."

He shrugged again.

The movie was a dog for the most part. Perhaps it had only seemed so to Stephen because he couldn't keep his mind on the story. The freeze frames of Sherry kept clicking through his mind. As Noah danced and played his pipes to lead the animals into the ark, Stephen reached out and took Sherry's hand in his. She didn't resist and her hand was warm and slightly damp. She didn't squeeze his hand, but she didn't let go either, though it was awkward to stretch with her other hand to reach the popcorn he held in his free hand.

They held hands through the rest of the film never letting go until he opened the car door for her. She sat closer to him as they drove toward home, not against him but closer. Neither spoke as they wove through the turns on the Hollywood side of the canyon road.

Stephen had a tightening knot between his stomach and loins. He could feel the coldness of his hands on the steering wheel. An agony of indecision grew more frantic as they drew closer to the crossing of Mulholland Drive and Laurel Canyon. It was almost a panic when the turn was within sight, but when they reached the traffic light the decision almost made itself. He turned left onto the dark road that ran along the ridges of the Hollywood Hills.

Stephen had been to Mulholland drive a few times before with Jan Melton when they were going steady, but it had never been like this. With Jan he had always kept everything in check, even holding her out of his fantasies by force of will. She had been something special to him and he didn't want to sully that specialness so they never did anything more than hold one another. He hadn't even tried to tongue kiss her, much less what he was thinking about now with Sherry. She had suddenly become special to him too, but in a different way. There was no love, or even infatuation, just a set-apartness that he couldn't define.

Stephen turned into a short dirt track shielded from the road by trees and shut off the engine. He left the radio playing softly. Before them was the expanse of the Los Angeles basin, covered with twinkling lights only a little obscured by the light smog that was almost never absent. He scooted over beside her, put a slightly trembling arm around her and kissed her gently.

Sherry was stiff at first, as though she was totally unpracticed at kissing, but soon she began to relax and respond a little. She stiffened a little again when he traced the tip of his tongue along the curve of her lips, but when the new sensation mellowed a moment she relaxed again and was ready when he hesitantly pushed his tongue into her mouth. She opened her lips and accepted it. In a little while she thrust her tongue into his mouth. After several open mouthed kisses it only seemed natural to bring his hand around in a smooth caress of her breast. He wasn't sure whether she felt his touch through her blouse and bra, but he was sure a moment later when he squeezed the resilient flesh. Sherry pulled away a little. She made no move to stop him or to protest, but he could see the questioning in her face. It battled with a look he couldn't quite make out. He knew it wasn't "cut it out, buster" look, but he couldn't read what it was. Then she turned her face up for another kiss and as he gave it to her he squeezed and caressed her breast again. His hand warmed with the round glow of her and he moved to unbutton her blouse. It wasn't the smooth opening of a practiced hand when he embraced her and tried to unhook the bra it defeated him. Sherry pulled away, reached behind her back and the bra went slack. Her breasts were free.

Sherry's hand was suddenly warm on his thigh. The feel of it brought Steven to raging hardness. "Are you sure?" he asked.

She hesitated a moment then nodded.

Stephen had never shown himself to a girl He was not sure now of whether he should go ahead, but her hand was magnetic, mesmerizing. He slowly undid his belt and pulled down his fly, then freed himself from his straining jockey shorts.

She stared at his hardness by the dim light of the radio dial then hesitantly reached out to touch him. As she did so he leaned in and held the creamy weight of her breast in his hand, then leaned down to kiss the cherry nipple. He felt it stir beneath his lips.

They kissed again and held each other. Stephen had never felt such warmth and comfort from anyone. Her arms were like a cloak around him, holding in closeness and warmth, but at the same time drawing shivers of wanting from his deepest self.

After a few moments Stephen decided to go all the way. He'd asked her what she would do if a guy tried to put his hand in her panties. Now he decided to find out. He slid his hand easily beneath her skirt, up her stocking legs and onto her bare thigh feeling her legs relax into a slight openness. She kissed him and laid her head back onto the seat as he felt the satiny smoothness of her panties then up to the elastic top. He pushed his fingers under the waistband and down.

Sherry's breath came in long sighs that were almost moans as they held each other. "Oh, Steve. Oh, Steve."

The music on the radio faded down and a voice laid over it said, "Twenty-Twenty News, at eleven twenty. In headlines, President Johnson addresses the press as Washington police break up anti-war demonstrations in Lafayette Park."

"Oh, God, Steve," Sherry gasped in recognition of the time. She hesitantly turned her hips away, bringing his fingers out of her panties. "We've got to go Steve. We've got to go or my folks will ground me till next year."

Stephen blinked, reading what she meant on her face. She was late, yes, but she wanted him more than she knew how to cope with and it frightened her. It frightened him too. Had they continued a little longer he might have gone beyond what his strict convictions could have accepted. He reluctantly drew his hand from beneath her skirt and put himself back in his clothing as she closed her bra and buttoned her blouse.

They drove to her house in an awed ecstasy of silence. They worked out no story to shield their lateness and it was agreed between them that no explanation would be forthcoming if her parents questioned her. Stephen walked her up the driveway and onto the lighted front porch. It was twelve-forty-five. There was a light on inside the house. Sherry unlocked the door and stood just inside it.

"Are your folks still up? I'll apologize to them and take the blame."

Sherry listened a moment, heard nothing and said, "I think they're asleep." She reached out and took his hand, squeezing it tightly. "It was as much my fault as yours," she said, smiling with a sweetness that sent a chill down Stephen's back. He kissed her chastely, lips closed, passion carefully, tightly reined in and she responded the same way.

"Good night, Steve," she said. "Thank you."

He smiled. "No, thank you."

She stepped farther inside and closed the door.

Stephen let the screen door close quietly and headed for home. As he drove a cold feeling of guilt began to develop in his belly, but he fought it back. *There was nothing bad about it.* He thought. *It was beautiful. For a few minutes we were as close as two people can be.*

The memory of it became precious to him over the following days. He put it away like a treasure to be held and loved in private moments.

The following Sunday, Sherry and Stephen spoke only friendly words of greeting to one another, but when they smiled the message of shared treasure passed between them. They did not go out again. It wasn't anything they decided, but they both seemed to know that the moment could not be caught again without tarnishing their shared treasure.

~ * ~

Stephen didn't have to be called to the breakfast table. He'd barely slept. He rose, put on his worn bathrobe, and went to the kitchen.

"Mike up too?" his mother asked, glancing up from the sizzling bacon.

"Nope, still snoring."

His mother smiled. Her teeth were slightly crooked, but she smiled so seldom almost no one noticed. Her hair was cut short and seemed shorter at the moment because it was done up in pin curls and covered with a heavy net cap. She was almost fifty but there was no gray in her jet-black hair. The only sign of age was the slight sagging of the flesh under her eyes and chin and the thickening of her body.

"He's not on his way to college," she said.

Instantly there were tears in her eyes. Not sadness, not joy, but some emotional mixture of the two.

"All right, Ma, cut that out," Stephen said gently and put his arm around her waist.

"I know, I know. Silly woman," she said lifting the corner of the apron she had on over her housecoat and wiping her eyes. "I'm just so proud of you I can't help it."

Stephen was embarrassed at all the spilled emotion. He covered it by going to the coffee pot and pouring himself a cup. "You want some now?" he asked his mother.

"Don't have enough hands," she answered.

Stephen carried his cup to the table and sat down in what was usually his father's chair.

"Did you sleep at all?" she asked.

"Not much. I'll sleep on the train. No loss."

"I thought you were having trouble. I saw your light on about two. Figured you were still reading or something. What were you reading?"

"*Origin of the Species.* It's enough to put a rock to sleep, but I could have been reading the phone book last night and it wouldn't have helped."

His mother glanced at him quizzically, careful to keep any look of disapproval from her face. She had nurtured Stephen's curiosity and desire to read when he was a child, but the fruition of that nurture wasn't exactly what she had in mind. Instead of studying the Bible and those things pertinent there too, Stephen became omnivorous in his reading. He always seemed to be swayed more by secular books than religious books. In fact, the religious books would have gotten pushed aside altogether had she not constantly slipped them in on him. With his penchant for the secular his decision to study for the ministry surprised and pleased her.

Truth be told, Stephen had chosen divinity studies more out of desperation than anything else. He didn't actually want to be a minister. He wanted to be an adventurer. He had been pretending to be a soldier of fortune for as long as he could remember, besides which there were many inconsistencies in the religion he'd grown up in.

The secular books he was allowed to read, even those not philosophical in nature, made much of his religious training seem wrong and benighted. History books told him of the crusades, the inquisition, the constant persecution of "God's chosen people," the Jews, all of which seemed to make a mockery of the teachings of Jesus. The Christian meek who would inherit the earth seemed suddenly to be armed barbarians who killed non-believers and believers alike if they did not agree with some particular interpretation of the teachings of Christ. Unsurely notwithstanding, Stephen was marching ahead to Mason College carrying the standard of the Lord.

A faint sound of music began and it grew louder as Stephen's father carried a portable radio from the bathroom toward the kitchen.

"Well," he said when he saw his son sitting at the table, "pretty early to see you."

There was a tension in his voice he couldn't conceal. It had been there for a long time, but seemed more noticeable this morning than usual. Maybe because he was about to be free of it. That "being free of it" was another reason this summer had been hard.

His father's grip seemed to tighten as his time to leave grew closer, and the tightening brought chaffing, which brought rebellion. Disagreements degenerated easily into screaming arguments and less than a week ago the argument had almost degenerated into a fist fight. Stephen couldn't even remember what it had been about now, but it had ended with his father saying, "Anytime you think you're big enough you just come on," as he lifted his hands into a rough fighter's stance. Stephen looked at him, seeing the silvery grayness of his hair, the leathery, tough appearance of his face and the still firm muscles of the tanned arms. In spite of all the friction between them Stephen still admired his father. Admired the fact the old man had been a Marine during the war and landed on many Pacific Islands. Stephen had asked him about the war, but his father would never speak of it.

I could take him, Stephen thought. *I could take him, but it would be tough. He's still strong.* He'd seen his father throw bundles of shingles weighing a hundred pounds onto each shoulder and climb a ladder without touching the ladder with his hands. Roofers had to be strong and agile to keep a job, but the strength and agility of the old man didn't scare him much. He was strong, thirty-five years younger and no stranger to fighting. The Sylmar neighborhood where they lived saw to that. He learned to fight viciously, and win very early. He gazed at this father that day and felt the eyes of his brother, his mother, and his grandmother boring into him from their places around the den. Hands down, arms rigid at his sides, he had swallowed and walked out of the room, then on out of the house toward the rugged brown hills a few blocks away. He climbed a steep jaggedly rocky path to a sheltered depression he and Mike had discovered years before and sat down.

I should have killed him, he thought. *I should have killed him.* But when the rage began to die, he recognized that he'd done well to walk out. It was an honor to his father and mother just as the commandment said.

The memory faded when his father came into the kitchen and said, "You ready to go?" He poured himself a cup of coffee.

"Just have to put my shaving kit in the overnight bag," Stephen answered, rising and moving to his usual chair as his father came to the table.

"Mike up?"

"No."

"Yes, I am," Mike called from the bedroom. "Do I have time to get a shower before we eat?"

"No," his mother answered, then called, "Grandma, are you up?"

"Yes, Lenora. Be there in a minute."

Her voice had a slight quaver in it. The quaver was not from age, but from Parkinson's disease, which was becoming gradually worse year by year. Her hands trembled constantly now and her facial muscles had a slack quality that allowed her chin to quiver as though she were always on the verge of breaking into tears. She bore it gamely, not blaming anyone or anything. It appeared not to have shaken her rock of faith in the mercy of God and the power of Jesus.

Mike came in wrapped in his checkered robe, his hair sticking up like the spikes of a hedgehog. Like all the Mitchells except Grandma he was tall, but he'd gotten his mother's propensity toward fleshiness rather than the disproportionate length of limb and stringiness of his brother and father. He was fourteen.

"Why don't you go comb that hair?" her father demanded.

"'Cause I'm just gonna mess it up again when I get in the shower."

There was a whiney quality edged into his voice but it was only a thin cover of the resistance already forming in him. He ran his fingers through his hair, not helping it much.

His father grimaced but didn't pursue the matter.

Lenora sat down and called, "Come on, Grandma."

"I'm here, I'm here," Grandma answered coming through the door and settling in her usual place.

"James, ask the blessing," Lenora said.

All joined hands and bowed their heads as the head of the house ran through the standard grace. They all answered "Amen" when he finished and began passing eggs, bacon, grits, and gravy around. A pan of biscuits didn't last long as Stephen, Mike, and James took two each, split them, and ladled gravy over them.

Lenora didn't make biscuits often now. She seldom had time between getting people ready for work and school and getting ready to go to her own bookkeeping job, but it made her feel a quiet warmth, a tie with the family's southern roots to see her men avidly eating them.

"The time is seven a.m.," the radio announcer said. "Time for the morning report." He continued into a summary of the news reporting heavy fighting around Tae Gu and another rocket attack on the airport at Long Bin.

"We better get a move on," Lenora said. "If there's any showering and such to be done."

~ * ~

Later, as Stephen wiped off the mirror Mike's shower steam had clouded, his brother asked, "What was it like when you went to get your draft card?"

Stephen thought a moment. "Nothin' much to it really," he said, raking canned shave lather off his face. "Just went in and talked to a guy at the counter. He gave me some stuff to fill out. I filled it out and took it to this other guy. He called me in a little while, asked me some questions, said my card would be in the mail in a couple of days, and that I'll get my classification in a couple of weeks. Said I had an IIS student deferment, and sure enough it was."

"What kind of questions?" Mike asked over the hiss of the shower.

"Was I a communist plotting to overthrow the government, and did I have any distinguishing marks on me."

They shaved and showered in silence for a couple of moments until Mike stepped out of the shower began drying himself. "You gonna have to go in the army?" he asked.

"Not so long as I stay in school."

"Would you go if they called you?"

Stephen swished his razor through the warm water in the sink before answering. He'd considered this several times. He was convinced that America was right to be fighting in Vietnam, but he also realized his conviction might be more a result of the constant conservative bombardment on the subject he got at school and at home. He smiled a little grimly thinking about Hardtwick conservatism. He'd been a target for it often during high school because he made no secret of the fact he was a Democrat and from a family of Democrats. His best friend, Rick Lamb, who was just a little to the right of Genghis Kahn politically, needled him by calling him "Libby", which was short for liberal though Rick knew Stephen was a pretty conservative Democrat.

"Yeah, I'd go," he answered. "I think I may go anyway if the war isn't over by the time I get through with school."

"Volunteer?"

"Yeah, volunteer."

"I hope it's over before I turn eighteen," Mike said, folding the towel and hanging it on the bar. "I don't think I want to go."

Stephen looked at his brother. The honesty of the statement and the clearness of the conviction made Stephen wonder about his own bravado. "You better not let Dad hear you say that. He'll be on you like a bad case of flu," he said.

"Yeah."

Stephen washed the stray bits of lather off his face, dried it, and put the razor into his shaving kit. "Anyway, it'll probably be over pretty soon. The commies can't keep taking losses like they have been. Marines at Danang counted eight hundred bodies. Said that probably wasn't half the casualties because the Viet Cong carry away their dead if they can."

"Mr. Lawson says those body counts aren't accurate. Says they're jacking up the numbers so it looks like we're winning."

"Mr. Howard, John Birch Society, Lawson of Hardtwick Academy, and the Valley Tabernacle Church said that?" Stephen said sarcastically.

"Yep. He's really down on President Johnson and the war and stuff."

Upon thinking about it, the thought wasn't so strange. Howard Lawson had been teaching Stephen's geometry class when Mrs. Compton, the principal, brought them the news President Kennedy had been shot. His was the only dry eye in the room when Mrs. Compton returned to say the president was dead. Lawson hadn't smiled or said anything, but there was something in his attitude that let everyone know he wasn't sorry about the assassination. It made Stephen bitterly hate Lawson. He could accept the fact many of the people at Hardtwick didn't like Kennedy's politics or his Catholicism, but not to feel some kind of sorrow or regret that a human being who had been the leader of America was dead was almost the same as having committed the murder.

After that Stephen had to grit his teeth mightily just to talk to Lawson and he considered the height of hypocrisy for Lawson to talk about Christian values and quote scripture against hate, which he did constantly.

"Well," Stephen said. "You gotta take anything he says with a grain of salt, or a whole box of salt, especially about politics. The war will probably be over before either of us have to worry about it."

Mike shrugged, "Yeah, I guess."

They went out. Stephen put his shaving kit into the scarred overnight bag and closed it. He looked at his watch. It was a quarter to eight a.m. *Guess there's nothing to do but get dressed and wait,* he thought.

Other books by G. Lloyd Helm
at
Rogue Phoenix Press

World Without End

When an author writes a story, creates a world and the creatures in it, does the literary world actually come into being in some parallel universe? Joshua Gordon, creative writing professor and writer of pulp fiction thinks so and is in fact so convinced it is true that when he is diagnosed with a terminal illness he sets out to find a protégé who he can convince to take over as the creator god of the world. He finds that protégé in the person of John Fisher.

Other Doors

Ben Fordham was a misfit destined to die in the gutters of L.A. until he found himself in a seedy bar trying to cadge a drink from an odd looking little fellow who claimed to be the best tattoo artist who ever lived. The next morning Fordham woke up with a beauty of a hang over, a beauty of a tattoo on his left forearm, and a beauty of a problem. He found himself chained to the slimy wall of a torch-lit dungeon with the threatening sound of soldiers' measured tread coming toward him--and his problems were just beginning.

Train Wheels, Flying Saucers
and the Ghost of Tiburcio Vasquez

Most of the people in these stories are at least tangentially based on real humans. Big Dave was a fellow I worked with many years ago and his description in the stories is accurate. The reader should also notice that all these stories start and mostly end in a bar somewhere. I don't play adventure games but, I am told that most of them start in bars as well. There are still several Big Dave stories to be told, and I am working on them, but I just couldn't get them done in time to come out in this book. Many elements of these stories are true. The fun and the trick is to figure out what is true and what is fantasy.

Borrowing a Moosehead from Cole Porter

In our time as members of the US Air Force we had lived in many places and gone through many things. We didn't expect that being stationed at Grissom AFB in Indiana would be the trial it turned out to be. We were leaving Germany, a foreign place, to come to middle America, supposedly home, but Grissom certainly didn't feel like home.

Between the circus that seemed to run the town of Peru, the god-awful weather and the hostile locals we felt like we had moved into a war zone. But, military families make the best of what they are dumped into so we did our best.